Karen McMillan is the author of 22 books, published in ten countries. She has written bestselling fiction, including *The Paris of the East*, *The Paris of the West* and *Brushstrokes of Memory*. Her non-fiction titles include *Love in Aotearoa*, which was shortlisted for the Ashton Wylie Award, *Unbreakable Spirit* and *Everyday Strength*, which represented NZ at the Gourmand World Awards. She is also the author of the popular *Elastic Island Adventures* books for children, which have been optioned for the screen, and *The Quokka Logic and Baking Book*, which placed third in the baking category of the prestigious Gourmand World Awards 2023.

Karen is a regular speaker at festivals and events. She was the resident book reviewer on The Café, TV3, for two years, and is a regular reviewer on radio and in print. An enthusiastic supporter of Aotearoa writers, she instigated the annual NZ Booklovers Awards.

Karen lives on the Hibiscus Coast with her husband. More information can be found at www.karenm.co.nz

Also by Karen McMillan

Fiction

Brushstrokes of Memory
The Paris of the West
The Paris of the East
Watching Over Me

Non-Fiction

Everyday Strength: Recipes and Wellbeing Tips for Cancer Patients
(with chef Sam Mannering)
Unleash Your Inner Seductress
Feast or Famine: A New Zealand guide to understanding eating disorders
Love in Aotearoa
Unbreakable Spirit: Facing the challenge of cancer in New Zealand

For children

The Quokka Logic and Baking Book
Elastic Island Adventures: Rarotonga
Elastic Island Adventures: Flip Flop Bay
Elastic Island Adventures: Kingdom of Blong
Elastic Island Adventures: Alphabet Resort
Blong the Cat's Costume Caper
Elastic Island Adventures: Rainbow Cove
Elastic Island Adventures: Port Mugaloo
Elastic Island Adventures: Jewel Lagoon

Turbulent Threads

KAREN MCMILLAN

Quentin Wilson
PUBLISHING

For Iain McKenzie, with love

First published by
Quentin Wilson Publishing
105 Moncks Spur Road
Redcliffs 8081
Christchurch
New Zealand
email: wilson.quentin@gmail.com
www.quentinwilsonpublishing.com

First published 2024

ISBN 978-1-99-110333-8 (Print)

A catalogue record for this book is available from the
National Library of New Zealand.

Published by arrangement with High Spot Literary

Front cover by Sugarcube Studios

Edited by Jane McKenzie

Page layout:
© Quentin Wilson Publishing, Christchurch, NZ
Typeset in 11.5/14.5pt Adobe Garamond Pro
Printed by Your Books, Wellington, New Zealand

Contents

Prologue

Instead of beauty, Greer could only see ugliness when she walked the Devil's Half-Acre that morning. The buildings looked rundown and sinister; broken bottles were strewn on the uneven footpath, the acrid smell of urine assaulting her nostrils. She passed a vacant lot and shivered in the cold morning air. She clutched the large flat bag she was holding more tightly and looked around. It was oddly deserted, which caused her to increase her pace. She had something important to deliver.

Suddenly, out of nowhere, rough hands were on her, brutally knocking her to the ground. She instinctively clutched the large bag to her chest. Two mask-wearing men loomed over her. They stank of ripe body odour and alcohol as though they had been sleeping rough.

"You won't be needing that," one of the men said, ripping the bag from her arms.

"No!" Greer screamed, fury and adrenaline surging through her body. In that bag was a treasure representing the hope of a new life and new beginnings, of finally following her dreams.

"She's a cherry that needs plucking," the other man said, turning back to her with a new expression in his eyes, and Greer instinctively backed away from him. What was to become of her? She looked around and realised the peril she was in. With her heart pounding, she watched anxiously when the first man grabbed his companion by the arm. She couldn't read his expression, and she suddenly felt very afraid and alone.

CHAPTER 1

October 1890

Fog clung to the hills and grief weighed down Greer's heart as the buggy travelled along the high road. Was it only two weeks ago her beloved papa's lifeless body had been lowered into the ground, surrounded by friends and neighbours dressed in sombre black? Was it only earlier today that she had, for the last time, looked around the humble cottage that had been her only home in the Devil's Half-Acre, now empty, the furniture sold to pay for her father's funeral? She clutched her only worldly possessions: one battered beige suitcase, one small sewing machine, and one case that housed her only family heirloom, a precious violin.

Greer barely noticed the wild beauty of the Otago Peninsula as the buggy rattled around another corner, taking her to a new life, far away from dreams of making something of her love of music, fashion or literature. It was a cold, drizzly spring day, and overhead a lone albatross soared in the sky and then gracefully skimmed over the water before ascending heavenward again. The coachman steered his horse around another bend and glanced at Greer with concern, but she avoided his gaze. She was already tired of the expressions of pity from strangers that had been her constant companion since her father's accident. The outpouring of tears from the first days had changed to a feeling of being hollowed out and undone, but her sorrow was unrelenting. Her anguish was a pane of glass through which she viewed her world. It was always there, the first thing she experienced in the morning and the last thing she felt at night.

"Almost there, miss," the coachman said, stealing another concerned look at her.

Greer nodded vaguely, smoothing down her black mourning dress in an unconscious movement, her mind a fog, like the patchy haze around them. But then they rounded another corner, and there was the castle on the hill. She was suddenly alert for the first time in days. Shrouded in mist, Larnach's Castle appeared grand and mysterious, perched high above the harbour, ideally situated on the vast grounds. It was the grandest building she had ever seen. It conjured up storybook castles Greer had read about, ethereal and fantastical, the mist adding to the atmosphere of a building that surely wasn't bricks and mortar. But then Greer blinked again, and she saw it was a solid, magnificent building, grounded very much in reality. Even to her inexperienced eye, it was also evident that it was constructed with the finest materials.

"Welcome to The Camp," the coachman said, bringing the horse and buggy to a stop outside the main entrance.

"It's not like anything I've ever seen before," Greer ventured to say, as he looked at her expectantly. They were the first words she'd uttered since they had left the city's outskirts.

"It's not, is it?" he replied neutrally.

The coachman jumped from the buggy and held out his hand to help her step down, Greer clutching her violin case. He turned back to retrieve her other belongings. A stout woman emerged by the castle entrance and strode towards them. When the woman got closer, Greer could see she had a kind expression, devoid of the dreaded mask of pity.

"You must be Greer Gillies. I'm Mrs MacGavin, the housekeeper. Welcome you to Larnach's Castle, or, as we like to call it, The Camp." She spoke with a soft, friendly burr, her voice like a warm bath, and Greer felt some of her apprehension about taking the role of a domestic servant dissipate. She realised how much she had been worrying about this moment.

Greer managed to find her voice. "It is an honour to meet you, Mrs MacGavin. Thank you for this opportunity."

"We are very pleased to welcome you. Follow me, and let's get you sorted." Mrs MacGavin glanced at the coachman. "Do you mind taking Miss Gillies' things to her accommodation?"

"I'm pleased to be of assistance," he said, picking up Greer's suitcase and sewing machine. He looked at Greer's violin case. She shook her head discreetly. Nodding, he disappeared around the side of the castle.

Mrs MacGavin gestured for Greer to follow her up the stairs and into the castle. "The family is out currently, so I want to quickly show you the floor you will be working on. However, please note you should avoid using the main entrance when they are in residence."

Greer nodded and followed in a daze, clutching her violin case to her chest. With some trepidation, she eyed the statues of lions that guarded the bottom of the stairs. They looked at her with menace. Further up the stairs, she was confronted by statues of eagles that seemed to view her with contempt.

"I am sorry for your loss," Mrs MacGavin said, turning back briefly with a look of compassion. "Your father was well respected in the community, and his terrible accident at the railyard is a true tragedy. Our deepest condolences."

"Thank you, Mrs MacGavin," Greer mumbled.

She paused on the entrance steps and looked up. A strange, smug-looking cat looked down on her, and further up, she was surprised to see a large carved owl, its wings spread in the spandrel between the two windows. She immediately thought of Shakespeare's words: *Out on you, owls! Nothing but songs of death*, and shuddered. Why had they chosen such an ominous symbolic bird to grace the front of the castle? The owl was associated with mourning and desolation; anyone with even a little education knew that. But then she noticed Mrs MacGavin was looking at her with concern, so she briskly followed her up the rest of the stairs and into the foyer, pausing only to admire the monogram on the floor's mosaic.

"'Sans Peur' is William Larnach's motto," Mrs MacGavin said, following Greer's gaze. "It means 'without fear'."

Greer nodded. The master of this castle must be without fear to build such a remarkable place.

"Follow me," Mrs MacGavin continued. "Then I'll let you get settled in the maids' cottage at the back of the castle."

The rooms they entered were undeniably grand. Greer almost dropped her violin case at one point, looking around in awe as Mrs MacGavin narrated this short tour. These were the rooms she would be working in. There was the elegant breakfast room with its marble fireplace. In the dining room, she gazed in astonishment at the ceiling with its carved flowers and birds. The furniture was carved to match the elaborate panelling.

Then there were the twin rooms. The feminine ladies' drawing room with soft green walls and a light pink chaise longue that Greer imagined sinking her weary bones onto, contemplating the mellow light of the gas-powered chandeliers above. The masculine library was darker than the drawing room, with rows and rows of leather-bound books in glass bookcases. But the music room most enchanted her, and the first thing Greer noticed was the elegant piano situated in the corner of the room. She had to stop herself from reaching out and stroking the smooth dark wood or the ivory keys.

Greer was soon feeling overwhelmed by so much grandeur, and was grateful when Mrs MacGavin led her outside the castle to a humble two-bedroom cottage that would be her new home, halfway between the castle and the stables. Soon she was on her own in the small, practical room she had been allocated, with time to unpack before joining the other servants for dinner.

She sat on the single bed and looked around the room. As well as the bed, there was a small wardrobe, writing desk and chair, everything spick and span. She sighed and began to unpack her suitcase. She had a small collection of books, Butterick sewing patterns and sheet music that she put on the writing desk. She hung her two dresses, both of which she had made, in the wardrobe. Greer had to admit she was proud of her sewing skills. One dress was moss green for daywear; the other was blue silk for special occasions. But she wouldn't be able to wear them for some time. She would have to continue to wear her black dress of mourning for at least a year when she was off duty. Otherwise, it would be the staff uniform already hanging in the wardrobe. A slate grey dress, white apron and white cap.

Greer glanced down at the dull black fabric of her mourning dress. It had been gifted to her by a member of her church. She had never considered she would need such a dress at the tender age of twenty. And while she was grateful for the dress at such short notice, the quality was inferior to her own dressmaking skills, and she was peeved at having to wear something so poorly made. It was a petty emotion amid her grief, which was hard and overwhelming – but somehow also pure and appropriate, given how close she and her father were. It had always been just the two of them.

Crossing over to the small mirror on the wall, Greer took off her simple bonnet and examined her reflection. She had pale skin naturally, but it seemed even paler today as she stood there in her mourning clothes. Her eyes were usually a piercing green but today appeared faded and grey. Her long hair, neatly tied up, seemed to be the only thing unchanged since her father's death. It was a deep auburn colour reminiscent of the most beautiful of autumn leaves. Her papa had said she was the spitting image of her mother, but she'd never known her mama. She had died not long after giving birth to Greer.

Greer sighed and turned away from the mirror. She hadn't thought of her mother in a long time, but with the sudden loss of her much-loved papa, she felt undone by the knowledge she was now an orphan.

There was a knock at the door, and before she had time to respond, the door burst open and a young woman erupted into the room. She wore the same staid maid's outfit that hung in Greer's wardrobe, but otherwise, there was nothing staid about her appearance. Her blonde hair had escaped from her bonnet, cascading wildly down the sides of her face, and the bright blue eyes were full of mischief.

"I'm Florence," she announced. "I just had to come and say hello as we'll be working together. I'm so pleased to meet you! I'm in the room next door. Most of the servants live in Portobello, but we are the lucky ones, like the nanny. Oh, and the stable hands. Oh, and bless, I mustn't forget the laundry staff and the cooks, as they also live on the grounds."

Before Greer could reply, Florence spied the violin case sitting on the bed, which she snatched up without asking first, causing Greer to wince. "Oh, you play the violin! How exciting! Not to blatherskite, but Mr Larnach's daughter Kate plays the violin as well. I don't know, but maybe you might be able to join in one of the concerts. That would be ever so nanty narking." She snorted. "Not that that will happen with you being a servant!"

"Um –"

Florence put the violin case back on the bed and turned her attention to Greer's sewing machine resting on the floor. "Oh, and you must sew, too. That will be ever so helpful! I always seem to be tearing my uniform. My mama tells me I'm a scatter-brained scapegrace, but I swear I don't know how I do it, so I can get you to do the repairs from now on!"

"Well –"

Florence linked her arm through Greer's. "It is so wonderful to have someone my own age to work with. The last maid was a bit fusty, I must confess. She was always telling me off for the quality of my work, which I thought was unfair, as I couldn't see her work was any better. She was as miserable as a bandicoot, if you ask me. I'm sure you won't be like that!"

"I –"

"And you have arrived at the best time, you know," Florence continued enthusiastically. "Mr Larnach will be here in the coming days with Constance, and things are always much livelier when he's around. They are engaged to be married early next year, did you know? She's ever so pretty, but she's so much younger than him. It's a bit scandalous if you ask me. But then he did marry the sister of his first wife last time around, so he's not new to scandal. Goodness, imagine getting married three times; who'd do that? I wouldn't have the energy and I'm young. He's quite an old cove, you know!"

Florence spied the two dresses that Greer had hung in her wardrobe, and she darted forward and stroked the fabrics. "Oh, these are corkers! Such fine quality. Did you make these?"

For the first time, Greer managed to get a short sentence finished. "I did."

"I am very impressed! Now, let's begin an unofficial tour of the castle and grounds while we have some time, and then we can join the others for dinner." Florence linked arms with Greer again and steered her towards the door. "Come on, chuckaboo."

Greer had time to look back at her lodgings briefly as they stood in the small corridor that separated their two rooms before Florence closed the bedroom door and led her out the cottage's front door, still chatting nineteen to the dozen. Just what had she got herself into? She resolved to put on a brave face, but her stomach was knotted with anxiety as Florence led her back towards the castle.

CHAPTER 2

Settling In

With Florence by her side, Greer noticed for the first time that despite its grandeur, Larnach's Castle was also a family home. There were boxes of board games, card games and shell collections in the drawing room, tennis racquets in the library, and croquet sets and targets for archery in the back. The place looked lived in. She was intrigued to notice that there were washbasins in many rooms, including the billiard room.

"Now, anything you need to know, do say, chuckaboo," Florence said. "Mrs MacGavin mentioned you haven't worked as a maid before, but you'll soon get the hang of it."

"Thank you, Florence, you are very kind."

Florence cocked her head to one side and looked at Greer closely. "You know, you are a bit of a toff when you speak, but a nice one. Shame all the children here are grown up, you could have been a governess."

"I did apply for a couple of governess positions," Greer confessed.

"Did you now? So what happened?"

Greer frowned at the memories. "The first position seemed good, but when the little boy was alone with me for a moment, he tried to bite me."

Florence roared with laughter. "What a brat! Well, you don't want to work with a child like that! What happened with the other position?"

"The mother had so many rules and regulations, it made me doubt I could live up to her expectations."

"Good job you don't have to work with someone as mean as a bandicoot," Florence said cheerfully. "It's no wonder you took this position instead."

Greer bit her lip. It had been hard to accept, that for now at least, her options in life were limited. But when she heard of a position in far-off Larnach's Castle, suddenly it held appeal, even if it was as a lowly maid. Walking the streets of Dunedin had become insufferable. On every corner there was a painful memory of her previous life when her father was still alive. Larnach's Castle held no memories, and it provided income and a roof over her head. She realised with a jolt that Florence was still talking.

"You will be much better off here. Most of us are nanty narking. Now let me show you the rest of this place while the family are away!"

It was a whirlwind tour of the castle and some of the grounds, and afterwards, Greer found herself seated next to Florence as the staff gathered for their supper around a large wooden dining table in one of the two kitchens, a long row of black coal ranges along one wall. There were a bewildering number of servants, perhaps around twenty, and Greer found herself suddenly grateful for Florence's non-stop chatter, as she didn't need to engage beyond the odd "hello" or nod.

There were two cooks and two undercooks. Five women were employed to do all the laundry, housed in a building remote to the castle. Besides Florence and herself, there were other maids tasked with looking after the general cleaning and dusting. Greer was just thankful she didn't have the monotonous job of attending to the many kerosene light fittings, cleaning, replenishing and replacing. Each family member also had a personal maid; there was a butler, gardeners and stable hands, and of course, the coach driver. He caught her eye and smiled. Greer noticed he had kind eyes, and he appeared ageless, neither a youth nor an old person. He seemed a steady presence, like Mrs MacGavin, who appeared to have a kind but firm hand with the household staff. But what of the rest of the staff?

Greer ate her dinner – succulent lamb medallions served with mint sauce, steamed vegetables unlike anything she had tasted before, and dreamy jacket potatoes. It was a meal far superior to anything she had ever had, and even though she hadn't had any appetite since her father's passing, she found the food too delicious to refuse. Greer observed the others through a tired fog. She'd given up trying to remember everyone's names; there was plenty of time for that. But it was clear one of the stable hands was keen on one of the kerosene maids, that a couple of the laundry women were at odds with each other, and the butler perhaps thought he was better than everyone else. He had severe dark hair and a pinched expression as he surveyed the table and he left as soon as he'd finished his meal without a word to anyone. Mrs MacGavin followed Greer's gaze.

"Mr Bentley has got a lot on his plate," she said in a mild voice. "Mr Larnach will be here any moment with his fiancée, so there is much to do to prepare their rooms and his office."

"Oh, I see," Greer mumbled, embarrassed that Mrs MacGavin seemed to sense her uncharitable thoughts.

Florence and Greer were making their way back to their rooms after the meal when Florence gave an excited giggle. "Blow me down; they're here already!" she whispered, pointing into the drawing room from the hallway. They both paused to observe the couple.

William Larnach strode into the room ahead of his fiancée. He moved with great confidence, although he was slightly portly; an older man with a drooping grey moustache and a receding hairline. He had charisma, however, and his personality filled the room. Constance followed a step behind, a petite figure with her light brown hair styled in a fashionable roll. She had perfect posture, and her brown eyes were clear and direct as Larnach turned, and they smiled at each other with obvious affection.

"I do believe the evening was a great success, my dear Connie," William said. "It looks like The Agricultural Company will be wound up soon, which is a relief."

"It is a great relief, my darling."

"I'm sure I was the envy of everyone in the room, having you on my arm."

"My darling, you are much too kind."

They were both dressed to the nines from their recent event. William Larnach wore a dark dinner jacket and trousers and a white shirt, a smart but unremarkable ensemble for a man with money. What made Greer envious was the exquisite dress Constance was wearing. It was truly spectacular; a dusky mauve silk with a delicate gold leaf pattern, the bodice embellished with heavily encrusted amber beads attached to intricate lace. It must have taken the dressmaker hours and hours to create this fine detail, Greer thought, before Florence jabbed her in the ribs, causing her to begin walking again.

"We aren't supposed to gawp at them, you know," Florence whispered with another giggle when they were out of earshot, stepping outside the castle into the cool night air. "But I can see why you did. She's beautiful, isn't she?"

"Yes, she is," Greer said thoughtfully.

"I don't know what she sees in him, though. He's an old cove."

"But he's rich and powerful," Greer said after a moment. "He does offer her a certain position in society. She'll never have to be a maid. And they do look to be fond of each other."

Florence looked taken aback by Greer's observation. "Well, regardless, when I marry, I'm marrying for love. And my husband will be young and dashing. We will make beautiful babies together."

Greer had to smile slightly at Florence's enthusiasm, but then tiredness overwhelmed her, and she started to yawn as they arrived at the door of their cottage.

"Oh, it's been a long day for you, chuckaboo!" Florence said sympathetically. "You get a good night's rest, and I'll show you all you need to know in the morning. I promise things will be nanty narking. It won't even feel like work with me by your side!"

***

The next few days were a blur, an endless round of lighting fires, cleaning and dusting. Florence and Greer were tasked with looking after the breakfast, dining, drawing, and music rooms, and library. The music room was undeniably Greer's favourite in the castle. Thanks to the tall windows framed by sage curtains, it had plenty of natural light. A large tartan rug in soft tones of beige and brown graced the floor. A chandelier above added just the right amount of sophistication to the room. Numerous artworks adorned the walls and several chairs were scattered around the room. Greer couldn't help her eyes wandering to one of the dramatic paintings of a stormy sea more than once. The raw, unrestrained power of the elements created by brushstrokes was mesmerising, and it tugged at her emotions. She'd never had the opportunity to experience art like this, but Florence just rolled her eyes when she tried to describe how she felt.

"All of this must be so different from what you are used to," Florence mused. "How did you spend your days before?"

"Well, after I finished my schooling, I kept house and did the cooking, but there were violin lessons, I was studying English literature, and I was part of a dressmaking group."

"Very fancy!" Florence flicked her duster over a surface.

"Well, it's not as though I was going to achieve a university degree, but Papa wanted me to get as much education as possible within our means, so he paid for private tutors."

"Sounds like a lot of work to me," Florence shrugged. "I enjoy relaxing when I've got time off. Don't fancy studying."

Greer dusted the piano in the corner of the music room and thought of her beloved violin, wondering when she would be able to play it again. She couldn't play it in her room – she was sure the noise wouldn't be welcomed; it was much too close to the castle – but if Greer didn't play soon, it would be another loss if her ability suffered through lack of practice. Music always lifted her spirits, the swell of the notes taking her mind to another realm. Her papa had said she had inherited her musical talent from her mama and grandmother, and while they never had much money and had lived in the Devil's Half-Acre in a small cottage, he'd never skimped on extras to supplement her education. She'd had violin lessons from a young age, he'd bought her the sewing machine when she'd shown a talent for dressmaking, and he'd always made sure Greer had any of the books she had her heart set on. Slightly battered and earmarked copies of *Wuthering Heights* and *Pride and Prejudice* were part of the small collection of literature in her room.

She must have drifted off into a daydream, as her thoughts were interrupted by Florence.

"Greer? Greer? Coo-ee! Are you listening to me?"

"What? Sorry." Greer turned her attention to her fellow maid.

"You always look a million miles away when you dust that piano. Can you play?"

"Just a little."

"Anyway, as I was saying, would you mind covering for me for a few moments? I just wanted to pop out and see Albert. He said he had a little something for me."

Albert? Who was Albert? Greer racked her brains and then remembered the young gardener who had been making eyes at Florence last night at dinner. Florence had been uncharacteristically quiet while they ate, when she thought about it.

"Of course, take your time."

Florence beamed at her, gave her a spontaneous hug, and rushed from the room. Greer returned to her dusting and her daydreams of playing the violin. She didn't notice that a petite figure had entered the room, so she started when she glanced up and saw Constance looking at her with a neutral expression. She was holding some sheet music.

"Good morning. You must be the new maid."

"Ah, yes, ma'am."

Constance gestured at the piano. "I thought I might countenance playing for a time."

"Of course, ma'am," Greer said, gathering her things.

Greer snuck a look at Constance under lowered eyelashes, admiring her well-made light-blue day dress. Constance took a seat, spread out the sheet music, and began to play. Immediately Greer recognised the notes of *Moonlight Sonata*. She walked as slowly as she could towards the doorway, wanting to enjoy the beauty of the music for just a few precious seconds longer. Constance suddenly stopped playing and Greer turned to look at her, alarmed she might have done something wrong. Mr Larnach had an excellent reputation with all the staff for being kind and generous, but the opinion about his new fiancée was undecided at this point, so Greer was suddenly fearful she was going to get a telling off. But she was relieved when she saw Constance's kind expression.

"I do believe you were walking in time to the music," Constance said.

"Was I? It's just such a beautiful piece, ma'am. I think that is my favourite of Beethoven's sonatas."

"We have that in common, then. I always feel uplifted playing this piece. Of course, it's got a melancholy feel, but it's exaggeratedly beautiful. Like brilliant autumn leaves, similar to the colour of your hair."

Greer patted the hair peeking out from her white cap, slightly embarrassed by the compliment.

"May I ask, do you play?" Constance continued.

"Only a little on the piano." Greer suddenly felt brave. "The violin is the instrument I love," she added in a rush. "I have studied it since I was a young girl."

"I'm delighted to hear that you play the violin! Such a noble but uncompromising instrument." Constance paused and looked at Greer thoughtfully. "And speaking of uncompromising, I am passionate about rights for women. I am curious, are you a supporter of women's suffrage?"

"I am," Greer said firmly. It was something she had discussed at length with her father. They both agreed. Why couldn't women have the vote?

"Excellent," Constance said, nodding her approval. "May I ask your name?"

"It's Miss Gillies, ma'am."

"Well, Miss Gillies, I'll ask Mrs MacGavin to drop off Mrs Sheppard's pamphlet, 'Ten Reasons Why the Women of New Zealand Should Vote', for you and the other maids. It's important that we all sign the next petition to get the law changed. At the moment, women are in the same category as criminals and the insane, which is ludicrous." Constance turned her attention back to the piano.

"But I mustn't hold you up," she said as she began to play again, her fingers gently stroking the keys. "I will leave you to resume your work."

It was Greer's cue to leave, so this time she walked more quickly from the music room, only to find Florence bustling along the hallway, her hair beneath her bonnet even wilder than usual. She pulled a single red rose from her apron and thrust it in Greer's face.

"Look what Albert gave me! The most corker of red roses, grown by his own hand. How romantic is that?"

Greer thought briefly that the rose actually belonged to William Larnach, but seeing Florence's ecstatic expression – she was almost swooning – she vowed not to be a killjoy.

"It's a splendid rose."

"Albert has invited me to picnic with him on Sunday! I simply can't wait. It's only two days to go, but never has time felt so long!"

Sunday was Greer's day off, too. She resolved to walk the grounds and find somewhere she could practise her violin. Mrs MacGavin had mentioned that staff were welcome to enjoy the vast grounds. After all, there was quite a community of people living on the estate when you factored in the house staff, stables and nearby farm, but she urged discretion and if Greer wanted to enjoy a moment in the sun in her spare time, it should be away from the main house.

Greer had a sudden urge to play *Three Romances for Violin and Piano* by Clara Schumann. It was a piece she played competently, but she would be rusty after all this time. She just hoped there would be somewhere suitable on the estate to play in privacy.

CHAPTER 3

Sunday Music

Sunday was a temperate, cloudless day after the early hours had blanketed the place in thick fog. Florence had already departed with Albert on their picnic, not wanting to waste a moment of a beautiful day with her intended. The last couple of Sundays Greer had stayed in her room reading, not wanting to do anything else. Her grief still weighed heavily on her heart. But today she felt a slight flutter of anticipation, of excitement even. For the first time in a long time, if she found the right spot, she'd be able to play her precious violin.

Greer picked up her violin case and made her way out of the cottage to the front of the castle. She stood for a moment on the raised lawn admiring the marble fountain she had been told by Mrs MacGavin came all the way from Pisa in Italy. It was hard to imagine it travelling so far! A peacock strutted past her as she admired the view. Here and there, guinea fowls roamed. Dogs barked in the distance, sounding happy and content. It felt as if all of nature was in harmony at that moment, and Greer felt her spirits lift.

Suddenly she was aware of a presence and turned to see a young man watching her, puffing on his pipe. From photographs, she recognised him as William Larnach's favourite and youngest son, Douglas. He walked with a discernible limp. Florence had told Greer just the other day that he'd been thrown from his horse as a schoolboy in England, and he'd suffered numerous broken bones. She'd described him ghoulishly as being "weakened", but from this distance, he looked a picture of health with a fine head of brown hair and a tanned complexion.

Douglas had been tasked with running The Camp for a few years. Florence, always a fount of knowledge (or gossip), had told Greer that Mr Larnach had wanted his youngest son to study medicine in Edinburgh, but Douglas had decided to come home and be a farmer. It seemed he didn't have the enterprising nature of his father, but Greer thought there was no shame in farming, and he looked happy enough as he approached her with a smile.

"Good day. You must be the new maid. Welcome to The Camp."

"Thank you, sir."

He glanced at her violin case curiously. "You play the violin?"

"Yes, sir. I was just looking for a place to practise without disturbing others."

Douglas puffed on his pipe before he spoke again. "We have vast grounds, so I'm sure you will find a private spot away from the main house. In the meantime, you might want to enjoy a moment in the pergola just ahead."

"It looks beautiful, sir." Greer looked at the pergola with interest. "Are they laburnum flowers?"

"Indeed, they are. Enjoy your day of rest." Douglas doffed his hat and made his leave to go before turning back. "I'm not musical myself. I take after my father in that regard, but I hope you get to hear my sisters play when they visit. And, of course, Connie is very musically accomplished."

Greer wondered if she should mention that she had already heard Constance play, but thought better of it. She was just a maid, after all. Not his equal.

"Thank you, sir."

Douglas turned towards the farm while Greer made her way to the pergola. Inside, she breathed in the gentle fragrance of the flowers, enjoying the dappled sun on her face. It was picturesque, but as Douglas had indicated, it was too close to the castle. She would need to find somewhere else.

She made her way through an arch in the hedge and stopped to admire the reflection pool before continuing. Mrs MacGavin had mentioned that the gardens were set over thirty-five acres, and today they looked particularly magnificent. Birds sang from a small arboretum of beech trees, underplanted with foxgloves – widely known to be Mr Larnach's favourite flower. Native and exotic trees and shrubs flourished everywhere Greer looked, and she played a game with herself to see how many she could recognise in this wonderland: tōtara, walnut, oak, poplar, flax, cabbage trees. But she soon gave up and moved on.

Greer made her way through a narrow pathway until she stood in another small pergola entwined with roses and creepers, yet again underplanted with foxgloves. The situation offered the most spectacular view of the Otago Peninsula, sea and land intertwined to create a vista that would be worthy of paradise in the afterlife. She had found her spot, a place that moved her soul with its natural, wild beauty, but also a place far enough from the castle not to bother others.

With a light breeze gently caressing her face, Greer set down her violin case and opened it reverently, taking out her most precious possession, her mother's violin, her only tangible link to her family; an Amati violin originally owned by her grandmother. She stroked the warm wood, a naturally luminous gold, and lifted the instrument and her bow from the case. Resting the violin against her neck, Greer ran the bow expertly across the strings. Not surprisingly, the instrument needed to be tuned, so she took a moment to do this, the discordant quickly becoming harmonious.

She took a deep breath before beginning to play the first section of Clara Schumann's *Three Romances for Violin and Piano*. The only accompaniment was the birds in the nearby trees. As the notes soared into the air, she felt the lightest since her father's death. She lost herself in the swell of the music, her soul restored for a moment by the splendour of the music, the sun on her face, the transcendent beauty of the garden around her and the scenic vista before her.

Some time later, Greer made her way through the garden back to the castle. Apart from Douglas working on the farm, the rest of the Larnach family were away that day, so she took the shortcut by using the front steps rather than going all the way around the building. The lions looked less menacing today, the eagles less haughty. The owl was now benevolent, not an omen of doom. She stopped to admire the wood carving and panelling in the foyer. Thanks to Florence, she had recently discovered that the panelled walls were a mixture of Spanish mahogany, mottled kauri and Burmese teak. No expense had been spared in this large mansion, and now the tiredness from her early days as a maid had lifted, she was starting to appreciate more of the fine details of the building. However, she did wonder about the glum-looking European wildcat in the window and the puzzling motto, 'Sans Peur'. It seemed William Larnach had a sense of humour, even though he was such an important man, given this odd pussy cat.

Greer turned to see Florence rushing into the foyer wearing her Sunday best, a sunny yellow dress that clearly suited her upbeat mood. Greer glanced down at her black mourning dress and felt suddenly very shabby. Florence's hair was typically escaping in all directions from under her bonnet, but her smile was wide and inviting. Outside, Greer caught a glimpse of Albert disappearing with an empty picnic basket on his trek back to Portobello, where he lived.

"What a corker of a day," Florence said, linking her arm through Greer's. "We had the most romantic picnic. Albert is the most thoughtful man I've ever met. He'd organised all the food himself, and we even had a little wine. Although I agree in principle with the temperance movement, I couldn't resist trying, and it was just the smallest of glasses on the best of days."

Florence giggled and skipped as they made their way out the back of the castle to their cottage. "Albert has invited me to go cycling next Sunday – he has a bicycle I can borrow. He's thought of everything, chuckaboo! And he said I must be his date for the Christmas party."

"Christmas party?" Greer asked, clutching her violin case to her chest, feeling ill. It would be her first Christmas without her beloved papa.

"It's a tradition. It's the best nanty narking! The Larnach family comes to the servants' kitchen on the night of the twenty-third of December, and they give us the most generous gifts. Then we enjoy a corker feast, and they really don't mind that we carry on partying for as long as we like." Florence beamed at Greer, not noticing Greer's face drop and her eyes moisten.

"Of course, we all need to work on Christmas Eve and Christmas Day. It's such a busy social time for the family, but we have Boxing Day to look forward to, having the day off to spend as we like." Florence laughed. "I really love Christmas. You'll see, working here, they make it something special! They really make a fuss of it!"

Greer sighed as she finally closed her bedroom door a little later, alone in her small sanctuary. After an afternoon of being transported by the power of music, sunshine and nature, she suddenly felt herself crashing back to earth. Christmas would usually be a time of joy, but this year it was an ordeal Greer would have to somehow get through.

CHAPTER 4

December 1890

The lead-up to Christmas had been a whirlwind of parties throughout November and December. William Larnach had hosted a succession of functions for business friends, with Constance at his side, and Douglas had had plenty of his own parties with friends from Dunedin. It seemed he had many friends and acquaintances who were very happy to accept invitations to come to The Camp. They had gay picnics or partied in the evening, often staying over. Despite Greer's growing concerns about getting through the Christmas season without her father, it made the castle a lively place to work. But mostly, Greer was too busy to think about her loss as the staff worked even harder than usual as more of the Larnach family began to arrive.

But now she was getting ready for the servants' Christmas party, replacing her uniform with her black mourning dress. Greer scowled at herself in the mirror. She really didn't want to go to a party, but there was no way out of this, so she closed her bedroom door and headed to the staff kitchen. Earlier in the day, a side of beef had been delivered, along with dozens of eggs, butter from the dairy, vegetables from the kitchen garden and buckets of strawberries and raspberries.

She was a few minutes late, so the rest of the staff were already there when she arrived. Florence waved at her, and she found a place next to her friend, who linked arms with her as she customarily did.

Members of the Larnach family were there, too, with a pile of presents nestled under a Christmas tree decorated earlier in the day. William Larnach was in good spirits. He made a rousing speech about how much the family appreciated their hard work throughout the year and the importance of Christmas and family. He was an excellent speaker, charismatic and confident, but Greer found her mind wandering as he spoke.

Greer had only had glimpses of Mr Larnach's daughters before this occasion, but she nonetheless had an impression of their characters. And as she watched them hand out the presents, she observed them quietly.

Kate, the eldest of the daughters, was clearly the favourite with everyone. She had been away nursing in Wellington, and Greer could see she was well suited to the profession. Kate was gentle and unfailingly kind to everyone, including her new stepmother-to-be, Constance. It was clear her father adored Kate as William Larnach watched his favourite daughter hand a present to one of the grooms. She was attractive with a warm, open face and long wavy hair that she had tied back. Her dress was likewise simple and sensible. The only fault Greer could find was that she wasn't gifted musically, despite her father investing heavily in music lessons. According to Florence, Kate couldn't play a note on the piano or violin without sheet music, and when she did have her music, she often butchered the tune. But tonight there was no hint of her musical impediment, only her natural grace and warmth.

Colleen was the second eldest daughter, and she didn't have the beauty of Kate. Instead, her brow was heavy and her eyes were hooded; her dark hair was pulled back severely under an unflattering hat. Alice was the third of the daughters, only a couple of years older than Greer, and her dress and manner were more flamboyant than those of her sisters, with a restless energy about her. She looked a little bored by the proceedings, her lips slightly pursed in a smile that didn't reach her eyes. But by all accounts, Colleen and Alice's musical skills were a significant improvement on Kate's. They both played the piano, and Colleen learned the harp while Alice studied the violin. But they didn't seem to want to be at The Camp, and when away from their father, were overheard complaining how dull things were there and that they couldn't wait to leave.

Worse still was the blatant rudeness they displayed towards Constance. Clearly, they disapproved of her marrying their father, and they seemed to take pleasure in rubbing this in her face, when their father wasn't around, of course. Even tonight, on their best behaviour, with smiles on their faces, they kept their distance from Constance, subtly turning away from her whenever they had the opportunity. When their father was absent, Colleen and Alice had long faces and scowls whenever Constance entered a room. Greer had observed that they kept commandeering the music room, just at the time when Constance would usually like to play the piano. It didn't seem like an accident, more a small-minded way to take some pleasure away from her day.

Gladys, the youngest, was only thirteen and seemed sweet in a gangly way, all awkward upper and lower limbs, and she clearly loved Christmas with all the enthusiasm of a young person. But it appeared she wasn't very keen on having Constance as her stepmother-to-be either, from the awkward way she interacted with her. According to Florence, Gladys had been very fond of Mary, William Larnach's second wife, so Greer understood a new woman would have a hard job of capturing her heart.

Donald, the oldest son, was based in Melbourne and wasn't going to be with them for this Christmas, so Greer had no idea about him, apart from the gossip from Florence. By all accounts he was more handsome than his brother, with darker hair than the others, and he had the confidence of being the firstborn and of being Oxford educated. He'd displeased his father by marrying an actress, a woman William Larnach never referred to by name but only as "the wife". The word from Florence was that Donald wasn't pleased about his father's marriage to Constance, either.

Apart from Kate, the only sibling to show any kindness to Constance was Douglas, Greer observed. He was a bit awkward around her tonight; perhaps it was the eight-year difference between them that caused that, but he was friendly and had a ready smile for her as they handed out more presents.

Constance was a figure of elegance, and she looked completely comfortable in her upcoming role as the lady of the house. She had small words of praise for each servant she spoke to. With a jolt, Greer realised Constance was now talking to her, handing her a wrapped gift. She had been in such a daydream!

"Mrs MacGavin told me the other day that as well as being talented musically, you love to read," Constance said, looking Greer in the eye in the direct way she had. "I do hope you will like this."

"Thank you, ma'am," Greer replied, taking the gift. She carefully opened the wrapping paper to discover a copy of *A Christmas Carol* by Charles

Dickens. Constance smiled when she saw Greer's reaction. Everyone had said how generous the family was at Christmas, but this exceeded Greer's every expectation.

"This is wonderful!" Greer said sincerely. "Oh, thank you so much. I will enjoy reading this."

"And now you have a party to enjoy," Constance said brightly.

Greer nodded and then glanced at her fellow staff members, busy opening presents, with the kitchen staff beginning to lay out their feast. Everyone was in high spirits, but Greer felt as if she was encased in a bubble away from the rest of them, observing them through a slightly distorted lens. Next to her, Florence was excitedly opening some scented soaps given to her by the young Gladys. The other members of the Larnach family were already slipping away from the kitchen, leaving the servants to enjoy their own time. Greer looked down at her black mourning dress. Constance followed her gaze and her expression softened.

"I don't feel much in the mood for a party," Greer confessed.

"It's your first Christmas without your father, isn't it?" Constance asked gently.

Greer nodded.

"I remember how hard the first Christmas was without my papa, too," Constance confided, and Greer looked up in surprise. She didn't know her father had passed.

Constance frowned and then her eyes lit up. "I have an idea that pleases me if it pleases you."

Greer waited expectantly to see what she would say next.

"Music can be a wonderful solace, so I propose that you fetch your violin, and I will play the piano. It will take you away from the party for a short time. I seldom get to play a duet, so it would be a treat for me, and I have time while the others are getting ready."

Constance must have noticed Greer's astonished expression – a maid playing with the soon-to-be lady of the house was unheard of.

"We are entering a new era," Constance said, as though understanding Greer's unvoiced thoughts. "Women are now being educated and can choose to make their own decisions about how they pass their time in this life. Why can't I play a duet with whomever I choose?"

Constance looked defiant, but then faltered for a moment. "Naturally, discretion is called for, but it is Christmas time, so let's enjoy some music and good cheer in the privacy of this home. What do you say?"

Greer swallowed, not quite believing what she was hearing.

"What piece do you want to play?" she asked haltingly.

"Something of your choosing."

"What about *Three Romances for Violin and Piano* by Clara Schumann?"

"An excellent choice! That is one of my favourites." Constance looked around. The rest of the Larnach family had departed the kitchen.

"Shall I meet you in the music room in ten minutes? I have time to play before I go out to dinner, and that gives you time to come back and enjoy the feast – if you feel like it, that is."

Greer felt an unexpected glimmer of happiness. "Yes, I would like that very much."

Constance made her way out of the room and Greer turned to Florence. "I have an, um, errand, so I'll be back in about twenty minutes. Just in case anyone asks."

Florence looked surprised, but then Albert put his arm around her shoulders, and her attention moved to him. "Well, don't be too long!" she said as Albert whispered something in her ear that made her giggle.

No one else noticed as Greer slipped out of the kitchen, her new book in hand. When she reached her room, she placed it carefully next to her existing book collection before smoothing down her hair and adjusting her cap, picking up her violin case and making her way back into the castle and the music room. In a moment of serendipity, they arrived simultaneously, Constance carrying some sheet music.

"I was contemplating playing this with Kate on Christmas Eve, so it will be timely practice to play this with you now," she said. "I very much approve of your choice."

"Thank you, ma'am." Greer smiled at the compliment.

Constance took a seat at the piano and arranged the sheet music while Greer took her violin from the case and readied to play. Constance glanced at her. "Do you want to stand where you can see the music?"

"It's all right, I know this by heart."

"Impressive. Are you ready?"

Greer nodded. Constance began playing the opening notes. Greer took a deep breath and then joined in, Constance looking up with admiration as

Greer made the violin sing. The acoustics in the room were excellent, and even Greer was suddenly stunned at her violin's beautiful, melancholy tone. They both lost themselves in the music, the violin and piano's melodies weaving and intertwining, Constance obviously appreciating Greer's musical talent and Greer admiring Constance's skills. They didn't notice at first that Kate, Alice and Colleen had gathered and were watching them.

"Oh, this is superb!" Kate said. "They play so well together."

"But what's a maid doing playing the violin?" Alice said, scowling.

"And where did she get a violin?" Colleen added, sounding outraged, her heavy brow creased. "It's not one of ours, is it?"

Their voices punctuated the daydream Greer had been in and she stopped playing abruptly, her bow making a discordant whine. Constance looked up and stopped playing as well. An expression of annoyance and awkwardness flashed across her face before she rearranged her features to something more neutral, straightened her back and turned.

"Can I help you, ladies?" Constance asked politely, looking at the three women with a steely gaze.

"That was simply wonderful!" Kate said, stepping forward. "Oh, please carry on."

"This is most unsuitable. This isn't right!" Alice said, her face reddening.

"What isn't right?" Constance queried, meeting Alice's eye. "I have invited Miss Gillies to play this duet with me before we go out to dinner."

Greer took a step backwards. She could feel Alice's anger radiating toward Constance and herself.

"But she's just a maid!" Colleen sounded outraged. "You can't play music with a maid!"

"Why ever not?" Constance said in measured tones. "One day, all women will get the vote, and I can't see when it comes to music it matters about a person's station in life. Times are changing! I would have thought you would be more progressive in your attitude."

"Miss Gillies, you are very talented!" Kate said kindly, ignoring her sisters scowling next to her. "I wish I could play like that."

Greer bit her lip; she didn't know what to do in this situation.

"But where did she get the violin? It's an Amati, isn't it? How on earth can she afford that? And where did she learn to play? How is this possible?" Colleen demanded, looking angrier with each passing moment.

Constance turned to Greer with a compassionate gaze "Would you like to share some of your story, Miss Glllies? It's yours to tell if you would care to enlighten those present."

"Um," Greer began. She looked at the floor for a moment before turning her attention to her violin. "Both my grandmother and mother played the violin. This is their violin, handed down to me."

"No wonder you are naturally gifted," Kate said. "It's obviously a talent you have inherited from your family."

"But how could you afford lessons, as a maid?" Alice persisted.

Greer lifted her head and looked Alice in the eye, a fire igniting in her. "I may not have your wealth, but my father spared no expense in my education. Just because I am poorer than you does not mean I am uneducated!" She was beginning to get angrier now. "I am only recently a maid. Before my father's death, I was busy with my studies."

"Oh." Alice had the grace to look embarrassed. "I think we should leave," she said, turning to Colleen, who was still scowling. "Come on, let's get ready for dinner."

They stalked from the room, but Kate remained.

"I hope you don't mind if I stay?" she said, slipping into one of the dark leather seats. "I would really love to hear you play from the beginning. What I heard before was truly beautiful."

"I think we should pack up," Constance murmured, beginning to stand up.

"No, please don't," Kate implored. "Please just play once, to the end."

Constance looked at Greer, unsure, and Greer waited for her as she seemed to wrestle with the situation. It was one thing talking about change, but another taking action. But then Greer saw the fire return to Constance's eyes as she sat down again. "Shall we?"

Greer nodded, they began again, and soon Greer forgot Kate watching them, her grief, the staff party that was beginning without her; she was lost in the music. They played to the end without further interruption. Constance was right; it was a solace.

Kate showered them both with praise before she left to get ready for dinner.

Constance sighed and turned to Greer. "Please take no notice of that outburst from Colleen and Alice. Their behaviour was inexcusable, but

I feel they don't really mean harm." She sighed wearily again. "I fear you just got in the way of their feelings towards me."

Greer looked at Constance in surprise. So Constance had noticed the way they were treating her.

"But you are always so civil with them," Greer blurted out. "Even when they treat you with disdain."

"Well, I must be. I will be married to their father soon, and I know it may take them a little while to get used to the idea, but I am dedicated to this marriage and will do everything to make it a success. I recognise they may need some time to get used to the idea, however, so will be tolerant."

Greer picked up her violin case. "I admire your attitude very much."

"And I admire your musical talent, Miss Gillies," Constance said. "Thank you for this interlude, but let us now continue the evening as originally planned."

Greer left the music room, put her violin back in her room at the cottage, and then made her way back to the staff kitchen. Manners were important, her father had always said, and it would be rude not to stay for the feast the cooks had slaved over. And after playing the duet, her spirits were a little lighter, despite the hurtful words from two of the Larnach sisters.

When Greer got to the kitchen, everyone was very merry indeed, and she wondered what was in the eggnog. It tasted very strong. Florence was busy conversing with Albert and hadn't noticed her return, so Greer sat at the end of the table by herself, enjoying the meal, despite not having much appetite. It was a traditional Christmas feast with roasted goose served with sage and onion stuffing. But there was also roasted turkey that Greer couldn't believe was so juicy, beef that smelt and tasted heavenly, Christmas ham and roasted potatoes. Greer was just dishing herself some plum pudding and brandy custard when the coachman took a seat beside her, also carrying a pudding plate laden with food.

"They're a merry bunch," he commented, gesturing at the servants swaying together as the room erupted with discordant song.

"I guess they are," Greer said.

"Do you have plans for Boxing Day?"

Greer lowered her spoon and looked glumly at her uneaten food.

"It must be difficult, your first Christmas without your father," the coachman said kindly.

Greer nodded miserably, still looking at the plum pudding.

"Well, I think you should get away from The Camp on Boxing Day, for what it's worth." He paused. "A change of scenery may lift your spirits. I'm going into town to visit a relative for a few hours; I could give you a lift if you wanted?"

Greer looked up into the coachman's kind eyes and made a decision. She had fled the familiar streets when she took this position, but she suddenly yearned to see them again. "You know, yes, I would like that. It will occupy some of the day. So yes."

"In that case, meet me out front at ten in the morning, and I'll be ready with the buggy. I'm Edward, by the way."

Greer smiled at him gratefully. "Thank you."

She looked at her plum pudding with more interest and took a bite, the sweet but tart flavours a taste sensation in her mouth. At least now, some of Boxing Day would be occupied, which surely would be better than spending her day off alone in her room. A buggy ride in the fresh air would do her good, she decided, as she tasted another mouthful of pudding.

CHAPTER 5

Home Revisited

It was a fine, clear day as the buggy and horse rode along the high road towards Dunedin, offering stunning views of the Peninsula, a complete contrast to the fog that had shrouded the hills on Greer's arrival at the castle almost three months before. She observed the sheltered lake-like harbour and the bush-covered hills as they travelled. It had a wild, rugged beauty that made her think they were at the very end of the world, far from civilisation, just surrounded by natural beauty unspoiled by mankind. She thought of a quote by John Ruskin, a writer she had studied. "Nature is painting for us, day after day, pictures of infinite beauty if only we have the eyes to see them."

Greer glanced at Edward, the coachman, but beyond a few pleasantries at the start of the trip, he seemed content to let her keep to herself. She was grateful. This trip would likely take about an hour, so she let her mind wander as the buggy bumped along the road, the chestnut horse trotting confidently ahead, clearly knowing the track well.

The last two days had been a blur of work as the Larnach family had celebrated Christmas Eve and then Christmas Day. There had been extravagant presents and Christmas cards, carol singing and performances in the music room. Constance looked awkward when she saw Greer now, or was Greer being fanciful? But things felt different since they had played their duet. Greer had to admit she had been curious when Kate and Constance performed the same Clara Schumann duet and had felt a small amount of uncharitable satisfaction when she heard Kate playing poorly. Greer could hear every note clearly from the drawing room where she was cleaning. But then she felt a little ashamed, as Kate was kind and generous. It wasn't her fault if she didn't have the natural musicality for such a piece. Perhaps they should have selected something simpler?

Greer did get immense satisfaction when Alice and Colleen performed a duet, which wasn't as bad, but it certainly wasn't first-rate. All those expensive music lessons hadn't done them much good. But then she thought, if her father were here, he would have gently scolded her for her bad grace in thinking ill of others, and she felt a stab of grief. Grief snuck up on her at the most unexpected times.

Mercifully she had been too busy with her many tasks to think much more about anything during the Christmas festivities, but here she was now with the lull of the rocking buggy giving freedom for her thoughts to roam free. Her father, handsome with his expressive brown eyes and his ready laugh, came into her mind as if he was still there and she could reach out and touch his muscular arms. He had managed to be both strict and loving in bringing her up, so even when he was chiding her about something, he was also building her up.

And he had so much faith in her abilities! According to him, she had a great future in whatever she decided to do. There would be marriage one day, of course, although she had yet to meet a young man she admired as a potential life partner. But she could be a teacher, or writer, or perhaps she could start a small clothing business. Then there was her skill with the violin. Greer imagined having her own home one day and performing in the parlour as she and her husband entertained their guests. Her husband would play the piano, she'd be on the violin, and love would fill the room as they played together. Afterwards, their guests would compliment them on their performance. It would be one of many sparkling, happy occasions.

The buggy went over a rock and Greer winced as her transport was jolted around. So much for her dreams. No one could have predicted her father's untimely death. He had invested so much in her education, so there was little left after she'd paid funeral costs, just a small amount of money squirrelled away in the bottom of her battered suitcase. Being a maid seemed the only solution to put a roof over her head and food in her belly; well, at least for the time being, until she had formulated another plan.

She played with the dark fabric of her shabby mourning dress and sighed, and the coachman glanced at her with concern. She feigned a small smile and he turned his gaze back to the road. The problem was that she was just too tired to even dare to dream of anything. Playing her violin occasionally in the spot she had chosen in the garden overlooking the Peninsula was a respite, but she couldn't even concentrate on reading the new book Constance had given her at Christmas. She'd re-read the opening page at least a dozen times before putting it aside.

Greer was so deep in thought she was surprised when Edward spoke. "We are almost there. Where would you like me to drop you off?"

"Would it be all right to take me to Walker Street?" Greer had a hankering to visit her old neighbourhood. To walk the familiar streets and take in the sights and smells.

"It's on my way," the coachman replied agreeably, not showing the prejudice that many in Dunedin would have for the Devil's Half-Acre. It had been a squalid place of brothels and opium dens in the gold-rush days, infamous for its criminal activity, with dingy shops and warehouses and rotten tumbledown shanties. It was still a rough part of the city, but now Scots, Irish, Lebanese and Chinese families lived in the area in close proximity, their children playing together in the alleyways.

Greer remembered her childhood as one of street games and fun. It might be rundown, but it was a place of community and togetherness for many of the people who made their homes there. Of course, there was tension from time to time when strangers arrived and didn't fit in, but they usually left fairly quickly. You still had to be careful late at night, especially if near one of the taverns, but the people who stayed were there for a fresh start in a new country, and they wanted to leave the old-world quarrels behind. If anything, it was them against the rest of Dunedin and the prejudices they encountered in the wider city.

These days, her childhood friends were long gone; some married, some working, some studying. She thought it unlikely she would bump into anyone she knew, but that suited her perfectly. They would all be busy with their families over Christmas, whereas she was now utterly alone.

Edward stopped the buggy at the beginning of Walker Street and helped Greer down. "Usually, lunch with my mother takes until two o'clock." He consulted his timepiece. "So that gives you about three hours to explore. Is that agreeable to you?"

"Perfectly agreeable," Greer said. "Shall I meet you back at this junction?"

Edward nodded, doffed his hat and then climbed back into the buggy, taking up the horse's reins again. "I won't be late, so I will see you then."

Greer watched as the coachman disappeared from view before she began to make her way up the sloping street. It was all instantly familiar – Petersons Grocer with its faded signage, the Chinese Cookshop with its distinctive smells of oyster sauces and garlic, and the uneven walls of the warehouse that manufactured cordial. Further down was the Caledonian Hotel next to a vacant lot where she used to play with some of the local children. Not far from there were the serene duck ponds and Chinese gardens. The Rising Sun Hotel still stood proud, and further along was the St Andrew's Presbyterian Church.

She continued walking the street, somehow managing to walk in real time but also down the passages of the past. Here was the shop where her father used to buy her ice creams. There was the building where she did Bible class studies. She crossed over another side street, and there was the humble home her father had rented for so many years. Greer stood for a moment, grief punching her again – but she was determined not to give in to the distress. After a moment, she walked closer to the familiar front door, now painted a jaunty blue. The small garden out the front had been tended; a profusion of white sweet peas had been planted, their richly perfumed flowers in sweet contrast to the stench of some of the garbage in the gutters further along the street.

An even more delicious smell of food came from her old home, an aromatic blend of spices. Greer could recognise the fragrance of cinnamon and nutmeg, but there was also the aroma of ginger, cumin and ground coriander. She closed her eyes and breathed in the flavours.

When Greer opened her eyes again, the door had opened and a young woman was staring at her with evident curiosity, a baby resting on her hip. She had long dark hair, olive skin and sparkling brown eyes. And with just a glance, Greer could see the vivid pink dress she was wearing had the most exquisite embroidery detail.

"Can I help you, miss?" she spoke in accented English, her voice warm and melodic. "You have been standing outside our home for some time."

Greer's hand flew to her face in distress. "I'm so sorry, it's just the meal you are cooking smells so delicious. I'm sorry to be standing here like a fool."

"You are clearly not a fool," the woman said. "You obviously appreciate good food, which is a sure sign of intelligence."

Greer clasped her hands, so embarrassed to be having this conversation. The woman eyed her kindly. "It's not just the food, though, is it?"

"I used to live in this cottage."

The woman clapped her hands in obvious delight. "Well, then you must come in and join us for lunch! You must tell us of your time living here."

Greer began to back away, overwhelmed with too many emotions.

"Please don't go, we have plenty of food, and we would love to hear your stories," the woman implored. "My name is Jamelie George, and this here is my daughter Soraya."

As though Soraya understood what her mother was saying, the baby suddenly gurgled and smiled at Greer. She was a gorgeous baby, with perfect olive skin and big brown eyes like her mother's, and Greer couldn't help but smile back.

"Ah, the influence of the baby," Jamelie said. "She likes you, so you must have lunch with us."

Greer hesitated. "My name is Greer Gillies."

"Come, Greer Gillies!" Jamelie commanded, and Greer automatically took a step forward and then another, following her into the cottage.

Greer was astonished when she stepped inside her old home. It was still a plain worker's cottage with a narrow hallway that led to the front room and then the kitchen, and it had two bedrooms at the rear of the house. But the earthen floor beneath the intricate rugs was swept so clean she wondered if the floor was polished. The walls, once a grubby beige, had been painted a clean white. Greer followed Jamelie into the kitchen with the familiar stone fireplace and coal range. Instead of their old table, there was now a low table surrounded by brightly embroidered cushions, and Jamelie directed Greer to sit on one of them. Greer couldn't help but be impressed by the colourful, simple style. The cottage had a freshness and cleanliness she had never achieved in all her years of housekeeping. She then turned her attention to the people who were looking at her with hospitable smiles. They had been conversing in Arabic, but the conversation paused when she entered the room.

"As-salaam," Jamelie said. "Greer, let me introduce you to my husband, Gabriel."

Gabriel nodded at her in greeting. "As-salaam, welcome to, er, table." His English wasn't as good as his wife's, but Greer appreciated his warm tone.

Jamelie put her baby into a cradle in the corner of the room with practised ease and sat next to Greer. "Here are a couple of our neighbours, Frank and Wardi."

The couple nodded in greeting and then continued to eat, dipping bread into a plate of hummus that looked very appetising. Greer had only sampled hummus once before but remembered how much she had enjoyed it.

"Everyone, this is Greer Gillies," Jamelie announced. "She used to live in this house."

"When you, er, live here?" Gabriel asked.

"Until a few months ago." Greer paused. "My father died, so I had to leave."

She dreaded the looks of pity, but instead she felt a rush of empathy, a warm enveloping of understanding.

"It is so difficult to lose a loved one," Jamelie said, "My dear papa passed over to eternal life before we immigrated, so I feel for you, dear Greer, at this sad time."

Frank and Wardi murmured something in Arabic that sounded sympathetic.

"Where live you now?" asked Gabriel.

"I work as a maid at Larnach's Castle."

"I hear William Larnach is a good employer – is that true?" Jamelie asked.

"Yes, he is." Greer was pleased to suddenly find this was true.

"Please, do eat," Jamelie gestured at the food. "This is kibbeh, our national dish; it has pine nuts and spicy meat to waken your tongue."

"The best!" Gabriel said, taking one of the fried treats and eating it with gusto.

"And this is kafta, a lamb meatball filled with onion, parsley, bread-crumbs and spices," Jamelie continued. "There is hummus, rice pilaf, and we have two salads, the fattoush and the tabbouleh." Jamelie scooped some onto her plate. "Help yourself to the manakish bread, and at the end, you might want to try knafeh. It's a pastry finished off with orange blossom syrup."

Greer looked at all the food in amazement. "There are so many dishes, I hardly know where to begin!"

It was astonishing to see such a feast in these humble surroundings. Greer knew how difficult it was to prepare food in this kitchen. There wasn't even running water – it had to be obtained from an outside tap on the back of the cottage.

"Food is not simply about nourishing the body," Jamelie said, handing Greer a plate and placing a piece of manakish on it. "It's an important way people relate to each other in our culture; food gives comfort, love and respect."

"Tell, er, living here," Gabriel said.

They all turned to her with interest.

"Well, I lived here with my papa for as long as I can remember," Greer began. "It was always just him and me as my mama passed away after childbirth."

Jamelie touched Greer's arm with genuine sympathy. "So much loss for someone so young. May I ask how old you are?"

"I'm twenty."

"Well, I have five years more experience than you and my husband seven more, but I sense you have a strong spirit and will overcome your early loss. And you say your father passed away recently?"

"He worked at the railway and there was an accident."

"So sad," Gabriel murmured.

"But I hope you have many happy memories of living in this home," Jamelie said.

"Most assuredly, I do, and although it was just the two of us, life always felt very constructive and fulfilled. We had many things in common. Papa used to read books to me, and then when I was older, I read books to him. And we had a piano in the front room. It wasn't a very good one – it was impossible to tune – but Papa used to play and I'd play my violin." Greer smiled at the memory.

"A place of reading and music; I approve! And do you approve of what we have done in your old place?"

"I do," Greer said sincerely, looking around the room again. She felt strangely comfortable in the presence of these warm, friendly people. She'd spoken more about herself in the last few moments than she had since Papa had died. It felt good to remember some of the good times. She realised she was curious about Jamelie and her family. "Can you tell me a little about where you came from, about your culture?"

"We are Lebanese Christians," Jamelie said proudly, and her husband and neighbours murmured in agreement. "We come from the town of Becharre, nestled within the famous biblical cedars. This is a place where our blessed Lord Jesus Christ walked the mountain tracks and met with his mother. Some believe the adjacent Kadisha Valley was the site of the Garden of Eden. It is a place of great beauty and wonder."

"It sounds lovely. May I ask why you came on such a long voyage to New Zealand?" Greer took another bite of the manakish bread and savoured the new taste.

"Unfortunately, over the years there was a shortage of good land," Jamelie explained. "It became harder to support the lifestyle we once enjoyed, made more difficult with the recent decline in the Lebanese silk industry."

"So we came," Gabriel added.

"We came here for new opportunities," Jamelie said. "We very likely will go back one day, but we will make our living here in this new land for now."

"What do you do?" Greer was genuinely curious.

"My husband is one of the best hawkers around. He sells the best of items on his travels. He has the finest ribbons, buttons, needles, cotton, lace, gloves and other small items." Jamelie rose elegantly from the table.

"I will show you some of the lace I make for him to sell on his travels."

She left the room and returned a moment later proudly displaying an intricate piece of lace that looked like the Phoenician work that Constance wore on some of her expensive dresses.

Greer gasped. "Such workmanship! This is beautiful!"

Jamelie laughed with delight. "You are very discerning. First, you enjoy the smell of our food; now you see the quality of our lace."

Greer glanced down at her shabby mourning dress and felt embarrassed. "I didn't make this dress!" she blurted out. "It was given to me when I needed to wear black. I didn't have time to make one – I never thought I'd need a mourning dress at my age."

Jamelie looked at Greer's dress with interest. "It is not the best-made dress I have seen, I must admit, so I see why you are distressed," she said finally. "But possibly we can improve it a little until you can finish wearing mourning clothing and perhaps wear something of your own creation. I take it you can sew?"

"Yes, it's something I thoroughly enjoy. My father even bought me a sewing machine."

Jamelie smiled. "I know just the thing then."

She left the room again and returned with some exquisite black lace that she laid against the dress's bodice, nodding to herself. "Yes, this will work well. You must take this as a gift and use your sewing machine to attach it to the bodice. Although it is subtle, it will improve the dress significantly, so your dress will still be within the confines of what I see women here wear when in mourning."

Greer looked at the lace and immediately saw how it transformed the dress from shabby to something discreetly elegant.

"I can't," she said out of politeness.

"I insist."

"I don't know how to thank you," Greer said after a moment.

"That is easy, my new friend Greer. You must visit us again. Come here on Sunday. We will be here at midday after church. I will look forward to seeing you in your improved dress in a couple of days."

CHAPTER 6

Fireworks

Greer straightened her bonnet and smoothed down her maid's uniform before leaving her room. She couldn't believe it was already New Year's Eve. The Camp was abuzz with preparations for a party for family and friends that evening. There was much to do in the meantime as she joined Florence in the music room so they could give it a thorough clean. Greer had more of a spring in her step since meeting Jamelie and had joined the family for lunch on Sunday, where she had been able to show off her improved mourning dress with the beautiful lace. They had all commented on what a lovely job she had done attaching the lace, and she'd felt a small glow of satisfaction.

"You're looking bonny today, chuckaboo," Florence said cheerfully. "A bit of time off over Christmas has done you a world of good, I would say."

"Well –" Greer began, making a start on dusting the clock and two vases on top of the fireplace mantelpiece.

"Of course, I had a corker time with my family," Florence interrupted. "It was all very jolly, and my sisters were all agog when Albert visited for a short time. He gave me the most beautiful silver-plated hairbrush and hand mirror. I think of him every time I brush my hair."

Greer glanced at Florence and smiled. Florence's hair didn't look as if it had been brushed at all recently, and her blonde tresses were peeking out from under her cap in all directions.

"Once we've finished with all the preparations for tonight's party, Albert has asked me to meet him so we can go for a long walk together." Florence sighed dramatically. "He's so romantic!"

Mrs MacGavin bustled into the room and Florence immediately started dusting in earnest, but she ignored her and sought out Greer.

"Ah, Miss Gillies, just the person I wanted."

"Yes, ma'am."

"Miss de Bathe Brandon's personal maid is unwell, so you will need to attend to her room."

Greer tried not to let her surprise show at being asked to look after Constance's bedroom, but Florence was much less discreet and looked at Mrs MacGavin with wide, amazed eyes.

"If you could follow me to her room, I'll show you what needs to be done."

"Of course." Greer picked up her cloths, brooms, brushes and bucket and followed Mrs MacGavin out of the music room, along the hallway and up the staircase to the upper floor. Greer allowed her fingers to slide along the handrail, carved from solid kauri, while admiring the mahogany bannisters and the oak steps.

William Larnach's bedroom was opposite the first-floor landing, the master bedroom directly above the main entrance. The door was open and as they walked past, Greer had a glimpse of a large, plainly furnished, masculine room with three pistols on cases sitting on top of a bedside table. The window provided spectacular views of the raised lawn, fountain, and beyond.

On either side of William Larnach's bedroom were two bedrooms once occupied by Eliza, his first wife, and the other by Eliza's sister, Mary, who later became his second wife. Mrs MacGavin led Greer into one of these rooms and Greer looked around with curiosity. This room was much more feminine, and a carved wooden double bed dominated the space. There was also an elegant writing desk, a camphorwood chest and a small table with a Dresden tête-à-tête set. The marble-topped washstand with pink and white china was especially lovely. The room also had a fireplace, and sealskin rugs covered the floor. But what caught Greer's eye the most was the exquisite dress hanging in the wardrobe, the door of which was slightly ajar.

As Mrs MacGavin went through her instructions of dusting this and cleaning that, Greer couldn't help her gaze returning more than once to the dress, and when she was on her own, she stepped forward and opened the wardrobe door. Ignoring the other dresses, she examined it closely, although not daring to actually touch it.

Constance's wedding dress was made of cream satin, and Greer peered closely at the embossed sprays of lily of the valley; the workmanship was outstanding. There was a short fitted jacket on another hanger with a mandarin collar and puffed sleeves.

The sound of footsteps outside broke into her reverie and Greer hurriedly began her work, starting with stripping the sheets and making the bed. But as she worked, her mind returned to the dress and jacket in the wardrobe, and she allowed herself the luxury of pretending she might design and wear something as beautiful one day.

Greer was polishing the ornaments above the fireplace when there was a discreet cough and Constance entered the room.

"Oh, Miss Gillies, the violinist! Thank you so much for helping out today. It is much appreciated."

Greer paused in her work, glanced at Constance and saw she wore a warm smile without any signs of the awkwardness Greer had felt recently. "You are welcome, ma'am."

Constance opened her wardrobe and selected a blue jacket before closing the door firmly.

"It's the perfect day for a ride into the city to do some shopping before the party tonight." She paused to look at Greer. "Did you have a good Christmas?"

"Yes, thank you, ma'am."

"I am pleased." Constance smiled. "I feel the time is galloping along, though. It's not long to go until my wedding now. I feel there is so much to do, but the arrangements are finally coming together."

Constance started counting on her fingers. "I have my dress from Kirkcaldie & Stains." She laughed. "I've travelled with it, would you believe, as I couldn't bear to leave it behind. St Paul's in Wellington is booked, my brother will give me away, the invitations went out some time ago, and the catering is all organised."

She laughed and sounded a tad embarrassed. "Excuse me, I sound like a jittery bride, but I'm the first of my sisters to get married, so all of this feels exceedingly novel."

"I'm sure the wedding will be wonderful," Greer said. She felt privileged to be told some details of the wedding and had a sudden realisation that Constance didn't have many people to confide in about these things at the castle.

"I think it will," Constance said. "But it's being married to William that is the most important thing and the life we will achieve together. I have high hopes for our partnership." She paused. "To think that the one man, one vote law has been applied in the general election for the first time; next thing women will get the vote! We are living in a time of great change!"

Greer nodded, and Constance looked at her again with a warm smile before turning to leave. "I must let you get on."

It was only a few moments later that Kate knocked on the door.

"Oh, hello, Miss Gillies. I didn't expect to see you up here. I don't suppose you've seen Constance?"

"She just left to go into the city to do some shopping, ma'am."

Kate shrugged. "It's a shame I missed her. Oh well, I will catch up at the party tonight." Kate looked at Greer with friendly interest, her face open and warm. "You really are wasted doing housework, you know. I probably shouldn't say things like this, but Constance would approve. She's very progressive in her ideas about women in the world. You should be playing your violin or something else that brings you joy."

"Oh, um, thank you," Greer mumbled.

She was struck by Kate's kindness and was about to say something further when they were interrupted by Colleen and Alice spilling into the room. Greer retreated behind the bed and busied herself with dusting. She didn't seem to be noticed by the two newcomers, which was a common experience being a maid – it made you invisible to some.

"You're not looking for the wicked witch, are you?" Colleen asked, her brow creased into a frown.

"Don't call her that!" Kate said. "Look how happy Father is at the moment; it warms my heart to see them together."

"Heinous toad then," Alice said, adjusting the feathers on her hat. Greer stole a glance and noted they were swan feathers. "I don't know why you give her the time of day. I'll never accept her as my stepmother."

"You may have noticed that we aren't children," Kate's tone was reasonable, "so I'm not sure that is what she wants either."

Colleen snorted. "I've had enough of talking about *that* woman," she said. "So let's change the subject and go and find something amusing to do before the party tonight. The function will be splendid; Father never hosts a dud do. But I must admit I can't wait to leave this godforsaken place. I don't know why Father wants to spend so much time here. It's so remote! We might as well be living at the very end of the world!" She took Kate's arm.

"Let's go to town. Perhaps we can get you something new to wear. You never seem to treat yourself."

"Oh, I really don't need another dress!" Kate protested, but she laughed.

They left with Alice chattering about a new clothing design store in the city that she wanted to visit if they had time. Greer looked after them, sighed and then went back to work.

***

The festivities were well underway when Greer made her way back downstairs later in the afternoon. People from the city were arriving, and Edward was extra busy ferrying guests to the castle time and time again, this time using the grand carriage and four elegant grey horses. Greer joined Florence back downstairs, and they took turns peeking at the people as they arrived. Greer enjoyed the sight of the elegant dresses, while Florence was more interested in people's personal relationships.

"Oh, I predict a New Year's Eve kiss between those two," she mentioned several times. "But that one's a bit of a strumpet, and that one there looks as barmy as a bandicoot."

The castle was sparkling by the time the staff had finished. Greer and Florence walked to the servants' kitchen, taking a detour to peer into the ballroom where people were mingling, everyone in high spirits. The three fireplaces were lit even though the evening was mild.

"It's got a sprung floor," Florence whispered. "So everyone will have a nanty narking time dancing later!" She noticed Greer looking at the magnificent windows. "Those were recycled from the first Bank of Otago, so la-de-da!"

The servants' dinner that evening was another triumph from the cook. Although not as fancy as the dinner enjoyed by the family and friends in the ballroom, Greer thoroughly enjoyed the fillets of beef with Madeira sauce, followed by Rhine wine jelly. It was much later than their usual dinnertime, however. All of them had been kept busy with chores, but no one seemed to mind the late hour of the meal.

They were just finishing when Florence looked at Greer with a curious expression. "I think you should play something for us on your fiddle," she announced loudly.

"That's a splendid idea!" Albert said, sitting next to Florence with his arm slung casually across her shoulders.

"Oh, I couldn't." Flushed and embarrassed, Greer began smoothing down the black dress she had changed into for their dinner together.

"Just one tune!" Florence implored.

"Go on – it's New Year's Eve!" Albert said. "The master of the house and everyone are having music; we should have some, too."

"It would be pleasant to hear a tune," Mrs MacGavin joined in. "If you wouldn't mind."

"I'll get your violin," Florence said, and before Greer could protest, Florence ran from the room with Albert just behind her.

The couple was gone longer than expected, both looking flushed on their return. Greer had thought she might be able to avoid performing as they were away so long. But when she saw her beloved violin in its case, she had the urge to play, and she knew just the song – *Gavotte* by François-Joseph Gossec.

There were a few cheers and words of encouragement as she took her violin from its case before quickly checking the tuning. The servants hushed, and she began to play, her fingers flying, the song lilting and cheery enough to make some of the servants start tapping their feet in time to the music.

They applauded when she had finished. "That was superb," Mrs MacGavin declared with a smile. "Simply superb!"

"Do play another one!" Florence begged. "Go on, chuckaboo."

Greer thought for a moment "Well, I'm Scots, not Irish, but you might enjoy this tune." She began to play again, a Swallowtail traditional Irish jig that got some of them dancing, and the next song turned into another and another.

Much later, the staff began drifting away from the kitchen, Florence and Albert disappearing into the vast garden and far out of sight for a late-night walk. The noise from the party in the ballroom was louder, the staff at the party now working much harder in their duties. Greer was the last left in the servants' kitchen, so she packed her violin away in its case and stepped out into the hallway. Not looking where she was going, she collided with another person and dropped her violin case.

"I am so sorry!" she cried, looking up.

It was one of the guests from the party, a little inebriated and smiling at her with playful blue eyes. He cut a dashing figure in his expensive clothes, and he had a cheeky smile that lit up his undeniably handsome face.

"Well, this is my lucky night to encounter an angel like yourself."

Greer blushed as he observed her with evident appreciation, his gaze travelling over her face and then her body. She shifted awkwardly and picked up her violin case, holding it like a shield.

"An angel who plays the violin, too!" said her admirer. She noticed he had a slight Irish brogue when he spoke. "But where are my manners? I am Fergus Breslin, at your disposal." He gave a flamboyant bow and she suddenly felt tongue-tied.

"I'm Greer, er, Greer Gillies," she finally stammered.

"Greer Gillies, ah, that name suits you well, to be sure. The perfect name for an angel who plays the violin."

"I'm just a servant," she mumbled.

"I beg to differ! You are my angel, so I will call you Angel Greer from now on." Fergus ran a hand through his blond hair.

It was romantic and foolish, and Greer felt a lightness she hadn't felt in a long time as she stole a look at him and saw him smiling back with an infectious grin.

"It's not long until the fireworks. Can I escort you to the lawn outside? We would get a good view of the spectacular from there. I see they have put in some bench seats so we can watch the display."

Greer frowned. "Well, I don't know. Shouldn't you be with the other guests?"

"Goodness, no! And I won't take no for an answer. Fate has brought us together tonight, and I feel we must watch the fireworks from the front lawn."

"But I can't; I work here."

"You are off duty, and you are my guest. I assure you, you won't get into any trouble."

Greer hesitated and looked at her violin case, and then Fergus grabbed her arm. Startled by the sudden contact that sent a spark up her arm, she looked up.

"It's just a few moments to watch the fireworks; that's all I ask," he said, his eyes twinkling with mischief. Greer couldn't resist the look in his eye, and she wavered.

"Very well then." She looked at her violin case. There wasn't time to take it to her room as they counted down to midnight, but she didn't want to leave it lying around either.

"I can tell that's a precious instrument," Fergus said, sensing her discomfort. "Just bring your violin with you."

With that detail sorted, Fergus held out his arm, and Greer linked her arm through his. This time, it was more than a spark; instead, a bolt of something like electricity rippled up her arm, and she felt off-balance and breathless. They found their way out of the castle to one of the benches on the lawn, set up for guests to enjoy the view.

Fergus was right; it was the perfect place to sit and watch. The castle looked grand and enchanting, with people spilling out of the ballroom, sounding very merry.

"It's magnificent, isn't it?" Fergus was sitting nearby but not close enough to be improper.

Greer looked again and thought the castle now looked mysterious and a little forbidding, even when lit up on a night of celebration. But she found herself tongue-tied. She put her violin case on the bench next to her and avoided Fergus's gaze. "It's like from somewhere else," she said finally, her voice disturbingly breathless.

Fergus turned to look at Greer in the moonlight. "You are right; it has a certain atmosphere, doesn't it?"

Greer looked into Fergus's blue eyes. They were extraordinarily vivid, and she felt hypnotised by his gaze before abruptly looking away. Fergus cleared his throat and looked back to the castle.

"I say, good on Larnach for spending his wealth on the Peninsula rather than going off to Europe to spend it. Although many of the materials are from abroad."

Greer glanced at Fergus, trying to concentrate on what he was saying. "Is that so?"

"It is so indeed. There are fire bricks from Glasgow, black and white marble tiles from Belgium, and mosaics and other tiles from Rome. The mantelpieces are Italian marble. Have you seen the stable floors?"

Greer nodded. The maids' cottage was not too far from them.

"There are thousands of cobblestones there from Marseilles."

"You know a lot about all of this." Finally, her voice sounded normal again.

"I've travelled." Fergus stretched back like a confident cat. "And my family estate back in the United Kingdom is built in a similar style, so I recognise many elements."

Greer looked at Fergus again. So he was rich as well as handsome. And he'd just appeared from nowhere and was sitting next to her that very moment. She stopped herself from shaking her head at the absurdity of their meeting and focused instead on trying to breathe normally.

"But look, you can see the family on the roof of each turret!" Fergus cried, pointing skyward.

Greer turned her attention back to the castle. William Larnach was an imposing figure, with Constance looking elegant at his side. His children gathering on the turrets were carrying lanterns as their guests continued to spill outside from the ballroom. It was a moment of happiness captured, everyone in unity, as people began to countdown to midnight.

Beside her, Fergus picked up the count. "Ten, nine, eight —"

Greer joined in. "Seven, six, five, four, three —"

Fergus leant closer to Greer for a dangerous moment, and she feared he might kiss her. But then midnight struck, and the sky lit up with fireworks, and Greer turned to watch in awe as the family and friends outside the castle cheered and kissed and hugged each other, ringing in the New Year. But every time Greer dared to steal a look at her new companion, he was staring at her, not at the fireworks, and his vivid blue eyes were exceedingly intense. It made her shiver slightly, although she wasn't in the least bit cold.

CHAPTER 7

January 1891

To say the staff was divided in opinion about the wedding occurring that day in Wellington was an understatement. Two of the laundry staff weren't talking to each other after a violent disagreement, not that the two women got on in the normal course of events anyway. This was the day that Constance de Bathe Brandon was marrying William Larnach at St Paul's Cathedral, the bride thirty-five, the groom fifty-seven. Although none of the castle servants, apart from Constance's personal maid (who technically wasn't part of the castle staff yet), were part of the festivities, everyone seemed to be well informed on what was happening. As Constance's father was deceased, her brother Alfred de Bathe Brandon would give the bride away. Two carriages were needed for the bridal party as Constance had three brothers and three unmarried sisters. By all accounts, Constance was the best looking of all the sisters, but they were all well read and had progressive opinions.

"Do you know that one of the sisters, Annie, wears a bright orange wig all the time?" Florence told Greer as they dusted and cleaned the music room. "Can you imagine? It's no wonder Constance is the only sister to get married; the others sound as barmy as bandicoots."

"Well, I've never met them, so I couldn't comment!"

"They are all musical, though, so at least they have that going for them, unlike the Larnach family."

"They aren't that bad …"

"You put them all to shame with a single note from your violin!"

Greer had to smile. It was silly for Florence to say, but she appreciated the compliment. Life seemed to be much brighter with the start of a new year. Of course, she still missed her papa, but she had new routines that lifted her spirits. Instead of staying in her room and reading on her Sundays off, she was now in the habit of travelling with Edward the coachman in to Dunedin. She went to her old church and then had lunch with Jamelie and her family.

And since New Year's Eve, was she imagining that Fergus seemed to be making excuses to come to the castle? She was always running into him, and he always had a complimentary word to say – and he looked at her in a way that often made her blush. It was all a little exhilarating, if she was honest, even if she seldom managed to string a sentence together when she was in his company. Of course, being in mourning, it was much too soon to consider that he might ask her out – that just wouldn't be proper, but who knew what the future held? She wasn't exactly sure what Fergus did when he wasn't at the castle, but it sounded important, and it appeared from his stories he was very good at property investment and business dealings.

She also regularly practised her violin down in the garden in the small pergola with views of the Peninsula on days that would allow and when she had a spare hour or so from her housekeeping duties. Playing music was a tonic to her soul.

"It'll be a large congregation today," Florence continued, "although I hear that they don't have music at the church, so no chance of whooperups. When I get married, you'll have to play at my wedding. You will, won't you?"

"Of course, but I didn't know you were getting married!"

"Well, not yet!" Florence said impatiently, mopping the floor. "But I can see the way Albert looks at me, chuckaboo. I'm sure it won't be long until he asks."

"You could ask him; you always say you are a progressive woman, after all!"

"Don't be daft!" Florence flicked some water from her bucket in Greer's direction, and Greer laughed. They didn't have to be so serious in their duties with all the family at the wedding. It was a bit like being on holiday when the family wasn't in residence. "It's one thing to stand up for women voting in future elections, but it's still up to men to do the marriage proposals! Anyway, did you hear where Mr Larnach and Constance will be honeymooning?"

"I have no idea, and how would you know?"

"Her maid told me they are honeymooning on the North Island's west coast."

"Well, I imagine we won't see them back here for some time then."

"But when they arrive, Constance will be the mistress of the house, not just a guest." Florence pulled a face. "I hope she doesn't want to make too many changes. I like things just the way they are."

"We'll just have to see, won't we," Greer said. "But I sense she wants to champion causes with her new position, so I doubt she'll be much interested in the housekeeping and maintenance at The Camp. I think she'll just leave all of that to Mrs MacGavin."

***

Later in the day, Greer picked her way down the garden path to her favourite spot to practise her violin. She had a precious hour to herself before other duties. She took a moment to breathe in the scent of the roses and foxgloves and admire the sea view. It was sunlit and tranquil, a small spot of perfection, fragrant, even a little magical.

She reverently opened her violin case and took out her violin and bow. Resting the violin against her neck, she ran the bow across the strings. She paused, listening to the bird song for a moment, before selecting a tune from memory, deciding on the opening to Mendelssohn's *Violin Concerto in E Minor*.

She began to play, lost in the notes and rhythm, in a place of contentment and peace. As always, her soul was transported from her grief and the drudgery of servant life. As she played, everything was a possibility. Beauty, music, happiness, love even.

There was a sudden crack of twigs underfoot nearby, and she abruptly stopped playing, looking around. And there was a young man, slim and tall, with dark hair and brown eyes, staring at her. He was well dressed and had a new jacket folded over his arm.

"Please don't stop. You play beautifully." He had the grace to look embarrassed. "I wasn't meaning to spy on you or anything." He spoke

57

with a soft Scottish burr. He gestured at the jacket he was holding. "I work for Hallenstein's, the menswear store in the city, and I was just delivering this new jacket for the butler."

"So you thought you'd find him in the garden?" Greer couldn't believe she was being so irreverent, but there was something about this man that made her feel bold.

"No, not at all!" He looked flustered. "I came in by buggy and had just tied up my horse at the stables when I heard this tune in the distance. At first, I thought I was imagining it, so I just had to investigate."

"Like a detective?" Greer suppressed a smile.

"No, not like a detective! I work in a clothing shop, I work on the shop floor, and I sometimes run errands for Mr Hallenstein."

He put his hand to his forehead, sighed, and looked at her steadily. "Let me start again. My name is Hamish MacLeod."

"It's nice to meet you, Hamish MacLeod." She paused and he smiled bashfully. "I'm Greer Gillies."

"It's such a pleasure to meet you, Greer Gillies. Are you a musician?" Hamish coughed awkwardly when she arched her eyebrows. "Well, obviously, you are a musician to play as you do, but I wondered if you might be performing here as you were practising."

Greer decided to put him out of his misery. "I'm a servant at the castle." She began to put her violin and bow back in her case. "I like to come here and play when I have some time off from my duties." She looked around at the view. "It's very beautiful."

"Beautiful," Hamish echoed, looking at Greer.

She caught his eyes and smiled at his expression, wondering if he was slightly cross-eyed. He really did look a bit like an enthusiastic child, even though they were probably the same age.

"I need to get back," she said.

"Let me accompany you." Hamish's words came out in a rush, and his voice had a slight tremor. "I mean, I am going to the castle anyway, as I need to deliver this jacket to –"

"– the butler, who we have established is not in the garden," Greer finished, and they smiled at each other before walking in companionable silence back along the path.

Greer was aware of Hamish stealing glances at her, and she felt flattered by his attention, but she was also worried he was going to put his neck out from looking at her from such an odd angle, and several times he stumbled as he wasn't looking where he was going. When they reached the castle, they climbed the lion steps into the foyer and paused.

"Righty-o. I must do this delivery," Hamish said. "But perhaps I might see you again, ah, next time I must come here. I expect to have many deliveries in the future."

"Do you?" Greer's face was starting to hurt from so much smiling.

"Well, Mr Larnach appreciates good clothing, and you have so many staff …" Hamish spoke in a rush, then his voice trailed off and he looked at her a little helplessly, his face flushed.

"Well, if you have so many deliveries, I'm sure our paths will cross again," Greer said before exiting left.

She could feel his eyes on her as she disappeared out of his view, and she smiled once more as she made her way around to the back of the castle and then outside to her cottage. She would be more than happy to run into Hamish MacLeod again, even if he seemed like a bit of a goff – but thankfully, a likeable goff.

CHAPTER 8

Interludes

Several days later Greer had been playing her violin and was making her way back to her cottage when she was startled by footsteps behind her. She turned to find Fergus running towards her. He skidded to a stop in front of her, handing her a rose.

"Angel Greer! For you!" he announced before kissing her hand flamboyantly, sending tremors of sensation up her arm. "We are just off to the city, and I'm running late, but I'm so pleased I saw you before I must depart."

Before she could respond, Fergus turned and disappeared back up the path he had come, towards the stables. "Adieu, until next time!" he shouted back to her.

She brought the rose to her nose and inhaled the subtle fragrance before continuing to walk, a smile playing on her lips.

***

Florence was dusting in the drawing room vigorously, her hair even wilder than usual, if that were possible.

"What's going on?" Greer looked at her friend with curiosity.

"Oh, it's so romantic!" Florence exclaimed, throwing down her duster. "I thought you'd never ask; I was about to burst! Albert has written me the most beautiful poem." She pulled a piece of paper from her pocket.

"Oh, that's lovely," Greer said.

"Let me read it to you!"

"Oh, surely that is private!"

"Nonsense!" Florence snorted before clearing her throat and beginning to read.

Greer listened with half an ear – Albert's talents were clearly for gardening, not poetry, but it was charming nonetheless – and she found herself wondering if Fergus might write her a poem one day. She shook the thought aside, but butterflies took flight in her stomach.

***

"Now, my dear, do take a seat," Mrs MacGavin began, directing Greer to a chair in her tiny office, papers littering a small desk.

Greer dutifully sat down and wondered why she had been summoned. She clasped her hands firmly together.

"It's now been six months since you started with us, so I just wanted to tell you I am delighted with the excellent work you are doing."

"Thank you, Mrs MacGavin," Greer said in relief, her body relaxing. "I am so grateful to be working here."

Had it really been six months? In many ways, it felt like a lifetime. So much had changed since her father's passing. As though reading her thoughts, Mrs MacGavin reached out and touched Greer's hand lightly.

"It's not long since your father's untimely death, so do let me know if you ever need to talk to me about anything. Time is the only thing that can help a grieving heart, but I'm here to be of assistance if you need it."

"Thank you, Mrs MacGavin." Greer was touched by her thoughtful words. "I really appreciate that."

***

Greer always seemed to be running into Hamish whenever she was starting work for the day. Here he was again with a garment bag slung over his arm, looking about earnestly but then feigning surprise when he saw her.

"Another jacket for the butler, I presume?" Greer said. "Did you check for him in the garden first?"

He smiled back at her, his brown eyes twinkling. "Alas, he wasn't to be seen, so I must try elsewhere."

Greer laughed and noticed the tag on the garment bag, labelled "Douglas Larnach". She pointed to the tag. "I didn't know the butler had upgraded positions to being part of the Larnach family. A wedding we don't know about?"

"An elopement," Hamish said, proving quick on his feet. "You know how secretive the butler is!"

They grinned at each other before they were interrupted by Mrs MacGavin bustling towards the rear entrance to the castle. They both abruptly turned in different directions, Greer aware that Hamish's eyes were on her until she was out of view.

CHAPTER 9

June 1891

It was a misty winter's Sunday as Greer made her usual buggy ride with the coachman into Dunedin. They rode in companionable silence, Greer watching a lone albatross circling above the Peninsula before the bird turned and disappeared from view. The beauty of the rugged landscape eventually gave way to the city's outskirts, and it wasn't long before she was alighting from the buggy at the end of Walker Street. Edward nodded at her before carrying on up the street. There was no need to explain anything; they had their routine for Sunday well established.

After the church service, Greer made her way to her old home, although she seldom thought about the cottage that way anymore. It was now the George family home, a place that Jamelie and Gabriel had made their own, along with their daughter Soraya, who was now nine months old and becoming bonnier by the day. It was a home infused with their easy Lebanese charm and hospitality – and as always, she savoured the aroma of their special herbs and spices as she neared the cottage.

She knocked on the front door, huddled into the long dark coat with a hood Mrs MacGavin had recently given her. Was it really a cast-off from a relative? She would never know but was just grateful she had something warm and reasonably well made to wear in winter. Jamelie greeted her with a kiss and a hug, welcoming her inside.

"Gabriel is away still on a work trip," Jamelie said, leading the way to the kitchen after Greer had hung up her coat. "Luckily, one of the neighbours is helping me with Soraya, and her friend has also come to visit."

An old Chinese lady with bright eyes bowed her head in greeting when

Greer entered the room. Soraya was sitting on her lap, looking contentedly around the table.

Jamelie performed the introductions. "This is Zhang Ming," she told Greer, "and this," she turned to address Zhang Ming, "is Greer Gillies. She used to live in this cottage."

"I remember you," Greer and Zhang Ming said simultaneously, and they both laughed.

"Your bright hair is still the same," Zhang Ming said admiringly.

"You looked after me a few times when my father was away with work," Greer said, looking at Zhang Ming fondly. She was well known as the grandmother of Walker Street, always having time for the local children despite the demands of her own family. "Do you still live in the same house?"

"I do, and my daughter and her husband live with me – they run the greengrocer shop my husband used to run."

"It's so nice to have family living with you."

Zhang Ming nodded. "It's just sad that my granddaughter married and lives with her husband in Wellington, so I don't see them or my great-grandchildren so often. I have only just returned from a visit." She jiggled a happy looking Soraya on her lap. "But at least I get to see this baby as much as I like."

Jamelie looked at Zhang Ming affectionately. "You are such a blessing to us."

The well-dressed Chinese man sitting next to Zhang Ming, perhaps fifteen years younger than her, stood and bowed formally to Greer, his face lit in a welcoming smile. "I am Charles Sew Hoy; it is a pleasure to meet you."

"Choie was a great supporter of my husband before he passed away." Zhang Ming smiled at him. "Now he is a friend to all. A great man and trustworthy, too! If Choie Sew Hoy tells you that a stone rolls uphill, you believe him."

Charles Sew Hoy smiled at Zhang Ming and sat down. "You are too kind."

"As-salaam," Jamelie said. "Greer, please sit also."

Greer took her place on the colourful cushions opposite the Chinese guests and discreetly admired the beautiful tailoring of the clothes they were wearing; Charles Sew Hoy in a dark three-piece suit, Zhang Ming dressed in a traditional tunic with a Chinese collar in the most exquisite dark cheongsam fabric. Jamelie gestured to the food on the table, and Greer helped herself to manakish bread, which she ate while listening to the conversation unfolding. She noticed a dish of wontons, a Chinese addition to the Lebanese feast.

"Choie Sew Hoy is a great gold-seeker, miner and merchant," Zhang Ming said proudly. "My husband worked with him, first in the goldfields and then when he began importing Chinese goods. He gave my husband excellent advice. He helped with credit and provisions when times were hard and helped us establish our small greengrocery business."

Charles Sew Hoy bowed his head. "Anyone would have done the same."

"Not true!" Zhang Ming retorted fiercely. "Greed turned many men sour, so they stunk to the heavens with their ambition. You opposed opium smoking, while others went to their dens. You learnt the language here, so you are bilingual."

"And you speak both languages just as well," he complimented her.

Zhang Ming bowed her head in thanks and jiggled Soraya on her lap, who squealed with laughter. Jamelie looked at her daughter with an expression of great love and then poured some zhourat tea for Greer, who savoured the aromatic herbs and rose petals.

"He is the best-known Chinese person in Dunedin," Zhang Ming told Greer. "Did you know he formed the Shotover Big Beach Gold Mining Company, which has had great success? The 'Sew Hoy dredge' is a world-leading design."

"My dear Zhang Ming, you must stop talking about me as though I am not here," Charles Sew Hoy protested. "I must admit I have been fortunate in my business endeavours, but much of that has been luck."

Zhang Ming gestured dismissively with one hand, the other firmly on Soraya. "Luck has very little to do with your success," the old lady insisted. "It's been your vision and hard work that has resulted in your greatness. Goodness, you were just a boy when you first went to the goldfields in California and then later to the goldfields in Victoria before coming here. You were brave and courageous and still are."

"As were you, one of the few women at the time who decided to accompany your husband to a foreign land."

Zhang Ming smiled. "Some would say I was improper to do so, but I wasn't going to leave my husband's side."

Charles Sew Hoy nodded at Zhang Ming thoughtfully and turned to Greer. "I understand you work for William Larnach. Now, there is a great man. He is so many things! The Castle Builder. The Farmer. The Business Man. The Banker and Financier. The Family Man. And I know he lost the last parliamentary election, but I wouldn't be surprised if he is a Member of the House of Representatives again one day."

"I think, for now, all of his attention is on his daughter Kate," Greer said, frowning.

"I had heard she was ill," Zhang Ming said. "Is it something serious?"

Greer nodded sadly. "She has typhoid. She is gravely ill, and all the family is in Wellington."

"I am so sorry to hear that," Charles Sew Hoy said. "May health and prosperity be hers soon." He paused. "I am curious; in happier times, do you enjoy working at the castle?"

Greer frowned again at being asked such a direct question. She didn't really enjoy being a maid, but she did enjoy the feeling of belonging that came with working at the castle.

"Um, I –" she began.

"What a question to ask!" Zhang Ming tsked. "I remember Greer being a young girl with a love of music, fashion and books, so I think her life ambition wasn't to be a maid. Am I right?"

Greer smiled at Zhang Ming gratefully. "Mr Larnach is a great and wonderful man, and I enjoy being at the castle, but it's not what I thought I'd be doing with my life."

"So what do you want to do?" Zhang Ming asked. "What great things do you want to achieve?"

"I don't know about great things." Greer sighed. "But I must admit I never thought I'd be a servant. But with Papa ..." Her voice trailed off, and Jamelie reached out and held her hand for a moment.

"You are young and have all your life ahead of you," Charles Sew Hoy said kindly. "So dare to think about what you want to do while you are on this earth, and then make plans to do what fulfils you."

"A journey of a thousand miles begins with a single step," Zhang Ming said.

"It may be marriage, a business, your music," Jamelie offered.

"It may be all of that and more," Zhang Ming said with a twinkle in her eye. "There are so many opportunities for you in this country, unlike an old person like me. Dare to be great! This is a wonderful time to live and a great time to be a woman with many more choices than just marriage and children. My, the number of educated women now is to be applauded!"

Greer blushed at all the attention on her.

"Speaking of greatness," Charles Sew Hoy said, changing the subject and turning to Jamelie. "How is your dear husband's hawking business going?"

"From strength to strength," Jamelie replied. "Despite the many prejudices."

"Prejudices?" Greer asked.

Jamelie sighed and glanced at her Chinese friends.

"In many ways, this is the land of great opportunity," Charles Sew Hoy said. "But in other ways, there are many obstacles."

"A closed mind is like a closed book; just a block of wood," Zhang Ming said. "Some here are like this wood."

"I confess I resent that my husband and I are referred to as 'Assyrian hawkers' in a tone that implies we are inferior," Jamelie said. "We are honest business people providing a good service to our community."

"So true," Charles Sew Hoy said. "And let us not begin to discuss the many prejudices against Chinese in New Zealand. We could be here for hours at the injustices, but I like to concentrate on the positive, not the negative." He turned again to Jamelie. "I am so pleased to hear your business is going well."

"I miss Gabriel when he is gone so long, but his English is coming along nicely and our sales grow each month."

"Excellent," Charles Sew Hoy nodded. "You have a prosperous business. And I know you are a key part of this success with the laces and gloves and haberdashery you make."

Jamelie smiled and looked a little proud. "We have extended part of the business. I have now completed some commissions for dresses."

Greer already knew about this and smiled at her friend. She had seen four of the dresses Jamelie had made over the past few months – the fabrics and detailing had been exquisite.

Charles Sew Hoy looked at Jamelie and considered this new information.

"Dressmaking is potentially a very profitable business with the growing prosperity in Dunedin. I notice the ladies do like to be well dressed. My wife is just one example. I think this is something you can expand on."

"I am working on my next commission," Jamelie said. "And I've just had an enquiry this week about another dress, but I don't think I will have the time to complete it. Let me show you what they want."

Before the others could comment, Jamelie swept elegantly from the room, returning with a bolt of pink corded silk, some delicate beige lace and a sketch of an evening dress. Greer looked at the fabric and sketch with interest.

"Oh, that is such a beautiful colour, and the lace you have begun is perfect for this. I imagine you will include beading detail on the bodice?"

"Of course!"

Greer was so engrossed in looking at the fabric that she didn't notice the look Jamelie and Zhang Ming exchanged over her bowed head.

"What do you think about altering the design just a little?" Greer suggested. "Perhaps we have the lace on the bodice like so." She pointed at the illustration. "But how might it be if we run a fine strip of lace detail along the skirt here and here, and then finish with the lace on the frilled trim like this?"

"Yes, I like that very much," Jamelie said. "But I don't think I can do this dress and the black evening dress you saw last week. It's just too much work, even with Zhang Ming looking after Soraya."

"Then I can do it!" Greer said, looking around the room, and this time she did catch the looks the two women had been sharing. "Oh, you planned this to happen, didn't you?"

"Well, you are a talented seamstress," Jamelie said. "And I was just telling Zhang Ming the other day that you have a sewing machine you could put to good use." She paused. "Of course, you will make the profit on the dress. So what do you say?"

Greer looked at the beautiful fabric and sketch again and then back at Jamelie, calculating. She could give up her violin practice – it was too cold to practise outdoors in the middle of winter anyway – and she could always work in the evenings to get this done. Greer felt a wave of excitement at the project. She had the skills – she could do this!

"When do you need this done?" she said finally.

CHAPTER 10

July 1891

Greer sat in her room, slowly and carefully adding another bead to the bodice of the commissioned dress. She'd spent all her spare time the past three weeks working on the pink and beige dress and had been meticulous when measuring and cutting the silk, confident in the pattern that she and Jamelie had made after the client had given them a cast-off dress. The client hadn't wanted to do a fitting; she was too busy with ball season, but had assured them her shape had not changed. Greer hoped that was correct, but had allowed some ease in the seams if they needed to let the dress out.

The light was fading, so she finished the beading she had been working on and held the dress up against her body. It was coming together well. The beading still needed to be finished, and she had more lace to create and then stitch to the skirt, but it was now in a state where she could imagine it being worn at a ball. On impulse, Greer twirled around the room and imagined the dress being admired, the mannequin Jamelie had given her bare in the meantime.

There was a knock at the door, and for once, Florence waited until Greer had opened the door before entering. Greer took one look at Florence's strained face and knew she was the bearer of bad news. She discarded the dress on to the bed and thought of the large carved owl, its wings spread in the spandrel between the two windows to the castle's entrance, an omen of doom, and felt a chill creep through her body.

"It's about Kate, isn't it?" Greer said, clutching her chest. "Is her typhoid worse?"

"She's died!" Florence cried, bursting into uncontrollable sobs. "She became much worse overnight, and now she's gone!"

Greer gathered Florence into her arms and gave herself over to the injustice of the news. Kate, so young, caring, and full of life, was now gone at only twenty-six years of age.

***

The rest of the week was a sombre time at The Camp as the servants prepared for the master of the house and his new bride Constance to return to Dunedin with Kate's body following the funeral service in Wellington. Kate had been much loved by even the most disagreeable of staff, so all were in various stages of shock and distress.

What was more shocking was William Larnach when he finally arrived at his castle. He looked as though he'd aged fifty years and gone were the flamboyant clothes he liked to wear. The checks of large patterns and vibrant colours were replaced by black and more black. Constance looked strained and subdued, doing her best to support her grief-stricken husband. Greer felt great sympathy for Constance on the day they returned. This should have been a time of joy, of Constance establishing herself as the mistress of the house, but instead, Kate's body was placed in a coffin and displayed in the ballroom that had been built for her. Later, she was buried beside her mother and aunt at the Gothic family mausoleum, with its soaring spire that reached into the sky, in the North Dunedin cemetery.

For a time the castle was filled with family and well-wishers, and then just as suddenly, everyone had gone apart from William and Constance, the youngest daughter Gladys, who drifted around looking like a frail ghost, and Douglas, who spent even more time on the farm and away from the castle than he had before.

Greer observed their grief and sadness with compassion, but her own grief was amplified during this time, and it was all she could do to keep going through the motions of each day. Her heart nearly broke when she overheard William Larnach talking to his wife in the drawing room as she walked along the corridor.

"Family troubles knock me over more than anything. But this is a big one to face, my dear; good little daughter Kate, gone. Her death is a great blow to us all, but God's will be done. I must bear it with good grace."

Greer could just make out Constance's murmurings of sympathy and support, and she had a glimpse of an old, broken man being comforted by a petite but strong younger woman, full of compassion and love for her grieving husband.

***

A couple of days later Greer finished work to find Fergus loitering around the rear of the castle. He brightened when he saw her.

"If it isn't my own Angel Greer," he greeted her in his smooth Irish accent. "You are a sight for sore eyes."

Greer's heart raced at the compliment, and her sadness lifted a little as she met his eyes.

"I realise this is a sad time for the Larnach family, so I thought this might cheer you up a little if things here are a bit gloomy."

Fergus proffered a small bouquet of pink roses from behind his back.

"Oh, thank you." Greer smelt the roses and smiled for the first time since learning of Kate's death.

"'Tis so good to see you smile."

She met his eyes and blushed before returning her attention to the flowers. As always, her senses were heightened whenever she was around him. Every gesture and look were intensified; even the roses were more fragrant.

"These are beautiful," Greer said sincerely, focusing on the delicate petals. "And they perfectly match the dress I am making."

"And when might I get to see you wearing your new gown?" Fergus enquired with a cheeky smile.

"Oh, it's not mine," she said quickly. "I've been commissioned to make an evening dress."

She glanced at his handsome face again; she could get lost in his eyes, so clear and vivid were they. She sought refuge in the roses again.

"An evening dress, you say. Well, that will be worth a bob or two. I see the dresses the society ladies wear."

Greer glanced up, and he looked suddenly thoughtful and even more handsome, his square jaw in profile, his brow slightly furrowed.

"I'm almost finished it," she said a little breathlessly. "I'll need to deliver it next Sunday, before church, to my friend Jamelie."

"Jamelie? Oh, this is your Lebanese friend who lives on Walker Street?" Greer nodded.

"Well, good luck with getting it finished." Fergus bowed, and with a flourish, took her hand and kissed it, sending sensations spreading all through her body. He turned to leave, seemingly unaware of his effect on her. "See you again soon, Angel Greer."

Fergus disappeared around the side of the building. Greer looked after him and blushed again. She was still standing there a moment later, trying to regain her normal breathing as she stared at the roses, when another familiar figure came into view.

"Good day," Hamish said, carrying a jacket over his arm. He looked at the roses. "Nice flowers."

Greer felt strangely embarrassed at his comment, and she stared pointedly at the jacket he was carrying. "Is that another jacket for Mr Bentley, the butler? I didn't see him in the garden." It was, of course, a running joke each time they met.

Hamish groaned. "You aren't going to let me forget that, are you? No, this is a jacket for …" his voice trailed off. "Actually, it doesn't matter. But I did want to say I'm very sorry to hear about Kate's death. My sincere condolences. It must be hard for the family and for you as well, as you will have known Kate."

Greer was touched by his concern, his brown eyes staring into hers with empathy and compassion. "Thank you, that is very kind. Most people don't even notice that all the staff are upset."

"Well, I'm staff, too, shop staff, and I think I understand what you mean."

Greer was perplexed. "How we can be there but be invisible to some people at the same time?"

"Exactly. Although sometimes I don't mind being invisible."

"True, there are times being invisible is a bonus." She thought of the Larnach sisters, Colleen and Alice. The only time they had ever acknowledged her was when she had played the duet with Constance, but she was grateful to be invisible again around them after they had been so unpleasant.

"And other times, it's good to be seen," Hamish said, holding her eyes for a beat too long before he blinked and cleared his throat.

They smiled at each other before Hamish suddenly looked at his timepiece. "Oh, I'm running late. I'd better get this delivered."

"To the butler in the garden."

"To the butler in the garden," Hamish repeated, going along with their nonsense before disappearing into the castle searching for whomever the jacket was really for.

Greer sighed, looked at her roses, turned, and made her way to the cottage. No more distractions; she had a dress to finish.

CHAPTER 11

A Dangerous Encounter

She had spent literally hours and hours working on her first commissioned dress, but the pink corded evening dress with the beige lace and beading was now finished and ready to be delivered. Greer looked at it on the mannequin for the last time and imagined once more the dress twirling around the ballroom floor, people admiring its beauty. One day she would wear something just as beautiful at a grand event. Greer daydreamed for a moment about dancing with Fergus. He moved with such elegant grace; she was sure he would be an accomplished dancer. She imagined being held in his muscular arms and then chided herself for being so foolish. He complimented her and gave her flowers and small trinkets, but it was not as if they were courting.

Greer gave herself a little shake, looking down at her black mourning dress and the reality of her life as a servant, and then carefully began to remove the dress from the mannequin ready for packing and delivering to Jamelie. She'd drop it off before church and join the family as usual for lunch after the service. Putting on her coat, she headed outside.

She was thankful it was a dry day as she sat in the buggy by the coachman. Edward glanced at the packaged dress before taking up the reins. "I see you have finished?"

"That I have," Greer said, as the buggy began moving. "I'm hoping the client will love this – I know I do!"

"Well, if you are happy, I'm sure she will be, too."

They settled into a comfortable silence and enjoyed the ride into Dunedin, the coachman stopping the carriage at the usual place on Walker

74

Street. He tipped his hat after Greer had alighted on to the street. "I will see you after lunch."

"I am most grateful," Greer said.

Walker Street was unusually deserted this morning, Greer thought, as she walked along clutching the precious dress in its bag, noticing more rubbish strewn around than usual. It looked as if there had been a wild party, with bottles lying broken in the gutter, and there was the distinct and unpleasant smell of urine when she walked past the Caledonian Hotel. Usually she only noticed the beauty of the Devil's Half-Acre, the cottages that had been tidied up and boasted small gardens, but today all the other buildings looked dilapidated and rundown, oddly sinister and menacing in the wintry morning light.

She walked past one of the vacant lots and shivered in the cold morning air. Greer couldn't wait to show Jamelie the finished dress. She was very proud of her workmanship and the design ideas she had incorporated. Greer planned to put the money aside for the future. Jamelie had said she could do more dresses if she had time, and she was excited enough to start daydreaming about their owning a fashion store one day. The more she thought about it, the more she liked the idea.

She was paying no attention to anything when suddenly rough hands were on her, and she was brutally knocked to the ground, instinctively clutching the dress to her chest. Two young men loomed over her, their faces obscured by masks. They looked rough, as if they had been sleeping on the street, and they stank of alcohol and ripe body odour.

"You won't be needing that," one of them said, ripping the bagged dress from her arms.

"No!" Greer screamed, fury and adrenaline surging through her body as she began to get up from the ground. They couldn't take the dress she had spent so much time creating!

"She's a cherry that needs plucking," the other said, turning back to her with a new expression in his eyes, and Greer instinctively backed back away from him.

The first man grabbed his partner by the arm. "Leave her. We were told to get the dress, nothing else."

The second man shrugged off the other's hands. "All right, all right, settle down. Let's get out of here then."

Leaving Greer stunned and gasping for breath, they disappeared down a side alley, soon out of sight in the labyrinth of tiny alleyways that were a feature of the area.

Greer sat for a moment checking that nothing was broken and then got to her feet gingerly. There was no one around to help her. The streets were abandoned, and drift weed tumbled down the alleyways. No one had seen the attack, and it felt unreal, like a terrible nightmare. She looked down and saw her coat and black dress were torn in places and would need to be repaired. Her hand was grazed and bleeding.

She limped her way down the street until she was at the front door of the Georges' home. Still catching her breath, she knocked and Jamelie opened the door.

"You are right on time!" Jamelie smiled warmly, but her expression changed to one of horror when she took in the sight of her friend. "Oh, Greer, what happened?"

"Two men," Greer gasped before sobs wracked her body, and Jamelie gathered her into her arms. "The dress!"

Jamelie pulled Greer into her home, closed the door firmly and bundled her into the kitchen after removing her ripped coat. Gabriel was playing with Soraya, who was laughing at something he had said. He looked up with alarm when he saw Greer's state. Zhang Ming was making some tea, and her eyes also widened when she saw Greer.

Jamelie placed a sobbing Greer on one of the cushions. Soraya stared at Greer, put her thumb in her mouth, and immediately became quiet.

"Husband, would you mind taking Soraya into the other room."

"Of course." Gabriel scooped up Soraya and kissed his wife on the cheek before exiting the room. Zhang Ming quickly poured tea for them and set the steaming cups on the table.

"My poor dear." Zhang Ming stroked Greer's hand, frowning when she noticed that her other hand was bleeding. "I've got some bandages so we can get that hand fixed up. I will be right back."

She left the room and Jamelie took a seat next to Greer, who was still sobbing uncontrollably.

"There, there," she soothed until Greer's sobs gave way to hiccups. Zhang Ming returned, washed Greer's grazed hand, applied some ointment and then bandaged it. Greer remained numb throughout the process.

"It is just a surface wound," she said reassuringly. "It should heal very quickly. You will be playing your violin again soon."

"Thank you," Greer found her voice again. It was small and squeaky; she sounded as timid as a mouse.

"You are safe here," Jamelie said, putting her arm around her friend. "Can you tell us what happened?"

"There were two men; they just came from nowhere," Greer began, shaking her head. "Before I knew it, I was on the ground, and they had taken the dress." She began to sob again. "The dress! It's taken me weeks to make it, and now it's gone. The client will be so disappointed!"

"The client will understand," Jamelie said firmly. "It's not your fault that it was stolen."

"Can you remember anything about the men?" Gabriel asked, standing in the doorway. "Perhaps I can go out and look and see if I can find them and recover the dress?"

"They were masked, and it all happened so quickly, I really don't remember much," Greer said.

She did remember the animal expression in one of the men's eyes, the inherent violence in his stance, but it wasn't something she could put into words. She only knew instinctively that things would have been very different if the other man hadn't been there.

"They will be long gone, I predict," Zhang Ming said, resignedly.

"I've put Soraya in her cot, so I'm going to have a quick look anyway," Gabriel said.

"Be careful, husband!"

"I will," Gabriel said, giving his wife another kiss. He disappeared from the room.

Greer wasn't sure how much later it was when Gabriel returned empty handed, but she felt a great depression descend on her, despite the kind reassurances of Jamelie and Zhang Ming that it was just a minor setback in the scale of things.

She knew it was just a dress, and that although the wealthy client would be disappointed, she would just buy another one. But that dress represented so much more to her. Greer had been able to dream about life away from the drudgery of being a servant. She had dared to dream of something shiny and beautiful in her future. The dress symbolised new beginnings, perhaps the chance to start a business one day, get married and have children.

A barely recognised thought was now front and centre of her mind. Fergus would only be serious about her if she proved herself worthy of a successful man such as him. But the brutal reality was she'd been a fool to dream. She was an orphan with no prospects and no future – she was at the bottom of the heap of life.

After some prompting, Greer eventually agreed to lie down in Jamelie and Gabriel's room. They all agreed she couldn't go to church in her distressed state. At lunch, she barely picked at the delicious food she usually enjoyed, oblivious to the concerned looks that passed between the others. Even Soraya had picked up on the unhappiness in the room and was looking at Greer with concern, sucking her thumb.

When it was the usual time for Edward to pick her up, Jamelie bundled Greer into her ripped coat and stood by her friend outside the cottage as the horse and buggy came into view.

"Let's talk about this again next Sunday," Jamelie said, walking with her before giving her a farewell hug. "You may have a different perspective on things with a little time."

Edward stepped down and helped her up into the buggy, his gaze travelling over her torn clothing, but he didn't say anything. He glanced at Jamelie with a puzzled expression, and a look passed between them, but she discreetly shook her head.

"I think," Greer began in a small voice before stopping. She started again. "Um, I hope I am not being uncivil, but I think I will need to decline your invitation for next Sunday."

Jamelie took a step back, looking wounded, but then forced a smile. "Of course, I understand. Please come again when you feel ready. We are always here for you, my dear friend."

Greer nodded, the coachman climbed up next to her and they set off. Greer closed her eyes, ignoring the concerned glances from her travelling companion. Her only true companions now her aching hand, ruined dreams and bleak misery. Why had she even dared to dream? What was the point? Life was just drudgery and decay, and then finally death.

She thought of the words by Shakespeare as the buggy rattled towards the castle. *I shall despair. There is no creature loves me; And if I die no soul will pity me.* Her mother dead, her father dead, even young, generous Kate extinguished suddenly like a flame flickering and then dying. And the dress, which was so much more than a mere dress, gone. Too much loss, suddenly heaped one on top of another. No one else would understand, much as they might try. She felt utterly alone in her misery.

CHAPTER 12

August 1891

It was a bleak winter's day, torrential rain and an unforgiving wind buffeting Larnach's Castle. Florence had disappeared to do an errand for Mrs MacGavin, so Greer was cleaning in Larnach's library by herself, and she was grateful to have a task away from Florence's incessant chatter. She knew her friend meant well, but she didn't seem to understand that all Greer wanted right now was to be on her own.

Since the theft of the dress, Greer had taken to having a tray of food in her room so she could avoid the other staff. She hadn't touched her violin or read a book. When she wasn't working, she just stared out the window, watching the rain plummet down. It had rained every day for weeks, keeping visitors away from The Camp. William Larnach was seldom to be seen, but when he was, it was always with a concerned Constance by his side.

Greer signed and continued dusting the bookshelves. The library was a very masculine room, and said to be Mr Larnach's favourite room in the castle. She had heard that he'd spent many an evening there debating the pros and cons of giving women the vote, Larnach often acting as an umpire between politicians with opposing views. But he had spent little time there since his favourite daughter's death.

Greer cast her eye around the room. Mr Larnach had an extensive collection of leather-bound books that included early American and Australian history and natural history – topics that interested him. Usually Greer would have been interested too, but her spirit was so bleak that her curiosity had been extinguished. Oil paintings and watercolours, oleographs and engravings all fought for space on the walls. There were guns in leather cases, field glasses, microscopes, and other objects – so many things in one room. But what was the point of it all, Greer wondered. All that was certain in life was death. Her mother, her father. Mr Larnach's first two wives, and now his daughter. She'd seen the anguish in William Larnach's eyes the odd time she had encountered him around the castle, and she recognised the grief that he was burdened with. It mirrored the grief that she felt. The loss of her parents, but now also the loss of possibility and dreams, of being stuck in a purgatory of cleaning and dusting and somehow not living.

When Greer finally ventured outside the library, she was surprised to find an animated Constance in the drawing room, with several of the women staff gathered and hanging on her every word.

"Nine thousand signatures!" Constance cried, waving her hands towards the gathered women. "We achieved nine thousand signatures in the Women's Christian Temperance Union Petition supporting the proposed introduction of parliamentary votes for women."

"Blow me down, so many people!" Florence said, her hair even wilder than usual under her cap.

"It is, and I know many of you fine ladies put your signatures to this petition," Constance said "It was presented at Parliament by the Liberal Party, and they voted it in with thirty-three votes to eight. But on the bill's second reading in the Upper House, I am so sorry to tell you that it failed."

There were groans of disappointment from the gathered women.

"I know, I share your pain this wasn't successful. But I have been in communication with Kate Sheppard, and she has already said she will be working to organise another petition before long."

The women murmured among themselves, and Greer listened with mounting interest as they discussed developments.

"When will the men in Parliament understand that the country will be much better off if women can vote?" Mrs MacGavin said, looking uncharacteristically cross.

"It's a disgrace we are treated the same as juveniles, lunatics and criminals!" one of the laundry maids chimed in.

Florence snorted. "I think they like booze too much. Those old coves are scared if we get the vote, we'll want to ban the sale of alcohol."

"Oh, men are like children!" one of the cooks said. "They really need educating on the value we will add to all the issues the country is facing, not just the debate about prohibition!"

Greer felt a spark of life again, of being interested in something beyond herself. "How many signatures do we need to get them to take us seriously?" she asked, her words coming out in a rush.

Constance looked at Greer with steady eyes. "I don't know, but I know that we will not give up! It will only be a matter of time before women can vote. I feel confident this will happen in our lifetime."

"What does Mr Larnach think of the situation?" Mrs MacGavin asked.

Constance paused, clearly considering her words carefully. "Like many prominent men, he doesn't believe that women want the vote."

"Well, nine thousand signatures proves them wrong!" Florence declared.

"Yes, it does, but I can tell you that in our many discussions, my husband is very happy for another referendum to be taken throughout the country, and he tells me that if the vote is what women want, then we should have it."

There was a defiant, optimistic mood in the room now, and the women cheered, with Greer joining in.

"Mr Larnach is a good man," Mrs MacGavin said.

"Yes, my husband is," Constance said, smiling.

***

The following Sunday, Greer put on the black dress that she had mended, and for the first time since the theft, ventured beyond her room on her day off. As she was coming around the side of the castle to see if she could ride with the coachman as before, she was surprised to see Fergus moving up the stairs by the lion statues that patiently guarded the castle. She hadn't seen him since before the theft. He turned when he saw her.

"Angel Greer," he called down to her in his smooth Irish lilt. "You are a sight for sore eyes. I have missed seeing your beautiful face."

Greer blushed.

"It is such a splendid day, it makes me think we should go on a picnic," Fergus continued, to Greer's astonishment.

"But I can't –" she gestured at her black dress.

"I mean when you are out of mourning!" he said quickly, his blue eyes dancing in a way that made her feel a little lightheaded. "It's early October, isn't it, the anniversary of your beloved papa's passing?"

So he knew that about her. He'd taken the time to find out. She was flattered.

"The first Sunday in October it is then," Fergus said. "I'll pick you up in my buggy at ten, and we will picnic in the Botanic Gardens."

He disappeared into the castle, leaving Greer standing below the steps feeling elated at the invitation.

She had a smile on her face as she continued on to meet the coachman, but typically, he made no comment. They exchanged a few pleasantries about the day and made their way into Dunedin. Greer was thankful that Edward didn't ask her about the weeks she had missed riding in with him. They travelled, as usual, in companionable silence before he dropped her at the top of Walker Street.

Seeing the spot where she had been attacked caused Greer to feel faint, but this time the street had several families on their way to church, so she took a couple of deep breaths and stepped in with them to make her way to the church service. Later, she knocked nervously on Jamelie's door. She had been so rude to her friend last time; she hoped Jamelie would forgive her. But instead of her friend, Zhang Ming opened the door, holding Soraya in her arms.

"Ah, dear Greer," she said. "We have missed you. Please come in."

Zhang Ming leant up and kissed Greer on the cheek. "Come, come, Jamelie will be pleased to see you."

"Thank you," Greer said, following Zhang Ming into the home, but instead of going directly to the kitchen, they stopped in the front room where Jamelie was sitting on a chair, a rug over her lap, looking frail and tired.

"Greer," Jamelie murmured and gestured to the seat next to her. "I am so pleased you are here. I have been worried about you."

Greer sank into the chair next to Jamelie, concerned about her friend's pallid complexion and damp eyes. "Oh, Jamelie, I am so sorry about how I left last time."

"Please don't think of it. You were very upset."

"Oh, you are so kind, but I have been so worried I had offended you!"

"Not at all."

Greer peered more closely at her friend. "Are you okay? You aren't yourself."

"No, I am not," Jamelie admitted before turning to Zhang Ming. "Would you mind making us some tea?"

"Of course," Zhang Ming bowed her head slightly and left the room, still with Soraya in her arms, who was looking sleepy and ready for bed.

Jamelie sighed and shifted in her chair, making herself comfortable before placing her hand over her stomach and looking sad. "Gabriel and I were going to tell you our good news last time, that God had blessed us with another child, but unfortunately, the good Lord has seen fit to take our baby early, so that is why I am sad."

"Oh, Jamelie!" Greer clutched her hand.

Jamelie brushed away a tear with her other hand. "When the time is right, we will try again. We are blessed to have Soraya and hope she will have a little brother or sister one day, but in the meantime, I am allowing myself to mourn the child who went straight to heaven, bypassing her family here."

"I am so sorry," Greer said, feeling helpless.

"Thank you, my friend." Jamelie patted her hand. "This is life, isn't it? The good and the bad. I count my blessings, my faith, my husband, my daughter, our home, our business, and our friends. But I also count my losses; sometimes I miss Lebanon greatly and my family there, and I am sad that this is the second baby Gabriel and I have lost."

Greer wiped away the tears that welled up as Jamelie quoted some scripture.

"To everything there is a season, and a time to every purpose under the heaven: A time to be born, and a time to die; a time to plant, and a time to pluck up that which is planted."

Greer nodded while Jamelie spoke and quietly held her friend's hand before they were interrupted by Zhang Ming returning with tea on a tray.

"I've put Soraya down for her nap." Zhang Ming poured tea for all.

"I don't know what I would do without you," Jamelie said. She turned to Greer. "Gabriel was by my side for days, but he had to go back to work. Life has to go on, but it would be hard to manage now without Zhang Ming's help."

"It is important we help each other in life," Zhang Ming said. She stooped to look at Greer's hand. "I am pleased to see your hand has healed."

"Just as you said it would, it has healed very quickly."

"But how about your heart? How are you feeling now?" Jamelie asked.

"I confess, I have been very despondent. I just haven't felt like doing anything."

"It is no wonder!" Zhang Ming said robustly. "Such a shocking attack, and the dress stolen after all that work. But you mustn't give up on your dreams. You must not let this set you back. No matter how tall the mountain is, it cannot block the sun."

Greer looked at the Chinese grandmother and her Lebanese friend and realised how much she valued their friendship and encouragement. A thought had been forming for a few days; she'd even sketched her idea. She turned to Jamelie. "What happened with the client who ordered the dress?"

"Well, I told her about the theft, and she was very sympathetic. She is a kind woman and didn't even ask to be recompensed for the fabric she had paid for."

"That is kind. Do you think she would still be interested in having another dress made?"

"Oh, yes, she would. She was very disappointed when I said we couldn't make her another dress at this time. I have too much on to take this as well, and I hadn't heard back from you ..." Jamelie's voice faded away, and she shifted uncomfortably in her seat.

"I am so sorry!" Greer repeated. "But perhaps there is a chance to save this situation. Do you think I can get some more of the same fabric?"

"Well, yes, but I don't have the funds to purchase material now."

"I have some money from my father's estate. It will be enough to purchase more material." Greer looked at the two women with mounting excitement. "I am not going to let those two thugs ruin this. I'm going to do a slightly different dress and earn that commission."

She pulled a sketch from her pocket, and Jamelie looked at it with interest. It was similar to the original design but had different lace and beading details with a varied neckline.

"This is very good!" Jamelie said. "I'll need to check with the client if she is happy with this, but I can't see why she wouldn't be. This design is even better than the first dress."

"Well done, Greer," Zhang Ming said. "A clever person turns great troubles into little ones, and little ones into none at all. You are taking back control from the thieves who tried to ruin your dreams."

"Thank you!" Greer said, her eyes shining with excitement. "And then I'll make another and another – and you will too, Jamelie."

Zhang Ming clapped her hands in delight. "You will have premises in the city in the future! I can just see your rooms now."

Jamelie smiled. "I occasionally daydream about us starting a business together – it's not something I could do on my own – so perhaps something for the future when Soraya is older!"

Greer laughed; her previous despair was replaced with the most precious thing in life – hope. She hugged both women. "One dress at a time, of course, but I think we can do this, too!"

CHAPTER 13

October 1891

Greer carefully checked the second commissioned dress. It was even more stunning than the first dress she had created. It had the same pink corded material, but Greer had selected silver lace and beading, which gave the evening dress an added air of sophistication, and the scalloped neckline was much more flattering than the first. Satisfied, she carefully packed the second dress into a bag ready for transport. They were leaving nothing to chance this time. The coachman was arriving soon with Jamelie and Gabriel, who would transport the dress directly to the client.

Being attacked was still a blur, but whenever she replayed the events in her mind, Greer had the feeling the men had been waiting for her. She had mentioned the first dress to numerous people, who might have talked to other people, so she guessed somehow the criminals had heard of the dress, and it was an easy way for them to make some fast money. The dress hadn't been seen around town, so the consensus with Jamelie and Gabriel was that the thugs must have sold the dress to a buyer in another town.

But this time was different. No one knew about the new dress except Edward, Jamelie, Gabriel and Zhang Ming. This time, the dress was going straight to the client's home, with the coachman and Gabriel on hand in case of trouble.

Greer adjusted her bonnet and looked at herself in the mirror, checking the moss green dress she was wearing. It brought out the new sparkle in her eyes and complemented her auburn hair. It was now a little over a year since her beloved father's death, and she was finally able to retire her black mourning dress. She planned to give it back to the kind person who had given it to her. There would be no further need to wear black.

She looked in the mirror again, smiled at her reflection, and then made her way around to the front of the castle, carefully carrying the new dress in its fabric bag. A moment later the coachman came into view with his horse and buggy. Jamelie stepped down from the buggy and embraced her friend while Gabriel looked on with a warm smile.

"Oh, Greer. It's so lovely to see you wearing colour," Jamelie said.

"No more black," Gabriel said.

"It's still a sad occasion, a year on from your father's passing," Jamelie added, looking at Greer closely. "But I love your moss green dress – a colour of nature and new beginnings. It is time for you to start looking forward again."

Greer smiled at her friend as Jamelie squeezed her hand. She understood. The grief, the heaviness, but also the feelings of life stirring, of wanting to be young and carefree again.

Jamelie gestured at the dress in its bag. "And are you happy with the client's dress?"

"I am," Greer replied. She unfastened some of the bag so Jamelie could see the beading and lace on the bodice.

Jamelie looked at the bodice closely before nodding her head and smiling. "This is truly excellent. Mrs Taylor will love this."

"I hope so!"

They smiled at each other again. Jamelie and Gabriel were dropping the dress off to the staff on duty on Sunday at the client's home, and Jamelie had booked to visit on Wednesday to see if she was happy. It was a change from routine, but Greer was going to join Jamelie when she visited Mrs Taylor. Something that both excited and terrified her.

Greer fastened the dress bag back again and handed it to her friend. Jamelie took it, passed it to her husband, and climbed back into the buggy.

"So pray tell, are you still going on a picnic with this man you were telling me about?" Jamelie said, suddenly very motherly, although she was only five years older than Greer.

"It's just a picnic!" Greer was defensive about her change in Sunday routine. "There will be crowds of people at the Botanic Gardens. Florence tells me that any temperate Sunday it's overflowing with people and quite the place to be."

Jamelie laughed. "I am pleased you are going out, my dear friend. Enjoy your picnic. I will look forward to seeing you on Wednesday!"

The coachman prompted his horse to begin walking, and Greer watched as the buggy disappeared from view. She turned back to look at the castle. Some days it appeared moody and melancholy, but now with the sunlight illuminating the statues of the lions that guarded the bottom of the stairs, the building seemed beautiful and benevolent. The lions appeared to have joy in their expression and were welcoming rather than predatory. Even the eagles looked friendly. She turned towards the expansive gardens before another horse and buggy came into view. The horse was going a little too fast with Fergus in the driving seat, and the buggy came to a skidded stop in front of her.

"Angel Greer!" Fergus greeted her, looking daring and dashing and impossibly handsome. "You look beautiful! You are a vision!"

He leapt down from the buggy, and Greer felt flustered when he offered her his hand to assist her into the buggy. As always, any physical contact with Fergus sent shockwaves of sensation through her body, leaving her feeling off-balance.

She concentrated on breathing normally and made herself comfortable on the seat, noticing the picnic hamper and rug that occupied the rest of the buggy.

"This is impressive," she ventured to say, her eyes exploring the buggy as Fergus leapt back into the driver's seat, flashing her a winning smile.

"I've borrowed this from a business associate," he told her. "I'm thinking about a new buggy myself. I sold the one I had recently, so I might make an offer on this. I'm still considering."

Fergus took up the reins and the horse started to trot at a faster pace than Greer was used to, but she was distracted by Fergus, who began to chat about his latest business dealings. He was considering investing in a Dunedin hotel in the Octagon, but still had to do more research. He was also considering investing in one of the local businesses. There were so many who might like him to secure shares in their operation. He quite liked the thought of F. G. Dalgetys, Wholesale and Importing Company, William Gregg with their coffees, spices and cordials, or Duncan and Wilson. They were malt importers and whisky makers. Then again, there was also Moss Joel, the brewer, Speight's beer, Cadbury's chocolate or

Richard Hudson's Excelsior Biscuit Factory. Greer had never stopped to consider how many Dunedin businesses there were. Her ears pricked up when Fergus mentioned Charles Begg's business of musical instruments and sheet music, and she made a mental note to find the shop when she was next in town to have a look.

There was no need for Greer to contribute too much to the conversation as they travelled as Fergus needed little prompting to continue talking about his business ventures. Unlike her travels with the coachman, where they routinely travelled in companionable silence, allowing her thoughts to meander and expand, travelling with Fergus was a completely different experience. She felt her heart racing too fast, her palms sticky. Fergus kept looking at her with his vivid blue eyes, and each time he looked her way, she felt a bolt of electricity. She discreetly observed the shape of his lean muscles beneath his well-tailored clothes and enjoyed the subtle smell of sandalwood. She had to repeatedly force herself to look at the landscape to get some equilibrium back.

Then she saw them. Two large albatrosses were soaring in the sky, playfully weaving back and forth in an elaborate aerial dance. It was a magnificent sight. But then, just as suddenly as they had appeared, they turned and disappeared from view, rising high up to the heavens.

Was it an hour or five minutes later that they entered the Botanic Gardens? Greer had no idea; just that time had distorted to the beat of her heart and the twinkle in Fergus's blue eyes.

Florence was right; the Botanic Gardens were filled with people picnicking in small and larger groups. She worried they wouldn't find any free space, but Fergus expertly tied up his horse and then found a space in the sun by the rose garden. He positioned a blanket where Greer had a perfect view of the roses. There were glorious pink Bourbon roses, with their glossy foliage and slightly purple canes, their flowers full and fragrant. Greer also recognised the compact white and pink Polyantha roses, small enough to look ideal in a gentleman's buttonhole.

Greer sat on the blanket and looked with interest as Fergus unpacked the contents of the picnic basket, a generous assortment of sandwiches, cold meats, salads, small pies, cakes and tarts. As Fergus talked, she noticed how long his eyelashes were, the slant of his cheekbones, the contours of his nose, and the beauty of his square jaw. He was talking about his estate back in the Old World – it sounded very grand – but most of the words just washed over her as she took in his masculine beauty. It seemed the longer they sat on that rug, in the Botanic Gardens by the rose gardens, the more handsome he became, and each time he looked and smiled at her, she felt that jolt of electricity between them. It was exhilarating, exhausting, confounding and confusing.

"I'm sorry," Fergus said finally. "I've been talking so much about myself. I just get so enthusiastic about the projects I'm involved in. My father sent me out to the colonies to further our interests, and I take my responsibilities very seriously."

"I can see you do," Greer agreed.

Fergus produced some lemonade and she sipped on the beverage, appreciating how refreshing it was. "So thirst-quenching," Greer commented. She paused "Are you a believer in the temperance movement?"

"Actually, I am," Fergus looked away as he spoke and seemed to fidget as if his clothing was irritating his skin. "I enjoy alcohol only on rare occasions, but otherwise, I like to model myself on William Larnach. He doesn't drink and I admire that very much."

He turned and winked at Greer before continuing. "Of course, his second wife Mary was very fond of her drink, so some say he abstains now because of her drunkenness. They say she was often found passed out in the nursery."

Greer raised her eyebrows.

"Although I doubt his new wife has that tendency," he hastened to add. "I'm a big fan of William Larnach."

"What is it about him that you admire so much?"

"He's a very upright character. He's highly intelligent and has an inventive and enquiring mind with a scientific bent. I think he is very enterprising and adventurous, and I admire that very much."

"He's had so much tragedy. Losing two wives, and now the death of his daughter."

"Yes, he has," Fergus nodded. "But he's also had so much success and achieved things others wouldn't even dare to dream of." He finished the rest of his lemonade.

"It's clear that he's tried to emulate his Uncle Donald in many ways. He's been very influenced by Brambletye, his uncle's country estate in

Sussex. So that's the inspiration for his own castle. And did you know the Hamburg grapes on the Otago Peninsula are cuttings from the vines at Brambletye?"

"Oh, I didn't know that."

"I predict William Larnach's achievements will be remembered in generations to come. He's a man of vision." Fergus looked intently at Greer. "And you are a vision, my Angel Greer."

He picked up her hand and kissed it flamboyantly, and her heart fluttered more than ever. "You have made me a very happy man agreeing to this picnic. I hope you will allow me to see you again in the future."

Greer could feel herself blushing, but she managed to nod as Fergus released her hand. He suddenly jumped to his feet, plucked a Bourbon rose from its bush and handed it to her, bowing extravagantly. Startled, Greer took the rose and brought it to her nose, breathing in the full, heady fragrance. Fergus smiled and sat down next to her again.

"Well, I shall think about our next excursion. Maybe another picnic next Sunday?"

The rose resting now in her lap, Greer shook her head, feeling worried as she spoke. "I am sorry, but I have already agreed to have lunch with friends."

Fergus frowned and looked a little peeved, but said smoothly, "Well, then, definitely the Sunday following – another picnic in our beautiful Dunedin Botanic Gardens."

"That sounds lovely," Greer said.

But she was aware as she spoke that she felt oddly conflicted about the stolen rose. Such a beautiful rose, but she realised she was uncomfortable with its possession. It belonged back on its bush, but now with Fergus's action, its fate was to soon wither and die. She was elated at the prospect of another date, and becoming more mesmerised by Fergus's presence – his easy confidence, the way he moved and carried himself – but she also felt hesitant for some reason that she couldn't identify. Maybe she was still adjusting to life without her papa? Jamelie always told her that grief was not linear but would come and go until it wasn't so overwhelming. So maybe she was just having a flash of grief amid a happy day. But it didn't feel like the other times of despair. Whatever the reason, she felt unsettled.

CHAPTER 14

Better Days

Mrs Taylor, the client for the new dress that Greer had created, lived close to the Octagon in an elegant two-storey home with large bay windows. Jamelie and Greer looked around appreciatively at the tasteful furnishings in the drawing room before Mrs Taylor joined them.

"Mrs George, it is wonderful to see you again," Mrs Taylor greeted them before taking a seat.

"It is a pleasure to be in your beautiful home again," Jamelie responded. "Mrs Taylor, allow me to introduce you to my business colleague, Miss Gillies."

Mrs Taylor nodded at Greer. "Miss Gillies, it is a pleasure to meet you."

"It's a pleasure to meet you too, ma'am."

A maid entered the room and set some tea and cakes on the table before pouring the tea. Greer noticed that Mrs Taylor was impeccable in her clothing and deportment and was obviously well off – but that she also had very kind eyes.

"I was so upset to hear of your being attacked and the dress you had made stolen," Mrs Taylor said, taking up her tea with a friendly nod of dismissal to her maid. "But I am so pleased that you have clearly recovered from this brutality." Her gaze slid to Greer's dress. "And I very much admire the dress you are wearing. I take it this is one of your designs, too?"

Greer glanced down at her blue silk dress – she had deliberately changed into her best dress for this meeting. "Yes, it is."

"Miss Gillies has a flair for sewing and design," Jamelie said, also sipping her tea.

"She most certainly does. I was delighted when you called on me with the idea of making a slightly different dress from the original I had ordered. When I saw the sketch, I was immediately enchanted."

"And are you happy with the result?" Jamelie asked nonchalantly, but Greer could see a slight tremor when she put down her teacup.

Greer leant forward and waited for Mrs Taylor's pronouncement.

"The dress you delivered on Sunday is …" Mrs Taylor paused, searching for the right word. "The dress is divine! I don't think I've ever had such a beautiful dress in my wardrobe before, and the workmanship is exquisite!"

Greer discovered she had been holding her breath, so she let it out and grinned at Jamelie like a five-year-old before recovering her dignity.

"I am so pleased to hear that!" Jamelie said, somehow managing to stay composed, when Greer knew she would be feeling the same as her.

Mrs Taylor pulled an envelope from her pocket and handed it to Jamelie, who took it just as discreetly and put it in her own pocket.

"I plan to wear it to a ball next weekend, but I thought I would like something else for New Year's Eve," she said, before turning to Greer. "Miss Gillies, do you think you can design me something similar to your dress for my New Year's ball? I very much like the styling of your own dress as a starting basis, and that colour is perfect."

Greer put her head to one side and thought quickly. "I suggest we keep the skirt simple like mine, but add detailed beading to the bodice and perhaps alter the neckline as so," she said as she pulled out a small notepad and pencil from her pocket and began sketching.

"And maybe extend the beading and lace to the top of the sleeves?" Jamelie suggested, as the dress came to life on the paper.

"Oh, excellent idea!" Greer said, adding the embellishment as suggested.

Mrs Taylor picked up the sketch when Greer had finished. "Yes, this is perfect! Can you source fabric and do this in time?"

"I saw the perfect blue silk when my husband and I last visited the wholesaler," Jamelie said.

Greer smiled at her friend. They had a happy client and another order! "Yes, I can have this done in time," Greer announced with great enthusiasm that wasn't unnoticed by her business partner or client.

"Excellent!" Mrs Taylor said. "Mrs George, if you send me a bill, I will make a deposit so you can order the fabric and begin."

Jamelie set down her teacup. "That would be my pleasure."

"And the same fee as the last dress, but please add an additional ten per cent. My husband and I pride ourselves in paying for quality, and I can see this dress will be worth it."

Greer and Jamelie exchanged delighted glances before forcing themselves to make small talk until their departure. They waited until they were around the corner of the grand house before Jamelie took the envelope from her pocket and thrust it at Greer.

"This is yours!"

"No, you need to take a percentage for organising everything!"

Jamelie tut-tutted. "No more arguing! As we have already discussed, the money goes to you for this dress. Remember, you had to invest your own money to purchase the fabric, you didn't get paid for the stolen dress, and you are the one who designed and made the new dress. We will talk percentages about other dresses in the future, but not for this one."

Greer could see Jamelie wouldn't back down. "Thank you. You are a very kind person, my friend, and I am grateful."

Jamelie nodded with satisfaction while Greer opened the envelope and looked at the wad of cash. This covered the fabric she'd bought, but it was also a healthy profit. Greer resolved to save as much as she could, but she suddenly thought about organising gifts for Christmas. She hadn't done that last year – in her grief, she'd never even considered the notion. But a little something for Jamelie and Florence would be warranted, and maybe she'd get some nice gloves for Fergus now that they seemed to be courting.

"Do you want to get the buggy back with me?" Jamelie asked.

"Actually, I think I might have a quick look around the shops," Greer said. "I'll catch the ferry back to Portobello afterwards."

"You deserve to look around. I would join you, but I must get back to Soraya."

The two friends hugged, and Greer walked a short distance to the Octagon with a spring in her step, her hard-earned money deep in her dress pocket. She stopped to look at the latest paper at the newsstand. She was interested to see that the writer Rudyard Kipling was in Wellington. Apparently he was in New Zealand to "loaf" and not talk about his literary achievements, but he'd written a short story for one of the papers. She resolved to read it.

One advantage of working at the castle was William Larnach always had newspapers on hand that eventually filtered down to any staff who wanted to read them. However, Greer was careful about what she read. So far, the decade had begun with too much death and tragedy for her sensibilities. Before she'd even started work as a maid, she'd been appalled by the death of the artist van Gogh from a gunshot wound at only thirty-seven years old. And last year Neil MacLeod, a forty-four-year-old constable, was the first police officer in New Zealand to be killed in the line of duty. And was it any wonder that death stalked the Larnach family? Why did they have the owl on the front of the castle, an omen of death and destruction? Had they not thought to remove the offending statue?

Greer shook her head free of more melancholy thoughts and made her way through the front doors of the local pharmacy. She wanted to look for some gift ideas for Jamelie and Florence while she was in town.

There were many products on display competing for her attention. She was distracted for a moment by Dr Williams' Pink Pills for Pale People. Apparently, they were the "Talk of the Day" and "No Remedy ever Discovered has Effected so many Wonderful Cures". Goodness, they could even cure fatal diseases. Greer walked on. She might be pale, but she didn't feel she needed these pills.

Her eyes rested on another product, Loasby's "Wahoo" that "Positively and Absolutely Cures" sleeplessness, acute dyspepsia and chronic constipation. Greer was thankful she didn't have any of those ailments, and breathed a sigh of relief when she spied some scented soaps that would make wonderful gifts.

She purchased soaps for her friends and then stepped back out on to the busy street. She next found Hallenstein's and entering through its elegant doors, discovered a sophisticated store with an appealing array of menswear displayed to showcase their stock to best advantage. She had just found the glove display when a familiar person appeared behind the wooden and glass counter, welcoming her with a broad smile.

"Greer Gillies, how delightful to see you again."

"Hamish MacLeod, are you still looking for the butler in the garden? If so, you are in the wrong place."

Hamish laughed, and she enjoyed seeing how his brown eyes sparkled.

"That I am, but I'm on shop floor duty today, although it's always a pleasure to come out to the castle to deliver garments for the, er, butler."

"He seems to require a lot of new clothes," Greer said with a cheeky smile.

"That he does," Hamish said in his soft Scottish burr. "But what is it you require today? How can I help?"

"I was thinking about a pair of gloves for a … friend to give as a gift."

"A male friend?"

Did Greer hear a hint of jealousy in his voice? She glanced at Hamish, but his face was neutral. "Well, this is a menswear store, is it not?" she countered.

"Very true, so what sort of gloves do you think your friend would like?"

Hamish began to lift out trays of gloves from under the glass counter for her to look at. There was an impressive collection. Leather, cotton, linen, silk and knitted gloves in an array of colours – black, grey, tan, beige and white. Greer reached out and stroked a pair of tan kid-leather gloves. She could feel the leather was of the highest quality, and it felt smooth and soft to touch. She picked the gloves up to examine them more closely. The stitching was exquisite.

"I see you have good taste," Hamish said. "I've had my eye on those kid Monteith gloves since we got them in last week. I think they are the finest I have seen."

"I think you may be right." Greer cast her eye over the other gloves on selection. All of them were good quality, but this pair clearly stood out as the best of them all. She noticed the price, three shillings, and made her decision.

"I would like to put these on lay-by, please."

"Excellent! I like a customer who can make a quick, good decision," Hamish said cheerfully. "Let me just get the lay-by book."

He disappeared out the back of the store, which gave Greer time to discreetly take a shilling from her pocket for a deposit. A well-dressed man in his mid-to-late fifties, sporting a long, thick beard, approached Greer.

"Are you being taken care of?" he enquired politely.

"Yes, sir," Greer replied, just as Hamish reappeared.

"I was just getting the lay-by book," he said. "Mr Hallenstein, may I introduce you to Miss Gillies."

Mr Hallenstein bowed and looked at Greer with shrewd eyes. "It is a pleasure to meet you, Miss Gillies. I will leave you in the very capable hands of Mr MacLeod."

Greer watched as the store owner went to chat with another customer before disappearing out the back.

"He seems pleasant," she commented.

"I couldn't ask for a better employer," Hamish said. "He treats all his staff like family; he's always concerned about everyone's welfare. I've never met a man more generous. I hear he donated five hundred pounds towards building a new ward at Dunedin Hospital just the other day."

"That is generous." Greer thought back to their conversation before meeting Mr Hallenstein as Hamish did the paperwork, taking her shilling and noting it as a deposit. "I must ask, though, do some customers take a long time to decide on their purchases?"

"A few are decisive like you clearly are. Some just don't know what they are looking for. They may have come here for a pair of gloves, but they haven't thought what material or colour they want, so it takes them time to whittle down the choices." He looked up from his paperwork and smiled at Greer. "Others are exceedingly fussy, and they can't find anything that matches their expectations. But others are not discerning enough, and fall in love with all on selection, so then it can take many visits, often with friends and family in tow, before they can make their choices. But then there are the worst shoppers of all."

"Oh, who are they?" Greer was genuinely intrigued and stared at Hamish expectantly.

"The ones who change their minds all the time! They buy the gloves, but they feel they are not right when they get home. So they bring them back. The record for this is a person who brought back items – not gloves – but shirts – twelve times before they were finally satisfied!"

"Goodness! You must be very patient."

"I must be. In fact, I have to be, especially when I can never find the butler in the garden. It drives me to distraction but proves I'm patient!"

Greer laughed so hard that she gave an unladylike snort, which made Hamish laugh also.

"You'll need to make two more payments before Christmas, and then you can pick up the gloves and they are all yours," Hamish said when he'd recovered his composure.

"Excellent," Greer said in her most dignified voice, taking the docket Hamish handed her.

"I'll see you again, soonish," Hamish said, looking at her a moment too long.

Greer paused and smiled at him. He was such a goff, but so likeable. "Yes, you will."

CHAPTER 15

December 1891

Seated on an orange cushion, Greer looked around the low table at Jamelie and Gabriel's place. Jamelie had Soraya on her lap, and Gabriel was eating some fattoush salad with enthusiasm. Their friends Frank and Wardi had just helped themselves to kafta meatballs. The table was groaning with the most delicious array of Lebanese dishes and the aromas were heavenly. They had found a place for the iced cake she had brought to contribute to the meal.

Greer marvelled at how different everything was from the previous year. Had it been only a year since she'd stood outside her old home, bereaved, alone and despairing? Now she felt part of a family and had a place where she belonged. The Georges' home had become her second home, away from the castle, and she was so grateful to these warm and hospitable Lebanese people.

"It's so good you are able to share Boxing Day with us," Jamelie said, handing Greer some manakish bread, now one of her favourite foods.

"How are castle things?" Frank asked, and his wife Wardi looked at Greer with interest. A year ago, Jamelie and Gabriel's friends only spoke Arabic, but now they were attempting some English.

"The celebrations at the castle were quite subdued this year," Greer said, speaking slowly so they could understand her words, although Jamelie provided muttered translations from time to time as well. "It's their first Christmas without Mr Larnach's daughter Kate, so while the family has gathered, there haven't been the big parties they would usually host, with people coming and going."

"The first Christmas is always difficult," Jamelie said.

All murmured their agreement; each of them had lost someone.

"But the Larnachs still came and gave us presents at the servants' Christmas party, and William Larnach looks much less wretched than he did immediately after his daughter's death."

"He is a good Christian man," Gabriel said. "There is comfort knowing his daughter is with the Lord."

"It is still painful," Jamelie said, glancing at her daughter, who was now a bonny fifteen-month-old, happy and curious about the world around her. "I can't imagine the loss." She shook her head. "But his faith will bring him comfort."

There were more murmurs of sympathy for the Larnach family when there was a sudden knock on the door. Gabriel stood and said, "I'll go."

Everyone looked up with delight when he came back a few minutes later with Zhang Ming, looking especially happy and bright-eyed, wearing a traditional Chinese dress.

"I just came for a few moments to say hello," she announced to the group as Gabriel found a spare cushion so she could join them around the table. He found her a place next to Greer.

"Do you want some tea?" Jamelie asked.

"I would love some of your tea. Thank you most kindly."

Jamelie passed Soraya to Gabriel, who gurgled with delight when Zhang Ming made faces at her.

"I see your daughter is becoming more beautiful by the day. She is a precious treasure," Zhang Ming said as Jamelie poured her some tea. "I am sorry that this is the first I've been able to come this Christmas season, with all my family visiting."

"No apologies!" Jamelie said. "We know it is special to see family that is usually in Wellington."

"I am very blessed. Worldly riches I have few, but I have a family that brings me great joy and happiness, so I could ask for no more." Zhang Ming glanced at Frank and Wardi, aware they were childless.

"And my friends are also my family, another great blessing."

The couple bowed their heads in acknowledgement of the grandmother of Walker Street, known for her wisdom and kindness to all. "We are blessed you are here," Frank said.

Zhang Ming smiled at them, her vivid eyes sparkling. Although old, her spirit shone from her ageing body. She turned to Greer.

"And how are you today, dear Greer? Did you finish the latest commission for Mrs Taylor?"

"Yes, I did!"

"And Mrs Taylor was so impressed, she has ordered another dress for completion in the New Year," Jamelie said proudly. "And we've had several more orders from some of her friends as well."

"Busy times for both of you then!" Zhang Ming said with satisfaction. "I can see your dressmaking business growing in the future. You will need patience, and patience is always a bitter plant, but its fruit is sweet."

"What we are doing suits us for now, while Soraya is young," Jamelie said, "but we shall see for the future."

"And are you still seeing that young man of yours?" Zhang Ming turned to Greer.

"Fergus?" Greer blushed a little just thinking of him. "We've had a couple of picnics, and he took me out to Cargill's Castle last week."

"Oh, I haven't been there," Jamelie said. "What is it like?"

"It's not as big as Larnach's Castle, but it's very impressive. There are twenty-one rooms, and Fergus told me it's built in an Italianate architectural style. It also uses Portland cement, something new, and Fergus said this concrete construction will render the castle fireproof."

"Maybe Fergus is tempting fate by saying something like that," Zhang Ming said, a trifle tartly.

"It seems like one man trying to outdo another," Gabriel said.

"The folly of wealthy men!" Jamelie laughed.

"Well, Edward Cargill is another prominent man who William Larnach rubs shoulders with, so there may be some truth in that," Greer said. "But I can't see anything wrong with these grand homes they have built."

"True," Gabriel said. "Could have spent money overseas instead."

"And when do you next see this Fergus of yours?" Zhang Ming asked, sipping her tea and looking at Greer with interest.

"We've arranged to meet at the castle on New Year's Eve to watch the fireworks," Greer said, blushing slightly. "I have the night off, and the Larnachs always like the staff to watch the fireworks if they can."

Unexpectedly Zhang Ming frowned. "Just be careful around him," she said finally.

"He's the perfect gentleman!" Greer said, rushing to defend Fergus and confused by Zhang Ming's caution.

"Maybe he is, but I also don't think he is quite what he appears," Zhang Ming replied after a moment.

"Oh, I didn't know you knew him." Greer was feeling a little bewildered.

"I've simply observed him from time to time. I may be wrong, but I'd advise caution in any new relationship when you are still getting to know one another," Zhang Ming told her. "After all, there are only two kinds of perfect people: those who are dead and those who have not been born yet. So take your time to get to know him." She turned to Jamelie, clearly changing the subject. "Now I must ask you about that recipe we discussed on my last visit. Did you say it needed lemons or limes? I can't quite remember."

"Lemons," Jamelie said with a laugh.

Greer took a bite of her manakish bread and found it oddly bitter for the first time. She glanced at Zhang Ming, who was now talking with Jamelie about the recipe. It was so strange that she didn't like Fergus. It wasn't like her to be negative like that. But then Greer cheered up a little; perhaps she would have given the same advice about whomever she was seeing. Maybe it was just a protective streak? She thought of her beloved papa and considered he might have been the same – thinking no one was good enough for his daughter. She guessed that is what people did who cared about each other. They were protective. She was suddenly encouraged by the thought, and she eyed the knafeh, which looked deliciously sweet and tempting.

CHAPTER 16

A New Year Beckons

This New Year's Eve was the polar opposite of last year's festivities at The Camp, Greer thought as she dusted ornaments in the music room. Last year the Larnachs had hosted their massive party with fireworks – and of course, this was when she had met Fergus for the first time. Greer smiled at the thought. She never could have imagined that they would now be courting. But this year, it was only the family at the castle, and the plan was just a low-key dinner. Fireworks were still planned – on a much smaller scale – but still a spectacle for the family and staff to enjoy. Fergus was coming by later in the evening, so they could watch the fireworks together.

Florence was mopping the floor and humming to herself when she suddenly stopped, her hair typically wild under her maid's cap.

"Crikey! We need to hurry up and finish this room," she said, sounding panicked.

"What are you talking about?"

"Sorry, I forgot to pass on the message from Mrs MacGavin! I'm such a scattered-brained scapegrace sometimes! The family were going to have a music recital this afternoon." Florence glanced at the clock on the wall and gave a small shriek. "Blazes, we have twenty minutes to finish things and get out of here!"

The staff had been instructed to keep their distance from the family as much as possible over the Christmas period while they were still grieving. They had seen them all at the servants' Christmas party, dressed in expensive black mourning clothes, but mostly they were ghostly figures in the distance. Once it would have been acceptable to still be cleaning if the family came into the room; now they were expected to make themselves scarce.

"We can do this!" Greer said, also glancing at the clock.

They began to work twice as fast and had just exited with their cleaning products in hand as the Larnach family filed into the music room. Florence was on to the dining room that they also needed to clean, but Greer couldn't help discreetly pausing and observing the family for a moment.

They were a sombre group. Mr Larnach's face was drawn and grey, and although Greer could see he was making an effort for his family for the festive season, sorrow etched his features. He took a seat with Constance next to him, Constance glancing at her husband with obvious concern. She had the same direct way about her, and she looked around the room with the same intelligent eyes that Greer remembered from the duet they had performed the year before. It was clear that Kate's death had affected Mr Larnach profoundly. He was only now getting back to any semblance of everyday life, and he'd made some decisions that seemed extraordinary, even to her, a simple maid. It was widely reported that he'd sold his Kaitangata Railway and Coal Company shares for half their value. Then he'd become a major shareholder in the Colonial Bank, which was having difficulties. All of this she knew thanks to Fergus.

Colleen took her place at the piano while Alice readied her violin, both sisters wearing pinched expressions as though they would rather be anywhere but in this room. Greer had already heard Alice play and knew that the tone wasn't as fine as her violin, even though it was probably a more expensive instrument. She didn't mean to take satisfaction in the knowledge, but she did, despite what her papa would have said if he were still alive.

The youngest daughter, Gladys, took a seat next to her father. The poor mite was obviously desolate after losing a third family member at such a young age – she was still a schoolgirl, most often at boarding school. Douglas entered the room, and despite his limp, he brought new energy with him. He looked tanned and healthy, making his father look even more pallid. Douglas took a seat next to Constance. Greer couldn't make out what Douglas said to Constance, but it made her smile for the first time since entering the room. Colleen and Alice managed to turn their habitual

105

long faces into a scowl in their stepmother's direction, but William Larnach seemed not to notice as he said something to Gladys in a low tone.

The sisters began to play, a piece that at first Greer didn't recognise, as while they were competent enough, their playing was wooden and formulaic. Bach's *Violin Concerto No. 1 in A minor* was usually a piece she loved, but not this interpretation. She sighed and made her way to the dining room to help Florence with the cleaning, just as Alice produced a discordant note on the violin, as though a parting gift.

***

After dinner with the other servants, Greer returned to her cottage room to change into her moss-green dress, the most suitable of her two dresses for being outside at night. Fergus would be arriving soon. The last time she had seen him had been before Christmas, as he had been away on business. She contemplated that this would be like Christmas and New Year's wrapped into one, and Greer felt her heart race in anticipation. She checked her reflection in the mirror and satisfied with what she saw, picked up the package with the Monteith kid gloves that were his present and left the room.

She was making her way around the front of the castle, package in hand, when Hamish came into view, running up the front stairs. He was carrying a cloth bag and appeared to be in a great hurry until he saw Greer. Hamish stopped by one of the lion's heads, turned and faced her.

"You are going the wrong way if you want to find the butler in the garden!" Greer said, enjoying their running joke.

Hamish laughed and his brown eyes twinkled. He was a very ordinary looking young man, she thought, but he had a certain charm when he smiled. "Well, I'll have a gallop through the castle first, and then I'll head out into the garden."

"It's late to be doing a delivery," Greer said. The family would be busy with their recital for an age, so she climbed the steps to put them on the same level. "Don't you have plans for New Year's Eve?"

"Oh, not really. I've spent Christmas with my folks, and I'd just popped into the shop to pick up a jacket I'd accidentally left behind when Mr Hallenstein asked if I'd mind delivering this last-minute order."

"It's still very late to be doing deliveries. Did you get lost on the way?"

Hamish looked sheepish. "I had a problem with the company buggy and one of the wheels, so I had to do a rough repair to get me here. Goodness knows how I'm going to get back."

"I will talk to the coachman. He'll be able to help, I'm sure."

Hamish looked relieved. "Shall I deliver this and then we see if we can find him in the stables?"

"Excellent idea!"

They began to walk up the stairs together and stopped when they got to the foyer. Hamish looked at the parcel in her hand and frowned. "I thought the gloves were a Christmas present for your male friend, but clearly, I was wrong!"

"A late Christmas present, that's all," Greer said.

Hamish seemed about to say something else but cleared his throat instead. "If you wouldn't mind waiting for a moment, I'll deliver this and meet you back here."

Greer nodded, and Hamish disappeared into the castle, walking in his distinctive determined style. She suddenly felt foolish holding the gift parcel for Fergus, so she bent down and stashed it out of sight behind an ornate wooden chair that sat in one of the corners of the foyer.

Hamish was back quickly. Greer suspected he must have been running, as he was panting slightly. They smiled at each other and made their way companionably to the stables, although Greer noticed Hamish stealing glances at her as they walked.

The coachman was busy mucking out the stalls when they found him, and he greeted Greer with a nod and a smile. "How can I help you, Miss Gillies?"

"Edward, this gentleman, Mr MacLeod, needs your assistance," Greer said. "He's got a problem with the wheel on his buggy."

"Well, he's come to the right place," the coachman said, turning to Hamish. "I'd be happy to oblige."

"Thank you kindly," Hamish replied. "I was worried how I was going to get home."

"We can't have you stranded," Edward said over the noise. The place was a hive of activity as grooms and stable hands worked, watering, feeding and mucking out the stables, all with the din of the horses' hooves on the tiles.

"That's a handsome looking stallion," Hamish commented, gesturing at the white horse closest to them, which seemed to have a slightly haughty attitude.

"Horses are one of William Larnach's greatest loves," the coachman replied. "Which keeps me very happily employed. We have fifty-eight horses and four foals."

Hamish nodded admiringly. "It's always been a sight to behold when he comes into town with his carriage horses. Always lively and fast; I hope we get to see him come into town again in the future."

"I am sure you will. He has twelve carriage horses, by the way," Edward said as he continued to work. "Six light-grey horses and six black. He keeps the best bloodstock horses in the Stars and Stripes field. If you look in the future, you'll see the field is planted so it resembles the American flag."

"They have picnics and church bazaars in the field," Greer chimed in. "I haven't been to any as I've had to work, but you enter through an archway of whalebones."

Hamish laughed. "How dramatic!"

"Master Larnach also has eight buggy horses. Traveller is my favourite, such a wonderful horse," the coachman said. "For heavy dray work, he uses the Clydesdales, but the farm uses mules and oxen instead for some unmetalled surfaces."

"It's quite an operation you have here," Hamish observed, looking around at the spacious stables and beyond. Greer followed his gaze.

The stables had plenty of room for the grooms' quarters, with coach houses and harness rooms adjacent to the cow byre, forge house, poultry, piggery and goat houses. There were liquid manure pits and huge stone compost bins nearby, and Greer could make out the coachman's cottage, the farm workers' cottages and a four-roomed residential laundry nearby. Not for the first time, she thought it an impressive set-up. The estate was a hive of activity, with so many people working in different roles. And it struck her that Edward was the chattiest Greer had ever seen him. It seemed the stables were his preferred home. But then she realised the time.

"Oh, I'm sorry, Hamish, but I must be getting back. Can I leave you to it?"

"That will be fine," Hamish said, although he looked a little downcast she was leaving.

"As soon as I've finished this task, I'll look at your buggy wheel," the coachman told him. "If we can't get it repaired tonight, you are welcome to stay in the stable accommodation until we get it sorted." Greer left the two men talking about how much food the horses ate daily. Apparently, each horse needed to be fed four times a day, and a staggering twenty pounds of food was needed.

It was getting dark by the time Greer reached the castle, and she found Fergus waiting for her out the front, pacing back and forth.

"Where have you been?" Fergus sounded annoyed at being left to wait for her, and Greer rushed to apologise. He looked sulky, not an expression she had seen on him before.

"I'm so sorry, I was caught up at the stables with an errand," she stuttered. "But wait! I have something for you."

She raced up the stairs, scooped up the package and then ran back down again and handed Fergus the gift. Instantly he was back to the handsome Fergus she knew, his blue eyes sparkling with delight.

"A gift for me? My Angel Greer, you are much too thoughtful!"

"It's a late Christmas present. Go ahead, please open it!"

"Let's find a spot to sit," he suggested. "I know, let's go and reclaim our seat from a year ago when we first met."

Fergus led the way to the raised lawn where bench seats had been set up again for the fireworks. The lawn was ideal for viewing the castle, which was lit up and looked enchanting.

Unlike last year, the ballroom was dark and empty, but the family were gathering on the turrets for the annual fireworks while staff members were dotted about the grounds. They sat, and Fergus grinned at Greer, causing her heart to palpitate before he turned his attention to opening the package.

"Oh, these are splendid!" Fergus laughed as he tried the gloves on. "And they are a perfect fit. Thank you so much, Angel Greer."

He reached inside his jacket and produced a small package, which he handed to Greer. "And I have a little something for you as well."

Greer's hands shook slightly as she opened the wrapping. It was so sweet that he had given her a gift. When she opened the paper, she gasped with delight. It was a silver-plated hairbrush.

"Oh, this is beautiful!" she exclaimed.

"You can think of me every time you brush your hair," Fergus said in his beguiling Irish lilt. "And it's extra special for another reason."

Greer looked at Fergus expectantly.

"It belonged to my mother, Mary Jane, and she sent it over to me in the latest crate of things from home. Goodness knows, my darling mother spoils me so. She said I was welcome to pass this hairbrush on if I met someone special. Which I have, my Angel Greer. It is my pleasure that you have this now."

"Oh!" Greer was lost for words as she ran her hand over the silver-plated embossed design. She noticed initials engraved near the base. "Look, it has the initials RM," she said, somewhat puzzled.

Fergus suddenly shifted in the seat beside her and cleared his throat. "Oh, I hadn't noticed any initials. RM is the initials of my grandmother, ah, Ruby Mary. Mary is a family name, of course," he said smoothly. "So this hairbrush was my mother's and my grandmother's before her."

"That's very special," Greer said with feeling and turning to Fergus, who was looking at her intently. She blushed under the intensity of his stare.

"Do you like the gift?" he asked, almost aggressively.

"I think it's beautiful! I will treasure it always."

His expression relaxed into a smile, and he looked around. "Not long until midnight now; you can see everyone getting ready for the big moment."

Greer looked around also. William Larnach was issuing instructions from the top of the turret, and some servants were scurrying around below. His family was caught for a moment, as in a photograph, illuminated by the moonlight and castle lights. Constance was by his side, a supportive hand on his arm. Douglas was beside her, leaning towards her as though they were about to dance. The three sisters to one side, slightly divorced from the trio, huddled like black crows waiting to take flight. The eldest son, Donald, was once again missing and overseas.

Greer looked along and could see Florence and Albert nearby, with Albert going down on bended knee, just as the countdown to midnight began. Behind them, she could see Hamish and the coachman walking around the front of the castle. Next to her, Fergus removed his gloves and suddenly held her hand; she turned her face towards him, all her senses on fire.

"Ten, nine, eight –" the countdown had begun around them.

"Seven, six, five, four, three –" the counting continued as Greer gazed into Fergus's eyes. He leant towards her, and she could smell his breath. Surprisingly, he smelt of beer, but then she remembered that he did drink on special occasions despite being a supporter of the temperance movement. New Year's Eve would undoubtedly qualify as that, she justified. Then, as the countdown reached midnight, his lips were on hers. She surrendered herself to the sensation and his embrace before coming back to reality with fireworks exploding in the skies above them. She bit her lip, noticing the bitter aftertaste of beer.

"Happy New Year, Angel Greer." Fergus gently stroked her cheek.

Greer smiled at him, happiness rising like a balloon inside her. His expression was intense again, so blushing, she turned and found herself suddenly locking eyes with Hamish instead. In that moment, Greer saw Hamish was looking at her with undisguised anguish. She didn't know what to do, his distress was so evident, but then Hamish abruptly broke his gaze, turned and began to stride away.

Greer had no time to consider the strange, unexpectedly emotional moment because Florence was suddenly there, with Albert just behind, looking like the cat that had stolen the cream.

"Oh, chuckaboo, guess what?" Florence flashed her hand at Greer and then pulled her into a fierce embrace. "Albert and I are engaged to be married!"

CHAPTER 17

February 1892

Greer was woken from a dead sleep by someone banging on her door. Groggy and barely awake, she pulled the covers off as Florence burst into her bedroom, her hair even wilder than usual. She must have dressed in a hurry as many of her buttons were askew.

"Cargill's Castle is on fire!"

Greer had to get Florence to repeat her words, which finally penetrated her sleepy fog.

"Albert is a volunteer fireman, so he's getting ready to leave now. We should go with him in case we can help."

"Are you sure? What can we do?" but Florence was already pulling the moss-green dress from her wardrobe, thrusting it at Greer.

"Quickly, get dressed! The family isn't here, so no one will care we have gone."

That was true. The Larnachs had returned to Wellington and weren't expected back at The Camp for some time. Greer hurried to get dressed. A fire sounded serious. She wasn't sure what they could do to help, but maybe there was something.

Florence and Greer ran outside and past the front of the castle, most servants around the estate still asleep. They squashed into the buggy the coachman had ready, Florence practically sitting on Albert's lap to give Greer some room. Albert was wearing his dark City Fire Brigade uniform and long boots, completed with a silver pointed helmet. The buttons on his uniform matched his helmet, Greer noted, as he gave her a smile of greeting, although his eyes were grim.

Edward went faster than usual, so they all had to hang on as the buggy sped around corners. There was a fierce dry wind that Greer knew, with a sinking heart, would be only fuelling the fire. Cargill's Castle sat prominently on the edge of the cliffs above St Clair, visible from land and sea. It was a remarkable home in a spectacular position with rugged coastline and sea vistas, but when they neared, they could see fire billowing from the elegant building. Edward brought the buggy to an abrupt stop, Albert racing to join his brigade while the coachman found a spot to tie up the horse and buggy.

It was a scene of chaos. Large volumes of dense smoke filled the air, and the flames were spreading rapidly. The fire brigade was doing its best to hose the flames evident in an outhouse, but Greer could see them spreading through a connecting wooden beam to the main building, destroying the lavish woodwork.

Visibly shocked, Edward Cargill and his four daughters, servants and some friends were gathered in the garden as workers tried to pull down the veranda connecting the main building and the laundry. But they had to abandon their attempts when a massive body of flame burst through the pantry window into the main building. Greer did a double take when she saw Hamish working with the men. She hadn't seen him since New Year's Eve, but he immediately ran towards her when he saw her.

"What are you doing here?" he demanded, his sooty face looking at her with great concern.

"Albert is a volunteer firefighter, so we came with him and thought we might be able to help," Greer said in a rush. "But what are you doing here?"

"I was doing an early morning delivery." Hamish pointed at the Hallenstein's horse and buggy parked away from Cargill's Castle, with several clothing bags on the back seat. "But when I got here, the outhouse was already ablaze. At that stage, everyone was running around, getting the neighbours to help. We didn't think it was going to turn into this inferno!"

"This strong southwest wind isn't helping matters," the coachman said grimly as they watched the firefighters battle the blaze.

Florence was pacing back and forth, looking extremely agitated. Greer looked at Hamish helplessly. Why had they come? It seemed there was nothing they could do.

Albert suddenly left his fellow firefighters and returned to their small group.

"We can't save the building, it's doomed, but with everyone's help, we are going to rescue as many valuable pieces of furniture and other items as we can." His face was covered in soot, and he spoke quickly. "Don't get too close, but you'll see that we are starting lines with the help of the Salvage Corps. You can lend a hand at this end."

"Let's join these people," Hamish said, leading the way and taking Greer by the hand, his touch warm and secure, and somehow comforting.

Greer stood behind Hamish, with Edward and then Florence behind her. They passed small pieces of furniture and valuable china to each other at a safe distance from the home that was now fully ablaze. Through the smoky haze, Greer could see some men struggling with a grand piano, and there were cheers as they successfully brought the piano out of the castle. They continued to pass fine china plates and other items, but Greer could feel the tremendous heat even from this distance, and the smoke was becoming suffocating. There were cries of alarm when flames suddenly appeared in the upper part of the house, and the firefighters had to retreat as the staircase inside collapsed.

There was nothing anyone could do now but watch the house burn. The firefighters continued to hose water on the castle to stop it from spreading beyond the buildings, but urged everyone to pull back. The Cargill family looked on with shock and horror, realising that no more of their precious possessions could be salvaged. The fire was an inferno. Greer noticed that Mr Cargill was getting medical attention for a burn above his eye and hoped he would be all right.

She was shivering from shock, and when Hamish saw this, he quickly removed his jacket and put it around her. "Come, let's sit here for a moment," he said kindly, leading her over to the Hallenstein's buggy.

"Those poor people!" Greer exclaimed. "They have lost pretty much everything."

"It is deplorable," Hamish agreed soberly. "I know Mr Cargill had an impressive library and numerous works of art and jewellery that will all be lost now. At least he had insurance."

"Will it all be covered?"

Hamish grimaced. "I don't think so. I heard someone say that he

114

reduced his insurance policy barely weeks ago, so he'll only be covered for twenty-two hundred pounds now, if what I heard is correct. It won't cover anywhere near what he has lost."

"At least he has these new clothes," Greer gestured at the bags in the buggy.

"A small consolation, I suppose."

"You would think a castle like this would have plenty of water on standby," Greer said, looking back at the castle.

"Oh, that's the tragedy. There is a tank of about three or four thousand gallons under the laundry, but of course, that's where the fire started, so the fire brigade couldn't access the water. And there were two large tanks upstairs too, but they can't be accessed now."

Greer watched sadly as this family's dreams went up in smoke, as the firefighters continued to launch water at the blaze, and as the fire continued to burn and burn and burn relentlessly.

She was so distressed by the scene that she didn't notice Hamish had put his arm around her and was looking at her, his big brown eyes full of concern as her body continued to shake and shiver. But a little later, she stopped shaking and he discreetly moved his arm and led her back to Florence, Albert and the coachman. All of them were in shock, all upset for the Cargill family. But all were grateful that no lives had been lost in this terrible tragedy.

CHAPTER 18

Movements

Greer wasn't paying attention to where she was going, taking the long way back to the cottage after playing her violin in her favourite spot in the vast castle grounds. She discovered she had wandered into the rock garden, a space created by the leftover rock that stonemasons had brought up from Broad Bay by ox-drawn sleds twenty years earlier to build the castle. Now the garden was bursting with exotic plants, a sanctuary of nature. Just then she realised that she was intruding on a couple, whispering and caressing each other while they sat on a small ledge. Florence and Albert didn't even notice her, they were so intently focused on each other, and Greer carefully backed away, relieved she hadn't interrupted such a private and precious moment.

***

William and Constance Larnach were finally back in residence at The Camp, William looking a little more like his old self with a bit more of a spring in his step. Constance was even more vocal about her support of the women's suffrage petition, often hosting small groups of influential women in the drawing room. They discussed how to highlight the cause and help gain more signatures for the new petition. Greer briefly spied on one of the meetings from the hallway, the ladies sipping tea and discussing the importance of being allowed to vote.

"Women should have equal rights. It is time for women to get the vote," one of Constance's guests declared.

"But we must overcome men's objections if we ever hope to succeed," Constance said.

"That is true," another of her guests murmured. "They seem to think our interests are perfectly safe in their hands. I've heard that some fear that if women become involved in politics, the human race will die out, as we will stop marrying and having children."

The women burst into laughter at the absurdity of the idea as Florence sidled up to Greer.

"Chuckaboo, are you going to help me in the dining room, or are you just going to continue to stand here like a pumpkin?"

"Women getting the vote is important!" Greer whispered.

"Yes, it is, but so is getting our work done. Don't tell me if we get the vote, our work will magically be done. That we'll never have to do housework ever again!" The friends looked at each other and giggled.

***

"Miss Gillies, if you were agreeable, I would like us to play another duet," Constance said, a spark of defiance in her eyes. "We won't be disturbed as the family is in the city. If it would please you, would you get your violin so we may play?"

Greer swallowed her surprise and found she was pleased. "Yes, ma'am. I will be back directly."

"Do you know *Chaconne in G minor* by Tomaso Antonio Vitali?"

Greer was even more pleased. "I adore that piece!"

"Then I will see you soon," Constance said, smiling.

Moments later, Constance seated herself at the piano in the music room while Greer readied her violin. Constance played the opening notes, and soon Greer was joining her, the swell of the notes transporting Greer to another sphere – one of purity and beauty, the music perhaps a glimpse of heaven, with no sorrow or loss, just eternal love.

Constance's eyes looked moist when they finished. "Thank you, Miss Gillies. I've never had a musical partner who has played this piece as well as you do. That was … superb."

Greer began to pack her violin away and found the courage to say what was on her mind.

"Thank you, ma'am. But why do you invite me to play music with you? I am, after all, just a maid."

Constance looked at Greer and frowned. "I know you work here as a maid, but I don't define you that way. I see you as a talented young woman with great potential. And don't you think music transcends class or sex or any earthly status?"

"I do," Greer said. "Although not everyone would agree with us. In fact, some would violently disagree."

"I suppose I'm a rebel, then," Constance replied. "I must confess, I like to challenge the order of things when I can, in my own way."

CHAPTER 19

May 1892

Despite May being a bitterly cold time at The Camp, the entire Larnach family finally had some good news to celebrate after the death of Kate the previous year. Alice Jane Larnach was marrying the solicitor, Mr William Francis Inder of Naseby, and all the servants had been in a buzz about the prospect. While only Alice's personal maid had been invited to the small family wedding, all of them took turns to spy on as much of the proceedings as they could, making any excuse to walk past the ballroom where the reception was being held. Even Mrs MacGavin, usually a stickler for correct etiquette around the Larnach family, had strolled past the ballroom on a bogus errand to get a glimpse.

The couple had been married by the Reverend Dr Stuart only hours earlier, and Greer was interested to see that the bride wore a dress of white serge trimmed with white fur, sensibly keeping the cold weather in mind. Colleen and Gladys were the bridesmaids, and they were kept warm in dresses of cream serge trimmed with beaver. Greer managed to think of two excuses to walk past the ballroom so she could also spy on the proceedings.

She was delighted to see how happy everyone looked. The bride looked beautiful that day, her attendants just as lovely. Mr Larnach was dressed in black, but was back to his more stylish way of dressing, his clothing perfectly tailored. Constance looked her typical tidy and elegant self, while Douglas looked as if his clothes were irritating him, as he was constantly tugging at his collar or sleeve. But the scene was harmonious as they celebrated with the groom's family and close friends.

Greer was surprised that Fergus wasn't invited to the wedding – he'd been at the castle for many other auspicious events – but when she'd finally asked Fergus, he'd laughed and said it was a small family wedding and he didn't know the bride or groom that well, so he hadn't expected an invitation.

On her third visit to the ballroom, she was surprised to see Constance suddenly in front of her. Greer looked about in panic at having been caught snooping at the family wedding, but Constance simply smiled when she saw her.

"Miss Gillies, the violinist," Constance said warmly. "I was just thinking of you the other day, as I so enjoyed the duet that we last performed." She turned towards the ballroom. "It is wonderful to see the family in such good spirits today. Alice's wedding is just what we all need, and I'm pleased to see William looking more like his old self."

"Everyone looks very happy, ma'am," Greer ventured to say.

"I hope Alice has a lovely start to her married life. Goodness knows, the start for William and me was fraught with Kate's untimely death. It wasn't the start to my married life that I would have hoped for, but none of us knows what is around the corner, do we?"

"No, we don't." Greer bit her lip, unsure what to say at these personal revelations, although she was flattered that Constance felt she could confide in her.

"Anyway, I must return to the festivities. Soon we'll be back in Wellington, but I do hope we manage to play a duet again before long. Maybe at Christmas."

"I would like that very much," Greer said.

She looked on as Constance disappeared back into the ballroom, and then made her way to her room. She didn't dare try to catch a glimpse of the wedding reception again – what if it was one of the others who caught her next time? The trouble she might get into didn't bear thinking about.

Florence was beside herself with excitement much later in the day when she caught up with Greer. The newlyweds had departed to start their married life in Naseby. Florence was in the thick of her own wedding plans, with the chapel booked for a couple of months' time in Pukehiki, near where her parents lived. Greer had wondered why she didn't live at home, but Florence had said there was no room, and while she loved her younger siblings, they drove her to distraction, and, according to her, they were as "barmy as bandicoots". Albert was sensibly leaving her to do most of the wedding planning.

"Blow me down; you'd think the bride would have a better dress with all that money. Talk about a dreary gown," Florence said as she flopped on Greer's bed while Greer sat in the chair opposite, the book she had been reading resting in her lap.

"It was a perfectly practical dress for the cooler weather," Greer said mildly.

"Chuckaboo, you are still happy to do my wedding dress, aren't you?" Florence looked anxious.

"For the millionth time, yes! The fabric you wanted has been ordered and should arrive next week. I will make a start on it then. I have plenty of time – you aren't getting married until next year!"

"Can I see the sketch again?"

Greer nodded, opened a drawer on her writing desk, and handed the paper to Florence, who studied it carefully. Greer had insisted that the dress was a wedding gift, and Florence had finally agreed. The dress was completely different from Alice Larnach's creation. A tasteful cream organza silk, it was a design that was fitting and structured, featuring a high neck and leg-of-mutton sleeves, and a bodice with intricate lacing and beading. The dress would be completed with a train, and Florence would also wear a veil.

"Oh, I love this," Florence said, looking dreamy. "It's such a corker of a dress."

"Did you get the boots you were after?"

"Yes, I did!" Florence sat up in a hurry, her hair going in every direction. "They are the most nanty narking cream leather boots you could ever hope to find. I've got them on lay-by."

"And the flowers?"

"I've chosen orange blossom and lily of the valley."

"Perfect! You have the invitations ready to go soon; your ma will make the cake, so that just leaves you to start thinking about the reception menu."

"Did you see that they had haggis at this wedding? What a barmy idea! I definitely won't be having that!"

Greer laughed; Florence certainly didn't like haggis and often commented it was a "bag of mystery" that had no place on any dinner menu.

"Well, it's totally up to what you and Albert would like."

"I'm definitely having Tipsy Cake for dessert," Florence declared, and Greer couldn't help but smile. It was the perfect cake for her slightly scatter-brained but lovely friend, without any doubt. "And music, we must have music. You will still play the violin, won't you? I must have *Ave Maria*."

"Yes, I'll practise until it's perfect."

Florence nodded and suddenly changed the subject, as she was wont to do. "Did you know that they have almost twenty thousand signatures for the second women's suffrage petition! Not to blatherskite, but I overheard Constance talking about it earlier."

"Oh, wouldn't it be wonderful if it was successful!"

"About time the old coves in our country started paying more attention to us women and our rights," Florence said robustly. "Albert fully supports the petition, so it's corker I'm marrying a progressive man." She paused. "What does Fergus think on the subject?"

Greer hesitated before answering. On the odd occasion she'd brought the subject up, he'd been lukewarm on the idea and had usually changed the subject. "He's very supportive," she lied, worried that Florence would retort with "don't sell me a dog", but thankfully she didn't.

"I haven't seen him around much lately," Florence simply commented.

"Oh, he's been away on business, but he'll be back in plenty of time for the wedding."

"Blazes, I should hope so! It will be the wedding of the year! Forget today's wedding. Mine will be much more romantic and heartfelt!"

Greer smiled at Florence, in no doubt that her wedding, while humble in budget, would be bursting with personality and life.

CHAPTER 20

Intervals

Greer applied another bead to the latest commissioned dress she was making, the sumptuous dark velvet fabric soft beneath her aching fingers. The night was drawing to a close quickly, but she wanted to complete the last of the beading before she retired for the evening. Greer suddenly thought it would be the perfect dress for her next date with Fergus, but it wasn't ready, and she couldn't possibly wear a client's dress anyway! She decided sensibly that her moss-green dress would do admirably, although another part of her imagined wearing the beautiful new dress with Fergus's appreciative eyes on her.

***

Greer looked around Port Chalmers with interest, her hand resting lightly on Fergus's arm, trying to keep her equilibrium when in his presence. She hadn't been to Port Chalmers since she was a girl, but she recognised some of the grand buildings that lined the main street – the banks, the restaurants, the town hall. It was a clear spring day, and they wandered down towards the port, a hive of activity with a ship in port and men unloading goods.

"It was here, in February 1882, that New Zealand's first cargo of frozen meat left for London in the refrigerated ship *Dunedin*," Fergus informed her, dropping his arm and gesturing at the view in front of them.

"That is incredible," Greer murmured, somewhat distracted by Fergus's vivid blue eyes turning in her direction.

"It was a true innovation, and you can see how much prosperity refrigerated cargo has brought to the region." He turned to look back at the street they had just walked along, lined with people going about their day.

"Perhaps I should invest in a company here." Fergus looked thoughtful.

"Perhaps you should!"

"Let me share my ideas with you over lunch," he said, giving her his arm again, making her shiver slightly, although she wasn't cold.

"I would like nothing better," she replied. And she was being truthful. Greer loved hearing about his business ideas. She never had to contribute too much to the discussion, and she was free to just sit and admire him. It was intoxicating.

***

Greer was on her hands and knees scrubbing a stubborn stain on the dining room rug. One of the Larnach family had spilt red wine liberally around the room. Some young friends of Douglas had stayed the weekend, and now various rooms looked the worse for wear.

"If only they had thought to put salt on it at the time," Florence muttered, scrubbing another section. "This will be dog difficult to get out. What a bunch of foozlers!"

Greer looked at her friend with tired eyes. It was exciting for the family in the lead-up to Christmas, but so exhausting for the staff. And she'd been working on another commissioned dress that was proving to be much fiddlier and more time-consuming than she had anticipated. She was numb with exhaustion most of the time. Even Zhang Ming, a big supporter of Jamelie and Greer's fledgling business, advised them to take on less work and do things to nurture themselves.

"A smile will gain you ten more years of life."

"What did you say?" Florence sat back and looked at Greer with curiosity.

Had Greer actually repeated Zhang Ming's proverb out loud? She must be more tired than she thought.

"Nothing," she mumbled. "Let's just get this stain removed! And then we can get our normal duties done before the family arrives back from the city."

***

It was a dream come true, Greer walking on to the dance floor with Fergus by her side. Admittedly she wasn't wearing one of the beautiful evening dresses she had created for clients – but her blue silk dress was good enough. And admittedly, it wasn't one of the very fancy balls that the city hosted but a low-key local charity affair in a church hall. Still, she had to pinch herself that she was about to dance with Fergus, and her body was already sparking with that particular electricity he seemed to generate whenever she was around him. He was looking particularly handsome in his dark suit, too.

So she was dumbfounded when the band struck up a Viennese waltz and they began dancing to discover that Fergus was a clumsy dancer. He had no rhythm and stood on her feet more than once. Even more surprising, he never apologised and didn't even seem to be aware of his ineptitude. It was strangely disappointing, perhaps because Greer had imagined this moment many times, and in her imagination they had floated effortlessly around the floor, not this awkward stumble. But she chided herself over her disappointment; it was no reflection on his character that he couldn't dance. She had been reading one too many novels about romance, she decided, and she would still enjoy the evening in his company. Nonetheless, in her heart of hearts, it was a disappointment.

CHAPTER 21

December 1892

Greer had been looking forward to lunch on Boxing Day with Jamelie and her family. Jamelie had insisted she invite Fergus as well, and Greer was excited at the prospect of introducing Fergus to them. But as soon as Fergus had come to collect her in his horse and buggy, it was clear he was out of sorts, although she had no idea why.

"We are going to be late!" he snapped when he arrived at The Camp. "Hurry up and get in; we don't have a moment to waste. It's such an intolerable distance from here to the city."

Abashed, she climbed into the buggy, averting her eyes from his angry face. But then he noticed the present she was holding and his face softened.

"I am so sorry, my Angel Greer," he said, reaching for her hand and gazing at her. "I've just had a challenging day." He stroked her cheek. "I hope you are all right."

She nodded, and he glanced down at the present she was holding. This was the first chance they'd had to see each other over the Christmas break. "A gift?" he asked softly.

"Just a little something," she said, handing him the parcel.

Fergus ripped open the wrapping paper and smiled when he saw a black satin puff necktie. "This is so thoughtful!" he said, stuffing the necktie in his pocket and pulling out a gift for her. "And here is a little something for you."

Greer opened the package carefully. It was so lovely he had thought of getting her a gift. She smiled when she saw it was a box of Nestlé chocolates.

"My favourites, thank you." She resolutely thrust memories of the silver-backed hairbrush to the back of her mind.

"Well, let's be going," Fergus said, getting his horse to start walking. "Let's meet these friends of yours."

While Fergus seemed in slightly better spirits after their gift exchange, he was oddly quiet, and Greer kept stealing concerned glances at him. He was just as handsome as ever, but the usual twinkle in his eye was replaced by a dull stare, his mind clearly on something else. His eyes were also a little bloodshot, something that was very strange.

Greer turned her attention to the view and contemplated that if she were wealthy and living in Britain, she would have needed a chaperone to go on a trip like this, but rules for orphaned maids in New Zealand were much laxer. Even in America, the idea of a chaperone was going out of favour – they were living in advanced times, after all. But perhaps a chaperone would have eased the tense atmosphere she was enduring currently? Or was she just imagining this? Greer plucked up the courage to say something when they got closer to Walker Street.

"Fergus, I must ask, are you all right?"

"What?" He looked at her and frowned.

"It just appears that you seem upset about something."

He gave her a half-hearted smile and seemed to rouse himself. "Oh, just some business dealings that haven't gone my way. But it's nothing to worry about. It's what happens sometimes. You take a risk, and sometimes it doesn't pay off."

He looked around them. "Now, it was the infamous Devil's Half-Acre, wasn't it, where your Assyrian hawkers live?"

Greer was shocked by both his words and his dismissive tone. "My friends are Lebanese, not Assyrian, and it's Walker Street where they live – in the very cottage I grew up in!"

Fergus glanced at her. "Oh, I'd forgotten about that. So the road on the left?"

Greer nodded, feeling upset, and willed herself to calm down. She didn't want to introduce Fergus to her friends when they were in the middle of a disagreement. "It's this cottage on the left," she said after a moment, thankful her voice was normal again.

Fergus stopped the buggy and tied his horse to a railing, while Greer put the chocolates out of sight on the buggy floor. He then turned to help Greer from the buggy, and there it was, finally, the dazzling smile she was used to.

"Let us go to lunch, my Angel Greer," he said, extending his arm.

She linked her arm through his, and they made their way to the front door. Fergus knocked and soon Jamelie opened the door with a warm, welcoming smile as she greeted her friend with a hug and a kiss. She turned to Fergus.

"As-salaam, Mr Breslin, you are most welcome to join us in our humble home; please come in."

"Thank you, Mrs George."

"Please call me Jamelie."

Fergus inclined his head. "And please call me Fergus."

Jamelie led the way to the kitchen, introducing Fergus to Gabriel and then Zhang Ming, who had a bright-eyed Soraya on her lap, now more than two years old, playing with a small doll that had been a special present from Greer.

Greer noticed Fergus's surprised expression when he saw they were to be sitting on cushions around the low table, so she was grateful when he made no comment but simply took the seat next to her. She berated herself for not mentioning this detail. She had planned to tell him on the way over, but had forgotten.

"Have you sampled Lebanese food before?" Jamelie asked Fergus conversationally.

"I confess, I have not," Fergus said.

"Well, you might like to try the manakish bread to begin," she said, handing him a piece.

"This is my favourite bread!" Greer said, smiling at Jamelie. "In fact, I want to learn to cook some of these dishes, although I'm not very good in the kitchen. You must share how to make the tabbouleh salad with me, and I adore your kibbeh, your national dish."

Fergus looked at Greer in surprise, and Zhang Ming turned and scrutinised him closely.

"It is an auspicious occasion to meet you, Mr Breslin," the grandmother said. "Greer has been telling us many things about you over the past year, so it is good we finally meet."

"Please, call me Fergus."

"In that case, I will, Fergus." Zhang Ming paused. "I am curious; what is your favourite food?"

Fergus sampled the manakish bread, his face neutral, before responding to Zhang Ming's question. "I must admit I'm a bit of a traditionalist. I can never go past some good roast beef and potatoes."

"Then you may like the kafta meatballs," Jamelie said, passing him the plate. "Although you may find them spicier than you are used to."

"Thank you," Fergus said, serving some meatballs on to his plate.

"I'm used to our traditional Chinese food," Zhang Ming continued, "but I have come to enjoy the spicy flavours of my Lebanese friends."

Fergus took a bite of a meatball, and Greer watched him anxiously before he smiled at Jamelie with his easy charm. "Yes, more spicy than I'm used to, but it's delicious."

Gabriel joined the conversation. "We were just talking about recent law changes. What do you think of The Land Act?" he asked.

"The Land Act?" Fergus paused before replying. "That's right, it was passed a couple of months ago, wasn't it?"

"Among other things, it enshrines the rights of the public to access our country's rivers, lakes, coastline, forest and mountains," Jamelie said.

"I think it is an excellent law," Fergus replied, smiling at her.

"And what do you think about personal income tax being introduced for the first time?" Gabriel went on.

Fergus shrugged. "I must confess, I have given it little thought."

"And I have given it much thought with my business," Gabriel said with a small smile.

"Greer told us you are a businessman too," Zhang Ming joined in.

"Yes, I am. I deal a little in property development, and I'm currently looking at various companies to invest in."

"Oh, you might want to invest in Greer and Jamelie's dressmaking business then," Zhang Ming said, causing both Greer and Jamelie to look at her with surprise.

"I didn't know you were going into business," Fergus said, frowning at Greer. "What is all this about?"

"Oh, I think you know I've made a few dresses," Greer said, growing hot under Fergus's scrutiny.

"I thought that was just a hobby, not a business."

"It's the beginning of a business," Zhang Ming said. "Greer and Jamelie have a queue of women wanting their magnificent gowns."

"Opening a shop is just an idea for the future. I am happy for us to take orders and create dresses as we can for now," Jamelie said, smiling warmly. She turned to Zhang Ming. "You are a very mischievous woman, you know, bringing this up every five minutes."

"Well, someone has to point out some of life's possibilities," Zhang Ming said, pouring herself some tea. "Be not afraid of growing slowly, be afraid only of standing still." She paused. "It's fine for you and Greer to make dresses on commission, but you need to be thinking bigger. Like opening a shop. That's the only reason I mentioned it to this young man looking for investment opportunities."

Fergus's face had clouded, and he glared at Zhang Ming. "Well, this doesn't fit the criteria for what I'm willing to invest in," he said bluntly.

Greer and Jamelie exchanged a worried look. Zhang Ming looked back at him with a calm, penetrating gaze.

"Don't worry, Fergus," Greer said hurriedly. "We have no intention of opening a shop!"

"And I certainly couldn't take on the responsibility of a shop right now, when my daughter is so young," Jamelie glanced at her daughter, who was pretending to feed the doll, oblivious to the conversation around her.

"This dress shop business is a good idea, though," Gabriel said, smiling at his wife.

"I'm pleased you agree. It's certainly something to consider for the future," Zhang Ming said smoothly before turning back to Fergus. "So, young man, what do you think about the idea of women one day being allowed to vote?"

"Oh, it's not something we have discussed much," Greer said quickly, noticing how sullen Fergus looked.

"I would still be curious to know what you think," Zhang Ming persisted, her attention remaining on Fergus.

"Well, I don't think it matters what I think, as the petition failed earlier in the year," Fergus said after a moment.

"But there is a third petition underway so surely you have an opinion? It could be that soon Greer can vote just the same as you can now."

"Oh, I think that is unlikely. But we shall see." He shrugged and ate another mouthful of food, and Greer felt her heart plummet. He was so dismissive of the idea. She resolved that they must have a proper discussion soon, and she would then persuade him of the sense of the idea.

"Members of Parliament will be paid salaries for the first time next year," Gabriel changed the subject. "Do you have any thoughts on that?"

Fergus perked up. "I think it is an excellent idea. It means it will attract more people to go into politics, rather than just the wealthy."

"Greer has mentioned you come from a wealthy family," Zhang Ming said. "That is most fortunate."

For the first time since they had arrived, Fergus became animated and began talking about his family's estate back in England. Greer sighed with relief. Now he was presenting himself in a way that would endear him to her friends. He looked handsome and charismatic, and she admired him from beneath her lashes for a moment. But then she caught Zhang Ming's face and was astounded to see Zhang Ming looking at Fergus as though he was the devil incarnate. Noticing Greer staring at her, she rearranged her expression to one of neutrality.

"I must put Soraya down for a nap," Zhang Ming said, lifting the little girl up.

"Can Dolly come too?" Soraya had a sweet, clear voice and gazed at Zhang Ming intently, waiting for an answer.

"Of course she can! She probably needs a nap too."

Soraya nodded happily.

"I'm very happy to put Soraya to bed," Jamelie made as if to rise to her feet.

"No, you relax. You have been working much too hard lately," Zhang Ming insisted, leaving the room after one more piercing look at Fergus.

"We should be going," Fergus said, putting down his serviette and getting to his feet. Greer had no choice but to follow his lead.

"Oh, is that the time? Yes, we must be getting back. Thank you for a lovely meal."

"You are welcome anytime, my dear friend," Jamelie said, standing up to escort them to the door.

"Thank you very much for your hospitality," Fergus addressed Jamelie and Gabriel, impeccably polite but without his usual charm.

Before Greer could say anything more, they were out the door and walking towards the horse and buggy. Jamelie waved for a moment, and Greer waved back, all of them full of smiles, but Fergus turned to Greer in fury as soon as the door closed.

"That is the worst lunch I've ever had to endure," he said through gritted teeth. "How can you eat that foreign muck? And all those pointless questions about politics! And you didn't tell me that a Chinese hag would be there giving me the evil eye."

Greer's eyes widened, and she stepped back in alarm.

"Oh, don't look at me like that," Fergus snapped. "I'm just speaking my mind."

He readied the horse and jumped into the buggy, crushing Greer's chocolates under his feet in the process. She knew it was an accident, but the tears welled despite her best efforts. They had been a gift, and now they were ruined.

"Come on, don't just stand there. Get in, and I'll take you back to the castle. I have a business meeting I must attend afterwards."

Greer got into the buggy, and they rode in silence to The Camp. A lone albatross soared in the sky, and to her eye, the bird looked as miserable as she felt. Alone and friendless. But to her astonishment, when they arrived and it was time for her to step down out of the buggy, Fergus suddenly turned to her looking contrite.

"Oh, my Angel Greer. Please forgive me. I just haven't been myself today."

His look was so pleading that Greer couldn't help but forgive him. "Anyone can have a bad day."

"Do you forgive me?"

"Of course I do."

Fergus leant forward and pecked her on the lips gently, gazing at her in a way she found mesmerising. "You really are an angel."

Greer blushed a little.

"I must go, but I'll be in touch again soon," Fergus said, helping her down from the buggy.

She watched from below the lion statues out the front of the castle until Fergus had disappeared from view, a cold wind causing her to shiver. She looked for a moment at the lions with their bared teeth guarding each side of the entrance steps. The eagles with their talons eyed her arrogantly. Above, the carved owl, the symbol of death and disaster, looked down on them all.

Greer shrugged off feelings of discomfort and walked around the side of the castle to the cottage. She sincerely hoped she didn't bump into anyone, especially Florence, who was always so inquisitive. After such a distressing and confusing lunch, she needed time to absorb her thoughts. Was this just their first quarrel, something that any couple should expect? Surely she shouldn't overthink things, but it would be tough not to. Already her stomach was in knots and her thoughts were swirling.

CHAPTER 22

Discord

She read and reread the letter until the paper was crumpled and tatty. The letter had arrived the day after her disagreement with Fergus. It was obviously written in a hurry, the handwriting large and scrawled and, in places, misspelt and challenging to read. But there was no confusion about the meaning of the letter. Fergus was departing immediately on urgent business to England. He would have already left by the time she got this missive.

There was no hint of affection or anything to bring her comfort, and the more she read it, the more questions she had. Were they still courting? When would he come back? Would he come back? The uncertainty of it all made her feel ill.

***

Greer had mastered so many more complicated pieces, but her fingers refused to behave every time she practised *Ave Maria* for Florence's upcoming wedding. Midway through, the soaring notes turned to discord in precisely the same spot.

Eventually she gave up, her fingers numb from trying repeatedly. So she put her violin and bow back into the case and stared glumly at the view that usually enchanted her, the wind chill unforgiving, before noticing the clouds starting to roll in. She would need to get back to the safety of the cottage before the heavens opened. Greer hurriedly picked up her case and began to run, but moments later, the rain plummeted from above and she was quickly thoroughly drenched. Miserably, she sought refuge in her bedroom, flinging her violin case on the bed and turning to watch the water pour down the window. She stood for a time before realising she must be sensible and change into dry clothes or she would catch a chill.

***

Greer had pricked her finger again on the needle, and now she looked in horror at the blood ruining a section of Florence's wedding dress. Distraught, she threw the dress into the corner of the room and began to sob. Everything seemed to overwhelm her at the moment. This was just the latest in a string of mishaps.

A little later, her finger now wrapped, she picked up the dress and began carefully cutting out the offending panel, readying to sew a new piece of fabric in its place. She rubbed her tired eyes and told herself she wasn't going to bed until this was repaired.

***

Greer must have dusted this dinner set dozens of times, the unique set displayed in the china cabinet in the dining room. For some reason it was seldom used, but it was always on display; a Bridgewood Orient dinner set that had been a wedding gift to William and Constance Larnach. When it had first arrived, Greer had loved looking at the delicate oriental design, the birds and flowers in soft greens and pinks against a white background – the design ascetically pleasing. But right now, she hated this dinner set. It mocked her, made her despise the tedium of the tasks she had to perform over and over each week, time seeming to condense to a never-ending round of dusting and cleaning, dusting and cleaning, ad infinitum, as if she were a hamster forever running on a wheel.

CHAPTER 23

July 1893

Greer looked through the doorway at the congregation gathered inside the wooden Pukehiki church building, sitting in the pews in anticipation of Florence's arrival. Light filtered into the church through the arched windows, and everything was bathed in a soft glow. Albert was waiting at the altar, nervously tugging at his shirt collar as he waited for his bride to come through the church doors. The Reverend Alexander Greig talked to him in soothing tones, making no difference to the poor man's nerves. Albert's brother, the best man, an older, taller version of his sibling, patted Albert on the back.

The guests looked about them in anticipation, all dressed in their best clothes. There was Mrs MacGavin, seated next to her husband. Edward the coachman looked dapper, seated next to a female companion who Greer had discovered was his sister. Other members of staff were seated behind the bride and groom's family. Greer hadn't realised that Hamish was a good friend of Albert until she'd seen the invitation list, so he was there too, dressed immaculately as always. He caught her eye and smiled. Greer smiled back and then turned to Florence, who was standing outside the church out of view of the congregation, looking radiant and fidgeting, not with nerves but with unrestrained energy.

"Everyone is inside and waiting," Greer said. "And you look beautiful!"

"Thank you, Greer. It's all thanks to this corker dress you made me. Blazes, I feel like royalty, wearing this!"

After a couple of hiccups, Florence's wedding dress had come out very well. The organza cream silk perfectly suited Florence's complexion, and although it was modest, with a high neck and leg-of-mutton sleeves, it showed off her slim figure. For once, Florence's hair was sleek and tamed under her veil, and Greer fussed around making sure the train was straight.

"It was a pleasure to make this."

"And your dress has come up well, too, chuckaboo."

Greer glanced down at her bridesmaid's dress. It was pale orange silk that complemented Florence's flower bouquet of orange blossom and lily of the valley. It was a much simpler design, but with similar beading on the bodice to Florence's dress. It was a dress Greer would be able to wear again. Not that she had anywhere to wear such a lovely dress after this occasion.

Florence caught her eye and frowned. "You mustn't think of that nineteener, Fergus, today," she said imperiously. "I command it."

Greer dutifully laughed at Florence's expression, but inside she was still hurt and bewildered by Fergus's actions. How could he just disappear to England with only a scribbled note for her to read and reread? She hadn't heard anything from him since, which made her feel more despondent with each passing day. She straightened her back. This was Florence's happy day and not the time or the place for her to fret, yet again, about the situation.

She stepped back as Florence conversed with her father before he took her arm, and then Florence gave Greer a nod. Greer picked up her smaller bouquet of flowers and went to the church doorway to nod at the seated pianist, who began the wedding march. Greer walked up the aisle, suddenly bashful with all eyes on her, but thankfully, soon all the attention turned to the bride.

Greer didn't remember much of the service; just that it was heartfelt, and the Bible readings were well considered and beautiful. Her violin sat ready by the pianist, and part way through the service, she was invited to play. Luckily her fingers and instrument were once more in harmony, and the beautiful melody of *Ava Maria* soared, the church acoustics proving superb. Greer lost herself in the music, but she noticed that several women were dabbing their eyes with handkerchiefs when she finished. It was Hamish she couldn't ignore as she began to pack her violin away and the service continued. Hamish stared at her with genuine appreciation, and she was suddenly pleased that he had seen her play in this setting; she

137

returned his gaze with a small smile. Moments later, Florence and Albert were declared man and wife, and Albert was invited to kiss his bride. Greer was one of the witnesses to sign the wedding documents soon after.

Following the service, everyone made their way across from the simple white wooden church to the community hall that had been readied for the reception. Florence had spent a lot of time thinking about her menu, which her family had rallied around to cook and provide. The mains were roast beef, turkey, boiled fowls, and lamb served on platters with garnishes of rosemary, sage and flowers. Tipsy Cake and red wine jellies were for dessert, and the wedding cake was a classic fruit cake. Greer ate and watched her dear friend enjoy her big day, the love between the newlyweds evident as they exchanged smiles and caresses, and the celebration was one of great happiness. It wasn't long before Greer put aside her thoughts of Fergus and just enjoyed the reception.

After the speeches and the cake cutting, and the first dance had encouraged others on to the dance floor, Greer found herself standing at another table by a smiling Hamish.

"I was hoping I'd get a chance to talk to you," Hamish said, pulling out a seat for her.

"Still looking for the butler in the garden?" Greer said mischievously as she sat down.

"Alas, he appears elusive every time I go to the castle gardens. Maybe next time." Hamish sipped his wine. "I very much enjoyed your musical number today. Are you still playing the violin in the garden?"

"Not recently, because of the winter weather, but I'll get back to it."

Hamish nodded. "You should." He pointed at the carafe of wine. "Would you like some wine?"

Greer hesitated.

"Oh, you are not for temperance, are you?"

"Well, I am," she told him. "But I believe it is all right to drink on special occasions, so I will have a glass."

"Excellent," Hamish said, pouring her a glass and then looking around. "It's definitely a special occasion, so good to see Florence and Albert looking so happy."

"Yes, it is!" Greer sipped her wine. It had echoes of peach and other fruits, and was delightful.

"And on other auspicious news, it's only a couple of days ago that the latest petition for extending the vote to women was presented to Parliament, so I hope it gets passed this time," Hamish said.

"Oh, are you a supporter of women getting the vote?" Greer looked at Hamish with interest.

"I most certainly am! In my view, women are the superior sex. The world is a much better place for their company, and I'm sure society as a whole would be much improved if they could vote."

Greer smiled. People around them were dancing, but she suddenly felt she was in a private bubble with Hamish. "There are almost thirty-two thousand signatures, so I hope this time they take notice," she said.

"I hope so too! We live in progressive times, and I see women as equal partners to men. It's encouraging to see so many women seeking higher education, and they are now working in areas that would have once been only the domain of men, such as being a lawyer or a doctor."

Hamish sipped his wine. Not for the first time, Greer considered how open and kind his face was. His brown eyes shone with sincerity as he spoke.

"That's very true," Greer said. "I don't have any aspirations to do either, but it does seem there are more options now for women."

"So what are your aspirations?" Hamish looked at Greer with curiosity.

"Well, before I became a maid, I had thought I might do something with my love of fashion or books or music." The words tumbled out, and she toyed with the stem of her glass.

"You could be an author, musician, or dressmaker if you choose to be." Greer looked up, and Hamish gestured at what she was wearing. "I must say you look beautiful, and that dress is splendid. I know you made Florence's dress, so I'm assuming this is also your creation?"

Greer smiled at the compliment. "Yes, it is."

"And you have mentioned other commissions in the past. Are you still designing other dresses?"

"Well, I've been working with my friend Jamelie George, and between us, we have had quite a few commissions lately. But we can't take on too many. I still work as a maid, and Jamelie has a young daughter."

Hamish looked thoughtful. "I have met the Georges; they are a charming, hardworking couple. This is very interesting."

Greer studied his face and laughed. "You look like Sherlock Holmes considering a clue!"

"Sherlock Holmes?"

"Oh, I recently read his story, *A Study in Scarlet*. It was very well done, and you just remind me of Arthur Conan Doyle's character, sitting there with that contemplative look on your face, as though solving a mystery."

"Well, I have been contemplating my own life recently, and I've decided that I want to go into business – but it's only now that my pathway seems a little clearer."

"Does it? Do explain."

Hamish cleared his throat. "Bendix Hallenstein is an exceptional businessman and employer, and I very much enjoy working at Hallenstein's, but I've been hankering to have my own business. I have some money saved to invest. But then I've also been thinking, I really can't do everything on my own, and what I really need is a partnership. So I do wonder ..." His voice trailed off, and he looked bashful.

"You wonder?" Greer was genuinely intrigued.

"Well, it seems that you have the makings of a business already with your friend Mrs George, but perhaps all you need is investment."

"Investment?" Greer's heart quickened. Was Hamish suggesting what she thought he was suggesting?

"A shop, some staff to do most of the sewing, freeing you to design, promote, and deal with clients."

"Oh, I see," Greer said. "You sound just like Zhang Ming! Every time I see her, she tells us we need to get a shop."

"Ah, the grandmother of Walker Street!"

"You know her?"

"I think everyone knows her. And she is astute. She is one of only a handful of Chinese women who immigrated to New Zealand when there was a rush on our goldfields. If she thinks it is a good idea, then it is!"

"But I can't do this! I can't just give up my job! It's impossible." But Greer felt a glimmer of excitement as she spoke.

"Why not?' Hamish was looking animated. "Look, I can do up a proposal. I'm very good with accounts and numbers. And I can see what properties might be suitable." Greer's eyes widened at the thought – he made it sound so eminently feasible – and Hamish reached out and

140

lightly touched her hand. "Look, you aren't committed to anything, but just consider that you and Mrs George could do the design and run the sewing workshop and deal with the clients. I could handle the accounts and property and marketing, and I could probably deal with the suppliers. I'm sure I can get you better deals than you are currently getting for your fabric and other supplies."

Greer looked down at Hamish's hand holding hers. It was warm and strong and stable. He saw her gaze and moved his hand away. She had been thinking for a while about a dressmaking business with Jamelie, but it seemed too complicated and risky. But with Hamish's help, she could see it just might work; having someone with business experience would be invaluable. He seemed to know all the things they didn't.

She smiled at him. "You know, I will discuss this with Jamelie, and I will let you know what we think."

"Excellent." Hamish ran a hand through his dark hair and looked relieved. "In the meantime, I will do a bit of research!" He paused and looked a little bashful again. "I say … would you like to dance?" He gestured at the couples moving on the dance floor, people whom Greer had forgotten about during their conversation. "Oh, but are you still seeing that Fergus fellow? I don't mean to pry." The way Hamish said Fergus's name clearly showed how much he disliked him, and right then, Greer didn't know if she liked Fergus anymore either. She made up her mind.

"Fergus is in England, so I see no harm in a dance."

Hamish looked delighted, leapt to his feet and escorted Greer on to the dance floor. The band was playing a Viennese waltz, and much to Greer's delight, they glided around the floor with surprising ease. She had only danced with Fergus on that one occasion – to the very same tune, if she wasn't mistaken. But what a different experience. Fergus had been clumsy and stood on her feet several times, but Hamish took the lead and together they floated around the floor effortlessly.

"Well, this is a surprise," Greer said.

"What is?" Hamish asked amicably.

"That you dance so well. I just wouldn't have guessed."

"Thank you, my lady. I do like to keep you on your toes." And with that, Hamish spun Greer around, causing her to laugh a little breathlessly. "And you dance very well yourself."

"My father taught me," Greer said. "When I was little, I used to stand on his shoes, and he'd dance around the cottage with me perched on them." She smiled at the memory.

"And my parents taught me. Although I don't recall ever standing on anyone's shoes!"

Greer found herself gazing into Hamish's kind brown eyes, and she felt a contentment she had been missing the past few months. Hamish was a goff, but a very kind one, and she realised that she trusted him. She would look forward to discussing his business idea with Jamelie.

CHAPTER 24

September 1893

Greer almost collided with Constance as she rushed around the side of the castle and in front of the lion stairs without looking where she was going. She was late for her ride into the city with Edward, who she could see waiting patiently for her at a discreet distance.

"Oh, I am so sorry," Greer said, coming to an abrupt stop. Out of the corner of her eye, the lion statue stared at her and seemed amused by her fluster.

Dressed elegantly, Constance smiled at her with her usual steady eyes. "Do not worry, Miss Gillies. It's your day off, and I imagine you have plans for this lovely spring day."

Greer nodded.

"And I imagine you are pleased with the news from Parliament."

Just two days earlier, the Legislative Council had approved the Electoral Bill giving women the right to vote – the first country in the world to do so! All the women she knew had been quietly celebrating ever since.

"I'm thrilled," Greer said fervently.

"It's a monumental moment in our history," Constance replied. "I spoke to Kate Sheppard to congratulate her, and she was exhausted but triumphant. She has worked tirelessly for the cause." Constance paused. "I mustn't hold you up. I realise I have talked much too long on this subject, but it is only due to my excitement at this historic news. Do enjoy your day off." Greer nodded and scrambled ahead into the waiting buggy.

She couldn't help smiling as she travelled along with Edward on their usual Sunday excursion into Dunedin. There were hints of spring, flowers blooming everywhere she looked, and the Peninsula air was finally full of the promise of warmer days and sunshine. Even the albatross birds soaring through the sky looked playful and mischievous, almost as though they were showing off with their antics. Greer had many things to be happy about, apart from the news from Parliament. She was going to have lunch at the Georges to discuss going into business officially, and Hamish would meet her there to talk through his ideas. When they neared the Devil's Half-Acre and her old home, Hamish was already standing on the street waiting for her. He helped her down from the buggy.

"See you at the usual time," the coachman said, dipping his hat before steering his horse and buggy away.

Hamish was his usual well-dressed self in a smart three-piece suit and dress shirt, and he was holding a satchel under his arm. He turned to Greer with an excited expression.

"Still looking for the butler in the garden?" Greer greeted him as usual.

"Well, I might just find him at your friend's place today." He paused. "But Greer, seriously, thank you for organising this lunch. You have my full gratitude."

"And you have my full gratitude for all your research and hard work," Greer said, gesturing to his satchel.

"Shall we?" Hamish nodded towards the property, waiting for Greer to take the lead and knock on the familiar front door.

Jamelie and Gabriel opened the door, Jamelie hugging her friend in greeting, and Gabriel shaking Hamish's hand before inviting them inside, leading them through to the kitchen where the table was laden with the usual array of mouth-watering food. They had guests. Zhang Ming was wearing a traditional Chinese dress and she sat with Soraya on her lap. Next to her, Charles Sew Hoy was dressed in European menswear, and he stood up to greet everyone, bowing low as he introduced himself.

"Please, take a seat," Jamelie said. "Let us enjoy this feast."

"And let us hear your business ideas as we eat," Zhang Ming said. "I invited my esteemed friend Choie Sew Hoy to give an unbiased view of your business plan."

Hamish smiled at Zhang Ming warmly and turned to Charles Sew Hoy. "You may not recall, sir, but I arranged for several suits for you a couple of years ago. It is a pleasure to meet you again."

Charles Sew Hoy nodded as Hamish sat on a cushion next to Greer. "I do remember you well. It is my pleasure to meet you again also."

Jamelie began to hand out food to her guests; it was the usual Lebanese fare that Greer had come to love so much, with a couple of Chinese dishes added to the table. Soraya ate some meatballs with gusto after Zhang Ming had patiently cut them up for her.

"Do try some kibbeh," Jamelie urged Hamish.

"It's their national dish," Greer said. "And it's simply divine."

"Well, I must try it then," Hamish said, waiting for Jamelie to serve some of the spicy meat on to his plate. He sampled a mouthful and then another and looked at Jamelie and Greer, his eyes wide.

"This *is* divine! It's truly exceptional. I love the spicy flavour, and is that pine nuts?"

"Yes, it is," Jamelie confirmed.

"Have you had Lebanese food before?" Zhang Ming asked. "Or Cantonese food?"

"Whenever I can, I like to try different types of food. So yes, I have sampled some Lebanese and Cantonese food in the past, but this dish surpasses anything I have tasted before."

Jamelie beamed with pride at the compliments on her cooking.

"My wife is a wonderful cook," Gabriel said, also looking proud.

"I understand you still work for Bendix Hallenstein?" Charles Sew Hoy turned to Hamish.

"Yes, I do, I couldn't wish for a better employer, but –"

"But you wish to have your own business?" Sew Hoy finished. "You have ambition; that is to be commended. And Bendix Hallenstein will understand. In fact, you will probably find he is very supportive of you and your endeavours."

"I know it's not polite to eat and talk business," Zhang Ming put in. "But I'm an old woman and not very patient, so I'd love to hear of your ideas for the dressmaking business while we eat."

"Of course!"

Hamish ate a few more mouthfuls of kibbeh and then made space on the table and extracted some papers from his satchel. They all looked on in interest as he talked them through his ideas. Hamish had found several properties that might suit as premises – enough room for a shop and changing rooms, with either a workshop at the back or on another level. He'd done provisional budgets for employing three workshop staff, freeing Jamelie and Greer to deal with the clients and do the designs, with Jamelie working part-time so she could care for her daughter and having the option of working more hours in the future if she wished. Hamish proposed he take charge of sourcing supplies unless Gabriel wanted to do that, but Gabriel insisted that he wanted to keep his attention on the hawker business.

"Besides, this is my wife's dream," Gabriel added. "She's just taking a while to understand this." Jamelie smiled at her husband affectionately.

Charles Sew Hoy studied Hamish's documents and nodded in approval. "This is very sound. And you are willing to invest this amount?"

Hamish nodded. "I live with my parents, so I've been able to save a sizable amount of my salary each month. And I project we'd be profitable within the year, all going well."

Sew Hoy sat back. "I think you are right. So barring some unforeseen complication, I agree with your assessment."

Zhang Ming jiggled Soraya on her lap. "It looks like you would like to do this?"

"Well, yes," Jamelie said.

"I think so too," Greer said, excitement bubbling up inside her.

Charles Sew Hoy smiled. "So what about the timing?"

"I was thinking if I can get the right premises, we could look at doing this early next year," Hamish said. "I'd need at least that time to find a property and then organise to fit it out."

"Oh, but where will I live if I give up my job at Larnach's Castle?" Greer suddenly realised she hadn't really thought about that before.

"You will come and live with us!" Jamelie said. "You can share a room with Soraya. We consider you part of our family."

Gabriel nodded. "We welcome you!"

Greer was overwhelmed and clutched Jamelie's hand in gratitude. Was this really happening? Going into business and living again in her old cottage with these beautiful, generous people? But so soon? Was she ready for such a big move?

"Look, we don't need to rush into this," Hamish said, sensing Greer's feelings. "But with your approval, I can start making some preliminary

146

enquiries. We won't do anything until we all agree on it." Greer looked at him gratefully.

"And what will you call your business?" Zhang Ming asked.

The three business owners-to-be looked at each other in puzzlement.

"I'm not sure," Jamelie began.

"How about MacLeod, George, Gillies and Co?" Charles Sew Hoy suggested.

"It's a bit of a mouthful," Greer said, frowning. "Perhaps we should just have one name?"

"I don't think George should be part of the company name," Jamelie said a little sadly. "While many are welcoming to Lebanese people, some are not; so being pragmatic, George shouldn't be part of the business name, as here it is known as a Lebanese surname, not an English one."

"Yes, our family name could cause problems with some people," Gabriel said, frowning.

"I disagree!" Hamish jumped in. "George should definitely be part of the company name, or how are we going to change the perception out here? What I propose is that I'm in the background of this venture. I believe the focus should be on you two ladies as you are doing the designs, and our female clientele will be much more comfortable that way."

"What about Gillies and George Designs?" Charles Sew Hoy suggested.

Everyone looked at each other for a moment and then started to smile.

"I think we have the company name," Hamish said. "It's stylish, and I like Design rather than Dressmaker; it puts us in a better business category. It suggests far more possibilities."

"What do you think?" Zhang Ming asked Soraya, who looked up at the Chinese grandmother with interest. "Gillies and George Designs?" Zhang Ming made faces at the young child.

Soraya suddenly laughed and clapped her hands. "Gillies and George Designs!" she mimicked in her high, sweet voice.

"Well, it's settled then," Jamelie said. "Our darling child has decided our business will be called Gillies and George Designs!"

CHAPTER 25

Harmony

Greer and Jamelie sat in the front room of the Walker Street cottage, and Jamelie took her time looking through the sketches Greer had been working on the last few weeks.

"What do you think?" Greer chewed her lip with sudden nervousness. Jamelie hadn't said a word and had looked at each of her designs for a long time, her eyes serious and hard to read. Jamelie looked up at her friend, and her face broke into a wide smile.

"With designs like these, our business will be a success!"

Greer clasped her friend's hand excitedly. "I'm so pleased you like them."

"I adore them. Your designs are stylish, practical, elegant, and a little different. All the society ladies will want to wear them."

"We just need Hamish to find the right premises!"

"I have every confidence that he will." Jamelie closed the sketchbook carefully. "And remember, we have much to do beforehand!"

"Oh, I know!" Greer said enthusiastically. "But now we have decided to go into business, I confess I want to open the store tomorrow. And I want to tell everyone!"

"Well, it can't possibly open tomorrow, and remember you are best not to tell anyone until we are certain. It may take months for Hamish to find a suitable place at the right price."

Greer sighed. "You are right, of course. But it's hard to be patient."

"What would Zhang Ming say if she was here?"

Greer grinned. "A little impatience will spoil great plans."

Jamelie nodded. "So we can't have that, can we?"

***

Florence turned to look at Greer dusting the china cabinet in the dining room.

"Chuckaboo, you do realise you have been humming the entire time we have been in here?"

Greer looked at Florence with surprise. "Have I?" She picked up one of the dinner plates and admired it.

"Blazes, I thought you didn't like this dining set anymore."

Greer carefully put the plate back on display. "It's an elegant design. I have no idea where you got the impression that I don't like it."

Florence's eyes narrowed. "Did you get a letter from Fergus or something?"

Greer stopped what she was doing and realised she hadn't thought about Fergus in days; she'd been so busy with their plans for a business. Not that she could tell Florence yet, which she felt a little guilty about, but she would the moment Hamish had secured a place.

"No, I haven't had a letter," Greer said carefully.

"Crikey, I have no idea what is going on, but I'm glad to see you nanty narking," Florence told her friend. "Everyone deserves to be happy. Like me! I love being married; it suits me down to the ground."

Florence had moved out of the maids' cottage, and she and Albert had a small place in Portobello. "Albert and I would like you to come to dinner this weekend on our day off. What do you say, chuckaboo?"

"I'd love to." Greer had helped Florence move her things, but it would be delightful to visit as a guest and have dinner with them.

"Excellent!" Albert will bring the buggy to pick you up and bring you back afterwards."

"It's not too much trouble?"

"Blazes, of course not," Florence said. "Albert is pleased to do whatever I suggest."

Greer had a sudden insight that Albert must be a very patient man and hid her smile as she continued dusting.

***

"Thanks for meeting me during my lunch break," Hamish said.

Greer smiled. "And thanks for sharing a sandwich with me on my day off."

She bit into the tuna and cucumber sandwich he'd given her as they perched on one of the bench seats in the Octagon.

"How is the property hunt going?" Greer asked after a moment.

"I investigated that property over there," Hamish pointed at a three-storeyed building nearby. "But it was completely beyond our budget. We'd need to be royalty to afford the lease."

"King Hamish," Greer said, smiling wryly. "Your title didn't impress them? I'm surprised."

Hamish laughed. "Perhaps I should get Queen Greer to talk to the owner instead!"

Greer shook her head. "No, thank you. And all joking aside, I'm so grateful you are taking the time to look at all these properties on our behalf."

"I will find the right property," Hamish said, looking suddenly earnest and very boyish.

"I know you will." Greer paused. "But can you hurry up!"

Hamish looked at her in concern and then saw her teasing eyes. They both laughed before returning to their sandwiches. Their lunch was enjoyable, Greer suddenly realised. The sun on her face, a tasty sandwich to enjoy, and Hamish was always surprisingly agreeable company. She stole another look at him just as he broke off a piece of bread to give to a waiting sparrow.

"Oh, did I tell you about the fabric I saw the other day at the wholesaler?" he said. "It would be perfect for the sketch you showed me last week for Mrs Smith."

Greer leant towards Hamish. He was always finding different and exciting bolts of fabric – and he had impeccable taste. "Do tell me more!"

CHAPTER 26

November 1893

Greer waited for Florence outside the polling booth, situated in one of the school buildings on Walker Street. Despite warnings that "lady voters" might be harassed, the street today had a festive feel. Everyone was dressed in their best clothes, and there was a genuine feeling of celebration as locals smiled and chatted with each other. There was even a brass band. It was a historic day and Greer was happy to be part of it. Just ten weeks after the governor, Lord Glasgow, signed the Electoral Act 1893 into law, for the first time in the world, women had the right to vote in parliamentary elections, and despite the short timeframe, a staggering eighty-four per cent of the adult female population had enrolled to vote. Men who had previously said women really didn't want the vote were forced to eat humble pie.

"Chuckaboo, it's done!" Florence said, joining her friend and linking her arm through Greer's, as she typically did.

"Has Albert voted?"

"He's going to do so later in the day – he had a project to complete in the garden first."

"It was really wonderful of Mr Larnach to give us a half-day off work to be able to vote," Greer said.

"Blazes, I think you will find that was all Constance's idea!"

"I suspect that is true." Greer paused. "I thought I might go and visit my friend Jamelie before going back to The Camp."

"And I thought I might look around the shops before catching the ferry back. I'm going to look for a gift for Albert for Christmas."

"Hallenstein's has a good selection of men's clothing. And you have probably met Hamish MacLeod; he'll be able to help you."

"Hamish does seem to come to The Camp an awful lot and always finds time to look you out," Florence said. She seemed about to say something else but instead kissed Greer on each cheek. "I'll see you later on. We still have the drawing room to finish cleaning, chuckaboo."

"That we do," Greer agreed as she watched Florence cross the street with her usual impatient gait, her blonde hair flying in all directions under her bonnet. She was always the personification of a friendly whirlwind.

Greer frowned as she made her way to the Georges' cottage. She hadn't yet told Florence about the idea of going into business and she was feeling increasingly guilty about the omission. But Hamish and Jamelie had been firm that they shouldn't tell anyone until they had secured premises and were ready to begin. Hamish hadn't found the right property yet – they had been too expensive, too small, too run-down, or in the wrong location, so he was still looking. It might take many months before he found the right place with a progressive landlord, so they didn't want to compromise her job at Larnach's Castle or his job at Hallenstein's in the meantime. Jamelie and Greer continued to make dresses on commission when they could work around their other duties. Both were also filling up sketchbooks with design ideas. Greer put the difficulties out of her mind as she knocked on the cottage front door, but it was some time before Jamelie came to the door.

"I was just in the neighbourhood to vote and thought I'd pop in quickly," Greer said, before noticing how wan her friend looked. "Oh, Jamelie! Are you all right?"

"Please come in," Jamelie ushered her into the lounge. "Gabriel is away working, but he has taken Soraya with him today, so we are alone."

She sat in one of the chairs and gestured for Greer to sit in another.

"Can I make you tea?" Greer offered.

"Actually, that would be nice. I am feeling weary today."

Greer frowned at her friend, but busied herself in the kitchen, coming back with tea for both of them.

"Can I ask what has happened?" Greer asked after a moment. "I am concerned."

Jamelie sighed. "The Lord has seen fit to take another baby before we could welcome them into the world. A third child in heaven, away from their earthly family."

"I am so sorry to hear that!" Greer felt tears prick her eyes.

"Yes, I am sad, and now is the time for me to mourn. But I am blessed with Soraya, and I'm blessed with my husband and my friends – and my new business partners."

Greer didn't know what to say, so she patted Jamelie's hand.

"I must say the thought of our shop gives me hope for the future," Jamelie confided. "A new venture is just what I need after this."

"I'm excited about it too," Greer confessed. "Daunted, but I feel sure Hamish will find us a place next year and then we can put all our plans into action."

"In the meantime, how are you going with the dress for Mrs Brown?"

"It's progressing well. I hope to finish the beading on the bodice over the next few evenings."

"It will be nice when we can employ good staff to do this work," Jamelie said, sipping her tea. "I've been thinking of a few people who may be suitable, all from good Lebanese families and with excellent skills."

"That's superb," Greer said warmly. "And I'm so pleased that Hamish has budgeted so we can pay reasonable rates. I don't want us to be one of those terrible sweatshops with crowded conditions."

"No, we want a place that is a pleasure to come and work in. We will treat our staff well. It will be one of the core values of our business."

Greer could see that Jamelie needed to rest, so after they had finished their tea, she put everything away in the kitchen, kissed her friend on each cheek and made her way down to the ferry and then the buggy ride back to The Camp.

When she alighted from the buggy at the castle, she was astounded to see Fergus sitting on the steps by the lion statues. She wondered if he was an illusion for a moment, but when she blinked again, he was very much real. Her heartbeat quickened at the sight of him.

"My darling Angel Greer!" Fergus cried, leaping to his feet. He thrust a bouquet of bright yellow flowers at her. "I was told you'd be back soon."

Greer took the flowers and looked at Fergus in confusion. He looked thinner than usual but just as devastatingly handsome, and she felt that exhilarating jolt of electricity when their hands briefly connected.

"I hope you got my note." Fergus stared at her intently, his brow furrowed.

"That you had gone to England?" Greer's voice wobbled. All this time without another letter or any sort of communication. Could she forgive him?

"Oh, I'm so pleased you got it!" Fergus flashed his dazzling smile, disarming Greer completely.

"I apologise sincerely that I had to go so abruptly, but urgent family business demanded my return home. Did you not get my letters while I was away?"

He'd written letters? Greer's heart softened. He hadn't just abandoned her after all.

"None arrived," she said demurely, looking at the flowers she held without seeing them.

"Oh, that is outrageous!" Fergus declared. She looked up and saw his blue eyes were even more intense than she remembered. "I penned dozens of letters to you. But none of them made it through? I am profoundly disappointed. I will make enquiries! But my Angel Greer, you must know I constantly thought of you during our time apart. So I hope you will forgive my absence, and I'd like to see you again soon. Perhaps a picnic on your next day off? Or something else – anything that your heart desires – and I will organise it for you!"

Greer gazed into his vivid blue eyes and blushed slightly when she replied. "I would be delighted to picnic with you on Sunday."

"I shall pick you up at ten sharp."

He leant in towards her and gently kissed her on the lips, causing her heart to race. "My darling Angel Greer," he murmured, stroking her cheek.

He began to walk away, and only then did Greer remember that she'd already made lunch plans with Jamelie, which she would now need to cancel. And that, oddly, Fergus was on foot and not with his usual horse and buggy. But she shrugged and skipped around the castle to her cottage, smelling Fergus's flowers, a bouquet of bright yellow carnations.

It was only when in her room and searching for a vase that Greer recalled that while yellow is a colour of happiness, yellow carnations were considered a gift of disregard. But then she shrugged. Fergus wouldn't have known that. Why would any man know that sort of detail? She smelt the flowers again, ignoring the slightly bitter aroma. Fergus was back and wanted to take her out; that was all that mattered.

CHAPTER 27

December 1893

It was yet another New Year's celebration at Larnach's Castle, the family gathering on the turrets to await the countdown to midnight and the traditional fireworks. Last year Greer had been too distraught at Fergus's sudden absence to even go to the festivities. She'd stayed in her room, turning pages of a book that she could not read beyond the first page. This year, though, everything was different; the night had a festive magic to it, the castle lit up and looking enchanting as guests spilt out from the ballroom to the grounds, the garden looking particularly well-manicured and maintained.

Greer glanced around. Florence and Albert were nearby, glowing with happiness. Married life suited them both, and they had enjoyed making the small cottage they had in Portobello a home. Greer dined with them from time to time, and Florence always had a new purchase or small household improvement to show her. Mrs MacGavin had been enjoying some of the punch served at their staff dinner, and her husband had arrived to watch the fireworks with her. Another happy couple who clearly doted on each other. The coachman was nearby looking after the horses; he'd had a busy day ferrying guests to the castle, and she'd heard him whistling as he'd worked. Even the normally aloof butler wore a smile and was drifting around outside the castle. Fleetingly she thought of Hamish – she had seen him earlier in the evening, but they hadn't had the chance to converse. If she found him again, she'd mention that he could really find the butler in the garden for once.

She'd observed the Larnach family over the Christmas period. William

Larnach was more of his old self, today dressed in a velvet coat and pants. She noticed he was exercising more, his steps and miles covered by the pedometer on his watch chain. And he took Constance with him everywhere, clearly delighting in her company and happy to show off his young wife. She was always immaculately presented, and she dressed exquisitely. Constance looked confident and happy as his wife, despite the obvious age gap between them, although all the children in the family, bar Douglas, continued to snub her. It was a pleasure to see Constance share a laugh with Douglas on more than one occasion, and Greer thought it good that at least one of the children had accepted her as part of the family. Colleen and Gladys still wore long faces whenever Constance was around, and despite being happily married, Alice looked the most miserable around her stepmother, even in the presence of her husband.

But for now, Greer only had thoughts for the man sitting on the bench next to her, on the raised lawn outside the castle. He had his arm slung casually around her shoulders. She turned and smiled at Fergus, drinking in his chiselled, handsome face and his expressive blue eyes. Since he'd returned from England he'd been incredibly attentive, and he'd taken her to picnics, plays and balls. She didn't care that his dancing hadn't improved any; it was a thrill to be held in his arms. She'd abandoned playing the violin, was behind on her dressmaking commissions, and hadn't caught up with Jamelie and Hamish about any business plans since Fergus had returned. She hadn't even read a book in ages, but she didn't care. The last few weeks had been a joyous whirlwind. Florence had kept teasing her about humming while she worked, but she was bursting with joy.

"My darling Angel Greer," Fergus murmured, reaching out to stroke her cheek.

The countdown to midnight began around them. "Ten, nine …"

Fergus slipped to one knee in front of her, pulling a ring box from his pocket. Greer gasped when she realised what he was doing.

"Greer Gillies, I know you're the only one I want to share the rest of my life with. I can't imagine growing old with anyone else, nor do I want to. When I look into your eyes, I can see a reflection of the two of us and the life I hope we'll share together." He opened the box, revealing a simple gold ring and solitaire diamond.

"Angel Greer, would you agree to be my wife?"

"Yes!" Greer felt her heart might burst from so much happiness as Fergus slid the ring on her finger and then kissed her passionately as fireworks exploded around them.

Florence must have seen the proposal because she and Albert descended on them a moment later, congratulating them on being engaged. Florence squealed loudly when she saw the ring. "Oh, it's beautiful!"

"It belonged to my grandmother," Fergus said.

"Congratulations," Albert said, thumping Fergus on the back.

Mrs MacGavin joined them. "Oh, what wonderful news! And when is the big day?"

Greer glanced at Fergus. "Well, we haven't had a chance to discuss –"

"I think around Christmas next year would be a splendid time to get married," Fergus said, putting his arm around Greer's waist. "That gives us plenty of time to plan everything, but there's something quite magical about the Christmas season, so that would be my thoughts on this."

He turned to Greer. "What do you think, my darling?"

"I think that sounds perfect." But was it? She wasn't sure. She'd like more time to consider the timing of the wedding when she suddenly remembered the dressmaking business.

"I do hope we won't be losing you," Mrs MacGavin said as others pulled Fergus aside to congratulate him. Greer glanced at Fergus and turned to Mrs MacGavin, feeling suddenly very awkward. How would her business plan progress with getting married? It had never been quite the right moment to talk about the shop with Fergus since he'd returned, but she would need to do so at some point.

"No, of course not," she mumbled. "Well, at least not for a long time."

Mrs MacGavin nodded and slipped away to talk to Florence and Albert. Greer recalled Edward and other staff coming to congratulate her when suddenly, a serious-looking Hamish was standing in front of her.

"I see congratulations are in order," he said stiffly.

Greer nodded. "Thank you." She usually felt so comfortable around Hamish, but now she felt unbelievably awkward. It was almost as if she had done something wrong in accepting Fergus's proposal.

"And is your fiancé happy for you to go into business with Mrs George and myself?" he asked, frowning.

"Well, I haven't discussed it with him yet," Greer admitted, her face flushing

"I see." Hamish sighed. It was a sound full of sadness.

"But I'm sure it will be fine!" Greer began to gabble. "Fergus said I can do anything that is my heart's desire, anything that will make me happy, which I know this business would. I've only ever known him to be kind and generous, so he won't deny me this opportunity."

Hamish seemed to be about to say something and then stopped himself. "Well, you have much to discuss with him in that case." He nodded at her formally and slipped back into the crowd of partygoers.

Greer watched him disappear and felt suddenly bereft, but then Fergus was again at her side, and all her thoughts turned to him and the glorious future they would have together. She gazed at Fergus, spellbound by his eyes and dazzling smile, the rest of the party disappearing into the background.

CHAPTER 28

January 1894

Greer knocked on the familiar door of the Georges' home and twisted her hands nervously, perspiring slightly from the heat of the day. She had been very remiss as a friend and hadn't seen Jamelie since the day she had voted in the election. The very same day that Fergus had dramatically returned to her life. Jamelie had sent her a message requesting she come by as she needed to talk to her about something of importance. She didn't say what, but it would have to be about their business that Greer had been shamefully neglecting. The door opened, and Jamelie greeted her friend with an enormous smile, looking elegant in a long purple dress with intricate beading.

"Greer, it is so lovely to see you; please come in. I'm so pleased you obviously got my message."

Relieved, Greer hugged her friend. "Oh, Jamelie, I'm so sorry I haven't seen you for such a long time."

"It is no problem. You are here now." Jamelie led Greer into the lounge, gestured to a seat, and sat next to her. "Please don't worry. I know you have been busy, with Fergus returning and now your engagement."

"You know about that?" Greer said in astonishment.

"Hamish came around last week, and he mentioned what had happened." Jamelie seized Greer's hand and admired her engagement ring. "Oh, this ring is beautiful! Do tell me everything. When did Fergus return? How did he propose? I only know the basic facts; Hamish was very lacking in detail, as men often are, so you must tell me everything!"

Greer recounted the recent whirlwind weeks and the romantic New

Year's Eve, and Jamelie seemed genuinely excited for her. Greer breathed a sigh of relief. She should never have doubted her friend's reception as she had never been anything but hospitable and understanding.

"But I must make us tea! Gabriel and Soraya are out at the moment, and I'm completely forgetting my manners in my excitement at your news."

"Let me help you."

Jamelie smiled, and they made their way to the kitchen, working alongside each other companionably as they made tea.

"I am truly thrilled for you," Jamelie said, sinking into a cushion around the dining table, Greer following suit. "I hope you will find married life most satisfactory, like I do. The most blessed and wonderful union."

Greer nodded and blushed slightly at the thought of actually being married and all that it would entail. She focused on Jamelie again. "I am very sorry that I'm behind on the latest dress with everything going on."

Jamelie waved her hand in the air. "Please do not worry; the client is on holiday, so we have some time. It was never urgent." She paused. "But that does remind me to ask you about something. Now you will be getting married, are you still able to proceed with our business, with going ahead with a shop?"

Greer stirred her tea. "I will need to discuss it with Fergus," she admitted. "And I will do so soon, but I don't expect there to be any problems. He says he wants to support all my endeavours."

Jamelie searched Greer's face for a moment, and did Greer imagine a flicker of anxiety? But then she was smiling at Greer again. "Well, that is good. Hamish mentioned he may have found a suitable place for us. In fact, he will be here soon to talk to us about the property."

As though on cue, there was a knock at the door. "Well, that will be Hamish now," Jamelie said, rising to her feet. "I'll let him in."

Greer stared into her teacup, not knowing if she should be excited or terrified. She still hadn't spoken to Fergus about their business idea. Every time Greer thought to say something, the moment felt wrong. But if Hamish had found a property, she would need to discuss this with Fergus as soon as possible. And she suddenly felt nervous about seeing Hamish again – things had been so awkward on New Year's Eve, but before she had time to fret more, Hamish strode into the room, smiling at her and sinking into the seat opposite.

160

"I've found the perfect place!" he announced as Jamelie poured him tea.

His excitement was palpable, and Greer found herself caught up in his enthusiasm as he took documents out of his satchel and began talking to them both about a building near the Octagon. It was a building where they could lease the lower floor, and there was room for a showroom with a workshop off the back. As they discussed the potential shop, all awkwardness that might have been there was replaced with easy comfortableness as they debated the pros and cons of the premises.

"It is perfect," Jamelie announced after they had finished their tea, and Hamish began tidying the documents away. "It's a good location, affordable, and has the space we need."

"Well done, Hamish," Greer said. "It is everything we are looking for."

"Shall we proceed?" Hamish's smile lit up his entire face.

"Yes, I say," Jamelie said.

"I say yes too," Greer said.

A look passed between her two friends before they turned back to her, and she read their unspoken question.

"Please don't worry. I will talk to my fiancé as soon as possible about this venture, but I'm sure I will have his full approval, and we will be able to proceed," Greer said, with more confidence than she felt.

Something faltered behind Hamish's easy smile, and he turned his attention to his satchel when he next spoke. "I shall begin the negotiations, in that case."

Greer felt a moment of discomfort, but the odd feeling disappeared when Hamish raised his head and she looked into his friendly, open face. All would be well in the end, she decided.

CHAPTER 29

February 1894

Greer looked around the spacious drawing room of the elegant three-level house and couldn't resist spinning around in a large circle. Fergus laughed at her childlike delight.

"This home is incredible! Are you really thinking of buying it?"

"I think this would be the perfect home for us. It's only about twenty years old and designed by Henry F. Hardy, an excellent architect, so it's well constructed. And it's in a good part of the city."

"And so spacious!" Greer had counted at least six bedrooms so far, and they hadn't explored the top floor yet.

"Plenty of room to raise a family," Fergus said, gathering Greer into his arms and kissing her deeply, making her feel deliciously off-balance and languid. "I hope you are looking forward to raising a family with me, as I am with you."

"Yes, I am."

But the truth was much more complicated. Greer couldn't wait to be a married woman and all that entailed, both in and out of the bedroom. Fergus made her desperate with desire, although he was always the perfect gentleman and hadn't pressed her beyond kissing and hugging. And she loved children and one day looked forward to having her own – but she was terrified about the prospect of childbirth. It had claimed her beloved mother, so was that also her fate? The thought was frightening, so she pushed it away every time it entered her head. The wedding wasn't until the end of the year, so there was no need to think of such things yet.

"Let me show you the master bedroom," Fergus said, leading her upstairs to a room with a garden view, the sunlight streaming through the window making it light and beautiful. Greer looked around with interest. It was a stunning room. Fergus led her to the double bed and gestured for her to sit next to him.

"Imagine us living here," he whispered before kissing her. She responded passionately, her heart racing, and then his hand slipped down, cupping her breast. She enjoyed the sensation for a brief instant, but then pulled away.

"Fergus, we mustn't."

He sighed, put his hand on her waist and stared into her eyes, making her melt again into his embrace.

"Angel Greer, you drive me to distraction! You have no idea what you do to me."

She looked away, blushing.

"But you are right; we can wait. It's not that long before we are married, although it seems an intolerable time away right at this moment." He stood up and looked down at her. "So, do you want me to purchase this house? We can live here after the wedding."

"I love it."

He nodded. "Then I will begin negotiations, and I'm sure we can agree on an acceptable price."

"It would be wonderful."

Greer stood up and looked out the window, adjusting her dress. The garden was particularly beautiful, and she daydreamed for a moment about sitting outside serving tea to her friends when she was the lady of the house. She turned to Fergus.

"This home is so wonderful! We have room to have a library and also a music room. I'll be able to play my violin for our guests."

Fergus smiled at her and gathered her into his arms. "I can't wait! As you know, I am not musical, but I will look forward to you playing whenever you choose."

He was looking at her with an expression of love and desire, and she suddenly felt brave enough to broach the subject she had been avoiding.

"Fergus, there is something I need to discuss with you."

"The guest list for the wedding?" Fergus smiled. "I'm still waiting to hear back if my parents will be able to come over for the celebrations."

"Oh, that would be wonderful if they could make it," Greer said distractedly. "But no, I wanted to talk to you about what we do after we are married."

He raised his eyebrows suggestively, and she laughed nervously.

"I meant for my work."

"Well, we have discussed you resigning from working at Larnach's Castle," Fergus said. "It's much too far away from the city, and besides, I don't want you working as a maid. You will be busy looking after our home and then, in due course, a family."

"Yes, I agree," Greer said fervently. "I have no desire to be a maid once we are married, but I would like to work. I would like to open a dressmaking shop with Jamelie George."

Fergus eyes darkened and his entire body stiffened.

Greer spoke in a gabble. "It would just be a small shop, but it would allow Jamelie and me to increase the dressmaking we can do by taking on staff. I have so many design ideas; I have sketchpads full of designs. Dresses that are up to date and elegant, just right for this modern era."

Fergus relaxed and stroked her cheek "I don't mind if you make the odd dress for people here and there as a hobby, and you must concentrate next on your wedding dress. Have you begun?"

"I got some fabric the other day. But Fergus, I'd really like to go into business. I think Gillies and George Designs could be successful."

"So you already have a name!" Fergus abruptly stepped away from her, his eyes flashing with anger.

"Well, it's just an idea," Greer tried to keep calm, although her voice broke when she spoke. "But Hamish has found premises that we think could work really well."

"Hamish?"

"Hamish MacLeod," Greer said, knowing as she spoke she'd made a fatal mistake by mentioning his name. "He is willing to invest in the company."

"The store boy?"

"He works for Hallenstein's. I didn't realise you knew him."

"He seems like a permanent feature at Larnach's Castle, so I've seen him."

Suddenly, Fergus grabbed Greer's wrist and twisted it slightly, making her wince. "I will say this once and only once. You are not going into business, and certainly not with the store boy and the Assyrian. You are to be my wife, and I expect you to make myself and our home and family your priority. In fact, when I think on this further, I don't want you making dresses anymore for other women. Understood?"

He looked so furious that Greer turned away, tears welling in her eyes.

"Yes," she said miserably.

Fergus let go of her arm, and she flinched for a moment when he reached out and stroked her cheek.

"Angel Greer," he began in a softer voice, gathering her into his arms again. "Put aside these thoughts. You will be so busy in our life together you will have no time for this nonsense. You haven't thought things through clearly. My business dealings are going so well there is no need for you to work, and certainly not as a common dressmaker. We will be busy having a gay time. You will be on my arm for balls and parties – you will be part of society, darling. We will have others make your dresses in the future!"

Despite Greer's disappointment about his reaction to her business – he would never approve of the idea, she realised sadly – she couldn't help but get caught up in the world he was describing. They'd create a library; eventually, there would be a nursery. They would host parties, and she would be able to play her violin at small gatherings, something that had been a childhood dream. She found herself believing in this future.

"I am right, aren't I?" Fergus said eventually. "There is no time for a dressmaking business in this glorious, wonderful life we will be enjoying."

"Yes, I see," Greer said. Although, she kept the thought to herself, she wasn't going to get anyone else to make her own dresses, but that could be a conversation for another day.

Fergus kissed her, and she lost herself in the sensation, as always, her body reacting to Fergus's handsome virility. She gazed at him for a moment afterwards, losing herself in his vivid blue eyes, before he glanced at his watch.

"We must go, but I'll start discussions with the owner about purchasing the house."

Fergus took her arm and they walked down the stairs and then out the front door, which he locked carefully behind him. It was nowhere near as large as Larnach's Castle, but it was definitely a small mansion, and Greer felt a surge of happiness that they would be living somewhere so grand once married.

"Would you like me to give you a ride back to the castle?" Fergus enquired, his face full of concern and love for her. It was as if they had never disagreed.

Greer realised she needed to tell Hamish that she couldn't go into business, and the sooner she did this, the better. It would only be more arduous if she thought about it too long.

"I think I'll stroll into the city," she said. "I have some shopping to do before going back to The Camp. I'll get the ferry back after."

"You don't need a ride to the stores?"

"It's a nice day, so I think I would like a short stroll."

"Very well," Fergus said, walking towards his horse and buggy. "I will pick you up on Sunday from the castle."

"I look forward to it."

Fergus kissed her again and then leapt into his buggy and headed off briskly. Greer watched him disappear from view before setting out. It was a lovely day and only a short walk to the Octagon.

She almost lost her nerve when she came to the elegant doors of Hallenstein's but forced herself to walk through them. Fortunately they weren't busy and Hamish was alone at the counter. He greeted her with a broad smile.

"I thought I might go out in my lunch break to see if I can find the butler in the garden," he joked, but then he saw her face and frowned. "What's happened, Greer?"

There was no way to soften this. "I can't go into business."

"Oh, I see. You've finally spoken to your fiancé? I take it he forbids it." Hamish stared at her, and she lowered her eyes.

"Well, not forbid exactly," Greer said, feeling flustered.

But Fergus was forbidding her, wasn't he? She could now vote in the country's elections, but not make up her own mind about her own life. She pushed the thought away. Fergus loved her and they would have a beautiful life together. It was extraordinary that a wealthy man would want an impoverished orphan as his wife. She should be grateful. She was grateful.

"It's just I won't have time once married with my duties as a wife and, later on, a mother." Greer glanced up at Hamish and searched his face to see his reaction. He looked undeniably sad, and it made her want to cry.

"I see," Hamish said. "Well, I think you need to tell Jamelie yourself about this." He picked up a pen and began tapping it repeatedly on the counter.

"Of course," Greer said quickly.

"And I'll tell the agent we won't be proceeding."

"Oh, but you can still do this with Jamelie!"

Hamish frowned. "Jamelie won't do this without you, you know that, don't you?"

Greer sighed. She wanted to deny it, but she knew what Hamish was saying was the truth. Jamelie had mentioned that a shop wouldn't work without Greer's help, such was the anti-Lebanese sentiment. She was clear that only together would they succeed.

"I'll go and see her now," Greer said miserably.

Hamish nodded at her and set down his pen. "Good day, then," he said formally, dismissively, a little coldly.

"Go-ood day," she stuttered.

Greer retreated from the store and made her way to Walker Street, feeling more miserable with each step. By the time she knocked on the Georges' door, dread clutched her so hard she felt she couldn't breathe.

"Greer!" Jamelie cried, opening the door. "What a pleasant surprise, do come in. I was just working on beading the latest dress you designed. I hope to have it ready soon." Then she saw her friend's face and gathered her into her arms as Greer burst into tears.

"Oh, Greer, what has happened?"

"Fergus won't let me go into business," Greer whispered, sobbing.

"Come, come, let's get you a cup of tea," Jamelie led her friend to the kitchen.

Zhang Ming was clearing up as they entered.

"I've just put Soraya down for her nap." She then noticed Greer's tears. "What is going on?"

"Her fiancé has said she can't go into business with me," Jamelie said, looking uncharacteristically cross.

Zhang Ming exclaimed in rapid Cantonese for a moment, and Jamelie and Greer looked up in surprise at her tone.

"Well, it's not specifically you," Greer said, turning to Jamelie. "He doesn't want me to go into business with anyone."

"So you give up your dream just to please him?" Zhang Ming snapped.

"But he loves me, and he's right; once married, I'm going to be busy with our life, running our home, and eventually having a family. I don't know what I was thinking!"

"You were thinking of a full life!" Zhang Ming said. "We live in new times, and you and Jamelie can do things I never dreamed of. And you throw it all away!"

"Oh, Zhang Ming, don't be too harsh on Greer," Jamelie protested. "She is getting married at the end of the year, and of course, she needs to consider her future husband's wishes."

"A man of empty promises," Zhang Ming said robustly. "You say he tells you that you can have whatever your heart desires, but he says no when it comes to something you actually want!"

"Well, it was more that he pointed out how impractical it would be," Greer tried to defend Fergus, but as she spoke, she could hear the uncertainty in her voice. She turned to Jamelie.

"But you could still open the shop. As you know, Hamish has found a suitable property."

Jamelie shook her head. "It won't work," she said simply. "It was only going to succeed if it was the three of us – without you, this venture is doomed."

"You could find another dressmaker! You mentioned some Lebanese people that you were considering as staff. Maybe one of them could be a business partner?"

Again, Jamelie shook her head. "They are excellent seamstresses, but none have your design skills. And they are Lebanese, so we still have a problem of … perception."

Greer bit her lip. "I'm sorry, Jamelie."

Jamelie took Greer's hand. "I understand. Please don't think of it anymore. We don't need to discuss this further."

Zhang Ming snorted and stood up. "I'm going to check on Soraya," she announced and stomped from the room. "That man is a charlatan through and through, I can see the muck under his fine clothes," she muttered, to Greer's bewilderment.

Greer and Jamelie exchanged glances. "She will come around," Jamelie said. "You have to realise it was her dream too. She would have been the mentor for our business."

Greer felt a stab in her heart. Just how many people was she disappointing? As though Jamelie had read her mind, she patted Greer on the back before standing up to make them more tea. "But you have a wonderful future to look forward to with your husband, so you must concentrate on that." She paused. "Will you be able to continue to make dresses on commission, though?"

Greer made a quick decision. "Well, I will until I'm married." Fergus need never know, and she liked the idea of having a little more of a nest egg of her own before she married.

"That is good."

"But what is not so good is that I won't be able to make dresses on commission once I'm married," Greer added miserably.

"Oh, well, let's just take things as they come," Jamelie said soothingly. "He may change his mind."

They looked at each other in silence. They both knew that he wouldn't.

CHAPTER 30

Setbacks

Fergus had found them another spot by the roses in the Botanic Gardens and Greer enjoyed the sun on her face as they lounged on the rug together, having enjoyed the delicious food that Fergus had unpacked from his hamper.

"You always spoil me so," Greer said dreamily. "And you always manage to organise the most wonderful food for our picnics."

"Well, I do have a person who does this for me," Fergus said, sipping his lemonade.

"Oh, really?" Greer sat up a little to look at Fergus. "Who helps you?"

"No one important. Just a woman who deals with this sort of thing. But that reminds me, I must tell you my news."

Greer sat up a little more and gave Fergus her full attention. From his tone, this was something serious.

"I'm sorry to say that the house I had hoped to purchase ... well, it isn't going to happen."

"Oh, but why? We loved that home!"

"Yes, we did, but unfortunately the owners have changed their minds, so they will no longer be selling." Fergus held Greer's hand. "But don't worry, Angel Greer. I know you must be disappointed, but I'm sure I will find us something even better before our wedding."

Greer was crushed by the news but fought to put on a brave face.

"I will make it my mission!" Fergus declared with a fierce energy that impressed Greer. "I won't stop until I find us somewhere perfect."

***

Greer picked up her violin for the first time in some months. She couldn't remember the last time she had practised. It was a beautiful day at her favourite spot on The Camp estate, and she took a moment to tune the instrument. Greer had a brief hour before she was back to cleaning duties.

She thought for a moment about what she might play and eventually decided on *Caprice in A minor, Op. 1, No. 24* by Niccolò Paganini. She began to play, but was disappointed when her fingers fumbled and the lyrical tune quickly became discordant. She eventually gave up and stared at the view like a blind woman, not seeing a thing. What was wrong with her?

***

Greer was dusting the Bridgewood Orient dinner set yet again. She contemplated that she would one day have her own china in her own home with Fergus, and felt a shiver of anticipation. Perhaps his parents might give them a set as a wedding present. According to Fergus, they were very generous. It would be lovely to select something herself, but she was sure Fergus and his family would have excellent taste if they decided to give them a set.

She had gone from admiring the Bridgewood china to despising it, to admiring it once more, so she would be pleased to have a similar set. The delicate green and pink design of birds and flowers against a white background was very appealing. Or maybe she should go for a darker colour if she had a choice?

She was so distracted by her thoughts that she didn't realise until it was too late that one of the cups had slipped from her fingers and smashed on the kauri floors.

Florence turned as the delicate teacup shattered into several pieces on the hard surface.

"Oh, no," Greer whispered, tears welling in her eyes.

"Chuckaboo, don't you worry!" Florence said firmly. "I'll sweep this up, and we'll go and talk to Mrs MacGavin about it."

"She'll be so angry with me!" Greer said, appalled at her clumsiness.

"No, she won't … I've broken many things in my time working here, being the scatter-brained scapegrace I am, and she has always been kind and reasonable. It's just an accident, Greer, and accidents happen."

Greer wiped her eyes.

"Now don't you worry a jot," Florence put her arm around her friend. "Obviously, you are distracted by the wedding coming up, so Mrs MacGavin will understand!"

CHAPTER 31

July 1894

It was a bitterly cold day, and the castle was particularly draughty and uncomfortable as Greer made her way down one of the hallways, slightly late for meeting up with Fergus. She slowed her pace and bowed her head when she encountered William and Constance Larnach walking towards her. She had been under the impression they were in the city, so regretted she hadn't braved the weather to walk around the outside of the castle.

"Good day, Miss Gillies," Constance greeted Greer with her customary direct gaze and ready smile.

"Hello, Miss Gillies," Mr Larnach said. He looked full of energy today, a man with a mission, a sense of renewed vitality about him that had been missing since his daughter's passing.

"Good day to you both," Greer replied, nodding her head again. "And congratulations, sir, on being elected for Parliament again."

"Why, thank you, Miss Gillies. I have a lot of work to do, but I'm looking forward to the challenges."

"We will be getting ready to go to Wellington next week," Constance said. "You won't see so much of us back at The Camp for some time." She and William exchanged a smile before Constance turned her attention back to Greer. "Anyway, we mustn't hold you up on your day off. I hope you have something pleasant planned."

"Thank you, ma'am."

Greer carried on her way, and Fergus was waiting with his horse and buggy at the bottom of the lion statue stairs, pacing around impatiently. But when she got closer, his face lit with a smile.

"Angel Greer, you look radiant this morning," Fergus declared before kissing her and helping her into the buggy. "And I have good news – I have found another home that I think will be perfect for us. And the owner has already agreed to my price, so we won't have a situation like the last house."

It had undoubtedly been a disappointment when Fergus had told Greer that the small mansion they had both looked at, which she had loved, wasn't able to be theirs. It had taken her some time to adjust to the news, although she had kept her disappointment hidden from Fergus.

"Oh, that is wonderful news!" Greer said, genuinely excited.

She would be happy if this new place was anything like the last home they looked at. She knew that Fergus had excellent taste. Fergus chatted about his latest business dealings as they travelled along the high road to Dunedin. He'd invested shares in several local companies, and they were doing exceptionally well. He was considering buying a parcel of land to develop. It was wonderful that things were going so well. All his business ventures were on the up and up. He mentioned that others weren't doing so well. Just last month, the government had passed urgent legislation to guarantee two million pounds to the Bank of New Zealand to enable it to continue making banking transactions. Fergus had cleverly intuited that the bank had problems, so he had moved his funds to another bank. Greer was grateful he was so good with his investments.

So it was a surprise when Fergus stopped the buggy in the Devil's Half-Acre, not far from Walker Street. Greer got out of the buggy, looking around uncertainly.

"Fergus, I thought you didn't like this part of town?" she ventured to say.

He laughed and smiled that dazzling smile of his that so enchanted her. "I thought it might be special for you if we had a home not too far from where you grew up. And the houses in this part of the city are much more affordable, which will free up my cash for the property development I was telling you about. So let me show you our home!"

He walked enthusiastically up to a small cottage, with Greer following behind looking about her with growing unease. There was a small picket fence that desperately needed a coat of paint, and the small garden out the front was filled with dead flowers. There was rubbish in the gutters. Fergus found the key in his pocket and opened the front door. It creaked in protest as he led her into the property.

It was similar in layout to her old home, now the Georges' home, with the front room, kitchen, two small bedrooms and an outhouse. But it was there the comparison ended. The Georges' home was immaculately clean and beautifully presented and always smelt deliciously aromatic. Here, the paper was peeling from the walls and the floorboards creaked and groaned as they moved around, dust rising and making her sneeze. It smelt musty and disused.

"I realise this house needs work," Fergus said, "but I can easily tidy this up before we move in. So imagine this space when I've done things."

Greer nodded, trying to imagine a different space, but all she could see were more flaws in the property. One of the walls looked crooked, and the ceiling was uneven, too. It would take a lot of work to make this into a home. And it was as cold as an icebox. She could see her breath and huddled into her coat in an attempt to keep warm, resisting the urge to put the hood over her head.

"So what do you think?"

"It's very different from the last place you showed me," she said uncertainly.

"I'm pleased that I wasn't able to purchase that property. It would have been much too large for us as a first home," Fergus said as he led her into the main bedroom. "This is a perfect size, and it will be a good investment once I've done it up. It will be a suitable first home for us before moving on to something grander."

Greer nodded; she could see sense in his words. She was on the verge of saying it was a bit on the small side, but remembered she currently lived in a tiny room, and this house was a similar size to the cottage she had grown up in. Greer would be close to the Georges, making it easier to visit them. She brightened at the thought and turned to Fergus, who was looking at her intently. She felt breathless under his gaze; he always had some sort of power over her when he looked at her that way.

"Are you happy if I complete the deal?" he asked, coming close and putting his arms around her waist.

"Yes," she said, and he leant in and kissed her, and she responded passionately. But then his hands began to travel over her body, and it was only when some of her bodice had been undone that she came to her senses. She pushed away from him.

"Fergus, we mustn't."

Fergus groaned and ran his hands through his hair in frustration. "Oh, Greer, what you do to me! I don't think I can wait much longer."

"It's not long until our wedding," Greer said, adjusting her clothes and blushing a little.

"Maybe we should bring the wedding forward," Fergus said suddenly. "Let's not wait until December; let's get married in a few weeks."

"But what about your parents?"

Fergus began to pace the room like a caged tiger. "I had word yesterday that they won't be able to come. Mother isn't well enough for the long voyage and Father won't come without her."

"Oh, I'm so sorry!"

Fergus turned and clasped her hand. "It's no matter. But you see, with this news, we can marry sooner!"

Greer's mind raced. She couldn't wait to marry Fergus, but at the same time, doing so in a few weeks was too soon for her. She had so many anxious thoughts about their wedding night – a combination of anticipation and fear of what it would be like. She had heard the bawdy banter of some of the women who worked in the laundry, which had been off-putting. She supposed it might be good to talk to Florence about her concerns, now she was a married woman, but she hadn't found the right moment. And then there was the terrifying thought of eventually giving birth. She just needed a bit more time to adjust herself to these things.

"But I haven't finished my dress," she said finally, although it was almost done. "And we'd need to redo all the invitations, and we'd need to rebook the venue, which might not be available."

"All things that can be sorted," Fergus said, kissing her again.

"But I like the magic of getting married at Christmas, like you said," Greer tried another tack. "Getting married in the middle of winter seems so … bleak."

Fergus sighed. "Oh, you are right, my Angel Greer. Forgive my impatience! Let's proceed with our December wedding, which you have so expertly planned. It will be unforgettable."

"It will be magical!" Greer said before Fergus kissed her again, this time with more restraint.

A little later, they made their way back outside. Some driftwood tumbled down the street and Fergus promised her a glass of hot chocolate in a warm restaurant soon. Greer suddenly realised that her engagement ring had slipped off, probably because of the cold day and her having recently lost a little weight. She hastily retrieved it from the dirty pavement and was about to put it back on her finger when she noticed an inscription inside. She'd never seen this before, because she hadn't taken the ring off since Fergus had placed it on her finger.

To JR, with love, the inscription read.

Greer stared at the ring for a moment. *JR?* But this was Fergus's grandmother's ring, and her name was Ruby Mary. There must be some mistake?

Fergus turned to Greer, and she hastily put the ring back on her finger. Surely there was an explanation, but she didn't have time to say anything as he helped her into the buggy, his hand on hers. All thoughts about the initials on the ring went out of her mind as she gazed into his eyes.

CHAPTER 32

Dreamworld

"Do you have everything organised for your big day?" Florence asked, flopping on Greer's bed like the old days before Florence married Albert.

"I think so. The venue is booked, and invitations have gone out. I've chosen the menu for the reception dinner."

"And you have me as your matron of honour, chuckaboo! Not to blatherskite, but I'll be the best matron of honour in the entire world. Now I must ask, how is my dress coming along?"

"Dresses for you and Jamelie are progressing very well!" Greer couldn't help laughing at Florence's boasting.

"And how about your dress?"

"It's done!"

"Can I see?"

"Not right now! I will show it to you another day."

"Spoilsport," Florence said, tossing a hairbrush at Greer. They looked at each other and giggled.

***

After Florence had left, Greer tried on the dress and looked at herself in the mirror. She had told Florence the dress was finished, which technically it was, but something about it wasn't right. Perhaps the neckline was too high, and the sleeves were too long? She looked at herself sideways in the mirror. It didn't sit right around her waist and created bulk where there was none. She looked more closely at the bodice and saw the embroidery was uneven in places.

Greer hated to admit it, but she really had done a terrible job. It was shoddy work, and she would probably need to unpick and redo the dress. Of all the dresses to fumble on, why did it have to be her wedding dress? Despondent, she began to change out of it. She would need to do a lot of work to get this just right.

***

The closer Greer got to the wedding, the stranger her dreams became, and she often woke up drenched in sweat with her heart racing. She dreamt of her father, but instead of the loving man she remembered, she was forever chasing him in her dream world, with him walking away from her, his back her only view of him. She dreamt of Hamish, who repeatedly turned to look at her with an anguished expression before dissolving before her eyes, whatever he was about to say lost forever. She dreamt of Zhang Ming, talking like a woman in a delirium. She could only decipher some of the words. "An inch of gold," she kept saying, "an inch of gold will do you no good."

Greer told herself not to be silly. These dreams meant nothing. Her waking moments were all about Fergus and their future together. But she realised something was troubling her at a primal, fundamental level. Was it just natural nerves about getting married, which was expected, or was it something more?

CHAPTER 33

December 1894

Greer paused outside the elegant glass and wooden doors of Hallenstein's. She hadn't been there since she'd told Hamish she couldn't go into business and hadn't seen him since. A different person had taken over clothing deliveries to The Camp. But she'd promised Fergus she would get him a new necktie for their wedding, and Hallenstein's had the best selection in town. She steeled herself and entered the store. Mr Hallenstein was on the shop floor and greeted her warmly.

"Good day," he said with a smile. "Are you looking for anything in particular?"

"A necktie."

"Then Mr MacLeod will be able to assist you."

Mr Hallenstein directed her to where Hamish was standing by a counter. When he saw her, his brown eyes were filled with surprise tinged with sadness, which he quickly replaced with a neutral, professional expression.

"Miss Gillies."

"Mr MacLeod." Oh, so formal! Greer bit her lip as Mr Hallenstein excused himself. "How can I help you today?"

"I was wanting a necktie."

"I see. This is for your fiancé?"

She nodded. Hamish rummaged under the counter and then produced a tray of neckties for her to consider. She pulled several out, fingering the different fabrics; silk, cotton and linen.

"And the big day is soon?" Hamish enquired, not looking at her.

"In two weeks." Greer couldn't meet his eye either, but then Hamish

180

grabbed her hand, causing her to look at him in surprise.

"Greer, are you sure about this? Do you really want to marry that man?"

"Of course," Greer said. She withdrew her hand and pointed at one of the neckties. "I'll take that one."

"The best of them all," Hamish said with a rueful smile. "You have good taste when it comes to clothes." His unspoken words hung in the air between them: "good taste, except for men".

She fumbled in her bag to extract the money and dumped the coins on the counter while Hamish wrapped the necktie, his face creased into a frown. Suddenly he seemed to make a decision, and he snatched a piece of paper and scribbled an address on it. He handed her the parcel, but her eyes were only on the piece of paper and its address.

"What's this?"

Hamish sighed. "Just to be sure, I think you should visit this address before getting married." He glanced at his watch. "He's sure to be there at this time on a Friday."

Greer took the parcel and piece of paper and stared at Hamish for a moment. "I don't understand."

Hamish took a deep breath. "Fergus Breslin is not who you think he is."

"You sound just like Zhang Ming!"

"She is a very astute woman." Hamish paused. "Just go there. That's all I ask."

"I don't owe you anything!" Greer snapped.

"I know," Hamish's voice fell to a whisper. "But you owe it to yourself to find out the truth."

Greer spun on her heel and stomped from the store, feeling Hamish's eyes on her back. How dare he criticise Fergus; he didn't even know him! But outside the store, she stood for a moment and stared at the address. It was in the Devil's Half-Acre, and she realised it was The Rising Sun Hotel, an establishment she had walked past many times. She had never been in, of course, as only women of ill repute would enter a hotel like that, and she was a respectable person.

She walked and argued with herself until she eventually gave in. She would go to the hotel, there would be nothing to see, and she would go back and tell Hamish so. She had thought he was a friend, but he was clearly jealous of Fergus.

When she arrived at The Rising Sun Hotel, she stood outside for a moment, debating what she should do. It was unseasonably, bitterly cold, but thankfully her coat had a hood that sheltered her from the icy chill. She'd never stopped to look at the hotel properly; previously, it was simply a landmark she walked past. And now, it wasn't the weatherboard building itself that captured her attention, but the people she observed coming and going from the establishment, men who looked decidedly rough, the few women clearly disreputable. She was about to turn and leave when she recognised a male figure, hunched into his coat and walking with his head down, who didn't see her standing across the street. She was stunned to see it was Fergus. So Hamish had been right that he would be here. But that led to the following question: What was Fergus doing at this hotel?

Minutes turned into half an hour; half an hour became closer to an hour before she decided she needed to go into the hotel. She would go in quickly, see what Fergus was doing, and then leave. Perhaps he was meeting a client? Although it looked like a place of drinking, not business, but what did she know about such things?

She kept her hood pulled low as she entered the hotel. It was dark and crowded, and it took a moment for her eyes to adjust to the gloom as she hovered inside the entrance. A long bar ran across the far wall, serving alcohol to the patrons who perched on stools at small tables scattered around the room. No one noticed her standing quietly against the wall. The room was noisy, and men were busy drinking and talking. Some were gambling, and some had women with painted faces and less clothing than was modest sitting on their laps. It wasn't a place she wanted to linger. But then she saw him.

Fergus was seated with two men who had their backs to her. It was a Fergus she had never seen before. He was inebriated and he looked mean. His face was screwed into an expression of self-congratulatory arrogance. A patron drunkenly bumped into Greer as he walked past and startled her, but he just continued on. She edged closer to hear what Fergus was saying, keeping her head down and her hood pulled low.

"How did the last job go?" one of the men asked.

So it was business after all. Greer sighed with relief. Although it was a surprise to see Fergus looking the worse for drink, but maybe that was the way of business. Fergus had been vocal that he only drank on special occasions, but what special occasion could this be? Fergus gulped a large mouthful of beer and burped; Greer frowned, her momentary relief dissipating.

"It was easy pickings. Foolish toffs even left their door open when they went out for the day." Fergus rummaged in his pocket and showed the men the contents. "I just took a selection, but I picked the best."

Greer was astounded to see a variety of jewellery tumbling onto the table. Rings, necklaces, bracelets, and silver hairbrushes. In an instant, she realised her hairbrush and engagement ring had been stolen. No wonder the initials didn't match his grandmother's name.

"They will fetch a pretty penny," the other man said. "Do you want me to sell these?"

"Splendid idea," Fergus said, pushing the jewellery towards his friend, who deposited the loot into his own pockets. "Let's split things the usual way. Good of you to do this; I don't want another stint in the slammer."

"You don't want to give anything to your pretty bride-to-be?"

"Nah. I'll get her something else in the future. For now, I need cash."

"But you'll have plenty of cash once you are married, won't you?"

"True," Fergus said, tossing back another mouthful of beer. "Father's allowance is a pittance for me to stay here, but at least I'll get a decent lump sum once I'm married and I get the inheritance I've been promised once it's all legal."

The men laughed and thumped Fergus on the back. "A win-win situation; money and a pretty filly in your bed."

Fergus gestured to the waitress to bring them more beer, and Greer watched with growing disbelief as the young woman sauntered over to the table with a tray of jugs of beer for the men. The waitress put the tray on the table and then sat on Fergus's lap, and they kissed each other, Fergus groping the tart's breasts.

"See you later tonight, darl?" she asked.

"As always!" Fergus said as she strolled away.

"You're going to miss that when you get married," one of the men said.

"Not at all," Fergus smirked. "We have an understanding. Lizzy is happy to accommodate me, and my new bride need never know. I'll be respectable, but still able to have my fun. It will be the best of both worlds." He took another gulp of beer. "I was fortunate to discover such a naïve beauty at Larnach's Castle. The resident son would scarcely give me the time of day, despite my best efforts and socialising at his dull parties, but it's all worked out well in the end."

The men roared with laughter, and Greer felt ill as his words washed over her, so much so that she was shaking. He was a thief, a drunk, a womaniser. Fergus had been in prison. He'd led her on; he'd lied to her. And to find out he was one of those remittance men, sent to one of the colonies so as not to embarrass the family – well, his mother and father were never coming to their wedding, were they?

She felt sick, and then she felt embarrassed. How many other people had known Fergus was a scoundrel? Clearly, Hamish did – so did everyone know he was a man of disrepute? She stared at Fergus across the room, and she wondered that she had ever found him attractive. His vivid blue eyes were now glassy and bloodshot. His chiselled features now more resembled a rat. He dressed like a peacock but underneath was a stinky, revolting pig. As though in a trance, she stepped forward several paces, and she was now at an angle where she could see Fergus's two companions.

She was so shocked when she saw their eyes that she gasped and grabbed the bar's edge to steady herself. They were the men who had attacked her and stolen her first commissioned dress. Fergus had sent them to steal the dress. He'd known where she would be. Without regard for her well-being, he set those thugs on to her to make some quick money. No concern either about the time she'd invested or the dashing of her dreams by his actions. No wonder he'd never enquired about the stolen dress after or that she hadn't seen him until her injuries had healed. He was a weasel.

A patron bumped into her, causing her hood to slip down. His eyes lit up when he saw her face and auburn hair, clearly liking what he saw.

"Dollymop, you here for a good time?"

He grabbed her around the waist and pulled her to him. His breath stank in her face.

"Get off me!" She pushed him away, and he was so drunk he just wobbled into the bar.

Greer fled. The wind was bitterly cold on the street, even colder than when she first went into the hotel. Tears poured down her face as she stumbled up the road. What a fool she had been. She had pushed aside

184

Fergus's mood swings, strange absences, and little things that didn't add up. She realised now she had never had proof of any of his so-called investments, presumably all of them a lie. No wonder he didn't want her to go into business. He wanted her trapped at home, or only on his arm as he decreed, so he could live a double life. If she hadn't gone to the hotel, she would never have known his true character.

"Greer!"

She turned to see Fergus running out of the hotel after her, looking panicked and distraught. "I can explain!"

She stopped, and as he came closer, her grief turned to cold, hard fury.

"It's not what it looks like!" he panted.

"So you are not a thief, womaniser, and conman?" Greer challenged, surprised to hear how firm and cold her voice sounded.

"Well, I only stole a few trinkets to pay for our house!" Fergus's voice came out in a high-pitched whine.

"And the lump sum for our wedding – you were marrying me to get your inheritance, weren't you? It was all about the money!"

"Of course not, Angel Greer. You know how much I adore you."

"Stop calling me that!" Greer spat. "I'm a real-life person, not some celestial being." She narrowed her eyes. "You never went back to England to see your parents, did you? That's when you were in prison! Oh, I think you aren't even English, are you? All that talk about holidays in Ireland, to explain your accent. You're Irish, not English!"

"Yes, I'm Irish; what of it? But I can explain everything else," Fergus pleaded. "I only took risks for us, so I can give you the life you deserve."

"You mean that run-down eyesore of a cottage you've bought?"

Fergus frowned.

"Oh, let me guess, you haven't actually bought it yet."

"I was waiting for the money to arrive from Father."

"More lies!" Greer was furious and trembling, but managed to twist her engagement ring from her finger. "We are over, Fergus." She flung the ring at him, and it bounced against his chest and clattered on to the pavement. "I never want to see you ever again."

"But wait!" Fergus cried, grabbing her arm.

Greer stared at his hand on her arm and then looked him in the eye – the same eyes that had once mesmerised her. The scales fell from her own eyes, and she finally saw Fergus as he really was – narcissistic, opportunistic and shallow. A well-dressed piece of contemptible excrement.

"Let go of my arm," she said, her voice a cold, low rumble, and she saw him finally see the expression in her eyes and realise the charade was over. He let go of her arm, and she walked away from him without looking back, the cold wind making her eyes sting, but she vowed to shed no more tears for this person who had deceived her so utterly.

CHAPTER 34

Tonics

Greer spoke to Mrs MacGavin in the small room she used as her office.

"Now don't you fret about that silly young man. He hoodwinked us all," Mrs MacGavin said kindly, patting Greer's hand.

Greer dabbed at her eyes with her handkerchief.

"We are just happy to have you staying on here. You are family to us."

***

Constance handed over the wrapped Christmas gift and Greer opened it carefully. Another book. It was *Frankenstein* by Mary Wollstonecraft Shelley. Greer had heard of the book, but had never had a chance to read it. *Frankenstein* was very different from a romance novel, and for that, Greer was grateful.

"Oh, thank you. I will look forward to reading this. You are very kind."

"William and I appreciate all you do here at The Camp," Constance said. "And would you countenance playing that duet we spoke about a few days ago? How about later today?"

"Perfect. It will be just the tonic I need."

***

It was a delight to have the music room to themselves; no sullen family to make barbed comments to either of them. Constance sat at the piano and spread out the sheet music.

"Are you ready?"

Greer nodded, and Constance played the opening bars of *Caprice in A minor, Op. 1, No. 24* by Niccolò Paganini; then Greer joined her, lost in the swell of the notes. The melody came effortlessly from Greer's violin, and she wondered why she had had so much trouble playing this piece before. This time, the music and she were one. She didn't notice Constance glancing at her with open admiration from time to time.

***

Greer dusted the music room with Florence, who was humming to herself. Greer sighed as she ran her duster over the piano keys. Florence turned and frowned at her friend.

"Chuckaboo, you must stop thinking of him, you know," she said. "Whenever you make that sigh, I know he's on your mind. So just stop it. Think about something good and nanty narking."

"I don't feel so sad now. I mainly feel embarrassed," Greer confessed. "As if I were the only one who didn't know he was a scoundrel."

"I had no idea," Florence said. "Nor did Albert, so I don't think many people realised he was a blatherskite nineteener, and that everything he said was a lie." She suddenly spun in front of Greer with her mop as a prop. "Anyway, Miss Misery Chops, I have some exciting news to share with you that will make you smile."

Greer stopped what she was doing, giving Florence her full attention.

"I'm going to have a baby!"

"Oh, I'm so pleased for you!" Florence was right; the news had made Greer smile. The two friends hugged.

***

Greer was now back in the habit of visiting Jamelie for Sunday lunch after church. It was a safe haven of love and support as she recovered from the shock of Fergus's betrayal. But today, she knew something was terribly wrong when she saw Jamelie's drawn face and red eyes.

"Oh, has something happened?"

188

"It's Zhang Ming," Jamelie said, ushering Greer into the cottage. "Her daughter came around to tell me she is gravely unwell."

"Oh, no!" Greer put her hand to her mouth in distress. "What is wrong with her?"

"She's had a bad cough, but suddenly she couldn't breathe. Thankfully her doctor could visit quickly, but he has confirmed she has pneumonia."

Greer clasped her friend's hand. "I feel so helpless. Can we visit? Can we do anything else?"

"We will visit her this afternoon if you like, and we will look after each other, and we will pray."

***

Greer briefly conversed with Zhang Ming's daughter, who looked exhausted, before taking a seat by Zhang Ming's bed. She was asleep, so Greer sat quietly by her bedside, holding her hand, noting it was bony, like a bird's claw.

Zhang Ming looked no better than the last time Greer had visited. The grandmother of Walker Street looked nothing like her usual self in her small bedroom. Her face had a waxy pallor, her breathing was laboured, and she looked frail and old, her spirit diminished. Greer felt utterly helpless. She had to get better! Greer realised how much she would miss Zhang Ming if she didn't recover. Her kindness, her proverbs, her inherent wisdom – Greer couldn't imagine her life without Zhang Ming in it.

"You have to get better," she whispered, but there was no response.

CHAPTER 35

February 1895

As Greer knocked on the door of the Georges' home for another of their regular Sunday lunches, with the warm breeze on her face and the flowers blooming in their front garden, she contemplated how grateful she was to her dear friends. Zhang Ming was back to good health, although they had been worried for a few days, spending many hours by her bedside. Jamelie and Gabriel were well also. But Greer was still nursing a wounded heart. Despite vowing not to shed any tears over Fergus, tears had spilt, Florence there to mop them up, but Jamelie had been the most helpful.

"The virtuous flourish like palm trees and grow as tall as the cedars of Lebanon," she would often say, quoting Psalm 92:12. "Fergus was not virtuous, so you are better off without him. You deserve better, Greer."

Greer realised she *was* better off without Fergus – the life she would have had with him would have put her into a locked cage. But she had loved him, even though she doubted now he had ever loved her, and his deception hurt. Greer had licked her wounds and continued doing positive things away from duties at The Camp so as not to sink into a depression. She had sold the wedding dress, thanks to help from Jamelie. Greer had made a new commissioned dress, read more books, and played the violin down in the garden as often as she could and when weather permitted. All these things lifted her spirits, but she found she was feeling restless. She was twenty-four years old; was this her lot in life?

"Greer," Jamelie said as she opened the door. "Please do come in. It's wonderful to see you."

"These are for you." Greer handed Jamelie a bunch of flowers, and

Jamelie accepted them with a gracious smile. There were two surprises when she went into the kitchen. Zhang Ming was at the table looking bright-eyed and well, the first time she had been at Sunday lunch since recovering from her illness. The other surprise was that Hamish was there, and he stood up to greet her when she entered the room.

"Greer," he said warmly. "It is good to see you again."

They hadn't seen each other since the day she had discovered Fergus at the hotel, and she realised how much she had missed Hamish's company. She'd been too embarrassed to seek him out, but as she looked into his warm brown eyes, she realised her worries had been pointless. She felt as easy around him as she always had and took the seat next to him as offered, smiling at him.

"It is good to see you again, too, Hamish," she said before turning to Zhang Ming. "And gracious, Zhang Ming, it is wonderful to see you looking so well."

"I am grateful to be returned to good health," Zhang Ming said, smiling at Greer with great fondness. "It is true that without our health we have nothing."

"Please don't scare us like that again!"

"I will try not to."

Greer turned to Jamelie. "Is Gabriel away on business?"

"He decided to take Soraya to the park. He will be back a little later."

"He wanted to give us time alone to talk," Zhang Ming said, handing Greer some tea.

Jamelie smiled at the grandmother and shook her head. "Always so impatient!"

"I'm allowed to be. I am old, I may be dead soon, so I want you young people to get on with things."

Greer looked at everyone in surprise, and Hamish laughed heartily.

"I think what the esteemed Zhang Ming means is that we might discuss our business plans again, now that you are not getting married and are free to make your own decisions." He frowned. "I'm very sorry, by the way."

"No, you're not!" Greer challenged him.

"I mean, I'm not sorry you are not marrying that conman, but I'm sorry that you had to find out his true character."

"Why didn't you tell me sooner?"

"I had my suspicions that he was a fraud, but it was only about a week before I last saw you that I had information that he wasn't who he said he was." Hamish shook his head. "Quite by chance, an acquaintance happened to mention that the investments of a certain Mr Breslin were in doubt and that he kept dubious company at the address I gave you. And then I wasn't sure if I should tell you or not. I really wrestled with saying anything."

Greer paused before speaking. "I owe you a debt, Hamish MacLeod. I didn't think so at the time, but I've come to realise it since."

"Good, good," Zhang Ming spoke briskly. "Let's not waste time talking about the toad. Talk does not cook rice."

"The toad?" Greer was amused, despite herself.

"Stinky toad. I didn't know exactly what Fergus Breslin was up to, but I could see he was a stinky compost pile under his nice clothes. He reeked of badness. No good. Not like my dear husband or my friend Choie Sew Hoy. You must have quality people to make life okay – and good health," she added.

Jamelie cleared her throat as she handed around food for them all to enjoy. "We invited Hamish for lunch so we could talk about possibly reviving the idea of Gillies and George Designs."

"And I thought it was a wonderful idea," Hamish said, sipping his tea. "I'd need to start looking again for a suitable property, but I'm ready to commit to this business venture if you are."

"I am," Jamelie said. "Gabriel and I have had long discussions, and I have his full support. I confess I want more than just making dresses on commission. A shop will be exciting and allow us to build a proper business. I might even be able to pass it on to Soraya one day."

They all turned to look at Greer.

"So it just depends on you," Zhang Ming said.

Greer looked at her friends and realised nothing was holding her back from this venture now she wasn't with Fergus. And as she turned the idea over in her mind, she found she was even more excited about it than when it had first been raised.

"Let's do it!"

Zhang Ming clapped her hands, and Jamelie breathed a sigh of relief. Hamish touched Greer's hand lightly before helping himself to the manakish bread. "You won't regret it!"

192

"I'm sure I won't, although you still need to find the butler in the garden."

"I'll need to go back on deliveries in that case," he said, causing Jamelie and Zhang Ming to look at each other in confusion.

Greer smiled at Hamish. Suddenly everything felt right again in the world.

CHAPTER 36

Cadences

Florence stopped dusting and rubbed her back before patting her slight baby belly. Greer stopped to look at her friend.

"Are you all right?"

"Chuckaboo, I've never felt better," Florence said cheerfully. "Although I have to pee every five minutes, which is driving me batty."

Greer had noticed the many toilet breaks, but Florence now glowed with her pregnancy after a period of morning sickness. She'd never looked so beautiful. Even her hair looked silky and less wild.

"Do you think it will be a boy or girl?" Greer asked.

"I don't mind either way, as long as he's healthy."

Greer laughed. "So you prefer a boy!"

"I have lots of sisters, so I think a boy would be nanty narking. I've even started making a list of names." Florence pulled a notebook from her pocket and began to read. "Felix. Theodore. William. John. Ezra. Oscar. Silas, or perhaps Oliver."

"What does Albert think?"

"He likes them all, but by blazes, I'm the one having this baby, so I'm going to make the final decision. I will know the minute he comes out which name is the best fit."

Greer laughed again and not for the first time thought Albert had the patience of a saint.

***

Another Sunday lunch and the table was packed with people talking over each other as they feasted on the Lebanese and Chinese food spread before them. Charles Sew Hoy was there with his much younger European wife, Eliza, who seemed utterly devoted to him. She had previously been his English-language secretary, and was an attractive woman with pale skin, curly hair and a ready smile. Zhang Ming was there with her daughter and son-in-law, a kind, industrious pair – and Charles Sew Hoy was suggesting some business ideas that might make their lives easier as greengrocers. Frank and Wardi were discussing a possible house they were thinking of buying. Soraya was now four and half years old and was chatting non-stop with a young friend who went to the same Bible class. Her poor friend couldn't get a word in, Soraya was talking so much. Jamelie and Gabriel discussed the details of his next work trip and how long he planned to be away.

Hamish caught Greer's eye and smiled before leaning in to whisper in her ear. "Everyone is so noisy today."

Greer looked around again and felt the love and energy in the room. She felt utterly content. "I wouldn't change a thing."

These were her people, an eclectic mix of Scottish, Lebanese and Chinese – their commonality that they were quality human beings with big, generous hearts.

"Nor would I," Hamish said, looking at her for a moment too long before helping himself to more food.

CHAPTER 37

June 1895

Greer, Jamelie and Hamish stood in a line outside the three-storey building near the Octagon on Stuart Street and admired it. The building was painted in a soft grey, and the windows were framed in white with pleasing ornate fretwork that gave it a sophisticated look. They crossed the street, Hamish opened the wooden front door, and they walked around the empty ground level. It was a bare space with kauri floorboards, but it was clean and fresh, and there was plenty of natural light that filtered in from the two front windows on each side of the front door and a side window.

"We'd have plenty of room to create eye-catching window displays here," Greer said, gesturing towards the windows.

"We could put a counter along this wall," Hamish said, pacing the space out.

"And we'd have mannequins and comfortable lounging chairs in this area," Jamelie said, and Greer could see precisely what she meant, picturing it all in her mind. A place for women to linger and look at their designs.

"The fitting rooms would be along here," Hamish gestured to the space along from the imaginary counter. "We'd have room for two generous ones, so you can do measurements and fittings in a private space."

"Oh, yes, that would be perfect," Greer said.

"And look at this space on the second level," Hamish continued, leading the way upstairs to a carpeted space. He bounded up the stairs like an agile mountain goat, enthusiasm in every step. "This has ample space to be the workroom. We can easily accommodate three sewing machines and staff here, and we could have a large cutting table along that wall. And the carpet will muffle any sounds to the shop below."

"And it's wonderful there is a small bathroom just off this room," Jamelie said, peering into the room. "Makes it so easy for everyone working here."

"There is more!" Hamish led them up to the third level, another space that was also carpeted. "We can use this as an office and for storage."

Greer looked around with interest, peering out the windows to the street below. After a moment, they traipsed back down to the ground floor again.

"It's a great location, and the lease is reasonable, well within our budget. And the landlord thinks our business will be profitable, as Dunedin is prospering, and he feels the timing is perfect for a new women's clothing store," Hamish concluded. "So, what do you think?"

"Let's take it!" Jamelie said.

"It's perfect!" Greer agreed.

Hamish nodded as the women hugged each other. "I'll talk to the agent today and get the paperwork sorted, so we can all sign it."

"I'll hand in my notice as soon as the paperwork is signed," Greer said, turning to Jamelie. "Are you still sure it's okay to move in with you?"

"Of course it is! You are part of our family. And we have so much to do before we open the store, so I need you nearby! We need to hire staff, and we need to have at least twenty dresses ready to make the shop attractive."

Hamish handed them each a sheet of paper. "I've made a list of what needs to be done, and you will see I've allocated who does what against each item."

Greer scanned the list. She would need to source and organise mannequins and lounge chairs. Jamelie was to organise the staff they needed. Both she and Jamelie were required to produce the initial batch of dresses they would need to open the store before the staff came on board. Hamish was organising the signage for the store, machinery, counter, fitting rooms, lighting, curtains and furniture for the workshop, as well as booking advertising closer to the shop opening. They all had a lot to do.

Greer smiled at Hamish. "You are very organised. You still haven't found the butler in the garden, though!"

Hamish smiled back at her. "And I won't have much time to look for him from now on as I'll need to hand in my notice at Hallenstein's as soon as possible, so I won't be doing deliveries to The Camp anymore."

They chatted about their plans for the store as they had another good look around the space, all of them making notes as they looked again. But soon, their talk turned to the news dominating all the newspapers; Scottish-born Williamina "Minnie" Dean had been found guilty by a jury of murdering a baby in her care, Dorothy Edith. WINTON BABY-FARMER FOUND GUILTY, the headlines screamed.

"I still can't believe anyone, let alone a woman, would murder a baby," Jamelie said.

"She was only convicted for the one murder," Hamish said, "but two bodies and a skeleton were found in the garden at The Larches in Winton."

Greer nodded. "Her lawyer claimed the evidence was circumstantial. She claims she is innocent, but it seems unlikely after the discovery in the garden of those remains."

"I'm not surprised it took the jury only half an hour to deliberate," Hamish said.

Jamelie shuddered. "It's a terrible thing. I just don't understand why anyone would harm a baby, let alone murder one."

"What is going to happen to her? Will they really execute her?" Greer asked.

"If they do, she'll be the first woman to be hanged in New Zealand," Hamish said grimly.

Greer sighed. "It's terrible what she did, but I don't know if I agree with her being executed. It seems as barbaric as her crime." She gave herself a little shake. "I can't bring myself to think any more on the subject. For now, we need to concentrate on our shop – we have so much to do!"

"Don't worry, Greer. We will get this done. I hope we can open our doors in a couple of months," Hamish reassured her.

"Gillies and George Designs!" Jamelie smiled at her friend. "It does have a stylish ring to it, doesn't it?"

"Stylish and sophisticated, catering for the modern woman," Hamish said. "I'm sure the business will be a great success!"

Greer was filled with hope and excitement for the future. Running a business would be a dream come true, and she couldn't think of two better people to be doing this with.

CHAPTER 38

Possession

Greer had been dreading handing in her notice, but she needn't have worried. Mrs MacGavin was typically kind and supportive of her new venture when they sat together in her small office.

"I am very sorry you will be leaving us, but I knew a talented girl like you wouldn't be with us forever."

"Thank you, Mrs MacGavin."

"And your new business sounds wonderful!" Mrs MacGavin seemed genuinely enthused. "Gillies and George Designs. I will make sure I visit when you open and tell all my friends."

"That would be most appreciated, Mrs MacGavin."

What was surprising was the reaction of the cook, who had clearly been loitering outside the door.

"Think you are too good for us, don't you?" she sneered. "And how can you go into business with an Assyrian? Mark my words, your business won't last five minutes."

Greer walked past her, too shocked to reply.

***

Greer was greeted by Florence's mother, sisters and the local midwife when she arrived at Florence and Albert's home. After emotional hugs and kisses, the family directed her down the hallway to the bedroom. There was Florence, looking tired but elated, with Albert sitting on the edge of the bed. They were both gazing intently at the bundle Florence was holding, but looked up when Greer knocked on the door.

"Chuckaboo, come in," Florence commanded. "Let me introduce you to John Albert Taylor."

Greer put the flowers she had brought with her on the bedside table and peered at the sleeping baby, swaddled in a soft blanket. "Oh, he's a bonnie lad. He's beautiful!"

"And the minute he arrived, by blazes, I knew he was definitely a John Albert."

"It's the perfect name for him," Albert said, gazing at his son in wonder.

***

Greer put her precious possessions in the bedroom that Jamelie had prepared. Her sewing machine was now in the business workroom, leaving her clothes, violin and books to house here. Not many things, but all precious to her. Jamelie had cleverly partitioned part of the room, so Soraya had her bed and toys on one side, but Greer still had her own space. It was cosy but, as always in this home, tastefully done.

"Are you sure it's okay to stay here?" Greer turned to Jamelie.

"For the thousandth time, yes, we will love having you here. Soraya is thrilled you will be staying with us – she has talked of nothing else since we told her. But don't worry, we have instructed her that she is not allowed to touch any of your things, and she ends up in our bed at some stage most nights, so I'm sure she won't bother you."

"Oh, I'm not worried about Soraya bothering me. I love her immensely. I just worry about being an inconvenience!"

Jamelie tsked at her friend. "You are never a bother, my dear friend, and I appreciate you contributing to the household expenses. And we have our exciting business venture to keep us occupied! It will be so much easier to get through the work with you living here."

At that point, Soraya ran into the room and jumped up and down on her bed.

"I'm so pleased you are staying with us, Aunty Greer. This is the best thing that has ever happened to me!" She paused for a moment. "And I promise not to touch your violin or books or clothes, but I do hope you will play with me sometimes, and you can share my toys." She grabbed a well-worn teddy bear and cuddled him before handing the toy to Greer.

"That would be my pleasure!" Greer accepted the teddy bear, touched by the little girl's generous spirit and enthusiasm. "Does your bear have a name?"

"Teddy, short for teddy bear," Soraya said seriously.

Greer smiled. "Of course, Teddy is the perfect name!"

***

Greer sat in the lounge and sewed another bead on to the dress she was making, Jamelie companionably sewing also. Gabriel had put Soraya to bed a couple of hours earlier and had since been away doing an errand. He arrived back, took his coat and hat off, and smiled at them.

"Are you ladies ready to retire yet?"

"Perhaps in half an hour," Jamelie said. "I'd just like to get this finished."

Greer looked up at him. "And I only have a few more beads to add."

Gabriel nodded and smiled. "You are both very industrious. I must applaud your hard work."

"And I must thank you, husband, for all your support." Jamelie looked at her husband with great affection.

Greer smiled, looking at the pair. This was what true love looked like. Respect, mutual understanding, kindness. One day she hoped to find this for herself, but she had work to do for now, a business to open soon with her friends!

CHAPTER 39

August 1895

Greer wasn't sure if it was a bad omen that they were opening their store the day after Minnie Dean had been executed by hanging in Invercargill. It was all anyone could talk about. When asked if she had anything to say at her execution, Minnie replied, "No, I have nothing to say, except I am innocent." As the hangman was about to carry out his task, her final words were reported as, "Oh, God, let me not suffer." Greer felt a chill run down her spine thinking about the scene, but then turned her attention to the display at the counter, where there was a selection of fans and gloves they all hoped would be popular with their clients.

She looked around the store and felt a flush of pride. It looked beautiful, from the welcoming Gillies and George Designs sign outside to the clothing displayed in the window to the comfortable seating strategically placed so women could sit and look at the dresses on display. Beautiful velvet curtains graced the two generous fitting rooms and the stairs that led upstairs to the workshop and the office on the third level, with plenty of space for additional bolts of fabric.

Greer disappeared upstairs to see how things were going in the workshop. Jamelie had found three lovely Lebanese women to work for them, who, although shy, had proved to be friendly, courteous and industrious in just a few days. There were sisters Abila and Dasia, two dark-haired beauties who looked very similar, and their friend Ferwa, slightly cross-eyed but just as charming. They spoke to each other in low murmurs, punctuated by gentle laughter, and under Jamelie's leadership, the workshop had a very happy and productive feel. Greer went back to the ground floor in time to see Hamish bursting through the front door, carrying some last-minute boxes and wrapping paper supplies.

"Are you ready for us to open soon?" he asked as he unpacked the purchases behind the counter.

"I think so."

Greer felt both excited and nervous. Soon they would open their doors for the very first time. She straightened one of the folders they had created with sketches of designs for their clients to choose from. Greer had a sketch pad ready to create new designs as needed. They had many bolts of fabric in the workshop and the third-floor office they could bring down to show customers, and thanks to Hamish's excellent bargaining skills, the fabric had been acquired at much better rates than Jamelie and she had ever achieved. Women might now have the vote, but they sadly couldn't achieve the same rates in business as men.

She smiled at Hamish, and he grinned back, his brown eyes twinkling. She and Jamelie could not have done this without him. He might not have wanted his name on the store, but he was crucial to their three-way partnership. But then she thought about all the risks of what they were doing and frowned.

"I hope we have some customers, though!" she added.

"I don't think you need to worry." Hamish glanced at his watch. "I saw a number of potential clients in the nearby café, so I predict we'll be busy when we open in twenty minutes."

Jamelie came downstairs to join them, and they fussed and straightened things, although everything was perfect and didn't need any more attention. Greer felt more excited as the time ticked by. She thought of her father and knew he would be proud of what she was doing. She thought how kind Mrs MacGavin had been when she went to resign her position, and William Larnach had passed on some additional money for her final day with a note wishing her well in her business and thanking her for her service. He was a very kind and generous man. She felt she had a lot of support for this venture, despite the odd mean comment from people who disapproved.

Hamish glanced again at his watch. "It's time."

Jamelie and Greer hugged and then nodded at Hamish to open the door.

"I won't stay long." Hamish had made it clear that he didn't think he should be on the shop floor too often. He felt it would be better as a domain for women, and he had enough to do with the accounts and their suppliers to keep him busy anyway. "But I can't resist being here on the shop floor when we open."

"Of course!" Jamelie said. "This is a momentous occasion for all of us."

Hamish opened the door and the first person through was Florence, her blonde hair in disarray, but her smile as bright as ever.

"Oh, this place is a corker!" she exclaimed, looking around, touching the fabric of the displayed dresses. Greer was grateful her friend had decided to come on their first day. "I couldn't resist coming on opening day, and my mother is looking after wee John for me."

Several other women entered the store straight after Florence. One of them looked Florence up and down and then departed back out the door with her nose in the air. Greer shrugged; they didn't need a customer like that anyway, and she turned her attention to the other women who were admiring her designs.

"Oh, I do love this dress," one of them said, stopping to look at a lemon silk dress on one of the mannequins. "And it looks my size, too. May I try this on?"

Jamelie was at her side in an instant. "Of course. I'm Jamelie George, one of the owners. Let me just remove this from the mannequin, and you can take the first fitting room."

"Wonderful! I'm Mrs Jones, by the way. I very much like your store."

"Thank you so much!"

One of Mrs Jones' friends had taken a seat and was looking through one of the folders with design sketches, oohing and aahing as she turned the pages. Greer was about to talk to her when Constance Larnach came through the front door, looking about for a moment before approaching Greer.

"Miss Gillies, your shop is a credit to you. This is very well done, as good as anything I have seen around New Zealand or abroad."

"Thank you!"

"We have many formal occasions when William and I return to Wellington. I thought I might get you to design me a dress, if you would be so kind."

"Of course! What did you have in mind?"

Constance pointed at the dress closest to the counter. "I do very much like this style, but I'd like this in a dusty pink if that were possible."

Greer smiled; she knew just the fabric. "If you'll excuse me for a moment, I'll return with some fabric I think you will love."

"Excellent." Constance moved on to look at another dress.

Greer whipped upstairs to the workroom; the three Lebanese women were busy with beading dresses – they were keeping any machining work to outside shop hours for the opening. She selected the bolt of pink fabric from the shelving that Hamish had designed and returned downstairs to the shop floor to show Constance.

"Oh, yes, that is perfect," Constance said when she saw the silk taffeta material.

Greer pointed at the display dress. "I suggest that we alter this design a little for you. Just a slightly lower neckline, say an inch lower, and we extend the lace into panels here and here." As she spoke, Greer indicated the dress sections she was talking about.

Constance thought for a moment. "Yes, I like that very much."

"Would you have time for me to take your measurements today?"

"Of course."

Greer picked up a notebook and a measuring tape. "Let's use this fitting room," she said, leading the way to the second fitting room.

It was a generous space with floor-to-ceiling mirrors on two sides, a comfortable chair and a coat stand.

"Let me take your coat."

Constance removed her coat and handed it to Greer, looking about with approval. "This is very nicely done," she said as Greer took measurements.

Although Greer had taken measurements for other clients before, it felt oddly intimate this time. She could smell the lavender of the fragrance that Constance wore, she noticed a small birthmark on the exposed part of Constance's back, just above the neckline, and she also noticed how smooth and pale her skin was, reflecting her lifestyle of privilege.

"You are very talented, Miss Gillies," Constance said conversationally, and Greer realised she had been holding her breath, slightly in awe of making a dress for her former employer's wife.

"Not really," she murmured.

"Yes, you are. Not only do you play the violin better than anyone

I know, but your designs are also lovely. Fashionable, but original and stylish Something a little different. I especially love the beading and lace work on your creations."

"That is thanks to my business partner, Mrs George," Greer said. "I do believe she makes the finest lace I have ever seen. And as for the beading, all our Lebanese workers excel at this skill."

Constance smiled. "I think your business will do very well and I will be sure to mention your shop to everyone I know."

"Thank you, that is very kind."

"We women must support each other. We live in a modern era where we can do things that were denied to previous generations, so we must make the most of everything."

When Greer had finished recording the measurements, they both stepped back into the store. Hamish was wrapping up a pair of gloves for Florence, and Jamelie was wrapping up the lemon silk dress for Mrs Jones. Already they had their first sales and their first commission, and more women were coming into the store. It was a relief that the day was off to such a good start. Greer felt a glow of satisfaction. With luck, Gillies and George Designs would be a successful business many years into the future, despite the few naysayers.

CHAPTER 40

November 1895

Greer sat next to Hamish in comfortable seats in the Dunedin City Hall. Hamish had somehow managed to get them tickets to the "Mark Twain at Home" lecture series, which was a blessing as the show had sold out almost as soon as the tickets had gone on sale. Mark Twain had recently arrived from Bluff and was doing a thirty-eight-day lecture tour of New Zealand. It was a rare treat from working, and Greer had been delighted when Hamish had surprised her with the tickets.

Greer had enjoyed the novels *Tom Sawyer* and *The Adventures of Huckleberry Finn*, but she was surprised to see that Mark Twain wasn't at all what she had expected. The advertisement in the *Otago Daily Times* had billed him as the greatest humorist of the century and assured the public of a night of wit and wisdom. But he didn't look like a humorist. He was older, on the short side, stockily built, and had a head of messy white hair. As he spoke, in a subdued, deliberate voice, he appeared to be delivering a serious lecture, but as Greer listened, she found his words to indeed be funny, although he seldom smiled.

"In New Zealand, the rabbit plague began at Bluff," Mark Twain was saying in his nasal drawl. "The man who introduced the rabbit there was banqueted and lauded, but they would hang him, now, if they could get him. In England, the natural enemy of the rabbit is detested and persecuted; in the Bluff region, the natural enemy of the rabbit is honoured, and his person is sacred. The rabbit's natural enemy in England is the poacher; in Bluff, its natural enemy is the stoat, the weasel, the ferret, the cat, and the mongoose. In England, any person below the Heir who is caught with a rabbit in his possession must satisfactorily explain how it got there, or he will suffer a fine and imprisonment, together with extinction of his peerage; in Bluff, the cat found with a rabbit in its possession does not have to explain – everybody looks the other way; the person caught noticing would suffer fine and imprisonment, with the extinction of peerage. This is a sure way to undermine the moral fabric of a cat. Thirty years from now there will not be a moral cat in New Zealand. Some think there is none there now."

Greer looked around the hall; there were as many women as men seated in the audience, and they were as mesmerised as she was by the way he presented his material. He had a slow deliberation and a kind of absent-mindedness that made his words irresistibly mirth-provoking.

"In England, the poacher is watched, tracked, hunted—he dare not show his face; in Bluff, the cat, the weasel, the stoat, and the mongoose go up and down, whither they will, unmolested," Twain continued. "By a law of the legislature, posted where all may read, it is decreed that any person found in possession of one of these creatures (dead) must satisfactorily explain the circumstances or pay a fine of not less than £5, nor more than £20. The revenue from this source is not large. Persons who want to pay a hundred dollars for a dead cat are getting rarer and rarer every day. This is bad, for the revenue was to go to the endowment of a university. All governments are more or less short-sighted: in England they fine the poacher, whereas he ought to be banished to New Zealand. New Zealand would pay his way, and give him wages."

The crowd roared with laughter and Greer turned to look at Hamish. They worked six days a week together now with their store, and he'd grown in her estimation. He was unfailingly hardworking, cheerful and full of innovative ideas. She found she trusted him completely, and enjoyed his ready smile and the familiar twinkle in his brown eyes. And while it was early days for the business and it would be some time before they were making a profit, everything was going well. The three of them were the perfect business combination. Jamelie worked part-time to have time with her daughter, but supervised the workshop, contributed to the designs, and helped out in the shop when they were busy. Greer had become the front person for the business, she did the majority of the designs, and at Hamish's suggestion, she modelled the dresses in the store, so each day, she wore something different. Hamish was in and out of the store all day or upstairs in the office, dealing with the suppliers, making deliveries, doing the accounts and anything else that came up. Hamish caught her eye and smiled at her, and she thought how handsome he looked in his well-tailored jacket and trousers, his dark hair grown slighter longer and almost in his eyes.

She focused back on Mark Twain and his lecture, a happy, haphazard browse at random among the pastures of his published work, but he also tailored it to the local audience. He spoke about Dunedin and the Scots. "They stopped here on their way from home to heaven – thinking they had arrived." He spoke about women's suffrage in New Zealand and "how women have the right to vote for members of the legislature, but they cannot be members themselves". He revealed sympathies and outspoken views concerning Māori, which were well received by the Dunedin audience, but Greer wondered how these views would be received in other parts of New Zealand.

At the conclusion of his performance, the hall echoed to the sound of cheering and stamping, followed by a rollicking rendition of *For He's a Jolly Good Fellow*.

"Did you enjoy that?" Hamish asked as they made their way to the exits.

"Very much!"

"I wondered if you might like to have dinner with me? It's getting late, and neither of us has eaten."

"An excellent idea. Very sensible. Now I think about it, I'm famished."

Hamish directed them to a small restaurant, its interior cosy with dark English oak panelling, a magnificent oak and stone fireplace, and lead lights and stained-glass windows. They were seated in a private corner.

"It was extraordinary to see such a famous man in real life," Greer said after they had ordered some food. "A real-life celebrity in New Zealand!"

"He's on a year-long tour," Hamish told her. "He has already toured Sydney, Adelaide and Melbourne, and by the time he has finished, he'll have lectured in places like Hawaii, Fiji, Ceylon, India and South Africa."

"Imagine doing all that travel!"

"Would you like to travel one day?"

Greer pondered. "I've never thought about it, really. It has never seemed something that would be possible."

"Well, maybe in the future, we can send you to somewhere like London or Paris to look at the latest fashions," Hamish said with a smile. "When the business is more established, of course!"

"I would like that very much!"

They were interrupted by the waitress bringing them their meals. They had ordered the same thing – lamb medallions served with Champagne-minted sauce and a variety of steamed vegetables.

"Tell me something about you that I don't know," Hamish said conversationally.

"Oh, I don't know … I'm a maid turned seamstress."

"Designer and business owner," Hamish corrected. "Okay, tell me about … tell me about your violin. It's an Amati, isn't it? How did you come to own it?"

"Well, this story involves my grandparents. They emigrated from the Scottish Lowlands to Dunedin in the 1860s. My mother was then a teenager."

"My grandparents emigrated about the same time," Hamish said, nodding.

"Well, before my grandparents married back in Scotland, by all accounts my grandfather was a restless young man, and he was not that happy about working on the family farm – although he was very keen on a lass who lived in the local area, who captivated everyone with her ability to play the old fiddle she owned. But she always yearned for a classy violin that really showed off her musical skills."

"Your grandmother," Hamish said, and Greer nodded.

"So the couple began courting, but the lass was confused and upset when my grandfather suddenly disappeared for several months. When he returned, he said he had been in London, and he presented her with an Amati violin and an engagement ring, which sealed their love forever."

Hamish sat back in his chair. "That is quite a story! Do you know where your grandfather got the Amati violin?"

"He apparently never said where he obtained the violin, but a rumour did circulate about a late-night, high-stakes poker game with a young man from the gentry who was down on his luck, and instead of the pot of money on the table, my grandfather asked for a violin instead. The down-on-his-luck man was happy to hand over the family violin instead of losing his money. No one played it and it was just gathering dust anyway. My grandfather would never confirm or deny what really happened."

"Incredible!" Hamish said. "What an amazing love story. And how did your parents meet? Mine met at a local dance, and not long after, they were engaged. So not a whirlwind romance exactly, but a short and successful one."

Greer laughed. "Actually, I do have a story about my parents. And it's not what you would expect."

"Oh, do tell me more!"

"Well, it is quite the story, for you see, my grandfather disapproved of Papa. This is after my grandmother had passed away, and it sounds like he wasn't the same man after this. Anyway, he threatened to shoot my father if he ever came near their place."

Hamish's eyes widened. "But they obviously got married, so what happened?"

"Papa wasn't going to be put off that easily, so he made some plans. First, he arranged with a minister to be ready to marry them when they arrived on a certain day. Then my uncle was persuaded to get my grandfather out of the way, so Papa could slip in unobserved with an extra horse to get my mother out."

"Ingenious!"

"Well, not quite, as my grandfather could smell a rat. He thought his son seemed too eager to get him out of the way, so he didn't go very far. But Papa still had time to travel a fair distance before my grandfather began riding after them."

"So he gave chase."

"Yes, he did. My parents arrived at the minister's home, excited to be getting married. They were early and discovered the minister working in his garden. Of course, Papa was looking over his shoulder and requested he marry them immediately. But the minister had other ideas."

"What was that?"

Greer laughed and continued her tale. "The minister quite naturally replied that he needed to wash his hands first, but Papa was having none of that. He told the minister that the 'old fellow' was after them and never mind his hands –they needed to be married with haste. So they were safely married before grandfather arrived, and then there was nothing he could do about the situation. By all accounts, he was livid, and it was probably only having the minister there that stopped him from making good on his threat of shooting Papa."

Hamish considered the story for a moment. "Did you ever meet your grandfather or your uncle?"

"No ... my grandfather died not long after, and my uncle moved away, and Papa lost touch with him after my mother died."

"So he might be alive?"

"Unfortunately, no; some years ago, Papa got a lawyer's letter letting him know that he'd passed away."

Greer had no family. They were all gone. Hamish reached out and took her hand, sensing her sudden melancholy. She looked at his hand, his long, square fingers. It was a hand that was reliable and dependable. She felt a warm glow from the pit of her belly through her entire body. Hamish went to move his hand, but she held it a little tighter, looking deep into his brown eyes. She realised that with Hamish, she felt at home. Not the breathless excitement she had experienced with Fergus, but something much deeper and more profound.

Hamish gazed into her eyes and seemed to see her realisation as they held hands and stared into each other's eyes in the soft candlelight.

"Greer," he cleared his throat, his voice a little husky. "I've been wanting to ask you something for some time."

"What is it, Hamish?" But she already had an idea where the conversation was going.

"Would you agree to us courting? I would like to see you outside of work and be more than a business colleague to you."

Greer smiled and felt complete contentment as she answered. "I would like that very much, Hamish MacLeod."

He lifted her hand to his lips and kissed it gently, and they gazed at each other for a moment until the spell was broken by the waitress arriving to clear their plates and bring them dessert. Greer had never felt so content as they ordered brandy snaps.

"Would you like to have lunch at my parents' home at the weekend?"

"It would be a pleasure to meet them," Greer said sincerely. It was only right and proper if they were courting that she meet them. Rather than being nervous, she found she was looking forward to this.

CHAPTER 41

Song

As soon as Hamish's parents opened the door to their stylish two-storey home in North Dunedin, Greer immediately liked them.

"Greer, it is so wonderful to meet you," Hamish's mother greeted her with a kiss on the cheek.

"Please come inside," Hamish's father insisted. "We have heard so much about you!"

They were exceedingly warm and welcoming as they invited her into their home. Hamish looked a lot like his father, with the same dark hair and brown eyes, but he seemed to have inherited his mother's warmth and cheerfulness.

Greer looked around the lounge as Hamish took her coat. It wasn't an ostentatious home, but it was charming and clearly a place of warmth and love.

"You must be Greer," a taller, stockier version of Hamish said, coming towards her.

"Andrew is my older brother," Hamish said, playfully punching him on the arm. Andrew frowned at Hamish.

"You can shake her hand if you like," Hamish offered.

Andrew stuck out his hand somewhat cautiously, and Greer shook it before Andrew turned when his wife called him to help with something in the other room. Two children chased each other around the lounge, paying no attention to the guest.

Hamish followed her gaze. "That's Andrew's children, and you'll meet his lovely wife in a moment. She's the outgoing one of the pair."

It had struck Greer that Andrew seemed shy, and it was intriguing to meet someone who looked so much like Hamish but who also seemed so different.

"What does your brother do?"

"He works in the bank. They keep him out the back where he doesn't have to deal with people."

Greer raised an eyebrow, and Hamish laughed. "My brother is wonderful. And he's got an amazing talent for numbers, but he prefers to let others hold the conversation, which suits me just fine."

"More time for you to do all the talking?"

"Exactly!" Hamish grinned. "Now, let me introduce you to the two rascals who seem to be trying to destroy the room. If we can get their attention, of course!"

***

Greer knew everyone had noticed the change in their relationship when she went to sit beside Hamish at the Georges' dining table the following Sunday. They'd managed all week to keep their new relationship under wraps, but she knew the game was up as soon as she saw Zhang Ming looking at them intently.

"Something has changed," Zhang Ming pronounced. "Now, don't waste an old lady's time. What precisely is happening, and when did things change? Remember, a bird does not sing because it has an answer. It sings because it has a song. Tell me about your song."

Hamish turned to Greer, reached for her hand, and then addressed the group while Jamelie and Gabriel watched them affectionately. Soraya had her head to one side with open curiosity. Next to them, Charles Sew Hoy reached over and held his wife Eliza's hand.

"Greer and I are pleased to announce that as well as being business partners, we are officially courting."

Everyone clapped and offered their congratulations.

"I very much approve," Zhang Ming said. "And it is about time. I thought this day would never come!"

Greer looked at her friends and then at Hamish, and they both burst out laughing.

CHAPTER 42

February 1896

Being a Sunday, Greer and Hamish had a day off work, and after church they decided to go for a picnic at the Botanic Gardens. Hamish found them a spot in the shade under the magnificent weeping ash tree, with views of the band rotunda where a string quartet was playing one of her favourite tunes, *Plaisir d'Amour*. It was a beautiful summer's day, neither too hot nor too cold, with just the perfect mix of sunshine and a cool breeze. Hamish unpacked the basket of goodies he had organised, a selection of sandwiches and cakes that they could wash down with some refreshing lemonade.

"It's such a beautiful day!" Greer said, looking around.

"A beautiful day spent with a beautiful woman, I can think of nothing better," Hamish said. "I feel so grateful to be living right now, in this moment."

Greer smiled at his compliment. "Speaking of living now, that reminds me, did you read in the newspaper that the University of New Zealand has announced the country's first woman medical graduate?"

"I remember seeing that," Hamish replied. "Such a wonderful achievement passing her final examinations, and she is only twenty-two." He handed her some lemonade.

"I do love living in this decade. I remember the 1880s; it was all gloom and doom and recession, but this decade it's all about prosperity and advancement." He laughed. "I saw the other day that you can now watch something called a motion picture in Auckland through Edison's Kinetoscope."

"How extraordinary. If we ever go to Auckland, we must go and see."

"I will make a note. And when business isn't making so many demands on us, we shall travel to Auckland and anywhere else you may like."

"Wonderful! When thinking about advancements, I must say that I love that women generally have more rights and opportunities than ever before."

"So do I. For you, my dearest Greer, I hope you will always follow your dreams and achieve all you want in life. You have my full support in all your endeavours."

"Thank you, Hamish. I so appreciate everything you do for me. I wouldn't be in business if it wasn't for your persistence and hard work."

"Ah, but I could see the opportunity with you and Jamelie, beautiful designs that are a little different." He laughed, a sound she loved to hear.

"It's actually fulfilling my dream, too, of having my own business. And while I love fashion as much as you do, I didn't want to set up a menswear store in competition with Hallenstein's. Bendix has been much too good to me. And women's fashion is much more exciting, I must say. Much more glamorous, and more profitable, too. Men can be cautious with what they spend on their clothes, but for men and women, that all goes out the window for a special dress for a particular engagement."

"Yes, and we do have some wonderful clients now," Greer reminded him. "I must thank people like Mrs Larnach and her contemporaries for recommending us." She sighed. "It's just a shame about some of the society ladies who come in, take one look at Jamelie, or me sometimes, and walk out again."

Hamish shrugged. "We don't need customers like that. And they are missing out on your beautiful designs, so it's their loss."

"You are kind. But I do worry that I will run out of design inspiration at some point. I had a complete block the other day when I was with a client, and usually the ideas come so freely."

"Well, don't give that a moment's thought. I've subscribed us to some design magazines from Paris and London, so you'll have these for inspiration from now on. Of course, you and Jamelie add your signature touches, but that way, we will be up with the fashion trends from Europe."

"You are always thinking ahead," Greer said, looking at Hamish gratefully.

"Thank you, dearest." Hamish cleared his throat. "I must say again, you look beautiful today and I really admire that colour on you."

After Fergus's overblown hyperbole, Greer enjoyed Hamish's direct manner of compliments; it made her feel valued and loved. She glanced down at the blue organza dress she was wearing, one of her favourite designs from the shop and one she had decided to keep for wearing outside the store. It perfectly complemented her smooth, pale skin and highlighted her green eyes and auburn hair.

"Thank you."

"Shall we stroll to your favourite duck pond?"

"I can't think of anything better," Greer said happily, so they packed up the blanket and picnic basket and placed them in Hamish's buggy nearby before walking to the duck pond, where they typically visited.

The pond was tranquil, and their two favourite paradise ducks were walking near the edge of the pond in tandem before gracefully entering the water together. Greer had never seen them apart and was sure she'd heard that paradise ducks mated for life. But then she noticed that Hamish had gone strangely quiet, and when she looked at him, he seemed a little pale under his lightly tanned skin.

"Hamish, are you all right?"

Hamish cleared his throat and suddenly went down on one knee by the pond.

"Greer Gillies. I remember the first time I met you, playing the violin in the garden at Larnach's Castle, so beautiful and accomplished. And since then, I have come to know your character, that you are loyal, hard-working and talented."

Hamish swallowed, and Greer looked at him with a balloon full of love in her heart and soul, so large, she imagined it might lift her into the sky, such was the love she felt for him.

"Greer, will you make me the happiest man in the world by agreeing to be my wife? I love you more than I have words to express. I want to eventually grow old with you. Will you marry me?"

Greer found her voice, and to her astonishment, it was clear and composed. "Hamish, I love you, and I would be honoured to be your wife."

Hamish sprang to his feet and swept Greer into an embrace, and they kissed passionately. The perfect kiss, on a flawless summer's day, full of excitement and longing for their future to unfold. Tender, sensual, and carrying the promise of the wonder of marriage that would be theirs in the future. Greer had never felt more right about any decision.

Eventually, they surfaced from the timelessness of their kiss and Hamish broke into a beaming smile. "I haven't even given you the ring!" he exclaimed, hunting for it in his pocket. "Very careless of me!"

"I would have said yes even if there wasn't a ring," Greer said tenderly.

Hamish found the jewellery box and handed it to her, and she paused before opening the box slowly. "But of course, I am very keen to see what you have chosen."

She gasped when she saw the ring. It was an elegant emerald engagement ring surrounded by diamonds on a plain gold band. Hamish slid it onto her finger.

"Oh, it fits perfectly! And it's so beautiful!"

"I had it designed especially for you," Hamish said, a little proudly. "It was easy enough to work out the ring measurement from the day I got you to try on all those sample gloves."

"Oh, I remember that day. You are so clever! I never thought you had an ulterior motive!"

"And I wanted the emerald to match your beautiful eyes, symbolising new beginnings, so I thought that apt. And the diamonds symbolise sincere love that lasts forever – which will be us. And this gold band has no beginning or end and is, therefore, a symbol of infinity."

Greer's eyes filled with joyful tears. His choices were impeccable and so incredibly heartfelt. She looked forward to their life together, and with Hamish, she knew she'd found the right man to be her husband, lover and partner.

"It's perfect."

Hamish gathered her into another embrace, and she lost herself in the sensations of their kiss, his mouth tasting of lemonade, his subtle scent of sandalwood, his warm, strong hand at the base of her neck. In his arms, she was safe and loved, cherished and adored. She couldn't wish for anything more.

CHAPTER 43

Overtures

"Oh, let me look at your engagement ring again!" Florence grabbed Greer's hand excitedly. "It's a corker and suits you perfectly."

Greer admired the ring also. "Hamish has excellent taste."

"Well, chuckaboo, he does marrying you!" Florence said kindly, stopping to rock baby John, who was growing bonnier by the day, on her lap. He chortled and smiled at them just as a waitress brought the tea they had ordered.

"So we must discuss the important things," she continued. "Will I be your matron of honour?"

"Of course! Both you and Jamelie will be my attendants."

Florence looked strangely uncomfortable before speaking in a rush. "And our dresses? What of our dresses?"

Greer pretended to think about something she had already decided on. "Well, I do know how much you love the dress I made you for my wedding that didn't go ahead."

"It's gorgeous!" Florence said. "I'd be happy to wear it! It would save you having to make another! But I just wondered if it might be strange for you, considering everything …" her voice faded out.

Greer took pity on her friend. "Florence, I'm pleased for you to wear the dress. And I've spoken to Jamelie, and she is happy, too. Of course, I will have a new wedding dress. The last was a disaster, an omen, looking back, and long gone anyway. But there is nothing at all wrong with the dresses I made for you both."

Florence sighed with relief. "I'm so happy. I can't wait to wear my dress. I'll be like a princess wearing something so corker on the day." She sipped her tea and then noticed Greer's raised eyebrow. "Oh, you will be too. But I'm so happy to wear my dress." She paused. "Now, what about your wedding cake and what dessert are you going to have?"

***

It was another visit to Hamish's parents' home, but this time Hamish had asked her to bring her violin with her.

"It would be wonderful to show off your talents to my parents," Hamish had said, so she wasn't surprised when Hamish asked if she would like to play something after Sunday lunch.

But she was surprised when Hamish sat behind the baby grand in the corner of the drawing room. He opened the lid and did a couple of accomplished scales up and down the piano keys before turning to her with a cheeky smile.

"What would you like us to play?" he asked his parents as they found seats nearby.

"I didn't know you played!" Greer said, laughing. Of course, she'd admired the piano on other visits, but had always assumed either his mother or father played.

"Well, I play, but you don't know if I'm any good, so what piece do you suggest we try?"

Greer thought quickly and selected something that was reasonably well known. "What about Bach's *Sonata in B minor*?"

Hamish nodded, got up, and rummaged in the piano stool seat. "Excellent choice. We even have the sheet music."

He settled himself and Greer readied her violin.

"Shall we?"

Greer nodded, and Hamish began to play the piano. She soon joined in and it was a revelation to learn that Hamish played well, and they had an effortless rhythm together. Perfect timing, in fact. Even though Greer was the superior musician, Hamish was an able accompanist. Anyone would have thought they had played together many times.

Hamish's parents applauded when they finished, and Greer and Hamish looked at each other, slightly flushed but triumphant. There was no need for words. What a revelation to discover they had this musical compatibility in common. What other talents was Greer still to discover about her future husband? The thought brought a smile to her lips as she packed away her violin, stealing glances at Hamish as he put the sheet music away.

***

It was a pleasant Sunday, and as the sun was beginning to set, Hamish and Greer sat on a bench seat at the Botanic Gardens. He put his arm around her shoulder and kissed her tenderly on the lips. Kissing Hamish was one of Greer's favourite pleasures. It felt so natural; she felt safe, loved, and nurtured, his mouth warm and welcoming. It was always a moment of stepping outside time, a feeling of languid infinity. Greer now had butterflies and sensations similar to those she had once experienced with Fergus, but this time the connection was more spiritual and emotional, perfectly in tune with her body's desires. In Hamish's embrace, she was home.

"I can't wait to be married to you," she said after a moment.

He smiled and stared into her eyes. "I can't wait either, but Greer, just think about it; once we are married, we have the rest of our lives to get to know each other."

He stroked her hand and then turned it upside down, drawing little circles with his finger, causing her hand to tingle.

"I want to get to know every part of you," Hamish whispered, his voice husky.

"And I every part of you," Greer whispered back, but then her underlying fear of childbirth caused her to stiffen.

"I know it worries you," he said, not for the first time, softly into her ear.

"You know I'm not worried about our union," she said, also not for the first time. "I desire it more than anything else."

"I know, my love. I feel the same. But I, too, would be terrified of childbirth if my mother had died as yours did. It is only natural. But we may not be blessed with a child straight away, and if we are, you will have help from women who know about these things."

She relaxed back into his embrace as he continued to murmur words of comfort, and the most important thing was he reassured her over and over that he would be there with her, no matter what. They would face her fear – and now his fear – together.

***

Greer and Hamish strolled along St Clair beach arm in arm, Greer enjoying the breeze and the sun on her face. It was a beautiful day, made even better by the man at her side.

"It's so nice to have a break from the shop," she said conversationally. "It was a lovely idea to come out here for the afternoon. A change of scenery is wonderful. I feel refreshed and ready for the week ahead."

"We have much to do," Hamish said, smiling at her. "More houses for me to look at, more dresses for you to design."

"You must tell me the instant you think you have found a home that will suit us. I want to be part of the decision, husband-to-be, not left on the sidelines."

"And you will be, my darling wife-to-be. In fact, I insist that you have the final say on where we live."

Greer smiled at Hamish and thought, not for the first time, that she'd found the perfect man to share her life with. Someone who made her feel safe and valued and very much loved.

CHAPTER 44

May 1896

It was a sunny but cool autumn morning as Greer and Hamish walked up the steep street to view a house that Hamish thought might suit to be their home once they were married. He'd looked at numerous houses in the past few weeks, and this was the first he thought would be appropriate for them. He hadn't been remotely interested in any of the others, he assured Greer. It was a short walk to their shop, so it was a great location and not far from where Hamish's parents lived.

They stopped outside the home so Greer could view the house from the street. It was a generous two-storey villa, the weatherboards painted white and the window trims in grey. The home was a little off the narrow road behind some shrubbery and a white picket fence. The fretwork around the doors and windows was outstanding, and Greer took her time admiring the workmanship before Hamish took her arm and they crossed the street.

As soon as Hamish opened the wooden front door and they stepped into the long hallway, Greer instantly fell in love with the sunny, generous property. Off the hallway there was a large lounge with a fireplace, and dining and kitchen to the rear of the lower level that opened up on to the generous back section. A small bathroom was situated down a passage between the lounge and kitchen. There was a coal range in the kitchen and an open fireplace in the dining room also. Greer looked up at the high ceilings that added so much space to the rooms. An elaborate dado rail separated the leafy patterned wallpaper at the top of the wall from the more straightforward design lower down. It was very tasteful. Greer spun around with delight.

"Oh, Hamish!" Greer felt giddy with excitement. "This is beautiful!"

"Wait until you see upstairs!" he said, watching her reaction with delight.

He kissed her gently on the lips and then led her upstairs. The master bedroom faced the street, and there was a study off this room with a balcony situated over the front door. "This can be our home office and library."

"Look at the view!" Greer said happily. "We can see much of the central city from here."

"We can't see our shop, though."

"But it's only a half-hour walk away!"

There was another small bathroom down a passageway, two generous additional bedrooms, and a long veranda with views over the large section and garden.

"I love it!" Greer declared, stepping out on to the veranda and looking at the view. She particularly liked the blue hydrangeas that were in full bloom.

"I love it, too," Hamish said. "Not as much as I love you, but a close second."

Greer laughed as he gathered her into an embrace, and they kissed again, Greer welcoming his mouth on hers.

"We will have plenty of room to entertain," Hamish said after a moment.

"And we can put your piano in the downstairs lounge; there is plenty of room for it. Oh, to think I once thought it belonged to your parents!"

"There is plenty of room to raise a family, too," Hamish said, and when he felt her body stiffen, he stepped back and looked her directly in the eye, his brown eyes filled with love.

"I know you are concerned, my dearest, but we must put our faith in God that we are even blessed with children," he said gently. "And I know your fears about childbirth are completely understandable, but if and when the time comes, I will make sure we are surrounded by women who have experience in these matters."

Greer relaxed and felt her anxiety dissipate. They had discussed Greer's concerns at length, and each time the subject was broached, she felt stronger and braver.

224

"You are right."

"And let's try not to worry about something that hasn't happened yet, or may not happen. We will have a fulfilled life whether children come or not. So what do you think? Do you want to purchase this home?"

"I do!"

"It's not a Larnach's Castle."

"I want a happy home, not a grand castle."

"In that case, I suggest we go to the lawyer's office to sign the documents immediately and make this place our own," Hamish said. "I'm sure Jamelie won't mind looking after the store for a little longer, so we can get the paperwork done."

"She did say not to hurry back."

"Just as well. I made an appointment with the lawyer then. I had a feeling you'd love this place as much as I do." Greer laughed, happy that Hamish had again thought ahead.

She seldom thought about Fergus these days, but she recalled the mansion he had pretended he would purchase for her – she knew now that was a lie. And then the shack he really was considering buying – but then the excuse of waiting for money before purchasing. She suspected they would have been stuck in that awful hotel where she had last seen him if the wedding had gone ahead.

Everything with Hamish was so different. True, she hadn't viewed the previous properties with him, but they had decided with their business commitments it was best for him to look first, and she'd look when he thought he'd found something suitable. Hamish was transparent and honest, and she felt they were equal partners in everything they did.

When they arrived outside the lawyer's office, they were surprised to see William Larnach stepping out of the building with William's youngest son, Douglas, and Constance just behind the politician, the pair murmuring to each other behind William's back. Greer was shocked to see how unwell and unhappy William looked. He was hunched over in his long coat as though in pain, his face pale and pallid. Then she recalled Florence mentioning that he'd had an accident travelling into Dunedin in his buggy with Constance and Douglas. An axle had broken at Anderson's Bay, and while Constance and Douglas hadn't been injured, Larnach had been thrown onto the road, breaking several ribs and dislocating his shoulder. But that had been months ago, so had William Larnach met with some new misfortune? Fortunately, Hamish wasn't as slow on the uptake as she was.

"I am very sorry to hear of the loss of your Uncle Donald," Hamish said, dipping his hat to William. "Terrible news from London. Our sincere condolences."

"Thank you," William said, nodding at Hamish. "It is another sad occasion for our family, but I appreciate your kind words."

Greer couldn't help but notice how old William suddenly looked; standing behind him, Constance and Douglas were a picture of glowing health and vitality, and they both looked composed and happy.

"Our deepest sympathies," Greer said to all of them.

"Thank you, Miss Gillies," Constance said, smiling at her fondly. "But on a happier note, we understand that congratulations are in order. We hear that you are engaged to Mr MacLeod."

Greer took off her glove to show Constance her engagement ring, something she always took great pleasure in. "Yes, we are. We are planning for a spring wedding."

"I'm so delighted for you both, and your ring is beautiful, don't you think, Dougie?"

"I don't know much about rings, but to be young and in love is a precious gift," Douglas said.

"The most precious," Constance agreed, staring at Douglas.

Something about how they looked at each other caused alarm bells to ring in Greer's head. But then she blinked and saw Constance taking her husband's arm affectionately – in an almost motherly way. "We mustn't hold you up, so I wish you a good day."

"Good day to you also," Hamish replied, dipping his hat once more.

Hamish and Greer watched the trio make their way to their buggy.

"Poor William Larnach," Hamish said when they were out of earshot. "I'm not talking out of school to say that he's made some poor financial decisions of late, and he's created a logistical problem in needing to be in two or three different places at the same time between his political, business and family obligations. He's greatly over-extended. And now the death of his uncle, who I know he greatly admired, will be a huge blow."

"I don't think it's a happy family life either," Greer said thoughtfully. "Florence keeps me up to date on all the news, even though she is busy with her wee John. Albert seems to know all that is going on. The oldest son Donald is apparently struggling to make ends meet in Melbourne, but his father is putting his foot down about continually sending money. And Colleen is at odds with her father and never visits The Camp, preferring to remain in Naseby. And Alice's firstborn son died before his first birthday."

"That's incredibly sad."

"It's good to see Douglas has mended his disagreement with his father, though. Florence was telling me that they had such a massive fight he disappeared to Naseby for a time."

"But doesn't Douglas run the farm at The Camp?"

"Yes, he does. I don't think the argument was about the farm, but something to do with the telephone installed at The Camp. Apparently, Douglas was sick of being a telephonist when he just wanted to be outdoors looking after the farm, so it's good to see that Douglas is talking to his father again."

"And looking rather chummy with Constance as well," Hamish said after a moment.

"Oh, so you noticed, too?" Greer paused. "Well, it's good that one of the children likes Constance, at least – Florence says the other children still openly despise her, which must be difficult."

Still, something about seeing Constance and Douglas standing close together, a little behind William, had seemed odd. But then Greer shrugged the thought away.

"Shall we?" Hamish opened the lawyer's door. "Let's purchase our first home!"

"It's so exciting!" Greer followed Hamish through the door and into the next part of her future.

CHAPTER 45

Presents

Greer followed Hamish's mother into the DIC department store, the older woman chattering away as they entered the grand shop.

"I'm so happy you are now part of our family, and we've decided we'd like to give you and Hamish a dinner set for your own home."

The two women went further into the shop until they stood in front of the dinner set displays. Greer studied them, feeling overwhelmed by the choice and the generosity of this kind offer.

"Now take your time, but let me know which set you like the best, and that will be our wedding present to you and Hamish."

"Are you sure?" Greer turned to her future mother-in-law, who smiled back with obvious affection.

"I'm getting a daughter, so you deserve the best. Now, which set would you like?"

Greer's eye fell on a burgundy and gold set, a little oriental, but so stunning in colour, she instantly loved it. She picked up a plate and looked at it carefully. "This is perfect."

"You have excellent taste!" Hamish's mother smiled at her for a moment. "I'll just have a quick word with the sales assistant, and then let's go and enjoy afternoon tea together."

***

Soraya wrapped her arms around Greer's neck as Greer sat on her bed. Soraya was now a spirited five-year-old and had blossomed since she

228

started school earlier in the year, doing well, especially with her reading and writing.

"I'm really going to miss you when you get married, and you can't share my room anymore."

"Don't worry, Soraya," Greer said, turning her head so their faces were side by side. "You will still see lots of me. I'll be working with your mother during the week, and I'll come and visit often. And you can come and visit me in my new house!"

Soraya jumped off the bed in excitement. "I would love that! When can I come and see your place?"

Greer laughed at her enthusiasm. "You can be one of our first guests after getting married."

Zhang Ming appeared in the doorway. "Soraya, I just need to talk to Greer for a moment. And you need to do your homework."

"Okay," Soraya said, dutifully moving to her side of the room and taking papers and pens out of her schoolbag. "I'll tell you when I've finished!"

"Of course."

Greer followed Zhang Ming into the kitchen and saw that she had already poured them some tea.

"Take a seat."

Curious at Zhang Ming's serious tone, Greer slid into the seat opposite.

"It's not long until your marriage, and we have a saying that when the lovers are finally together, all shall be well. However, I wanted to give you some advice before the wedding day."

Greer looked at her curiously, wondering what aspect of marriage Zhang Ming would discuss.

"I want to share the greatest secret of a marriage with you," Zhang Ming continued as she handed Greer her tea. "What do you think it is?"

Greer frowned. "Love?"

Zhang Ming smiled. "That is important, that is true, but there is something even greater." She paused. "Patience is the most important. Patience is power; with time and patience, the mulberry leaf becomes a silk gown."

Greer smiled at the image it brought to mind as Zhang Ming continued.

"You must realise that although you love Hamish and he loves you, gold cannot be pure, and people cannot be perfect. So you will have disagreements; that is just the way of life. But if you are patient in one moment of anger, you will escape a hundred days of sorrow."

Greer nodded. "That is excellent advice, Zhang Ming. I am grateful for your wise words."

Zhang Ming nodded, clearly happy to have passed on this advice. "Now, how are all the last-minute arrangements coming on?" she asked, sipping her tea.

CHAPTER 46

September 1896

Greer looked at herself in the mirror as Jamelie made some last-minute adjustments to her wedding dress. Jamelie and Greer had made it together. The dress was made of cream cannelle-weave silk with a simple fitted bodice, a wide low neckline and short sleeves. Over this, Greer was wearing a matching fitted V-neck jacket with long leg-of-mutton sleeves. It boasted silver brass hooks and tiny eyelet holes, and the sleeves and neckline and back of the jacket had Valenciennes lace that matched the panels of lace on the skirt. The ensemble was completed with a parasol, a pair of pure silk stockings and cream leather ankle boots.

"You look beautiful!" Jamelie stepped back to admire Greer. "You make the most radiant bride."

"Thank you so much for helping me make such a stunning dress," Greer said, turning to hug her friend. "And thank you for letting me stay in your home for so long."

"You are family to us, dear Greer. We will be sad to see you go – although, thankfully, I still get to see you most days at the store!"

Greer looked around the bedroom she had shared with Soraya for just over a year. Her possessions were now packed up for the next part of her life. Once, she'd only had one battered beige suitcase housing some clothing and books, one small sewing machine, and one case that housed her precious violin. But now she had an extensive wardrobe suitable for her new position as a dress designer, and a small library of books thanks to friends' generous gifts over the years. The silver hairbrush she had been given by Fergus had been tucked away and forgotten until Zhang Ming had helped her pack. When Zhang Ming heard this particular story of deceit and that Greer planned to throw the brush out, Zhang Ming claimed it for herself, which had pleased Greer. It wasn't the hairbrush's fault it had been stolen. Now it would be appreciated once more.

She had loved being part of the George family over this time; she had felt a great sense of belonging, and when Greer wasn't at the shop working, she'd helped Jamelie cook, played with Soraya, put her to bed and read her stories. She'd enjoyed listening to Zhang Ming humming in the kitchen when she came over to help – or just visit for a chat – occasionally with her daughter and son-in-law accompanying her. She'd seen more of Jamelie and Gabriel's friends Frank and Wardi, and as their English improved, she'd been able to converse with them more, finding them warm and intelligent people. Florence and Albert had come to visit with their wee boy John, and everyone had got on swimmingly. She was excited that Florence and Jamelie would be her attendants today.

"You look beautiful, too," Greer said, looking at her lovely friend.

Jamelie was wearing a soft green dress, complementing her dark hair and skin tones. Like Florence's dress, it had been made for another wedding, but was being worn for the first time today.

"Thank you," Jamelie said.

She picked up Greer's orange blossom flower bouquet and checked the matching flowers in Greer's hair one more time. Greer had a veil, and they had styled her auburn hair pinned up, with curls cascading down, the flowers perfectly complementing her vibrant hair colour.

"I'll take these and give them to you at the church," Jamelie said, kissing her friend before leaving the room. Gabriel and Soraya were already in the buggy. Zhang Ming and her daughter and son-in-law were travelling separately, and Florence and Albert would meet them at the church.

"See you soon," Greer said, checking her reflection again.

A shiver of anticipation ran down her spine. Today was the day she married Hamish, and she couldn't wait to be his wife. Her only sadness was that her beloved papa couldn't be with her. She had thought for some time about who to ask to escort her down the aisle, and when she thought of the perfect person, she berated herself for not considering him earlier. Edward, the coachman, had always been kind and was like a father figure to her, and he'd accepted immediately when she had asked him.

Greer looked around the room one more time before picking up her parasol and walking out onto the street where Edward awaited her, looking dapper in his jacket and trousers. It was a mild spring day, a little overcast but otherwise sunny.

"It is an auspicious day," he commented, helping her into the buggy.

"Thank you for being with me on my special day," Greer said, as the horse began walking.

"I wish you and Hamish as much happiness as I had with my beloved wife, Anne."

"Oh, you are married?" This was the first he had ever mentioned a wife.

"Unfortunately, Anne passed away after an illness. But we had many happy years together that I will always treasure."

"I'm sorry."

"No, don't be. I just know I'm blessed to have had so much happiness in my life, and I can see you and Hamish are well suited and will have a happy marriage."

"Yes, I think we will," Greer said, and they continued in companionable silence as Greer thought about Hamish. His qualities were numerous. Kind, caring, thoughtful, intelligent, honest and trustworthy. Not that he was perfect, of course, but she even loved his imperfections. She teased him about being a tight Scots with money, but he would always retort that they would be better off in the long run by being careful, something that she had to agree with. And he could never remember the punchline to a joke, which was funny in itself, but that was hardly something he could do anything about.

He was handsome: tall, dark and attractive. It was strange to think Greer hadn't seen his masculine charms immediately. Instead, she had considered him a goff. But then the scales had fallen from her eyes, and she'd finally seen the real man. He was lean but had a strong, muscular physique; his face in profile was classically handsome and his brown eyes usually alight with warmth and love. She loved the way his dark hair often flopped over his forehead. She loved watching him play the piano, his long, square fingers confidently caressing the keys. She imagined his fingers on her body and felt a flush. He'd been the perfect gentleman throughout their engagement – plenty of kisses and embraces – but nothing more. No furtive groping or pressure to rush their marital pleasure. But the more gentlemanly Hamish had been, the more she had found herself desiring him. In the days leading up to the wedding, she could barely be in the same room with him without heat flooding her body, her heart thumping while she became breathless.

Greer was roused from her thoughts when the buggy suddenly jolted forward, and she had to clutch the sides to stop falling out. Edward cursed under his breath and leapt down to investigate.

"What is it?" Greer looked at him anxiously.

"The axle has broken," Edward said. "I am so sorry. Of all the days for this to happen. And I see my horse has lost his shoe."

Greer thought quickly. "It will be quicker to walk the rest of the way than for us to wait for you to repair the buggy and replace the horseshoe. We must be halfway there." She began to get down from the buggy, grabbing up her parasol. "Shall we?"

Edward regarded her with admiration. "Yes, that would be the best plan. I will tie up my horse and let us continue on."

He sorted the horse and buggy and offered her his arm, which she gratefully accepted, but they had only walked a few blocks when Greer noticed the skies darkening. "Oh, it looks like it's going to rain!"

"We must hurry then."

They picked up the pace and walked another couple of blocks before the rain started. Greer hastily put up her parasol – meant to ward off sunshine, not rain – but she thought it was better than nothing.

"If I may?" Edward swept her into his arms, and he began to jog, Greer so surprised she didn't find her voice for a moment. "This will be faster." Indeed, he was jogging briskly, and she could see the elegant polychromatic brick of All Saints' church now coming into view as the rain began to pour down. "Rain on your wedding day is good luck, you know," Edward said a little breathlessly.

"Really?" Greer said, trying to keep dry under her parasol.

He slowed down a little. "Rain is good luck because it symbolises that you will be cleansed from the tough times and sadness in your past and be given a new chapter in your life."

Greer promptly stopped worrying about her appearance. "That's beautiful," she said. "And I'm certainly not going to let a few raindrops stop me from marrying Hamish."

Edward grinned and picked up the pace again. "That's the spirit."

Jamelie and Florence were waiting inside the foyer of All Saints' church, peeking out through the archway in anticipation of Greer's arrival. Soraya, dressed in her flower girl dress, a miniature version of her mother's and looking impossibly pretty, held her mother's hand. Jamelie and Florence looked astonished when Edward and Greer came into view, Greer in the coachman's strong arms, laughing despite the rain, her parasol only keeping some of the water off her. Edward deposited her gently next to her friends in the foyer and stepped back while Jamelie and Florence anxiously fussed around their friend.

"Greer, what happened?" Jamelie asked.

"Blazes, chuckaboo, you know how to make an entrance, don't you!" Florence said.

Greer discarded her sopping parasol, and despite being a little damp, she looked at her friends with glowing vitality, her cheeks slightly flushed, making her even more beautiful. "Would you believe the axle broke, and then it started raining, so Edward just picked me up and carried me here."

Jamelie began fussing about rearranging Greer's dress and then examined her hair and flowers, helping her put the veil over her face. "The dress has survived the rain well, and your hair looks just the same, so I think you are ready to get married, my lovely friend."

Florence handed Greer her bouquet. "Are you ready?"

"Yes, I am," Greer said confidently.

Jamelie nodded and led the way into the church and down the centre aisle, with Soraya holding her hand and Florence following behind. A little later, Greer followed on the coachman's arm, her eyes only on Hamish, who was looking handsome and a little nervous in his dark suit with its buttonhole flower matching her bouquet. His face lit up when he saw her, and she felt herself float rather than walk up the aisle towards him. Edward nodded at her affectionately and took a seat in the congregation, but she barely noticed he had left her side.

"You look beautiful," Hamish whispered as she stood next to him before the minister. Florence, Jamelie and Soraya stood on one side, Hamish's brother Andrew on the other, along with Albert.

"So do you," she whispered back.

She didn't remember much of the service, just Hamish looking at her with love and admiration as he lifted her veil and they said their vows before he placed the plain gold ring on her finger. She took in her surroundings only after the minister had pronounced them man and wife. The rain had stopped, and the church looked glorious with sunlight streaming in through the stained-glass windows, the decorations and the flowers beautifully done. But it was the people that captured Greer's attention. Hamish's parents and the rest of their family. The George family, with Soraya looking about in wide-eyed delight at the proceedings. Zhang Ming, who kept wiping her eyes with a handkerchief. She had been very vocal in her approval of Hamish, as had Charles Sew Hoy, who was also at the wedding with his wife, Eliza.

There were friends from Larnach's Castle – Mrs MacGavin and her husband, Edward, of course, Florence and Albert and their wee boy. They'd even invited Mr Bentley, the butler, who had no idea he had been part of a long-running joke before their relationship became romantic – but he seemed to be enjoying the day.

Bendix Hallenstein was there with his wife and other local business owners. Of course, their Lebanese staff were there, and a selection of clients who had become friends, adding style to the proceedings, many of them wearing Greer's creations. They had also extended an invitation to William and Constance Larnach, who were quietly but prominently seated, beautifully dressed, but both looking stiff and awkward, not their usual charming selves.

Their guests began to move outside while Greer and Hamish posed inside for one wedding photo, a gift from Constance and William Larnach. The photographer had already prepared a small space in the vestry with a backdrop and had the camera ready to capture the moment. After standing and posing for the shot, the couple joined their guests outside the church. Constance was the first to approach Greer.

"Congratulations," she said quietly. "It was a beautiful ceremony, and I wish you every happiness."

Greer thanked her for the wedding gift, but noticed that Constance didn't look happy; her face was drawn, and she looked uncharacteristically downcast. "Are you all right?"

Constance blinked and rearranged her features into a semblance of a smile. "Oh, I just find weddings make me melancholy these days. Don't mind me." She paused. "Weddings start with so much promise, don't they?" she said cryptically before moving away.

Greer looked after her for a moment as Constance joined her husband. They exchanged a few words that Greer couldn't hear, but William's face hardened, and they then stood side by side without touching or looking at each, a very different picture from when they were first married. He seemed more like a stern father than a loving husband, looking older than his years, and her so much younger and in her prime, still beautiful in her melancholy. But Greer was roused from her observations by Hamish taking her arm.

"My dearest wife, shall we make our way to the reception?"

"Of course!"

Their wedding reception was at a nearby restaurant, and a Scottish piper played as they entered the venue, almost bringing a lump to the throats of the bride and groom before they caught each other's eye and laughed instead.

"It smells delicious in here," Hamish commented as he escorted his bride to the main table.

"It should smell good after all the effort we went to choosing the menu," Greer remarked, taking the seat Hamish pulled out for her.

He sat down next to her and they both scanned the printed menu on the table. There was creamed cauliflower and asparagus soup to start, followed by braised lamb cutlets baked in an Italian sauce, beef fillets served with macaroni tossed in seeded tomatoes, and shredded chicken marinated in a chive vinaigrette. For dessert, they had jellies and cream and assorted pastries.

"Good choices," Hamish murmured, setting down the menu and staring at Greer meaningfully. "I find I have another appetite in mind, though."

Greer fanned herself with her menu before setting it down. "Patience, husband. Let's enjoy our time with friends and family first."

The meal and the speeches felt like a glorious dream, and it seemed in no time they were ready to cut the wedding cake. They had chosen a traditional fruit cake that Hamish's mother had insisted on making, and Greer felt she had never been happier than when they cut the cake in front of their friends and family.

Much later, after Greer had changed into her new moss-green going away outfit, everyone gathered to wave at the departing newly married couple. Hamish had packed up his buggy with the items they would need for their honeymoon.

"So tell us again where you are going?" Albert teased.

"None of your business!" Hamish retorted, but he smiled. "Mrs MacLeod and I deserve three days on our own before we are back in town."

Mrs MacLeod.

Already her new name sounded good to Greer. And they had decided that when they returned from their honeymoon, the signage for the store would change to MacLeod and George Designs, and Hamish was good-natured when Greer teased him about getting his name on the building in the end. He refused to confirm or deny if that had always been his intention.

In reality, they weren't going far, and it wasn't long before Hamish stopped the horse and buggy outside the small cottage he had hired near Portobello, carrying Greer over the threshold and then returning to retrieve their bags and care for the horse.

Greer removed her coat and lit a few lamps, but barely registered the tasteful décor of the cottage. She only had eyes for her husband when he entered the cottage, loosening his necktie. He poured them both a small dram of whiskey before taking off his jacket. They took a seat on the chaise lounge, and Greer found she was mesmerised by his confident, languid movements. When he set down his glass and took her glass. too, and set it down, looking deeply into her eyes, he had never looked more handsome, and she could barely breathe from desire. When they kissed it was with unbridled passion, and soon he was unbuttoning her dress with urgency, his shirt undone, and the sight of his naked chest the most erotic thing Greer had ever seen.

Wordlessly, Hamish scooped Greer into his arms and carried her to the bedroom, and they were both soon naked, delighting in the texture and taste and exquisite sensations of each other. There was a brief, sharp pain, but then Greer found a rhythm with Hamish, her movements instinctively matching his until a crescendo of waves flooded her body, superior to any high note she could achieve on her violin. Breathless, they collapsed next to each other on the bed and stared at each other in the lamplight.

"I hope I didn't hurt you," Hamish murmured, gently stroking her cheek.

Greer gazed at him. "That was incredible …I've never felt so good."

He smiled at her in relief.

"In fact, that was so good; I'd like to do it all over again whenever you would like."

He laughed and gathered her into his arms. "I love you, Greer MacLeod!"

"I love you, too, Hamish MacLeod."

CHAPTER 47

December 1896

Greer was still overwhelmed with desire every time Hamish walked into the room. Even though it was now more than three months since their wedding day, Greer had discovered a sensual desire for her husband that consumed every waking moment. She didn't see the knowing looks from her female friends or the way clients envied her glow from the many nights of lovemaking with her husband, him as insatiable in his need as her. They had quickly agreed on a no-servant rule, even if it meant Greer had to do all the housekeeping. They relished their privacy too much. And having been a servant, Greer had no wish to have anyone do her housework. But today was Christmas Day, and she tried to focus her mind away from the many charms of her husband to the task at hand. They were hosting Christmas lunch for their friends and family for the very first time in their wonderful new home.

Even though Greer had been cooking for days, preparing Christmas lunch was a more significant task than she had imagined. She had become used to cooking alongside Jamelie at the cottage and now realised how competent her friend was in the kitchen and how she'd always naturally taken charge. Hamish checked in from time to time to see how things were going, but Greer affectionately shooed him away. She wanted to do this meal independently, but as she surveyed some of the food, she admitted it wasn't the best. Some dishes were burnt or undercooked; nothing was exactly as it should be.

They had tried to accommodate everyone's tastes. To celebrate their Scottish heritage, she'd done a roast turkey with all the trimmings and a cock-a-leekie soup made from chicken, stock and leeks. She'd also made some traditional butter shortbread and a Christmas pudding to be served with a brandy sauce. For her Lebanese friends she had made a koosa, a lamb-stuffed zucchini with a cinnamon-spiced tomato sauce, as well as tabbouleh and hummus. For their Chinese friends, she had made sweet and sour pork, wonton noodles and drunken shrimp.

Hamish came into the kitchen again and put his arm around her waist, kissing her cheek. "How is everything going, my love?"

"Not as well as I'd hoped," Greer said, feeling hot and bothered from the warm day and the cooking. "The turkey is overdone, I've burnt the koosa, and I should have baked the shortbread for longer."

"It all looks delicious to me."

Greer sighed. "There is hope, I suppose, that it might taste better than it looks. I hope people won't be disappointed."

"Greer, they aren't coming here to judge your food. They are here to enjoy Christmas Day with us."

She turned in his arms. "You are right, of course." She kissed him passionately before pushing him away. "But don't let it go to your head that you are right this time! Shall we set the table?"

"Finally, something I can help with!"

"Well, you did organise the tree, and you've made the punch, so you have been a huge help!"

They kissed again and then set about organising the table with platters of food, plates, glasses and cutlery – all welcome wedding presents as they were starting from scratch with their household items. Greer stopped to admire their lovely burgundy and gold dinner set, such a generous gift from her in-laws. In the kitchen they only had the minimum of cooking utensils and furniture while the dining room held just a table and chairs. In the lounge were Hamish's piano and a couple of sofas, and for now, a Christmas tree that they had decorated with offcuts of fabric tied into bows.

Upstairs they had a bed and wardrobe in their room and a writing desk in the so-called study. The other bedrooms were empty. But it didn't matter that they didn't have many possessions. They had each other, and they were fortunate to have their own home, and they would slowly fill it up with what they needed when they could. For now, their focus was on building their business. Greer was lost in her thoughts about their home and business when the front door sounded.

"Oh, our first guests! How do I look?" Greer asked.

Hamish smiled at her. "You look beautiful – as always – and that dress really complements your figure and complexion."

Greer looked down at the red dress she was wearing, a festive colour choice for the occasion and she smiled back at him. "Thank you, my husband. You look very well, too, I must say. Let's go and greet our guests."

Soraya was wearing a new blue dress, and she rushed into the house as soon as Greer and Hamish opened the door, wrapping her arms around Greer's waist and looking up at her with excited eyes.

"Merry Christmas, Aunty Greer!"

Soraya's parents came through the door just after, juggling presents and taking time to kiss Hamish and Greer hello, and moments later, their other guests were walking through the door, also full of Christmas cheer and goodwill.

Before long, all their guests were seated around the dining table after exchanging gifts in the lounge. Hamish said grace, and Greer looked around with happiness as everyone piled their plates with food. She held her husband's hand briefly, taking in the moment. No one seemed to have noticed that some of the food wasn't the best – everyone ate enthusiastically.

Next to her, Jamelie and Gabriel talked animatedly about Christmases past while Soraya played with the new doll she had been given permission to bring to the table. Zhang Ming's family was away in Wellington, so she sat next to Charles Sew Hoy and his wife Eliza, discussing what the New Year might bring. Sew Hoy predicted prosperous times, and Greer certainly hoped that would be the case. Hamish's mother and father praised Greer's cock-a-leekie soup, and his mother asked her for the recipe, so at least one of the dishes had worked out. Hamish's brother, wife, and children sat at the end of the table in quiet discussion about their upcoming holiday to Queenstown and preparations for leaving the next day until Soraya joined them and the children escaped to the lounge to play with their new toys. Florence and Albert couldn't be there as he was working at Larnach's Castle, but Greer looked forward to catching up with them the following day. She looked again at all the food she had prepared and realised that there would be plenty of leftovers and she wouldn't need to cook anything more for days.

"I'd like to propose a toast," Hamish said, getting to his feet.

"Hear, hear!" from Hamish's father.

Hamish raised his glass. "Here's to family and friends and being able to celebrate Christmas together."

"To family and friends," everyone responded, raising their glasses and drinking the punch.

"And here's to the New Year being one of health, happiness and prosperity," Hamish added.

"Health, happiness and prosperity!" everyone echoed as they toasted each other.

Greer gazed at Hamish – he looked so handsome and accomplished, and she was proud to be his wife. After being on her own for the past few years, it filled her heart with gladness that she was part of a team, never to be lonely ever again now that Hamish was by her side. Greer looked around at the group. There was so much love and happiness in the room. It felt tangible, as if she could reach out and grasp it. She imagined her mother and father looking down on the scene from heaven, which brought her great comfort. And she was confident next year would be wonderful. MacLeod and George Designs was flourishing. Of course, they were still in debt, but Hamish projected that they would be in the black by the end of the following year if they continued as they were. Life couldn't be better.

CHAPTER 48

Melody

"Now pay attention, chuckaboo," Florence said. "This is a corker of a summer pudding, and I'm going to teach you how to make it or my name's not Florence Taylor."

Greer sat in her kitchen juggling John on her lap as she watched Florence heating the berries in a pan.

"That's a lot of berries!"

"Raspberries, blackberries and blueberries," Florence confirmed. "I'm just making the most of all the summer produce. The next step is to use up that stale white bread."

***

"I'd like a dress just like the one on the mannequin," Mrs Bell said, pointing at the day dress with buff silk printed with a geometric spring design in a soft caramel. "But I'd like a different fabric. That's not my colour."

"Certainly, Mrs Bell." Greer looked at her client with a critical eye. "We have new fabric in, a printed wool and silk leno weave, which will suit you perfectly. The colouring would wonderfully complement your complexion." Jamelie was by her side and smiled at Greer.

"I take it you mean the navy and pink just in?"

"Precisely."

"Let me fetch it for you."

Jamelie disappeared upstairs while Greer made small talk with their client. It had been unseasonably good weather over the past week.

"Oh, I love it!" Mrs Bell enthused when Jamelie showed her the fabric. "When can you complete the dress?"

Greer felt great satisfaction. They already had Mrs Bell's measurements on file as they had only just finished a dress for her. Another order and it was only mid-morning. Everything with their business was going so well.

***

"I've found a new composer, and I'd love us to try this piece," Hamish said enthusiastically.

They'd had dinner and were relaxing in the lounge after a long day at work, both pleasantly tired but thrilled that MacLeod and George Designs was going so well.

"Oh, who is the composer?"

"It's a French composer, Jules Massenet." Hamish handed Greer the sheet music. She studied it with interest.

"*Meditation from Thaïs,*" she read, and then hummed the melody as she looked at the notes on the sheet music. "This is very good, yes, let's play!"

Hamish grinned at her with boyish enthusiasm. "I was hoping you'd say that!"

He took her hand and led her to the piano. Hamish readied the sheet music while Greer tuned her violin and then stood where she could see the music over Hamish's shoulder.

"It was only composed a few years ago," he told her. "I was fortunate to see this at Charles Begg's when I popped in today. Charles Begg played me a little of the tune, and I loved it so much that I bought the sheet music on the spot."

"I'm pleased you found this," Greer said, humming the opening melody again. "Shall we?"

Hamish turned his attention to the sheet music, frowning slightly with concentration. He played the opening notes, with Greer coming in a few bars later, her violin effortlessly soaring and entwining with the notes from the piano. They lost themselves in the swell of the music, and although Hamish's piano playing wasn't always faultless, they were perfectly in time. They played with fierce concentration but also musical abandon and joy until the final page.

The composition was one of the finest Greer had ever encountered, but there was no need to tell Hamish when she looked at his face. Her steady hands suddenly unsteady, she let her violin slip into its case before she found herself in Hamish's embrace, his mouth devouring hers. She was aware of him hastily undoing her bodice as she pulled his shirt from his trousers. They sank onto the nearby sofa, moving to that exquisite space outside regular time and dimension, her only focus them. Skin on skin, mouth on mouth, claiming each other in the most intimate but pleasurable of ways, creating their own beautiful swelling melody of ecstatic joy.

CHAPTER 49

April 1897

Greer and Hamish were in the habit of having breakfast and reading the latest *Otago Daily Times* before heading off to work – Greer to the shop floor, Hamish usually visiting suppliers or working upstairs at the shop doing the accounts and budgeting. The business was going better than anticipated with a recent flood of orders, so more bolts of fabric had been purchased. Greer had brought her sewing machine home and put it in one of the upstairs bedrooms to do additional sewing in the evenings to keep up with demand. She felt life couldn't be more agreeable as she smiled at her husband and served him tea, glowing from another night of lovemaking. While she could now look at her husband without losing her breath, the desire she felt for him was as strong as ever.

But then she sat down to read the lead story in the newspaper and her spirits plummeted. "Oh, Hamish, look at this!" He moved in his seat so they could both read the front-page news. With severe flooding in Hawke's Bay, the Tūtaekurī River had broken its banks, and twelve men had died, ten of whom were rescuers trying to help the people of Clive.

"Those poor men," Greer said sorrowfully. "Those devastated families."

"It's a terrible tragedy," Hamish said, putting his arm around Greer's waist and pulling her close. "It makes me appreciate all I have even more."

They continued their breakfast of sausages, ham and eggs, served with bread rolls, both feeling subdued, when there was suddenly urgent banging at their front door.

They looked at each other in alarm and rushed to the front door to find a distraught Jamelie outside, looking dishevelled.

"Fire!" she shouted. "Our shop is on fire!"

She was out of breath, and Greer pulled her into the house. "Come inside and catch your breath."

"Has the fire brigade been called?" Hamish asked urgently.

Jamelie nodded. "When I arrived, it was already alight, and a neighbour had alerted them."

Hamish looked at Greer and grabbed his coat. "I need to check."

"I'm coming with you," Greer said, also grabbing her coat.

"I'm coming, too," Jamelie said. "At least downhill will be easier than running uphill. It will be quicker than organising the buggy if we run."

They hurried out the door and set off briskly, the day early, so few people were around. When they arrived, the building was fully ablaze, and people started to gather in small groups as the fire brigade hosed the fire. Greer looked, but Albert wasn't part of the firefighting team.

Hamish hurried over to talk to the firefighters and came back looking grim. "They can't save our shop – they are just trying to contain the blaze, so it doesn't spread to the neighbouring buildings."

Greer watched in horror as flames consumed the MacLeod and George Designs sign, and they stepped back when the windows suddenly exploded, flames blazing out onto the street.

"Everyone get back!" some of the firefighters shouted while battling the blaze.

Abila, Dasia and Ferwa approached them, looking at the building in shock.

"How can this be?" Abila said, as Ferwa began to cry.

"Let's just be thankful that none of us was inside," Jamelie said, gathering the girls into a motherly embrace. "No one has been hurt, so that is the main thing."

Greer tore her eyes from the devastating sight and turned to Hamish. "We've lost everything!" She began to weep, all their hard work and dreams burning before them.

Hamish gathered her into his arms and stepped away from Jamelie and the staff. He waited until her tears had ceased before he spoke.

"All is not lost, Greer. The landlord is insured, so the building will be rebuilt, or we can find other premises. And we have insurance for our machinery."

"But all our dresses, all the fabric, all the furniture and fittings! It's all gone."

"We will find a way," Hamish said steadily. "It's admittedly a setback, and we will need to borrow more money from the bank, but we will work hard and recover. I promise you."

Greer looked into Hamish's eyes and felt comforted by his words. Her resolve grew. They wouldn't let this beat them.

A little later, the fire brigade had the blaze under control. Jamelie instructed Abila, Dasia and Ferwa to go home, telling them she would be in touch with them tomorrow. The girls left, looking dazed, as were the people on the street around them.

Hamish went to talk to the fire chief again and returned to Jamelie and Greer. "They are not sure yet how it started, but one of the neighbours heard an explosion, so they think it might have been a faulty gas lamp."

Greer gulped. "I'm just thankful no one was in the store at the time, but still …" She turned to look again at the smouldering building, and her words caught in her throat. Hamish pulled her close again.

"I think we should go home," Hamish said after a moment. "There is nothing we can do here. Jamelie, do you want to go home or come to our place?"

"Let's go to your place," Jamelie said, wiping tears from her eyes. "Let's make some tea and plan how we start again."

They were a forlorn threesome walking back up the road to Hamish and Greer's home, and after Greer had made them some tea, they sat in the lounge wordlessly, each lost in their own thoughts, the only sound the ticking of their recently acquired grandfather clock. Hamish broke the silence.

"My first step is to talk to the landlord, and I will also talk to the insurance company about a pay-out for our machinery." He sighed. "I regret now that I didn't insure the fittings and our stock, but at the time, it was just too expensive."

"You weren't to know this would happen," Greer said, taking his hand. "It's good you insured the machinery, and if the landlord doesn't rebuild, we can find another place to lease, so it is not the disaster it would have been otherwise."

"Thank goodness we had five customers pick up their dresses yesterday,"

Jamelie said. "So one silver lining is that they weren't destroyed in the blaze."

"And it's also good that I brought my sewing machine home so we can begin work again without having to wait for the insurance to buy more machinery," Greer said, also thinking of silver linings. "And I have three dresses upstairs that are nearly completed."

"See, that's good," Hamish said. "That gives us a little cash flow to pay wages and purchase more fabric."

"But we have lost so many display dresses!" Greer said, thinking of the stock that had been in the shop – twenty-three dresses in all if her memory was correct. "And all that fabric!" Her voice caught a little. "And we will also need to find new furniture and curtains." It suddenly seemed overwhelming.

Jamelie patted Greer's hand. "Let's try to concentrate on the positive. Five dresses were picked up yesterday that would have been lost otherwise. You have three nearly completed dresses upstairs, and I have another two at my home."

"Really?"

"We've had so many orders lately that I just took a couple home to work on the lace in the evenings to keep up with the demand."

"Thank goodness you did! But what about unfinished dresses that were on order and have been lost?" Greer thought through the orders. That left twelve dresses in the workshop that would need to be redone.

"I'll contact all the customers," Hamish said. "I'm sure everyone will be very understanding. We will make a list, and I'll go around personally to explain the situation."

"The Queen's Jubilee," Greer blurted out.

Hamish and Jamelie looked at her blankly. "It's Queen Victoria's Diamond Jubilee on the twentieth of June – we should aim for that date to reopen."

Hamish sat back and was clearly doing some calculations in his head. "It will be tight, but I think we can do that. And it would be great publicity to reopen on such a historic occasion."

Greer nodded and then had another thought. "My dresses!"

"What?" Hamish looked puzzled.

"I've got a full wardrobe of beautiful dresses upstairs. I'll just keep a couple, and my wedding dress, of course, but let's sell the rest or keep them aside for when we reopen as display stock."

"Are you sure?" Jamelie asked.

"That's a sound idea," Hamish said at the same time. "The less money we have to borrow from the bank to get up and running again, the better. And Greer can always make some more dresses in the future. She has already established herself as a style icon, so economising at the moment won't hurt her reputation."

Although tired and dazed from the shock of the fire, Greer felt a growing sense that they could rebuild and get back on track. "We can use the spare bedrooms upstairs as workspaces for our staff until the shop reopens."

Hamish grinned at her. "You are on a roll, my dearest wife. That will do very well."

Jamelie nodded and smiled, too. "You don't mind if I bring Soraya with me when Zhang Ming can't help?"

"Of course not!" Greer said. "She is welcome anytime, just like she is at the workshop at the store."

Hamish disappeared upstairs, returned with pen and paper, and began listing all they had to do. He needed to talk to the insurance company and the landlord. He'd need to estimate the amount they would need to add to their mortgage and talk to the bank, as well as organise the refit and visit all the clients. Greer and Jamelie and their staff were tasked with completing the existing orders as soon as possible and seeing if they could sell any of Greer's dresses. Then they would need to organise two more sewing machines, but Greer's would suffice in the meantime. And they would need to order more fabric as soon as they had funds.

There was much to do, but Greer could see the same steely determination in Hamish and Jamelie's faces as she felt. If they worked hard, they could do this.

CHAPTER 50

Signs

Greer looked around the crowded bedroom that now housed all the staff while the landlord was rebuilding their store. Jamelie was finishing the beading work on one of the outstanding orders. She looked exhausted, but Greer knew better than to try and send her home. Abila, Dasia and Ferwa were bent over their work, too. They would soon have two more orders completed, bringing in valuable income. Greer turned back to her sewing machine and began another seam. She was so tired, but she tried to focus on the task at hand, one seam by one seam rebuilding a business.

She looked up when Hamish entered the room, all of them pausing in their work. Hamish was grinning with boyish enthusiasm, although he, too, looked tired, with dark circles under his eyes.

"Afternoon, ladies," he greeted them. "Great news, the rebuild has officially begun. Tradesmen are working as I speak. As you know, the fire didn't reach the roof, and the bathroom is somehow still intact, so it's less work than we all initially thought."

There was a murmur of happiness before they tiredly returned to work, and Hamish slipped again from the room, back to the building site.

***

Greer was having a quick break from sewing, making a cup of tea and rubbing her aching neck when Hamish came into the kitchen with a definite spark in his eye. She looked at him questioningly.

"I have something to show you," he announced, taking her hand and leading her into their lounge.

"Oh," she said when she saw the sign resting on the sofa. It was their new shop sign, MacLeod and George Designs. "It's even more splendid than the original!"

"I know!" Hamish drew her into an embrace. "It's happening, my darling. We will be opening our business again soon."

"I do hope so," Greer said tiredly.

But there was still so much to do. It seemed insurmountable. Every day more jobs to add to an ever-growing list.

***

Hamish slid under the bedcovers next to Greer and spooned her from behind, his body warm and comforting.

"Sorry I'm so late," he murmured in her ear, "but the carpet is now in the shop, so it's good that it is all done."

"Did you manage to have supper?" Greer was so tired she could barely get the words out. "I left food for you."

"Thank you, my love; that was thoughtful."

He kissed her neck gently, and she felt a flicker of desire, but sheer exhaustion of the day was already claiming her, her breathing slowing, her last sensation the welcome weight of Hamish's arms around her.

CHAPTER 51

June 1897

The previous day all of New Zealand had enjoyed a public holiday to celebrate Queen Victoria's Diamond Jubilee. There had been processions through the main streets of Dunedin that included the fire brigade, brass bands, military volunteers and friendly societies. Oak trees had been planted at Jubilee Park. "Queen's weather" had prevailed, and today was mild also, as Greer, Hamish, Jamelie and their staff gathered outside their newly rebuilt and refitted shop. They paused to savour the moment, the new MacLeod and George Designs sign proudly displayed above the front door. The dressed mannequins – many featuring dresses from Greer's wardrobe as well as some new designs – were colourful and enticing, and Greer looked at the display with approval.

Hamish ceremoniously opened the front door, and Jamelie and their three Lebanese staff made their way upstairs to their newly constructed workshop while Greer and Hamish made last-minute adjustments to the shop before they opened their doors to the public for the first time since the fire. The shop was even better than before. They had taken all their knowledge of the previous store and made improvements. The counter was now rounded, not square, as previously they had collided with its hard edges. The fitting rooms were slightly longer to give clients a better view of themselves in the mirrors. They had a dedicated section of the store where customers could sit and look through the folders of designs, painstakingly redone by Greer and resting on an elegant coffee table.

The past months had been a blur, with the three business owners working long hours into the night. Greer still couldn't believe they were ready to open after such a short time and knew they couldn't have achieved this without Hamish's organisational skills. The landlord had completed a fast rebuild, not wanting to lose income from rent, the insurance company had paid up quickly, and the bank had extended their loan. But while Greer, Jamelie, Abila, Dasia and Ferwa finished existing orders and worked diligently to create more dresses for the shop's stock, Hamish had almost single-handedly done everything else, helping the landlord in organising builders, and buying new furniture, fittings and machinery. A massive job that had had him scurrying all around town.

Hamish smiled at Greer and gathered her into his arms for an embrace. "We did it," he whispered in her ear. "And I know it's expensive, but from now on, I've organised insurance for our stock and fittings as well, so we never have to worry about having to start over again like this."

They kissed and then readied themselves for the day ahead. Hamish had handed out flyers and advertised in the *Otago Daily Times*, so they hoped some people at least would know about their reopening and stop by to look.

They weren't disappointed when Hamish opened the door to the public half an hour later, and by the afternoon, Greer realised there had been a steady stream of customers – both old and new – visiting the shop. They had sold two dresses from the display mannequins and had orders for three more – so a great success.

Constance Larnach came into the store with Douglas, laughing at something he was saying, both looking happy and animated. She looked around the store with interest as Douglas waited near the door, now looking awkward as men often are in a women's wear shop.

"Oh, I love this shawl!" Constance exclaimed, taking one off a manne-quin and draping it around her shoulders. She turned to Douglas. "What do you think, Dougie?"

"It looks very fine on you," he said, a flash of appreciation lighting up his face.

Constance took off the shawl and put it on the counter. "I will take this, please. You have done so well getting your shop open again after such a short time."

"Thank you!" Greer said, wrapping up the purchase.

"Douglas was so kind to bring me into the city today, so I could visit you," Constance turned to look at her stepson with obvious affection. "William has to be at Parliament, so Douglas is a godsend when he is away. Of course, I'll be joining William again next week." Was it Greer's imagination, but was Constance over-explaining the situation?

"Do you prefer being in Wellington or Dunedin?" Greer enquired.

"That is a very interesting question," Constance said. "In Wellington, it is extremely busy, and William works incredibly long hours. I try to accompany him to everything I can, although there are limits to what I'm allowed to do, but we certainly attend many dinners and events. And in Wellington, there is a real sense of purpose, of making New Zealand a better society by passing good laws." She turned towards Douglas and looked a little dreamy.

"I must confess, at first I found life at The Camp a little isolated, but these days I relish its location on the Peninsula and its rugged beauty and the chance to unwind from the busyness of life." She turned back to Greer.

"Now, what do I owe you for this fine shawl?"

It didn't take long to complete the transaction, and Greer watched as Constance left the building with Douglas by her side. If she didn't know they were wife and stepson, they could have easily passed as husband and wife. They looked very comfortable together. But then Greer shook off the odd thought and considered it was all very superficial – they were just closer in age than Constance and William. At least one of the children was fond of Constance, Greer thought. By all accounts from Florence, relationships with the other children continued chilly in the extreme.

Greer turned to her next customer, a thin woman around her age with scraggly brown hair. Greer was alarmed to see she had a huge black eye.

"Oh, my goodness, how did that happen?" Greer asked, before realising it might be indelicate to enquire. The woman looked uncomfortable.

"Silly me, I walked into a door."

"Poor you," Greer commiserated, privately thinking it looked more like someone had hit her. "How can I help you?"

"It's my wedding anniversary, so my husband said I could choose something nice."

"Well, that is very lovely. And congratulations!"

"My husband always gives me thoughtful gifts, but this time I said I'd like to choose something myself." The woman turned with a troubled look to the man standing outside the door. Greer followed her gaze and was shocked to her core to see Fergus waiting outside. She hadn't seen him since she had broken up with him, and she found herself oddly detached looking at him. He no longer had any emotional hold over her. She observed that he was still well dressed and handsome, but looked surly and out of sorts. Greer turned back to her customer as she spoke again.

"I must confess he wasn't keen on the idea at first," Mrs Breslin said. Greer could picture where the black eye came from now. She could imagine his anger. Why spend cash when you could just steal something and pass it off as a gift? The poor woman.

"Well, it's good that he came around," Greer said slowly. This was a surreal situation, but she felt a great deal of sympathy for the woman in front of her. "What would you like?"

"I had my heart set on a new pair of kid-leather gloves. And I really liked the look of those." She pointed at a pair under the display counter, and Greer retrieved them so she could try them on.

"They are a perfect fit," Mrs Breslin said, admiring them. "How much are they?"

Greer told her the price and the woman's face fell. She would be pretty if she didn't look so thin and downtrodden. "Oh, I only have half that. I didn't realise they would be so expensive."

Greer thought quickly. She didn't know this woman, but as she had married Fergus, she felt a great deal of pity for her. She seemed browbeaten by life, and she deserved to at least have a nice pair of gloves to enjoy.

"But that's before the discount. Because of Queen Victoria's Diamond Jubilee, we have fifty per cent off today." Greer leant forward and kept her voice as low as possible, not wanting to offer a fifty per cent discount on any of their other sales. It was just for Mrs Breslin, and she knew Hamish would understand their making no profit on this sale when she told him about it later.

Mrs Breslin beamed and searched in her bag for the money. "Oh, that is wonderful! I have just enough in that case."

"Would you like me to wrap them?"

"I think I'd like to wear them and show them off to Mr Breslin."

"Very well."

Greer watched as Mrs Breslin joined her husband on the street, and she showed off the gloves. Fergus shrugged dismissively with a surly expression and began walking down the street. Mrs Breslin looked momentarily downcast, but then looked at her gloves again, shrugging and smiling to herself before following her husband. Greer watched until they were both out of sight. She sighed with relief. To imagine she might have married that man! Now he was showing his true character, devoid of any charm he might have once had. Greer didn't like what she saw.

Hamish burst through the door carrying new bolts of fabric and he smiled at her, his brown eyes twinkling with love and honesty. He winked at her, making her laugh before returning to her duties. A client was waiting and wanted to be measured for a new dress. Greer had little time to consider the remarkable difference in her husband's character compared to her once fiancé. Instead, she grabbed her tape measure and notebook and invited the customer to the fitting room.

CHAPTER 52

Romance

"I've found sheet music for *Three Romances for Violin and Piano* by Clara Schumann," Hamish announced after they had retired to the lounge after dinner. Greer clapped her hands with pure joy and stood up to retrieve her violin.

"Oh, you know how much I love that piece."

"I haven't had any time to practise," he warned her, taking a seat at the piano.

"Well, you've been too busy with our business," Greer said, tuning the violin. "I'm just so pleased that it's all going so well."

"So am I," Hamish said, placing his fingers on the keys.

Greer stopped to look at him. "Did you ever have any doubt?"

"Not with you at my side, my talented wife. We make a great team."

Greer smiled and then they began to play. While it wasn't perfect, they were effortlessly in time together, the notes swelling and falling, building then fading. Greer looked at her husband as she played and then anticipated their time in the bedroom afterwards. After the frantic time of exhaustion, Greer found her libido had returned with a vengeance. She stumbled on a note, and Hamish turned to look at her; from his expression, she could see that he could read her mind. He abruptly stopped playing and gathered Greer into his arms, the violin discarded to the floor as their lips found each other.

***

"What is this?" Greer asked as Hamish removed his hands from her eyes. They were standing in the garden in their backyard. Leaning against the back fence were two bicycles.

"Well, they look like bicycles to me," Hamish teased.

"No!" Greer laughed. "I mean, why do we have bicycles?"

"Well, you have mentioned that you would like to ride a bicycle, so I thought it would be fun to try it out this afternoon."

"You bought two bicycles?" Greer turned to look at her husband suspiciously. "I know the business is going well, but didn't you say we still need to be careful with spending?"

Hamish ran his hand through his dark hair and looked a little sheepish. "Well, you know my Scots side well. I've hired the bicycles. If you like riding, we'll buy them. But let's see if you like this first."

Greer grinned. "I did ride a few times when I was young, but I'm pleased to give this a try again!"

Hamish grabbed one of the bicycles and rode expertly around the lawn before stopping in front of her. "Your turn now."

Greer got on to the other bike and tentatively began to cycle. She was delighted to see that she hadn't forgotten. Hamish looked at her with admiration.

"Is there nothing my brilliant wife can't do?"

She smiled at him. "Shall we ride to the Botanic Gardens soon?"

⁂

Late Sunday afternoon, when Greer and Hamish arrived at the Georges' home for a quick visit, they discovered Zhang Ming and Charles Sew Hoy playing Mahjong on the kitchen table with Zhang Ming's daughter and son-in-law while the grandchildren and Soraya played in the front room. Everyone greeted them warmly before returning to their play.

"They have been playing Mahjong for hours," Jamelie said. "And I still don't understand how this game is played."

"It does look complicated," Greer said after a moment of watching them.

"Learning is a treasure that will follow its owner everywhere," Zhang Ming pronounced.

"Do you want to join us?" Charles Sew Hoy offered.

Greer and Hamish shared a look before Hamish answered.

"We may take you up on your kind offer another day, but we can't stay long as we are visiting my parents for dinner."

Charles Sew Hoy and Zhang Ming nodded and continued their game. Jamelie poured some tea for Greer and Hamish, and they made themselves comfortable at the end of the table, chatting about work for the upcoming week. Gabriel was packing and preparing for a week away. Greer sipped her tea and felt utterly content among her dear friends.

CHAPTER 53

December 1897

"Good evening," the butler said with a slight bow when they arrived at Larnach's Castle on New Year's Eve. "I am most pleased to see you both."

"Thank you, Mr Bentley," Greer replied. "We are very pleased to be here."

"You are very welcome, unlike someone else here tonight," the butler added darkly, causing Greer to look at him with curiosity, but he turned and led them to the ballroom as though he'd never commented.

It was the most magical of evenings as Greer and Hamish enjoyed time in the ballroom, their first time there as a married couple and as guests. The ballroom looked magnificent, a riot of decoration in the modern Gothic style, and Hamish and Greer stopped to admire many of the room's features that displayed the designers' talents and the skills of the craftsmen employed by William Larnach. There was so much to appreciate with the three open fireplaces, the sprung wooden floor, the arched wooden ceiling, and the shimmering chandeliers overhead. Of course, Greer had seen the ballroom before, but she could now sit and admire the design as a guest.

Everyone was dressed in their finest clothes, and Greer smoothed down her peach-coloured silk dress as they chatted with the people seated next to them. It seemed like a who's who of famous people. She couldn't believe she was mixing with Andrew Macandrew, who championed the commercial interests of Dunedin, poet Thomas Bracken, who had written the words to *God Defend New Zealand*, and medical practitioner Dr Hocken and his wife Julia. They had been close friends of William Larnach's first wife.

Bendix Hallenstein and his wife were here, as was Charles Sew Hoy and his wife. And there were plenty of politicians. Hamish pointed out Julius Vogel, Robert Stout, Richard Seddon and Joseph Ward seated at other parts of the vast table.

William Larnach presided over the evening, proving himself an excellent host, although he seemed a bit tired and forgetful at times. He had Constance by his side, gracious and beautiful, elegant in one of Greer's designs, which made Greer feel proud. Douglas sat next to Constance, and Greer noted that they enjoyed many a private joke between them, and there was a lightness in the way they communicated. Constance was more serious when talking to her husband and constantly seemed to be trying to reassure him about one thing or another.

The rest of the family was thin on the ground. Donald was still in Melbourne. Colleen and Alice had departed immediately after the Christmas festivities, according to Florence, who still had her finger on the pulse of activities in The Camp. So that just left Gladys, who looked alone and a little forlorn during the party.

"I wonder how he managed to scrounge an invitation?" one of the staff, whom Greer knew briefly from her latter days as a maid, muttered discreetly and nodded towards the end of the room before moving away.

It was a huge jolt to see Fergus and his wife seated at the far end of the vast room. Fergus glanced her way a few times with an expression she couldn't fathom, but they were seated so far apart there was no reason for them to speak, for which Greer was grateful. However, she was pleased to see that Mrs Breslin looked in good spirits, and Fergus seemed to be on his best behaviour. It would seem the Larnachs were none the wiser to his true identity, even if the staff knew he was a fraudster. Or had been, Greer corrected herself; after all, he might have reformed in the intervening time.

Greer recognised none of the other staff who were busy at work serving food and drinks. The first course was a mulligatawny soup, which was followed by stewed eels, and it took Hamish and Greer a moment to decide what else was in the dish. Greer identified the nutmeg, garlic and onion, Hamish the anchovy paste and port wine. They both agreed the fricandeau of veal with spinach was a triumph. Greer decided to pass on the next course, curried lobster and rice, as she was too busy contemplating the two dessert options.

"I can't decide which I prefer. The steamed pudding or the orange-flavoured cheesecake with almonds and candied orange peel?"

"Whatever you choose, I'll have the other," Hamish said. "Then you can sample both."

Greer was delighted. "Oh, you are very gallant to share dessert with me!"

A trio of musicians had been playing in the background throughout the meal, but once dessert was over, they struck up some popular dance tunes and around them, couples began to leave the table to waltz as staff worked hard to turn the ballroom from a dining room back to a place of dancing.

"Shall we?" Hamish stood up and pushed back his chair. He held out his arm to Greer, and she nodded at him.

"I'd be delighted."

They circled around the room with elegant ease, and Greer enjoyed the feeling of the sprung floor under her feet and being in Hamish's muscular arms. It had been a joy to discover how effortless it was to dance with Hamish, and as she gazed into his warm, loving eyes, she considered how much her life had changed over the last seven years. Greer had gone from being utterly alone after the sudden death of her father and thrust into the drudgery of being a household servant, to a life of richness and blessing. Now she was part of a thriving business and getting to enjoy one of the great passions of her life – designing beautiful dresses like the one she was wearing now. She was living her dream of dancing in a grand ballroom in an elegant dress – something that had seemed merely fantasy when she made her very first commissioned dress.

She loved her home and that when they entertained, Hamish would play the piano and she would join him with the violin. Another dream was fulfilled. They had a growing library in the study; another childhood dream becoming a reality. And her beloved Hamish, the love of her life, her best friend, lover, husband and business partner, dancing with her now – she never imagined she could feel so much love – he was the greatest blessing in her life. She had been welcomed into Hamish's family, and she thought of her dear friends, Jamelie and Gabriel, Zhang Ming, and Florence and Albert, and knew she was even more blessed.

A little later, as time edged towards midnight, the guests spilt out of the ballroom onto the lavish grounds, and Hamish put his arm around her as everyone counted down to midnight for the Larnach's traditional fireworks display.

"Ten, nine, eight –"

"Seven, six, five, four," Greer and Hamish joined in. Fireworks erupted at midnight, and Hamish gathered Greer into an embrace, kissing her passionately.

"I love you, Greer MacLeod."

"I love you, Hamish MacLeod."

It was a mild, moonlit night, and Greer and Hamish strolled through the vast gardens. On a whim, they made their way to the pergola with views of the Peninsula, where Greer had once played her violin.

"This is where I first met you," Hamish said. "I was enchanted by the music and then saw you playing and was enchanted by you."

"I took a bit longer to become enchanted with you, I must confess, but I'm completely enchanted by you now, my dearest Hamish."

He grinned at her. "I'm pleased you finally came to your senses, even if I've given up trying to find the butler in the garden."

"Well, he did greet us when we arrived."

"True, but I've never managed to actually be here while he is in the garden."

"I should let you in on a secret."

"What's that, my love?"

"He doesn't like the garden. He always grumbled under his breath about the expense and upkeep, so I don't think you will ever find him in the garden."

Hamish laughed and gathered her into an embrace, and they kissed passionately. He looked at her with an expression she knew so well, one of heartfelt desire.

"I think we should be getting home." He stroked her cheek gently.

"I think that is an excellent suggestion," she murmured.

"I'll need to ready the horse and buggy."

"Would you mind if I stay here for a moment? I feel the urge to enjoy this little piece of nature for a moment before we go. So special, our first meeting place."

"Of course! I won't be long. I'll be back soon."

Hamish set off at a brisk pace back towards the stables, and Greer stood for a moment under the pergola, breathing in the fragrance of foxgloves and roses. She remembered the first violin piece she had played in this spot; Clara Schumann's *Three Romances for Violin and Piano*, still one of her all-time favourites. She closed her eyes for a moment and, in her mind, heard the swell of music, the real-life sounds of cicadas with their summertime chorus providing accompaniment.

She was suddenly knocked off balance and found herself in Fergus's unwelcome embrace. Alarmed, she saw that he was very drunk.

"You think you're too good for me," he slurred, his breath hot on her face, his grip on her increasing. She began desperately struggling to escape his clutches.

"Let go of me!"

"You shouldn't have broken off our engagement!"

"That's in the past!"

"You should have married me!" Fergus lost his balance and fell on her as she struggled against him. "Nothing has gone right since you broke things off." He kissed her roughly, his mouth wet and foul and angry on hers.

"Stop it!" she gasped for breath as they tussled.

Suddenly Hamish tore into the space and roughly pulled Fergus off Greer.

"Get your hands off my wife!"

Greer looked up to see pure fury in Hamish's eyes as he shoved Fergus. She sat up as Fergus bellowed and went to attack Hamish, who deftly sidestepped his clumsy advance. In the background, Mrs Breslin appeared, breathless and distraught.

"Fergus! What are you doing?"

"Stay out of this, Jane," Fergus snarled, turning back to Hamish and lunging at him. Hamish swung his fist and punched Fergus directly on the nose, causing Fergus to fall back, blood streaming everywhere.

"You are a disgrace," Hamish said grimly, helping Greer to her feet and putting his arm around her protectively. "If you ever go near my wife again, I will kill you."

Greer trembled in Hamish's arms as he led her away from the scene of the attack. She could feel anger pulsating from his body. She looked back. Fergus was on the ground, holding his bleeding nose and cursing loudly. Jane leant over him and looked uncertain before standing upright and putting her hands on her hips.

"If you ever disrespect me like that again, or if you ever hit me or anyone else ever again, I am leaving you, Fergus Breslin. Do you hear me?"

Fergus looked at her with a stunned expression and nodded meekly, to everyone's astonishment. The mouse had become a lion, judging by the way he cowered before his wife's righteous fury.

"You can clean yourself up and make your own way home," Jane continued. "I'm going with them." She gestured to Greer and Hamish. "If that is all right," she added, looking anxiously at Greer. "My parents live in the city."

"Of course," Greer reached out her hand. "Wherever you need."

Jane turned back to Fergus. "I shall be home in the morning and I'm going to lay out new rules for our life together."

"Come home with me now," Fergus said, getting to his feet groggily. His voice was feeble and whiny. "My darling Angel Jane, forgive me. Let me make everything right again."

"In the morning," Jane said firmly. "When you are sober, we will talk. Not before. And my rules will stand or I'm moving back with my parents permanently." Jane turned and strode ahead, Greer and Hamish following in her wake.

"Are you okay, my love?" Hamish murmured.

"You arrived at just the right time. Yes, I am fine."

"I'm serious. I will kill him if he touches you again."

Greer looked into the eyes of her lover and saw he was serious. She nodded, not sure how she felt about her husband threatening to kill another man, but part of her realised she found his stance filled her with primitive, sweeping desire.

After they had dropped Jane off at her parents' home – which ended up being not far from their own home – they retired to their bedroom. With the moonlight illuminating the room, Hamish gently removed Greer's torn dress and then his own clothes, and they made love desperately, seeing in their love for the New Year, their passion earthy and primitive; two souls becoming one.

"You are my love and my life," Greer murmured as they drifted to sleep in each other's embrace.

CHAPTER 54

February 1898

Greer had noticed that Jamelie had put on a little weight, but thought nothing of it in the busyness of life until Jamelie pulled her aside when they were opening the shop one fine summer's morning.

"Greer, please take a seat," Jamelie said, directing her to one of their comfortable lounge seats in their shop. "I have some news I must share with you."

Greer looked at her quizzically, but then observed how Jamelie held her belly and immediately knew the news her friend was going to share.

"Gabriel and I are blessed to be having another baby!"

"Oh, Jamelie! That is wonderful news." Greer embraced her friend. "I am so pleased for you."

"I'm five months along, so by the grace of God, we will have a healthy boy or girl sometime soon."

Greer hugged her friend again. After three miscarriages, she knew what a blessing this child would be for the George family. Greer hoped she might have her own child one day with Hamish, having become a little less nervous about the thought of childbirth, but for now, they were too busy to worry that they hadn't been blessed in this way yet. However, this wasn't the time to think about herself, and she was genuinely pleased for her friend.

"I can't say enough how thrilled I am for you and Gabriel. He must be delighted."

"Happy, and a little worried, but mainly happy."

"And how about Soraya?"

"She's very excited. She has her heart on a little sister, so I'm not sure what we will do if we have a boy, but we'll cross that bridge when we come to it."

Hamish entered the shop carrying some bolts of fabric under his arm, and he stopped and smiled at his wife and business partner when he saw them holding hands and sharing a conspiratorial smile.

"Now, you two look as if you have good news to share."

"The best news," Greer said, smiling.

"Gabriel and I are having another baby!" Jamelie said, laughing when Hamish promptly dropped his bolts of fabric and gave her a warm hug.

"That is the best news! I am so pleased for you and Gabriel. That's two pieces of good news today!"

Jamelie looked confused, and Greer rushed to explain.

"Hamish was very excited to read in today's *Otago Daily Times* that the first two motor cars to arrive in New Zealand have just landed in Wellington."

"They were built in Paris by Benz and imported by William McLean, the politician," Hamish said enthusiastically, taking a seat next to them. "He's named them 'Lightning' and 'Petrolette'. Apparently, they are capable of speeds of twenty miles an hour."

Greer patted her husband on the knee. "I'm not sure we should compare cars and babies—"

"But good news on both counts, nonetheless," Hamish interrupted. "Just think, we'll have motor cars in Dunedin soon! We are living in times of great progress!"

"I can see you are excited by this news of cars. And as for my baby, I am due in June," Jamelie said, pre-empting the question Greer knew Hamish would ask next.

Hamish looked at the two women, his mind clearly working. "You will need some time off, so we will need to get someone else to manage your role."

Jamelie nodded. "I've been thinking of this, and I've taken the liberty of talking to Zhang Ming, who has recommended someone."

"Well, I'm always keen to know what Zhang Ming recommends," Hamish said.

"Her name is Mary Stewart; she's widowed and in her fifties."

"Scots and mature," Hamish commented. "That's not a bad thing."

"She used to run her own dressmaking business before she stopped to have children. Now they are grown, she is looking to go back to work. I had a cup of tea with Zhang Ming and Mary yesterday and was very impressed. I think she would be an excellent choice to run the workshop until I can come back to work."

"I wonder how Zhang Ming knew about her," Greer mused.

Hamish smiled at her. "Zhang Ming knows pretty much everything that goes on in this town. Why wouldn't she know about her?"

"True." Greer turned to Jamelie. "But you didn't want to promote Abila, Dasia or Ferwa to the position?"

"I haven't told them I'm expecting – I'll do that when they come in for work today," Jamelie said. "But I have sounded each of them out about a possible role. Ferwa flatly refused; you know how shy she is. And Abila and Dasia don't want the extra responsibility. They are all happy to continue to do their work as they are."

"Then when can we meet Mrs Stewart?" Hamish asked, glancing at his timepiece.

"Ah, in about five minutes," Jamelie said, looking a little sheepish.

Hamish laughed. "I approve! We will need to find your replacement quickly, so you can train them up before you have the baby. And business is going well. We can certainly afford to do this."

Jamelie looked relieved. "I had hoped you would like the idea."

Hamish stood up and busied himself with taking the bolts of fabric upstairs while Greer and Jamelie prepared the store for another busy day. Mrs Stewart knocked on the shop door precisely five minutes later, and Jamelie ushered her into the space.

"Please take a seat, Mrs Stewart," Jamelie said.

"Thank you, and please call me Mary." She spoke with a warm Scottish burr, and she had a kind face, open and honest, her light-brown hair pulled into a tidy bun. Greer noted the excellent workmanship of the muted green dress she was wearing, which was perfectly tailored to make the most of her voluptuous figure.

"Very well, Mary," Jamelie said. "These are my business colleagues, Greer and Hamish MacLeod."

"A pleasure to meet you both," Mary said, taking the indicated seat.

270

"The dress you are wearing is very fine," Greer said. "Did you make this yourself?"

"I did. I had my own dressmaking business for eight years before stopping to raise my family. But I've continued designing and making my own dresses ever since."

As Mary spoke about her skills and experience, Greer knew, without a doubt, that she would be a valuable asset to the business. She had a friendly but direct way about her, and she reminded Greer of Mrs MacGavin in how she spoke and moved.

"Would you also be happy to help serve customers and do fittings when we are busy?" Greer asked. "Or is that too much with running the workshop and managing our three staff?"

"Not at all," Mary replied. "I like variety, and it would be a pleasure to work with the clients as well as manage the production of the dresses."

Hamish glanced at Greer and Jamelie and nodded his head discreetly. They both returned the nod.

"Mary, we'd be delighted to offer you a position with us." Hamish named a generous figure, and Mary nodded.

"I'd be delighted to accept. When would you like me to start?"

"As soon as you would like," Jamelie said. "Perhaps next Monday?"

"That would be perfect."

They shook hands, and Mary left just as Abila, Dasia and Ferwa arrived for their work.

"I have some news to tell you," Jamelie beamed at the girls as she led them upstairs to the workroom space. Greer and Hamish smiled at each other as they heard the whoops of joy at Jamelie's announcement from overhead.

"So that's three good things for today," Greer said, turning and kissing her husband on the cheek. "Cars, babies and a new employee."

"We are experiencing a prolonged spell of good luck, my love," Hamish said. "So much good fortune coming our way!"

Greer had to admit that life was pleasing at the moment, and as they opened their doors for the public a little while later, she had an extra spring in her step.

CHAPTER 55

June 1898

There was a small gathering of women in the Georges' cottage that Sunday morning when they arrived, the local midwife, Wardi, and Zhang Ming's daughter, but it was Soraya, now a spirited seven, going on eight-year-old, who insisted on leading them to her parents' bedroom. Jamelie looked tired but happy when Greer and Hamish peeked around the door. Gabriel had been sitting on the bed and holding his wife's hand, but he stood up and waved them into the room.

"Congratulations," Hamish said, shaking Gabriel's hand, while Greer found a place to put the flowers they had brought, smiling at her friend.

"It is wonderful to have another daughter," Gabriel said, looking at his wife and new daughter with love.

"Oh, Jamelie, she's beautiful!" Greer peered at the tiny bundle in Jamelie's arms.

"We've named her Zaib," Jamelie said proudly. "It means beautiful in our language."

She was only a day old but already a gorgeous baby, with delicate features and a little bit of dark hair. She yawned and snuggled back into her mother's embrace.

"How are you feeling?" Greer took a seat by the bedside.

"A little sore," Jamelie confessed, "but it is worth it for this precious bundle. And the birth itself went well, nowhere as long in labour as when I had Soraya. Thank goodness for the midwife and for Zhang Ming."

"Oh, I didn't see her when we arrived."

"She went home to change."

There was a sound of someone clearing their throat, and Greer turned to see a beaming Zhang Ming putting her hands affectionately on Soraya's shoulders. "It's all right to go in," she said to the child.

Soraya ran into the room and sat on the bed, looking at her sister with great curiosity.

"She's still so little," she announced, which caused them all to laugh.

"Well, she will take a little while to get bigger," Jamelie said tenderly.

"When will I be able to play with her?"

"Not for a little while, but you can hold her if you like?"

"Really?" Soraya was wide-eyed with wonder as Jamelie gently helped her hold the baby correctly. Soraya looked at Zaib carefully.

"Her fingers are so tiny; she looks like a doll!"

"You looked a lot like this when you were first born," Jamelie said, stroking her eldest child's dark hair.

"Surely, I was never this small!"

"We all start out this small," Zhang Ming said from the doorway. "But acorns eventually turn into beautiful trees."

"So true," Jamelie said. She turned to the other guests "How is everything at the shop?"

"Nothing for you to worry about," Hamish reassured her, wiping his brow with a handkerchief. "Mary is managing the workshop well, so there is no urgency for your return."

"Just enjoy this precious time with your newborn," Zhang Ming told her.

"I will," Jamelie said, gently retrieving the baby from Soraya. "I definitely will."

They made small talk, but noticing that the baby needed feeding and that Jamelie was looking tired, they made their excuses and left, Soraya skipping past Zhang Ming and down the hallway ahead of them.

Zhang Ming looked at Greer and smiled. "You are glowing, my dear." Her gaze slid to Greer's belly.

Greer looked at Zhang Ming in astonishment and saw that Zhang Ming knew the news she planned to share with Hamish that evening. She'd just been waiting to see that Jamelie had her baby safely before telling Hamish that they were expecting. Greer stopped herself from stroking her belly, which she'd repeatedly done after talking to Florence about her growing suspicions. After describing her symptoms and the timing, Florence had crushed her with an excited hug and had told her in no uncertain terms that she was most certainly with child. She glanced at Hamish, but he clearly hadn't heard Zhang Ming's comment. He looked distracted.

Zhang Ming also looked at Hamish and frowned. "But Hamish, you look feverish."

Greer looked more closely at her husband and saw he looked pale and sweaty.

"Hamish, are you all right?"

"It's nothing," Hamish said abruptly, looking angry. "Don't fuss! It's just intolerably hot in here."

Greer and Zhang Ming exchanged worried glances as they bid the others farewell and stepped outside the cottage. It was not a day to feel hot. It was a cold winter's day, and the air had a nasty bite. And it wasn't like Hamish to be bad tempered.

"I'd convince him he needs bed rest when he gets home," Zhang Ming whispered as Hamish went to collect the horse and buggy from a little along the street. "And he shouldn't revisit here until he is well, as he may be contagious."

"But he never gets sick."

As Hamish returned, Greer could see her husband was very unwell, though. His breath was laboured, his face sweaty despite the cold. She'd never seen him with more than a passing cold, and worry filled her soul after she had said farewell to Zhang Ming and they made the journey home. By the time they arrived, Hamish was shivering violently and had begun coughing, which sounded full of phlegm.

"My love, we must get you to bed," Greer said, helping Hamish into the house.

"I have the most frightful headache."

Hamish's voice sounded weak, and he was like a child as he let Greer guide him to their bedroom, help him remove his clothes and put him in his sleepwear before tucking him into bed. She raced to the kitchen and began making chicken broth, checking on him regularly. By the time the broth was ready, he was even worse, coughing violently and alternating between shaking off the bedclothes with fever to shivering with cold. He had one spoonful of broth, but couldn't eat more.

Several hours later, Greer was extremely concerned. She had been putting cold cloths on his forehead to try to get the fever down, but by now, he was so delirious he didn't recognise her. She watched him with growing despair when there was a loud knock on the door. It was now early evening, and she raced downstairs to find Zhang Ming and a bespectacled Chinese man on her doorstep, holding a bag.

"I thought you might need some help," Zhang Ming said. "This is Dr Chen, and he will attend to your husband."

"Good evening, Mrs MacLeod," Dr Chen said. "If you could please lead the way, I will examine your husband."

Greer was overwhelmed with gratitude at her friend's thoughtfulness as she escorted the doctor to the bedroom, returning to find Zhang Ming making herself at home in the kitchen.

"I'm so grateful your doctor is here," Greer said. "I was going to contact the doctor in the morning, but I'm very worried as Hamish has taken such a turn for the worse, and so quickly. I have never seen him so ill."

"I didn't think you would mind, and Dr Chen is an excellent physician." Zhang Ming took some herbs out of her pocket and began making tea. The aroma was pungent and bitter.

"What is this?" Greer asked as she watched Zhang Ming at work.

"Something that will help reduce the fever. It's traditional Chinese medicine."

"Thank you, I am willing to try anything."

The doctor joined them in the kitchen a few minutes later and regarded Greer seriously when she asked how ill Hamish was. "My diagnosis is that he has the current strain of influenza circulating around New Zealand."

Greer put her hand to her mouth in horror. Only that morning had they been reading about the increase in cases; a dozen people had died the previous day. Everyone worried it might be as bad as the Russian flu earlier in the decade. Hamish had seemed fine at breakfast until she remembered that he'd mentioned a slight sore throat, but that wasn't uncommon in winter, and she'd thought nothing more about it.

"How would he have caught it?" she wondered. "We don't know anyone with influenza."

"Hamish is out and about in the community all the time," Zhang Ming said. "He could have caught influenza from any of his many visits."

275

"It's a very infectious disease," Dr Chen confirmed.

"What can be done?" Greer wrung her hands.

"You must keep your husband hydrated, so plenty of water and things like chicken broth. Fruit is also good. Honey and tea are good, too, and I see Zhang Ming has made a special herbal tea which will help. And sleep; expect your husband to sleep a lot."

Greer nodded, feeling overwhelmed.

"I will visit again in the morning to see how he is doing."

"And I will stay overnight, and we can take it in turns to care for him," Zhang Ming said.

"But you shouldn't!" Greer protested. "What if you become sick?"

"She is right," Dr Chen addressed Zhang Ming. "This is a highly infectious disease, and you can't risk being infected at your age."

Zhang Ming went to protest, but the doctor silenced her with a firm look. "You can visit when Mr MacLeod is well again, but until then, you must stay away." He turned to Greer. "Please wash your hands regularly and keep the room ventilated, so you don't catch this. And I understand you own a shop, is that correct?"

Greer nodded.

"You must keep the shop closed for the time being until we can be sure none of the staff have the illness. There is a chance they may have contracted it, but we won't know for sure for a few days."

"Oh, we visited a friend at home who has just had a baby!" Greer said in growing horror. "Will she be okay?"

"Were you there for long?"

"Perhaps fifteen minutes. Oh, Hamish shook the father's hand!"

"Let me alert the midwife and we can make arrangements at that end," Dr Chen said, looking at Greer and Zhang Ming kindly as he asked for more information.

"Well, I'm going to contact Mary and your staff," Zhang Ming said, clearly wanting to help in the situation. "So don't think more about the shop; just concentrate on looking after your husband."

They didn't hug or kiss as customary, and Zhang Ming and the doctor disappeared outside into the night air. Greer suddenly thought of Hamish's mother and father, who were having a midwinter holiday in Queenstown with the rest of the family, and she resolved she must get a message to them in the morning, although it would take time for them to journey back.

The next few days were a blur as Greer tended to her husband, who continued to have a high fever and was delirious. Dr Chen kept coming and going to check on progress, not saying what they were both thinking – that he wasn't getting better, he was deteriorating. Greer washed her hands regularly and kept the room ventilated, but she didn't care if she got sick, too. She spent most of her time watching Hamish anxiously and bathing him to try and reduce the fever. The good news was that Jamelie and her family weren't sick, nor were the staff at the store, but Zhang Ming was now bedridden and fighting for her life as well. She would never forgive herself if Zhang Ming didn't make it. And there was nothing she could do for her while caring for Hamish around the clock.

She took a moment at one point to look at their wedding photo, displayed proudly in their lounge. In the image they stared directly into the camera, and despite having to stand still for a time and not smile, they radiated love, happiness and health, both of them in their prime. She turned away from the photograph with a tearful sigh.

It was the fifth evening, around midnight, when she despaired that he was so unwell he might die. His skin was burning up and she gazed at him in the moonlight as she bathed his upper body again. He was everything to her. Her love, her life. She refused to imagine life without him.

"Hamish, you must fight. You mustn't give up."

His eyes were closed, but she saw his eyelids flicker. What she would give to see his eyes open again. He mumbled something incomprehensible, and she leant closer to see if she could understand him. His breath, usually so sweet, was now sour. He had been mumbling for days as she battled to get him to drink anything, and nothing made any sense.

She sighed and ran her hands over her belly. She hadn't even had the chance to tell him about the baby. But then she remembered the theory that when people were unconscious, they might still be able to hear what you said. She clasped Hamish's hand.

"Hamish, I have something to tell you, so I hope you can hear me. I have wonderful news – we are going to have a baby. So you have to fight to get well, for your child, and for me. For our family!" There was no response from Hamish, and eventually Greer gave in to an exhausted sleep next to her feverish husband.

When she opened her eyes, pale winter sunlight was peeking into the room, and Greer realised with wonder that Hamish was lying there watching her with his beautiful brown eyes locked on hers.

"You're awake!" She stroked his face tenderly and then felt his brow. He was no longer feverish; his brow was cool.

"What happened? How long have I been in bed?" His voice was weak and raspy.

"You don't remember?"

"I remember visiting the Georges and their new baby, then ..." his voice trailed away, and he frowned.

"You've been in bed for six days. You've been ill, but my love, your fever has broken. You are going to get better now. How do you feel?"

Hamish considered. "Tired. Weak. Hungry."

"Hungry?" That was a good sign. "How about some chicken broth?"

"Yes."

Greer kissed him gently on the cheek and returned quickly with chicken broth. She helped him sit up and spooned the broth into his mouth. He ate all that was in the bowl and then settled back into the pillows.

"I kept seeing your face," he said. "You were like an angel. And I dreamt about a little girl with your hair and eyes."

"Did you now?" Greer's heart was racing. "Do you remember anything I said when you were ill?"

Hamish shook his head. "No, I just had a feeling of your love, like a warm blanket. Like it was cocooning me."

Greer found that tears were sliding down her face. "I love you, Hamish MacLeod."

"I love you, my dearest Greer."

"And I have news. Good news. We are going to have a child."

She observed his response. He looked confused, and then his face lit up with delight. "A baby?"

"Yes, you are going to be a father."

Weak as he was, he gathered her into an embrace. "News of wonder," Hamish murmured. "We are blessed."

CHAPTER 56

Progress

"Mrs MacLeod, it is so good to see you," Mary welcomed Greer when she entered the store, feeling flustered and already worried she shouldn't be away from Hamish too long. "Do take a seat." Greer sank gratefully into one of their comfortable chairs.

"How is Mr MacLeod?"

"He's getting better, but the doctor has warned us he will need more bed rest before he is fully well again."

"That is to be expected," Mary said calmly.

"His family are looking after him at the moment; I couldn't keep them away after they cut short their holiday to come back."

"He will be in good hands. Now, I expect you have been anxious about the business on top of worrying about your husband. But I can assure you there is nothing to fret about."

Mary began to give a succinct account of the work in progress, new orders and the state of their supplies, and as she talked in her soft Scottish burr, Greer felt much of her worry dissipate. Not for the first time, she was thankful they had hired someone so competent and unruffled.

***

Florence knocked on Greer's door, holding a tub of soup.

"Chuckaboo, I won't come in," she said, thrusting the gift at Greer. "I just wanted to give you this and ask how Hamish was doing."

"He's getting better. He actually got out of bed for a few hours today, sat on the couch and read some newspapers."

"That's a corker sign! Blazes, he'll be back at work before you know it."

"I hope so. He's now at the stage of being a bit bored, but not well enough to do too much."

"He'll be as good as gold before you know it," Florence said firmly, patting her wayward hair.

***

Greer walked the hospital corridors until she found the room where Zhang Ming was residing. Charles Sew Hoy had insisted on moving her from her home to the hospital and had informed her yesterday that Zhang Ming was finally a little better and was probably well enough for visitors. But when she looked into the room, Zhang Ming was asleep as though dead. Greer was shocked to see how pale, small and lifeless she looked. Zhang Ming had aged terribly and still looked deathly unwell. She looked even worse than when she had pneumonia. It seems Charles Sew Hoy was mistaken in his assessment.

Not wanting to disturb Zhang Ming, Greer put the flowers she had brought on the bedside table and retraced her steps. A nurse passing by stopped her as she left the room.

"Are you a friend of Zhang Ming's?"

Greer gestured at the flowers. "Yes, I am. I was just ... she looks so ..."

The nurse looked at Greer with compassion. "Your friend has been very unwell, so it will take time for her to recover. But she has a strong spirit, so she has that on her side."

As she walked away, Greer thought how her fit, healthy young husband had suffered, and he was now only slowly recovering. She could only pray that Zhang Ming would recover also. Greer just couldn't bear the thought of losing her. She suddenly thought of the owl with its wings spread in the spandrel at Larnach's Castle and shuddered with a sense of impending doom.

CHAPTER 57

October 1898

For the rest of her life Greer would remember the exact moment she heard the news. Zhang Ming, now recovered from influenza and looking bright-eyed and alert, had just visited the store, nodding with approval over Greer's new designs as several clients browsed. Mary was busy in the upstairs workroom discussing a new technique of creating lace with the three Lebanese staff, who were excited to be trying a new style. Hamish had just delivered some packing material and was putting the bags and wrapping paper away.

An unexpected gust of wind caused everything in the shop to blow about as Florence burst through the door, her bonnet completely forgotten and her hair wild around her face.

"William Larnach has committed suicide!" she declared before flopping onto one of the chairs and throwing a newspaper onto a table. "He's dead."

Greer and Hamish had been pondering why their usual paper wasn't in their letterbox, but now they could see the headlines for themselves.

SUICIDE OF MR LARNACH. FOUND DEAD IN A COMMITTEE ROOM. A LOADED REVOLVER IN HIS HAND. CONSTERNATIONS IN THE HOUSE.

It was as though the world was in slow motion; everyone in the store looked at each other with shock and disbelief. Greer would remember later the widening of Hamish's eyes, the clients putting their hands to their faces, the women from the workroom running downstairs and joining everyone with shocked expressions, and Zhang Ming collapsing onto a chair, looking confused.

They pored over the newspaper report, and as the day progressed, a stream of visitors came to the store with further information until they had a fuller picture of what had happened.

The facts were undisputed.

The month before, on the twenty-third of September, William Larnach purchased a six-chambered revolver from the shop of William Henry Tisdall, a gunsmith in Lambton Quay, Wellington. The previous day, the twelfth of October, sometime after 4pm, William Larnach went to the "J" committee room, a part of the Parliament building seldom used when the House was sitting. Mr Kane, the parliamentary bill reader, was the last to see him alive and distinctly heard him lock the door, but simply thought he was writing some private letters.

When William Larnach didn't arrive home at teatime, Mrs Larnach expressed concern, and Mr Mills, one of the government whips, commenced a thorough search for him. When finding the committee room "J" locked, he sent for assistance and they forced the door open.

They discovered William Larnach sitting in a chair at the head of the table, quite dead, with his head thrown back. He had a six-chambered revolver in his right hand, one chamber of which had been discharged. The bullet entered the head almost in the centre of the forehead, slightly over the left eye.

"Why would the man do such a thing?" Mary was distraught. "He was such a successful person with his business and political dealings. And what about his family?"

"The papers say he was having financial difficulty," Hamish said, scanning the news again. "He'd lost heavily in the Colonial Bank shares and, according to this report, even sold valuable shares in the Kaitangata Railway and Coal Company to buy additional Colonial Bank shares before the banking troubles developed."

Mrs MacGavin, red-eyed and tearful, had joined the throng in the store. "But he has that beautiful castle he built," she said. "It's one of the showpieces of our district."

"Yes, although it must cost a fortune to maintain and run," Hamish said. "So the worry over finances must have been crippling."

"But he was a smart man," Mrs MacGavin said. "He would have made more money in the future. That was something he was good at."

"He was depressed, though," Florence said. "Albert said anytime he was at The Camp, he was totally unlike his old self. He was pale and quiet. And his wife didn't help matters."

"Constance? What do you mean?" Greer asked.

"Well, the way she was carrying on with Douglas, her stepson, you do know they were having an affair, don't you?" Florence said. "Mr Larnach must have found out, so that's why he committed suicide."

"They certainly were not," Mrs MacGavin said severely. "How can you say such a wicked thing!"

"No disrespect, Mrs MacGavin, but anyone could see how they looked at each other."

"Merely affection between a stepmother and stepson." Mrs MacGavin glared at Florence. "You shouldn't gossip like this; it's unseemly."

Edward, the coachman, had also joined the group. "Douglas was the only one of the children who had any time for Mrs Larnach," he said. "You have no proof they were anything more than just good friends."

"I know what I saw," Florence said firmly. "And I'm not the only one who noticed."

"It says in the newspaper that Mrs Larnach was devoted to her husband and was recently a constant attendant in the gallery of the House, which is occupied by the ministers' wives," Hamish said.

"A guilty conscience," Florence declared. "Besides, Douglas has been at The Camp, not in Wellington, so where else would she be?"

Greer had noticed the affection between Douglas and Constance, but she found it hard to believe Constance would act on her feelings even if she was attracted to Douglas. She always seemed a straightforward and honest person, and even if her marriage to William hadn't worked out as she had hoped, she was a responsible person, and you could see she cared for her husband, even if any attraction might have faded.

Greer thought of William Larnach, the man who had employed her during those critical early years. She remembered his generosity, flamboyant way of dressing, ambition for life, and many accomplishments. How sad that a man who had so much going for him had felt so much despair that he would take his own life. Greer brushed away her tears as Hamish put his arm around her.

"Are you all right, my dear wife?"

"It's such sad news. I can't believe it. He was always so full of life, a man that others looked up to. A man of ambition and achievement. What a loss to his family, but also all of us."

"He will be missed," Hamish said simply.

"He was a great man," Zhang Ming said. "Did much good."

Usual business was forgotten as Dunedin City was brought to a standstill with the shock of the news. Their flamboyant, generous, hard-working Member of Parliament was dead by his own hand. It was hard to comprehend.

CHAPTER 58

Farewells

William Larnach's body had arrived by the Government steamer *Hinemoa*, transported from Wellington to Dunedin after an inquest had been held at the Wellington Metropolitan Hotel. A verdict of suicide while temporarily of unsound mind was given by the coroner and accepted by the jury.

Crowds had waited at the wharf before seamen placed the coffin on the hearse, pulled by horses from Larnach's stable. Traveller, Larnach's favourite buggy horse, led the procession to the Northern Cemetery. Greer and Hamish were among the large crowd of mourners gathered as the funeral procession made its slow way to William Larnach's final resting place. Greer shivered slightly as a cool wind blew, and Hamish put his arm around her protectively.

Following the hearse was youngest son Douglas, Constance's brother Alfred de Bathe Brandon, and William Larnach's son-in-law, William Francis Inder. Constance, Alice, Colleen and Gladys travelled together in a mourning coach; when closer, Greer could see their faces were etched with grief.

Greer looked around the gathered crowd and saw many faces that she recognised, including Bendix Hallenstein and his wife, Charles Sew Hoy and his wife, other high-profile business and political leaders, and former and current staff from The Camp, everyone dressed in sombre black and wearing sorrowful faces. Zhang Ming was there with her family. Jamelie and Gabriel stood close to each other while their staff stood in a huddle, paying their respects.

After the hearse had finally stopped, a few Peninsula settlers carried the coffin from the hearse to the steepled family mausoleum. William would be interred with his first wife, Eliza, his second wife, Mary, and his daughter Kate. Greer understood that Larnach had commissioned the tomb as a memorial to his first wife. It was designed by the architect R. A. Lawson in 1881 in the form of a Gothic chapel. This was, of course, a period of time when Larnach wasn't plagued by financial problems.

The wind buffeted the crowd as Larnach was laid to rest amid the tomb of Oamaru stone and slate and stained-glass windows. A handsome wreath from the miners at Kumara was placed on the coffin by the mayor of Dunedin, Edward Cargill. Despite the wind, it was a beautiful, elevated spot.

After the service, people murmured to one another, many sharing stories of William Larnach's generosity. Even in the midst of financial problems, he'd helped so many, but Greer found herself thinking of the quote from "Romeo and Juliet": *Thou detestable maw, thou womb of death*. It seemed incomprehensible that William Larnach had committed suicide and was now in a tomb of decay.

Later, as Greer and Hamish were about to depart, Greer noticed Fergus and Jane in the throng. He had put on a little bit of weight, and had an air of contentment about him that was new. Florence had mentioned that he was now the bar manager at The Queen's Arms, and it seemed his criminal days were in the past. Greer realised that she wished him well, and as her gaze moved to Jane, she could see a different relationship between the couple. Jane looked confident and happy in herself, and Fergus seemed to defer to her as they quietly shared a word. When Jane stroked her belly, Greer looked again and realised that Jane was pregnant, and she couldn't help smiling.

Hamish followed her gaze and then protectively stroked Greer's growing baby belly, and she held his hand, both of them feeling their baby kick.

"It's a wonder," Hamish murmured into Greer's ear. It was a wonder. The miracle of life. While she was still nervous about giving birth, Greer felt much more reassured and had already forged a good relationship with the midwife. And she and Hamish had begun discussing possible baby names, their list changing all the time.

As Greer looked around the gathered mourners, she felt mixed emotions when suddenly comparing her life to the Larnachs. Although she had not long ago been an orphan without prospects, now she had a thriving business and lived in a beautiful home. More importantly, Greer had so much love in her life – her husband, her child growing within her, her wonderful friends. Looking now at the Larnachs gathered together, all she could see was their misery, despite their once having had it all: wealth, prestige, power, and opportunities. But even apart from the shock of William Larnach's death, they had been an unhappy family for years. And their wealth? Who knew what would happen next? Rumours were already circulating that there wasn't a will, and battle lines were already being drawn over who would get what of the little that remained.

For a moment, Greer caught Constance's eye as she walked to the waiting coach, utterly alone. Constance's eyes were red from crying, but still, she had the same firm gaze she had always had, and she held her back straight. Greer felt sympathy for her as they nodded to one another. Whatever her relationship had been with Douglas, she would find no comfort in the family she had married into. Behind her, Colleen, Alice and Gladys stood in a huddle, comforting each other, but offering Constance not even a sympathetic glance. And Douglas was far away from all of them and seemed to be lost in his own thoughts, his face unreadable, but his shoulders bowed with the weight of the world. Eldest son Donald wasn't present; he hadn't made it over from Melbourne in time.

As Constance walked away, Greer suddenly realised that this would be the last time she would see her. Constance wouldn't return to Dunedin; Greer knew that as a certainty in her heart of hearts.

"Come, Greer," Hamish cut into her reverie, "we should go."

Greer nodded. Yes, they should go. They had paid their respects to a great man, a visionary who had done so much for others. But he was also a man who had been unable to share his private anguish and now a man who had lived too much of a public life to be left in peace.

It was time for them to return to their own lives. It was a much simpler life than the one William Larnach had chosen – but a life Greer knew in her heart was infinitely richer in the things that really mattered – family, friendship and love.

CHAPTER 59

February 1899

"Keep pushing!" the midwife urged as Greer squeezed Jamelie's hand. Sweat poured from her brow and body, and she grunted as another contraction tore through her body.

"I can see the head! One more push, Greer. One more push!"

Greer used every last ounce of her strength to bear down, and her baby emerged into the world with a loud cry. Zhang Ming and Hamish's mother cried tears of joy and hugged each other.

"You have a healthy baby girl," the midwife said, examining her and then cleaning her up and wrapping her in a cotton blanket before turning her attention back to Greer.

Greer smiled groggily as the baby was placed in her arms and she could see the infant for the first time. Jamelie smiled at her friend, murmuring something that sounded like a blessing before she went downstairs to retrieve Hamish and his father, who had both been anxiously pacing the lounge floor. Jamelie left again soon after, wanting to give the new parents some privacy, and the others followed her downstairs shortly after.

"You did it, my beautiful wife," Hamish said, kissing Greer's forehead gently, and they both looked with unreserved adoration at their daughter. "She looks just like you."

She did look a little like Greer – she had a burst of auburn hair. But she had her father's limbs and his mouth. She was a beautiful, perfect combination of the two of them.

"Nora, welcome to the world," Greer said, kissing her baby, in awe of her tiny fingers, her smooth skin, her rosebud lips.

"So we've decided on Nora?" Hamish smiled at his wife.

Greer nodded, consumed by her baby girl. "She's definitely a Nora."

Hamish peered at his daughter. "Ah, that she is. Nora she will be forever from this day onwards."

Greer lay back with her baby in her arms and her husband by her side and thanked the Lord for this blessing, a bonny baby girl. Delivered safely after a relatively straightforward labour. All her fears had been cast aside, and now she felt just pure and overwhelming love for the bundle in her arms. Never had she experienced anything so profound. She looked into Hamish's eyes and could see he felt the same way.

Much later, after breastfeeding and resting, visitors started to return in dribs and drabs, all carrying gifts or flowers, all with good wishes for the new arrival. They also arrived with news and chitchat. Dunedin was still full of gossip about the Larnach family, facts and rumours circulating on a daily basis.

"Oh, your baby is a wee bairn," Mary exclaimed when she arrived. "As bonny as a baby can possibly be!" After some further small talk, Mary leant forward.

"But have you heard the latest about the Larnachs?"

Greer and Hamish shook their heads.

"Well, I'm not one to gossip, and you know that they all searched high and low at The Camp and the Wellington residence for William Larnach's will, and there was nought to be found. So dying intestate means the estate will automatically be split with one third to Constance as his wife, and the rest divided among the children."

"Well, that sounds fair in the circumstances," Greer said, not really paying too much attention to Mary; she only had eyes for Nora.

"Ah, but Douglas isn't happy. He claims that the estate was always promised to him." Mary shook her head as she spoke. "No good will come of that, I tell ye."

Florence and Albert arrived a little later. Greer let their words wash over her before the subject turned to the Larnachs, as it invariably did these days.

"Douglas Larnach isn't at all happy," Florence said, echoing Mary's words.

"Because he thinks he should inherit The Camp?"

"Well, that, but Constance is in England with her sister Annie, and who knows when she will ever return."

Greer gazed at Nora and nodded at Florence, who needed no encouragement to continue.

"Then there is the mystery of the letters."

"What letters?" Hamish asked, also gazing at his daughter.

"By blazes, you must have heard!" Florence exclaimed with delight. "On the afternoon of William Larnach's death, he received a letter that he was most upset about. Apparently, he read it and paced up and down the library in an agitated state afterwards. I think it was from Douglas revealing he was having an affair with Constance. That's the real reason William Larnach shot himself."

Greer looked up. "Really? Is there proof?"

"Well, the letter hasn't been found," Florence admitted. "But I swear I'm right. I know about these things. And then there are the other letters! On the day he died, William Larnach wrote several letters, and one of them he asked the librarian to post to Dunedin, putting a late fee on it, as he said he was most anxious that it got on the mail for Dunedin. But it's never been found! I think it was a letter to Douglas."

"You've been reading too many novels," Greer said mildly.

"Chuckaboo, real life is much better than a novel," Florence said cheerfully. "You couldn't make this tale up!"

Jamelie came back again, this time with Gabriel in tow, and when the conversation steered towards the Larnach family, Greer was more interested to hear what they had to say.

"It's an unfortunate state of affairs when a family fights over a loved one's estate," Jamelie said, cooing at the new baby.

"Gladys is siding with Douglas' claim that he should inherit the entire estate," Gabriel said.

Jamelie chimed in again. "Meanwhile, Donald, Alice and Colleen are claiming that they signed a deed in 1887 which they were misled into signing, and they want it overturned."

"Deed? What deed?" Hamish asked.

"It's complicated," Gabriel said. "Apparently, William made over his property to his second wife as insurance against the risk of bankruptcy."

Jamelie took up the thread. "But then she died, so he instructed his lawyers to prepare a deed of assignment for his children relinquishing their interests in his estate. He did this so he could continue to collect rents from The Camp during his lifetime – and he verbally told them the estate would be theirs after, but that's not stated in the deeds."

"It seems he got them to sign papers without letting them read them," Gabriel added.

"So Donald, Alice and Colleen are trying to get the deed overturned as they claim they were misled," Jamelie concluded.

"Sounds like they were," Hamish said.

"But it means if they win their case, Constance will get nothing," Gabriel pointed out.

"And what about Douglas?" Hamish asked.

"Douglas also signed the deed but says they weren't misled and that his siblings are only trying to get it overturned to stop Constance from receiving anything," Jamelie said.

"So if Donald, Colleen and Alice win, Constance and Douglas will get nothing," Gabriel reiterated.

"Goodness. It's so complicated," Greer said, turning to Hamish. "And who'd want to be part of the Larnach family? They are all turning on each other like sharks."

After a stream of other visitors, Zhang Ming was their last visitor that day, and she, too, had words to share about the Larnachs, but not what Greer or Hamish had expected.

"It's very sad. You should govern a family as you would cook a small fish – very gently. William Larnach was a great man but not so good with his family. Now, this is the final meal, the final result. Very sad."

291

CHAPTER 60

September 1899

Since the arrival of Nora, Greer and Hamish still had breakfast together before Hamish departed to go to work, but Greer was more likely to be in her sleep attire at the breakfast table after a night of getting up to look after Nora, who was proving to be a light sleeper. They had relaxed their no-servant rule to pay Florence to come in twice a week to do domestic chores. They had more furniture and possessions than when they had first moved in, but now their home was often strewn with baby clothes and toys. Although Nora was only tiny, she was like a baby hurricane when it came to her things around the home.

When Greer came downstairs with Nora after breastfeeding, Hamish had their breakfast laid out on the table, and there was a wrapped gift waiting for her.

"Happy birthday, my dearest wife," Hamish kissed her gently. "And how is my gorgeous baby girl?" He gathered Nora up, and the baby gurgled with delight when she saw her papa. Hamish watched Greer unwrap her gift, his attention alternating between his wife and daughter.

Greer opened the package carefully; the paper could be reused, after all. She gasped with delight when she saw what Hamish had given her. It was a pearl choker, and Greer put it on immediately, even though she was still in her nightdress. She stood up and modelled.

"Oh, Hamish, it is beautiful! Imagine this with a ball dress!"

"It looks just lovely with what you are wearing," he said, laughing at Greer posing this way and that, pretending she was dressed for a ball.

Nora chortled with delight, and Greer kissed her husband and then scooped up her baby and sat Nora on her lap while Hamish poured the tea.

"I can't believe I'm twenty-nine today," Greer said.

"You don't look a day older than when I met you."

"Charmer!"

"It's true!"

"I never dreamed I would have all this," Greer gestured vaguely around the room.

"You mean a dining room?" Hamish said teasingly.

"No, silly. A husband, a baby, a home, a business!"

"You deserve it all!" Hamish gestured at the food. "Do eat before it goes cold. And tonight, I've arranged for my mother to babysit so we can have dinner out."

"Oh, are you sure about being away from Nora?" Greer sounded alarmed.

"It will just be a couple of hours, we will be a short walk away, and you know how much my mother loves Nora."

"You are right. In that case, it will be a treat." Greer stroked her new pearls. "I'll make sure to find a dress that complements my lovely gift." They smiled at each other and began to eat their breakfast.

Greer jiggled Nora on her lap as Hamish studied the latest news in the *Otago Daily Times*. Premier Richard Seddon had proposed to dispatch a contingent of mounted troops to join Britain's fight against the Boer Republic in South Africa. The House of Representatives had recently voted by fifty-four votes to five in support, the first time New Zealand troops would be deployed overseas. The newspaper had daily reports on the decision, even going so far as to reproduce telegrams of congratulations from around the country. Hamish read some of them out to Greer, who listened intently.

"May the best fortune of war attend arms of our contingent. Know they will uphold New Zealand's honour, and trust they will return in triumph."

"Inhabitants of Port Chalmers join me in wishing the New Zealand Contingent every success and blessing in helping to maintain the flag of the Empire."

"If the day of our greatest peril should come, the sons of the Empire from all ends of the earth will gather to the field of strife to be victorious."

Greer frowned. "Am I the only person in New Zealand who is concerned about sending our men to a foreign war?"

"It seems it is just you and I who are concerned," Hamish said, scratching his head. "Everyone I speak to seems to think this is a glorious idea of supporting the British Empire, even though I can't see how a conflict in South Africa has anything to do with New Zealand."

"Oh, you don't think you will need to go, do you?" Greer suddenly felt ill. Nora looked at her mother and put her head to one side, noticing the change in her mood.

Hamish reached over to hold Greer's hand. "Men are racing to enlist, I think they will have more soldiers than they need, so there is no need to worry."

"Thank goodness," Greer said, and smiled, causing Nora to break into a toothless grin. "I couldn't bear for any harm to come to you."

Greer often thought about how close she had come to losing Hamish when he was battling influenza. She'd quietly kept an eye on the death notices for others who had succumbed and said a prayer for their families each time. Two hundred and nineteen poor souls had died due to this recent round of illness. But then she shrugged off these melancholy thoughts and focused on the day ahead. It was her birthday, after all, a time of celebration.

***

Hamish had just left for work when Florence burst through the door with kisses and a small gift of chocolates before vigorously tidying and cleaning, whisking around with a great deal of energy as Greer nursed her baby. Florence was very complimentary about Greer's pearl choker, but then, as Greer had half expected, she started talking nineteen to the dozen about the Larnachs, still her favourite topic of discussion.

"You'll read all about this in tomorrow's paper," she said, her hair wilder than ever. "But I have it on good authority that Donald, Colleen and Alice will win their case to overturn the deed they signed."

"How do you know this?"

"Albert has an acquaintance at court. They met up last night. Anyway, that means Constance and Douglas won't get anything from the estate, well, apart perhaps from a share of an insurance policy or jewellery, I suppose. But they both come away pretty much empty handed."

"That's a shame," Greer said, but her focus was on Nora, who was smiling at her. She had the loveliest dimples!

"I think it's revenge from beyond the grave, chuckaboo," Florence sounded gleeful. "It pays back Constance's lack of love and Douglas' unfilial behaviour."

"Oh, Florence! You must stop talking about them like they were lovers. There is no proof. They were just good friends."

"Not nearly as good a story!" Florence sniffed before stopping in her work to coo at Nora. "Who's a pretty baby then! Who's a pretty baby!"

Nora chortled with delight. She was certainly a happy baby, even if she was too alert to want to sleep at night.

"I'll put her upstairs for her nap," Greer said. She glanced down at her nightdress. "And I should get dressed."

Florence laughed. "When John was Nora's age, I don't think I got dressed for weeks!"

Greer put Nora down for her morning nap and managed to get dressed for the day, departing with Nora later to visit the shop, leaving Florence to continue with her work. Florence waved her away when she offered to help – something she would usually do when Florence was in the house. It was like old times working side by side with Florence, although much more satisfying doing this in her own home.

"Not on your birthday, chuckaboo!" Florence said. "You go and enjoy!"

It was a curious feeling going into MacLeod and George Designs, almost like being a customer, and she looked around the shop for a moment, nodding to herself at how well everything looked. The dresses on display were eye-catching, and the place looked stylish but comfortable. Mary was busy attending to a customer who was buying some gloves, and she nodded in greeting when Greer came into the store with Nora in her arms.

Hamish was nowhere to be seen, but Jamelie emerged from the upstairs workroom once the customer had left the store and handed her a gift; their three Lebanese girls emerging to wish her a happy birthday and coo over Nora before returning to their work.

"It's from all of us ladies," Jamelie said as Greer opened the parcel. It was a pair of satin gloves suitable for going to a ball.

"Oh, these are lovely!" Greer was delighted. "Perfect for wearing to formal occasions when Nora is a bit older."

Jamelie took Greer to lunch around the corner from the store, and as they sipped their tea and enjoyed the sandwiches and cakes, they chatted about their husbands, children, and their business, marvelling more than once at how happy they were. Jamelie and Gabriel had purchased a home, so their days of renting the cottage on Walker Street were coming to a close.

"It is the end of an era," Jamelie said.

"Yes, it is," Greer replied thoughtfully.

Zhang Ming was waiting for Greer when they returned to the shop and had a gift for Greer, a beautiful bouquet of flowers that Nora immediately lunged for and tried to eat.

"These are not for you, little missy," Greer said, moving them out of reach. "Thank you, Zhang Ming. These are beautiful."

"May you live to be a hundred and enjoy many happy years," Zhang Ming said, kissing Greer affectionately. "One day, you may be as old as me!"

"You are not a hundred!" Greer protested.

"I am certainly old. But happy."

Greer arrived back to an empty but clean house and was very grateful for Florence's help. She nursed Nora and put her down for her afternoon nap before lying on the bed near the cot to enjoy an afternoon nap herself. She was looking forward to dinner out with her husband, the first time they would have been out together on their own since the arrival of Nora.

CHAPTER 61

December 1899

Inspired by the mix of a beautiful day and old-fashioned curiosity, Greer stood outside Larnach's Castle, her baby in her arms and her husband by her side. She was dressed in the finest light-blue silk that perfectly complemented her glowing complexion. The lion statues looked down on them with regal calm; the eagles, further up, seemed ready for flight. The strange cat peered down at them just as smugly as always, but the ominous owl with its wings spread in the spandrel between the two windows was in bad repair. Parts had crumbled away.

None of the Larnach family had remained at The Camp after the court proceedings. Florence informed her that Constance was now living with her sister Annie in Wellington, next to her brother and opposite her sisters. Her brother Alfred was providing for her financially. Douglas was also in Wellington, living around the corner from Constance. The oldest son Donald had returned to Dunedin with his two eldest daughters. Florence wasn't sure where Colleen, Alice and Gladys were now, but Greer thought she'd probably have all the news next time they met.

Larnach's Castle looked just as grand as the day Greer had first laid eyes on the building, but so much had changed in a decade. It was rumoured that it was to become a nuns' retreat and that the furniture and chattels would be up for sale the following year. Most of the staff had been dismissed – just a handful kept their jobs to maintain the property. Mrs MacGavin was now retired, happily spending her time with her husband and tending to her own house and garden rather than being tasked with organising the housekeeping for such a large place.

Albert had started his own gardening business and was kept busy with a growing number of prosperous families who had the means to employ a gardener part-time while Florence continued to raise their family and housekeep for Greer and Hamish twice a week. Edward, the coachman, had surprised them all by marrying a woman out of the blue – no one knew he was even seeing anyone – and they had moved to Queenstown. He still worked with horses. As for the butler, he had found employment with Edward Cargill, so there was never a chance now that Hamish would find him in Larnach's garden.

As though reading her mind, Hamish smiled at his wife as they strolled through the gardens, Nora looking around at everything with wide-eyed interest. They made their way to the famous pergola with the spectacular views – famous to them, anyway – as the place they had first met years ago when Greer had been practising her violin.

"Look, Nora, this is where Daddy first accosted Mummy," Greer said.

"Accosted? Certainly not! Nora, this is where Mummy put a spell on Daddy."

"Spell? Now you are getting ridiculous," Greer laughed. "Let's start the story again for Nora."

Hamish put his hand to his chest in dramatic fashion. "Nora, this is where your Daddy first saw your Mummy and was mesmerised by her beauty, charm and talent."

"Much better!" Greer said, giving Hamish a kiss.

"And they eventually lived happily ever after."

"Eventually?"

"Well, you did give me the cold shoulder for years! You only had eyes for a scoundrel."

Greer shrugged. "Oh, well, I came to my senses and succumbed to your charms in the end."

They linked arms and walked back to their horse and buggy to start the journey home, Larnach's Castle soon disappearing from their rear view. Scores of young albatrosses soared in the sky, their joy and grace apparent, before swooping low over the water. Nora was enchanted, and Greer had a sudden memory of the lone albatross on the bleak day she had first travelled to the castle. She had gone from being a lone soul to finding her people, having treasured friendships, a loving family and being part of the wider community. She had the sudden notion of her beloved papa and mama looking down on their travelling buggy, and the thought filled her with great comfort.

They had a New Year's Eve party to organise for the evening, all their loved ones gathering, but everyone was helping somehow, taking the burden from Greer's shoulders. They were ringing in not just a new year but a new century! Despite the ongoing Boer War and the reports of the first New Zealand soldier to be killed there, Greer was filled with hope and anticipation for a bright future.

Playlist

Moonlight Sonata by Ludwig van Beethoven
Three Romances for Violin and Piano by Clara Schumann
Gavotte by François-Joseph Gossec
Swallowtail Jig a traditional Irish jig
The Opening to Felix Mendelssohn's *Violin Concerto in E Minor, Op. 64*
Violin Concerto No. 1 in A Minor by Johann Sebastian Bach
Chaconne in G Minor by Tomaso Antonio Vitali
Ave Maria by Franz Schubert
Caprice in A minor, Op. 1, No. 24 by Niccolò Paganini
Plaisir d'Amour by Jean-Paul-Égide Martini
Sonata for Violin and Piano in B Minor by J. S. Bach
Meditation from Thaïs by Jules Massenet

Victorian word glossary

As barmy as a bandicoot (Aust./NZ) – very eccentric.
As miserable as a bandicoot – extremely miserable.
Blatherskite – a boaster, skite, blowhard.
Chuckaboo – an affectionate term a good friend.
Cove – fellow, bloke.
Foozler – someone who tends to mess things up or is clumsy.
Goff – an affectionate term for someone foolish or awkward.
Nanty narking – good fun.
Nineteener – a bad person.
Scatter-brained scapegrace – forgetful rascal.
Whooperups – people who sing loudly without a good singing voice.

Acknowledgements

Many thanks to my fabulous publisher, Quentin Wilson, for his enthusiasm and guidance. A sometime violinist himself, his musical knowledge was invaluable in finessing this novel. Thank you to my hardworking agent, Catherine Wallace from High Spot Literary, and to the great team who worked on this novel: Jane McKenzie, for her insightful and skilful editing; Ana Aceves for her cover artwork, and my publicist Margaret Samuels.

It was a privilege to enjoy the Robert Lord Writer's Cottage Residency and I thoroughly appreciated my invaluable stay researching this novel.

I would also like to thank my dear friend Man Yin for kindly sharing her knowledge of Chinese culture, and Duncan Sew Hoy, who generously shared about the remarkable Choie Sew Hoy. Thank you also to Matthew Farry and Martin George for their invaluable help with information about early Lebanese immigrants to Dunedin.

Finally, all my love and thanks go to my wonderful husband, Iain McKenzie. His knowledge of Victorian Dunedin is without compare, and I couldn't have written this book without the extensive information stored in his mind. As a side note, Hamish and Greer's home in this novel is modelled on the beautiful two-storeyed villa that he restored when he lived in Dunedin.

Author's Note

Dunedin has a special place in my heart. My father was a manager for Hallenstein's and would visit the head office from time to time, taking his family with him. As a child, these trips to Dunedin felt magical. My husband was born in Dunedin and was a local for many years, and since being married, we have visited numerous times. To research this book, I am very grateful to the Robert Lord Writer's Cottage Residency for allowing me concentrated time to walk the streets back in time to the 1890s.

The 1880s in New Zealand was a time of depression and hardship, but the 1890s were exciting and prosperous times, especially for young women. Never before had they had so many opportunities in life, and I have tried to capture what it would have been like living in Dunedin in this decade. New Zealand became the first country in the world to pass a law so women had the right to vote in the parliamentary elections, but numerous other laws were passed during this progressive time that are the cornerstone of our society now.

Despite its bad reputation, the Devil's Half-Acre was a poor but thriving community in Dunedin, where Scots, Irish, Chinese and Lebanese lived side by side, often new immigrants supporting each other in their endeavours. It was wonderful to include characters that reflect this multicultural heritage.

Greer and most of the characters in this book are entirely fictional, but her story is counterpointed by the tragic story of the real-life William Larnach and his troubles later in life. That he had money troubles and

committed suicide at Parliament are undisputed facts. However, whether his much younger third wife Constance had an affair with her stepson Douglas, Larnach's favourite son, is speculative, so I'll leave it up to you if you think it is true or not. I tend to fall on the side that it was a malicious rumour, but we will never know the truth. I have taken liberties in the novel by having Constance stay at Larnach's Castle before her wedding.

There are cameo appearances of the real-life businessmen Bendix Hallenstein and Charles (Choie) Sew Hoy. I am forever grateful to the modern-day Hallenstein business for their generous support of my father when he was diagnosed with cancer, looking after him (and us) financially until his untimely death.

The more I have read and learnt about Charles Sew Hoy, the more impressed I am by this generous and successful businessman. Among his many achievements he set up the Cheong Shing Tong, a benevolent society helping the poor and elderly Chinese migrants. In 1883 the society was responsible for exhuming 230 Chinese dead and conveying them to Guangdong. Charles Sew Hoy died on 22 July 1901 in Dunedin, where he was buried. But his final wish was to be buried in Cheong Shing Tong's cemetery in upper Panyu. His body was disinterred in 1902 during another mass exhumation and placed on board the *Ventnor*, bound for China. Unfortunately, the ship sank off Hokianga, and his remains, along with most of the other 498 bodies, were lost.

You couldn't tell a story set in Dunedin in this era without including the stylish and industrious Lebanese families who immigrated here. I hope I have done justice to the many families who carved out new lives on our shores with my fictional George family.